Mary Balogh is a *New York Times* bestselling author. A former teacher, she grew up in Wales and now lives in Canada.

Slightly Sinful

Mary Balogh

piatkus

PIATKUS

First published in the United States in 2004
by Bantam Dell, a division of Random House, Inc.
First published in Great Britain in 2007 by Piatkus

5 7 9 10 8 6

A CIP catalogue record for this book
is available from the British Library.

ISBN 978-0-7499-3787-4

Printed and bound by CPI Group (UK) Ltd, Croydon, CR0 4YY

Papers used by Piatkus are from well-managed forests
and other responsible sources.

MIX
Paper from
responsible sources
FSC® C104740

Slightly Sinful

Chapter One

Having spent almost all of his twenty-five years in England and therefore isolated from most of the hostilities that had ravaged the rest of Europe since the rise to power of Napoléon Bonaparte, Lord Alleyne Bedwyn, third brother of the Duke of Bewcastle, had no personal experience of pitched battles. But he had listened with avid interest to the war stories sometimes told by his elder brother, Lord Aidan Bedwyn, a recently retired cavalry colonel, and had thought he could picture such a scene.

He had been wrong.

He had imagined neatly deployed lines, the British and her allies on this side, the enemy on that, flat land like the playing fields of Eton between them. He had imagined cavalry and infantry and artillery, all pristine and picturesque in their various uniforms, moving about neatly and logically, like the pieces on a chessboard. He had imagined the rapid popping of gunfire, disturbing, but not obliterating, the silence. He had imagined clarity of vision, the ability to see all points of the battlefield at all times, the ability to assess the progress of the battle at every moment. He had imagined – if he had thought of it at all – clean, clear air to breathe.

He had been wrong on all counts.

He was not himself a military man. Recently he had decided that it was time he did something useful with his life and had embarked upon a career as a diplomat. He had been assigned to the embassy at the Hague under Sir Charles Stuart. But Sir Charles and a number of his staff, Alleyne included, had moved to Brussels while the Allied armies under the Duke of Wellington's command gathered there in response to a new threat from Napoléon Bonaparte, who had escaped from his exile on the island of Elba earlier in the spring and was raising a formidable army in France again. Now, today, the long-expected battle between the two forces was being fought on a rolling, hilly stretch of farmland south of the village of Waterloo. And Alleyne was there in the thick of it. He had volunteered to carry a letter from Sir Charles to Wellington and to bring back a reply.

He was thankful that he had ridden out from Brussels alone. He might have been unable to hide from any companion the fact that he had never been even half so frightened in his life.

The noise of the great guns was the worst. It went beyond sound. It deafened his eardrums and pounded low in his abdomen. Then there was all the smoke, which choked his lungs and set his eyes to watering and made it virtually impossible to see clearly more than a few yards in any direction. There were horses and men milling about everywhere in the mud caused by last night's torrential rain, in what seemed like total confusion to Alleyne. There were officers and sergeants bellowing out commands and somehow

2

making themselves heard. There was the acrid smell of smoke and the added stench of what he assumed must be blood and guts. Even through the smoke he could see dead and wounded wherever he looked.

It was like a scene straight from hell.

This, he realized, was the reality of war.

The Duke of Wellington had a reputation for always being in the place where the fighting was most fierce, recklessly exposing himself to danger and somehow escaping unscathed. Today was no exception. After asking at least a dozen officers for information concerning his whereabouts, Alleyne finally found his man on an open rise of land looking down on the strategically placed farmhouse of La Haye Sainte, which the French were fiercely attacking and a troop of German soldiers was just as ferociously defending. The duke could not have been more openly exposed to enemy fire if he had tried. Alleyne delivered his letter and then concentrated his attention upon keeping his horse under control. He tried not even to think of the danger to his person, but he was painfully aware of the roar of cannonballs close by and the whistle of musket balls. Terror seeped into his very bones.

He had to wait for Wellington to read the letter and then dictate a reply to one of his aides. The wait seemed interminable to Alleyne, who watched the battle for control of the farm – whenever he could see it through the billowing smoke of thousands of guns. He watched men die and waited to die himself. And if he survived, he wondered, would he ever hear again? Or be sane again? Finally he had his letter, stowed it safely in an inner pocket, and turned to leave. He had never been more thankful for anything in his life.

3

How had Aidan tolerated this life for twelve years? By what miracle had he survived to tell of it and to marry Eve and settle to a life in rural England?

When he felt a sharp pain in his upper left thigh, Alleyne thought at first that he had twisted awkwardly in the saddle and pulled a muscle. But when he glanced down, he saw the torn hole in his breeches and the blood spurting from it and realized the truth almost as if he were a spectator looking down dispassionately upon himself.

'By Jove,' he said aloud, 'I have been hit.'

His voice sounded as if it came from a long way distant. It was drowned out by the pounding of the guns and his fuzzy-eared deafness and by the ringing sound within his head, suddenly turned icy cold with the shock of knowing that he had been shot.

It did not occur to him to stop or dismount or seek medical attention. He could think only of getting away from there, of returning without delay to Brussels and safety. He had important things to do there. For the moment he could not remember what any of those things were, but he knew he could not afford to delay.

Besides, panic was clawing at his back.

He rode onward for a few minutes, until he felt more confident of being out of harm's way. By that time his leg was hurting like the very devil. Worse, he was still bleeding copiously. He had nothing with which to bind the wound except a large handkerchief. When he pulled it out of his pocket he feared that it would not reach about his thigh, but corner-to-corner it was longer than he had estimated. With clammy, shaking hands he bound it tightly above the tear in his breeches, wincing and nearly fainting from the pain.

The ball, he realized, must be embedded in his thigh. Agony tore through him with every pulse beat. He was dizzy with shock.

Thousands of men were wounded far worse than this, he told himself sternly as he rode on – far worse. It would be cowardly to dwell upon his own pain. He must force himself to rise above it. Once he had reached Brussels, he would complete his errand and then get a physician to dig out the ball – perish the thought! – and patch him up. He would survive – he hoped. So would his leg – he hoped.

Soon he was in the Forest of Soignés, riding a little to the west side of the road in order to avoid all the heavy traffic proceeding along it in both directions. He passed numerous soldiers in the forest, a few of them dead, many of them wounded like himself, a large number of them deserters from the horror of the battlefront – or so he suspected. He could hardly blame them.

As the shock gradually subsided, the pain grew steadily worse, if that were possible. The bleeding, though somewhat retarded by the tourniquet he had fashioned, continued. He felt cold and light-headed. He had to get back to Morgan.

Ah, yes, that was it!

Morgan, his younger sister – she was only eighteen years old – was in Brussels, her chaperons having rashly waited there too long instead of leaving with most of the other English visitors who had flocked to the city during the past couple of months. The Caddicks were now virtually trapped in Brussels, since all vehicles had been requisitioned by the army – and therefore so was Morgan. But worse than that, they had allowed her out of the house alone today of all days. When he had ridden out of Brussels earlier, he had been startled to find her at the Namur Gates with some other women, tending the wounded who had already been straggling into the city.

He had told her he would return at the earliest possible moment and see to it that she was taken back to safety, preferably all the way home to England. He would beg temporary leave from his post and take her himself. He dared not think of what might happen to her if the French won the victory today.

He had to get back to Morgan. He had promised Wulfric – his eldest brother, the Duke of Bewcastle – that he would keep an eye on her even though Wulf had entrusted her to the care of the Earl and Countess of Caddick when she had begged to be allowed to come to Brussels with their daughter, Lady Rosamond Havelock, her friend. Good Lord, she was little more than a child, and she was his sister.

Ah, yes, and he had to deliver his letter to Sir Charles Stuart. He had almost forgotten the wretched letter. What was so important, he wondered, that he had had to ride into battle and out again merely to deliver a note and bring back a reply? An invitation to dinner that evening? It would not surprise him if it were something as trivial as that. He was already having niggling doubts about his chosen career. Perhaps he ought to have taken one of the parliamentary seats that Wulf controlled – except that his interest in politics was minimal. Sometimes his lack of direction in life disturbed him. Even if a man had enough personal wealth to carry him comfortably through life without any exertion on his part, as he did, there ought to be something that fired his blood and elevated his soul.

His leg felt like a balloon expanded to the point of bursting. It also, paradoxically, felt as if it were stuck full of knives and powered by a million pulse points. A cold fog seemed to be swirling inside his head. The very air he breathed was icy.

Morgan ... He fixed her image in his mind – young, vibrant, headstrong Morgan, his sister, the only one of his five siblings who was younger than he. He had to get back to her.

How much farther to Brussels? He had lost track of both time and distance. He could still hear the guns. He was still in the forest. The road was still to his right, clogged with carts and wagons and people. Just a couple of weeks ago he had attended a moonlit picnic hosted by the Earl of Rosthorn here in the forest. It was almost impossible to realize that it was the same place. Rosthorn, whose reputation was far from savory, had dallied with Morgan almost to the point of indiscretion on that occasion and had provoked considerable gossip.

Alleyne gritted his teeth. He was not sure how much farther he could go. He had not known it was possible to feel such pain. He felt jarred by every step his horse took. Yet he dared not dismount. He certainly would not be able to walk alone. He called upon every reserve of strength and willpower and rode onward. If he could just reach Brussels ...

But the forest floor was uneven, and his horse had undoubtedly been as frightened as he by the dire conditions of the battlefield and was now bewildered by the dead weight of the unresponsive rider on its back. The horse stumbled over a tree root and then reared in alarm. It was nothing that under ordinary circumstances Alleyne could not have controlled with ease. But these were not ordinary circumstances. He toppled heavily backward. Fortunately his boots came free of the stirrups as he did so. But he was in no condition to employ any of the defensive moves that might somehow have cushioned his fall. He fell heavily and landed hard, his head bouncing off that same offending tree root as he did so.

He was knocked instantly unconscious. Indeed, he was so pale from the loss of blood and from the fall that anyone coming upon him afterward would have assumed that he was dead. It would not even have been a startling assumption. The Forest of Soignés, even this far north of the battlefield, was littered with the bodies of the dead.

His horse pawed the air once more and galloped away.

The quiet, seemingly respectable house on the Rue d'Aremberg in Brussels that four English 'ladies' had rented two months before was in reality a brothel. Bridget Clover, Flossie Streat, Geraldine Ness, and Phyllis Leavey had come over together from London on the calculated – and correct – assumption that business in Brussels would be brisk until all the military madness had somehow been resolved. And they were very close to achieving the ambition that had brought them together in a working partnership and fast friendship four years before. Their goal, their dream, was to save enough of their earnings to enable them to retire from their profession and purchase a house somewhere in England that they would run jointly as a respectable ladies' boarding house. They had had every reason to expect that by the time they returned to England they would be free women.

But their dream had just been shattered.

On the very day when the guns of war booming somewhere south of the city proclaimed the fact that hostilities had finally been engaged and a colossal battle was raging, they had learned that all was lost in their personal world, that all their hard-earned money was gone.

Stolen.

And it was all Rachel York's fault.

She had brought the news herself, coming back into the city from the north instead of continuing on her way home to England as almost all the other British visitors to Brussels were doing. Even many of the local residents were fleeing northward. But Rachel had returned. She had come back to tell the ladies the terrible truth. But instead of raining down recriminations upon her head, as she had fully expected they would do, they had actually taken her in, since she had nowhere else to go, and given her the one spare bedchamber in the house as her own.

She was now the newest resident of the brothel.

The very thought of it might have horrified her just a short while ago. Or it might just as easily have amused her, since she had a healthy sense of humor. But right now, at this moment, she felt too wretched to react in any way at all to the simple fact that she was now living with whores.

It was well after midnight. It was not a working night, a fact for which Rachel might have felt thankful if she had been thinking straight at all. But she had been distraught all day yesterday and today too until she had arrived here and broken the ghastly news. Now she was merely numb.

Numb and horribly guilty.

They were in the sitting room, the five of them. It would have been difficult to go to bed and to sleep anyway, but there was the added distraction of the battle that had been raging all day. They had been able to *hear it*, even though it was being fought miles away from the city, if rumor had the truth of it. There had been a great deal of rumor and many waves of panic when the citizens who had not already fled had expected an imminent invasion by war-maddened French soldiers. But news had come late in the evening that the battle was over, that the British and her allies had won the victory and were chasing the French army back in the direction of Paris.

'A fat lot of good that will do us,' Geraldine had commented, her hands splayed on her magnificent hips. 'All those lovely men gone and us sitting here like a quartet of poor church mice.'

But it was not just the war news that had kept them all up. It was dismay and fury and frustration – and the burning desire for revenge.

Geraldine was pacing, her purple silk dressing gown billowing out behind her with each long stride while the violet nightgown beneath it molded her voluptuous figure, and her loose black hair bounced against her shoulders, and one arm sawed the air as if she were a tragedian onstage. Her Italian heritage was very obvious to Rachel, who sat to one side of the fireplace, hugging a shawl about her shoulders even though it was not a cold night.

'The slimy, villainous toad,' Geraldine declaimed. 'Just wait till I get my hands on him. I'll tear him limb from limb. I'll squeeze the life out of him.'

'We have to find him first, Gerry,' Bridget said. She was sprawled in a chair, looking weary. She was

10

also rather dazzling on the eyes, her shocking pink dressing gown clashing horribly with her improbably red hair.

'Oh, I'll find him, Bridge, never you worry.' Geraldine lifted her hands before her face and made it very clear what she would do with them if the neck of the Reverend Nigel Crawley had just been obliging enough to appear between them at that moment.

But Nigel Crawley was long gone. He was probably in England by now, a great deal of money that was not his own on his very handsome and pious and villainous person.

Rachel thought she would rather enjoy blackening both his eyes herself and knocking his perfect teeth down his throat, though she was not normally of a violent turn of mind. If it were not for her, he would never have met these ladies. And if he had not met them, he would not have made off with their savings.

Flossie was pacing too, somehow avoiding collisions with Geraldine. With her short blond curls and big blue eyes and tiny stature and pastel-colored garments, Flossie looked as if her head might be stuffed with nothing more valuable than fluff, but she could read and write, and she had a head for numbers. She was the treasurer of the partnership.

'We have to find Mr. Creepy Crawley,' she said. 'How or where or when I do not know since he has the whole of England to hide in – or even the whole of the world for that matter, and we have almost no money left to go after him with. But I'll find him if it's the last thing I do in this life. And if you have claimed his neck for your own, Gerry, I'll take another part of him and put a knot in it.'

'It's probably too little to tie in a knot, though,

Floss,' Phyllis said. Plump and pretty and placid, her brown hair always neatly styled, her clothes always plain and unremarkable, Phyllis looked the least like Rachel's image of a whore. And ever practical, she had just come back into the sitting room with a large tray of tea and cakes. 'Anyway, he will have spent all our money long before we find him.'

'All the more reason,' Geraldine said, 'to mash up every bone in his body. Revenge can be sweet for its own sake, Phyll.'

'How ever are we going to find him, though?' Bridget asked, pushing the fingers of one hand through her red tresses.

'We will write letters, you and I, Bridge,' Flossie said, 'to all the sisterhood who can read. We know sisters in London and Brighton and Bath and Harrogate and a few other places, don't we? We will put out the word, and we will find him. But we are going to need money to chase after him with.' She sighed and stopped pacing for a moment.

'All we need to do, then, is think of a way to get rich quick,' Geraldine said, sawing the air again with one arm. 'Any ideas, anyone? Is there some nabob we can rob?'

They all began naming various gentlemen, presumably their clients, who were or had been staying in Brussels. Rachel recognized a few of the names. But the ladies were not serious. They paused after naming a dozen or so and snickered merrily – a relief to them, no doubt, after the terrible realization today that all their savings were gone, stolen by a rogue masquerading as a clergyman.

Flossie plopped herself down on the settee and picked up one of the cakes from the plate. 'Actually there may be a way,' she said, 'though we would have to act quickly. And it would not be *robbing* exactly. A person cannot rob the dead, can she? They have no further use for their things.'

'Lord love us, Floss,' Phyllis said, sinking down beside her, a cup and saucer in her hands, 'whatever are you thinking of? I am not going about raiding any churchyards, if that is what you have on your mind. The very idea! Can you picture the four of us, shovels over our shoulders—'

'The dead from the *battle*, I am talking about,' Flossie explained, while all the rest of them looked at her, arrested, and Rachel hugged her shawl more tightly about her. 'Loads of people will be doing it. Hordes of them are already out there, I would wager, pretending to look for loved ones but really looking for loot instead. It is an easy thing for women to do. All we would need is a pathetic, slightly frantic look and a man's name on our lips. We would have to get out there soon, though, if we were to have a chance of finding anything of any value. We could make back everything we have lost if we were lucky – and diligent.'

Rachel could hear teeth chattering, realized they were her own, and clamped them firmly together. Raiding the dead – it sounded lurid. It sounded like the stuff of nightmares.

'I don't know, Floss,' Bridget said doubtfully. 'It doesn't seem right. But you aren't serious anyway, are you?'

'Why not?' Geraldine asked, both hands raised expansively. 'As Floss said, it wouldn't be exactly robbing, would it?'

'And we wouldn't be hurting anyone,' Flossie said. 'They are already dead.'

13

'Oh, goodness.' Rachel set both palms against her cheeks and held them there. 'I am the one who should be finding a solution. This is all my fault.'

Everyone's attention swung her way.

'It is *not*, my love,' Bridget assured her. 'It most certainly is not. If it is anyone's fault, it is mine for allowing you to notice me and for letting you come inside this house. I must have had rocks in my head.'

'It was not your fault, Rache,' Geraldine agreed. 'It was *our* fault. We four have oceans more experience with men than you do. I thought I could pick out a rogue from a mile away with one eye shut. But I was taken in by that handsome villain just as surely as you were.'

'So was I,' Flossie added. 'I had kept a firm grip about the purse strings for four years until he came along with his sweet talk of loving and honoring us because we shared the same profession as that Magdalene woman, and Jesus loved *her*. I would slap myself about the head if it would do any good. I gave him our savings to take back to England to deposit safely in a bank. I let him take the money – I even *thanked* him for taking it – and now it is all gone. It was my fault more than anyone's.'

'Not so, Floss,' Phyllis said. 'We all agreed to it. That's what we have always done – planned together, worked together, made decisions together.'

'But I introduced him to you,' Rachel said with a sigh. 'I was so proud of him for not shunning you. I brought him here. I betrayed you all.'

'Nonsense, Rache,' Geraldine said briskly. 'You lost everything you had to him too, didn't you, the same as we did? And you had the courage to come back and tell us about it when as far as you knew we might have bitten your head off.'

14

'We are wasting time with this pointless talk about who is to blame,' Flossie said, 'when we all *know* who is to blame. If we don't decide to get out fast to where the fighting was, there will be nothing left for us.'

'I for one am going, Floss, even if I have to go alone,' Geraldine said. 'There will be rich pickings out there, I don't doubt, and I mean to have some of them. I mean to have money to go after that blackest of black-hearted villains with.'

No one seemed to consider the fact that if they could acquire a great deal of money in such a way they might simply use it to replace their loss and restore their dream and forget about the Reverend Nigel Crawley, who might be anywhere on the globe at that moment or within the next few days or weeks. But sometimes outrage and the need for revenge could take precedence even over dreams.

'I have a client coming tomorrow afternoon – or *this* afternoon, I suppose I mean,' Bridget said, crossing her arms beneath her bosom and hunching her shoulders. 'Young Hawkins. I couldn't go out for more than a little while, and so it would not be worth my going at all, would it?'

Her voice was shaking slightly, Rachel noticed.

'And I *won't* go even though I don't have Bridget's excuse,' Phyllis said, looking apologetic as she set down her cup and saucer. 'I'm sorry, but I would fall into a dead faint at the first sight of blood, and then I would be useless. And I would have nightmares for the rest of my life and wake you all up every night with my screams. I probably will anyway at the very thought of it. I'll stay and answer the door to any callers while Bridget's working.'

15

'Working!' Flossie said with a groan. 'Unless we do something about our situation, we are going to be working until we are old and decrepit, Phyll.'

'I already am that,' Bridget said.

'No, you aren't, Bridge,' Flossie told her firmly. 'You are in your prime. Lots of the young bucks still come to you from choice rather than to any of the rest of us, especially the virgins.'

'Because I remind them of their mothers,' Bridget said.

'With *those* tresses, Bridge?' Geraldine said with an inelegant snort. 'I think not.'

'I don't make them nervous or afraid of being failures,' Bridget explained. 'I make it all right for them to be less than perfect their first few times. What man ever is perfect for a good long while, after all? And most never are.'

Despite herself, Rachel could feel herself blushing.

'You and I will go, then, Gerry,' Flossie said, getting to her feet. 'I am not in the least afraid of a few dead bodies. Nor am I afraid of nightmares. Let's go and make our fortune and then let's make that Crawley fellow sorry his father ever looked at his mother with lust in his eye.'

'I would go too,' Bridget said. 'But young Hawkins insisted upon coming today. He wants me to teach him how to impress his bride when he marries in the autumn.'

Bridget was in her thirties. She had once been hired as Rachel's nurse by the child's widowed father, and the two had quickly grown as fond of each other as if they were mother and daughter. But Rachel's father had lost everything at the card tables – something that had happened with disturbing regularity throughout

16

his adult life – and had been forced to let Bridget go. It was only a month or so ago that the two women had met again, quite by chance, on a street in Brussels, and Rachel learned what had become of her beloved nurse. She had insisted upon renewing their acquaintance despite Bridget's misgivings.

Rachel suddenly surged to her feet without at all realizing that she was about to do so – or that she was about to say what she did.

'I am going too,' she announced. 'I am going with Geraldine and Flossie.'

There was a chorus of comment as all attention turned her way. But she held up both hands, palms out.

'I am the one mainly responsible for losing your hard-earned money,' she said. 'No matter what you all say to the contrary to try to make me feel better, that is the plain truth. Besides, I have a grievance of my own against Mr. Crawley. He gulled me into admiring and respecting him and even agreeing to be his bride. He stole from my friends and he stole from me, and then he tried to lie to me, thinking, no doubt, that I was a total idiot instead of just foolish beyond belief. If we are to go after him, and if we need money to do it, then I am going to do my part to get some. I am going out there with Geraldine and Flossie to loot the bodies of the dead.'

She could have wished then that she were still sitting. Her legs suddenly felt as if someone had removed every bone from them.

'Oh, no, my love,' Bridget said, getting to her feet and taking a step in Rachel's direction.

'Leave her alone, Bridge,' Geraldine said. 'I have liked you from the first moment, Rache, because you

17

are a regular person and not one of those high-and-mighty ladies who poke their noses at the sky and sniff the air when they pass us as if we carry around two-week-old dead dogs in our reticules. But now tonight I like you a whole lot more. You have spirit. Don't you take what he did to you lying down – to borrow an image.'

'I do not intend to,' Rachel said. 'For the past year I have been a meek, mild-mannered lady's companion. I hated every moment of that year. If I had not, I surely would not have been so taken in by a smiling villain. Let us go now, without any more talk.'

'Hurrah for Rachel,' Flossie said.

As she led the way from the room in order to run upstairs to don warm, serviceable clothes, Rachel tried not even to think of what she was about to do.

I am going out there with Geraldine and Flossie to loot the bodies of the dead.

Chapter Two

The road south of Brussels looked like a scene from hell in the dusk of early dawn. It was clogged with carts and wagons and men trudging along on foot, some of them carrying biers or helping or dragging along a comrade. Almost all of them were wounded, some severely. They were streaming back from the battleground south of the village of Waterloo.

Rachel had never witnessed such sheer, unending horror.

It seemed to her at first that she and Flossie and Geraldine must be the only persons going in the opposite direction. But that was not so, of course. There were pedestrians, even vehicles, moving south. One of the latter, a wagon driven by a tattered soldier with a powder-blackened face, stopped to offer them a ride, and Flossie and Geraldine, acting convincingly the part of anxious wives, accepted.

Rachel did not. The bravado that had brought her out here was rapidly disintegrating. What was she *doing*? How could she even be *thinking* of profiting from all this misery?

'You go on,' she told the other two. 'There must

be many wounded men in the forest. I'll look there. I'll look for Jack and Sam too,' she added, raising her voice for the benefit of the wagon driver and anyone else who might be listening. 'And you look for Harry for me farther south.'

The lie and the deception made her feel dirty and sinful even though it was doubtful anyone was paying her any attention.

She turned off the crowded road to walk among the trees of the Forest of Soignés, though she did not go so far in that she would lose sight of the road and get lost. What on earth was she going to do now? she wondered. She could not continue with her plan, she was convinced. She could not possibly take so much as a handkerchief from a poor dead man's body. And even the thought of *seeing* one was enough to make the bile rise in her throat. Yet to go back empty-handed without at least trying would be selfish and cowardly. When Mr. Crawley had sat with the ladies in the sitting room on the Rue d'Aremberg and explained to them how potentially dangerous it was to keep a large sum of money with them in such volatile times and in a foreign city to boot, and had offered to take the money back to London with him and deposit it safely in a bank where he would arrange for it to earn some decent interest, she had sat beside him and smiled proudly over the fact that she had introduced them to such a kindly, considerate, compassionate man. Afterward she had thanked him. She had thought that for once in her life she had discovered a steady, upright, dependable man. She had almost imagined that she loved him.

Her hands curled into fists at her sides and she grit

20

her teeth. But the reality of her surroundings soon cut through pointless reminiscences.

There must be thousands of wounded on all those carts and biers, she decided, averting her face from the road to her left. All that suffering and yet she had come out here to find the dead and search their bodies and rob them of any valuable that was portable and salable. She simply could not do it.

And then her stomach seemed to perform a complete somersault, leaving her feeling as if she were about to vomit as she set eyes upon the first of the dead bodies she had come to find.

He was lying huddled against the tall trunk of one of the trees, out of sight of the road, and he was very definitely dead. He was also quite naked. She felt her abdominal muscles contract again as she took a hesi-tant, reluctant step closer. But instead of vomiting, she giggled. She slapped a hand over her mouth, more horrified by her inappropriate response than she would have been if she had emptied the contents of her stomach onto the ground in full view of a thou-sand men. What was funny about the fact that there was nothing left to loot? Someone had found this one before her and had taken everything but the body itself. She could not have done it anyway. She knew it at that moment with absolute certainty. Even if he had been fully clothed and had a costly ring on each finger, a gold watch and chain and expensive fobs at his waist, a gold sword at his side, she could not have taken any of them.

It *would* have been robbery.

He was young, with hair that looked startlingly dark in contrast to the paleness of his skin. Nakedness was horribly pathetic under such circumstances, she thought. He was an insignificant bundle of dead humanity with a nasty-looking wound on his thigh and blood pooled beneath his head, suggesting that there was a ghastly wound out of sight there. He was someone's son, someone's brother, perhaps someone's husband, someone's father. His life had been precious to him and perhaps to dozens of other people.

The hand over her mouth began to shake. It felt cold and clammy.

'Help!' she called weakly in the direction of the road. She cleared her throat and called a little more firmly. 'Help?'

Apart from a few incurious glances, no one took any notice of her. All were doubtless too preoccupied with their own suffering.

And then she dropped to one knee beside the dead man, intent upon she knew not what. Was she going to pray over him? Keep vigil over him? But did not even a dead stranger deserve some kind notice at his passing? He had been alive yesterday, with a history and hopes and dreams and concerns of his own. She reached out a trembling hand and set it lightly against the side of his face as if in benediction.

Poor man. Ah, poor man.

He was cold. But not entirely so. There was surely a thread of warmth beneath his skin. Rachel snatched back her hand and then lowered it gingerly again to his neck and the pulse point there.

There was a faint beating beneath her fingers.

He was still alive.

'Help!' she cried again, leaping to her feet and trying desperately to attract the notice of someone on the road. No one paid her any attention.

22

'*He is alive!*' she shrieked with all the power her lungs could muster. She was desperate for help. Perhaps his life could still be saved. But time must surely be running out for him. She yelled even more loudly, if that were possible. '*And he is my husband. Please help me, somebody.*'

A gentleman on horseback – not a military man – turned his attention her way and she thought for a moment that he was going to ride to her assistance. But a great giant of a man – a sergeant – with a bloody bandage around his head and over one eye turned off the road instead and came lumbering toward her, calling out to her as he came.

'Coming, missus,' he said. 'How bad hurt is he?'

'I do not know. Very badly, I fear.' She was sobbing aloud, Rachel realized, just as if the unconscious man really were someone dear to her. 'Please help him. Oh, please help him.'

Rachel had foolishly expected that once they reached Brussels all would be well, that there would be a whole host of physicians and surgeons waiting to tend the wounds of just the group to which she had attached herself. She walked beside the wagon on which Sergeant William Strickland had somehow found space for the naked, unconscious man. Someone had produced a tattered piece of sacking with which to cover him partially, and Rachel had contributed her shawl for the same purpose. The sergeant trudged along at her side, introducing himself and explaining that he had lost an eye in the battle but that he would have returned to his regiment after being treated in a field hospital except that he had found that he was being discharged from the

23

army, which apparently had no use for one-eyed sergeants. He had been paid up to date, his dismissal had been written into his pay book, and that was that.

'A lifetime of soldiering swilled down the gutter like so much sewage, so to speak,' he said sadly. 'But no matter. I'll come about. You have your man to worry about, missus, and don't need to listen to my woes. He will pull through, God willing.'

When they *did* reach Brussels, of course, there was such a huge number of wounded and dying about the Namur Gates that the unconscious man, who could not speak for himself, might never have seen a surgeon if the sergeant had not exerted the authority to which he was no longer entitled and barked out a few orders to clear a path to one of the makeshift hospital tents. Rachel did not watch while a musket ball was dug out of the man's thigh – thank heaven he was unconscious, she thought, feeling faint at the very thought of what was happening to him. When she saw him again, both his leg and his head were heavily bandaged and he was wrapped in a coarse blanket. Sergeant Strickland had found a stretcher and two private soldiers, who loaded the man onto it.

Then the sergeant turned to her.

'The sawbones thinks your man has a chance if the fever don't get him and if the knock on his head didn't crack his skull,' he told her bluntly. 'Where to, missus?'

It was a question that had Rachel gaping back at him. Where to, indeed? Who *was* the wounded man, and where did he belong? There was no knowing until he regained consciousness. In the meantime, she had claimed him for herself. She had called him her husband in a desperate – and successful – attempt to attract someone's attention back there in the forest.

But where could she take him? The only home she had in Brussels was the brothel. And she was only a guest there – a totally dependent guest at that, since she had almost no money of her own with which to help pay the rent. Worse than that, she was very largely responsible for the fact that Bridget and the other three had lost almost all of their money too. How could she now take the wounded man there and ask the ladies to tend and feed him until they could find out where he belonged and arrange to have him taken there?

But what else could she do?

'You are in shock, missus,' the sergeant said, taking her solicitously by the elbow. 'Take a deep breath now and let it out slowly. At least he is alive. Thousands aren't.'

'We live on the Rue d'Aremberg,' she said, shaking her head as if to clear it. 'Follow me, if you please.'

She strode off in the direction of the brothel.

Phyllis was up to her elbows in bread dough – their servants had fled Brussels before the battle – and Bridget was preparing to entertain Mr. Hawkins. She came out of her room at the sound of the commotion at the front door, red hair tied in a loose topknot with pink ribbon in order to keep it off her face, cheeks aflame with rouge, one eye heavily painted with blue shadow and thick black lines above and below the lids, the other startlingly naked in contrast.

'Lord love us,' Phyllis said, her eyes alighting on Sergeant Strickland, 'a one-eyed giant and I am the only one available.'

'Rachel is with him,' Bridget pointed out. 'My

25

love, what *is* this? Did you run into trouble? She did not mean any harm, soldier. She was just—'

'Oh, Bridget, Phyllis,' Rachel said all in a rush, 'I was searching through the forest, and I came across this man on the stretcher here. I thought he was dead, but then I touched him and realized he was still alive, but he had been shot in the leg and had a horrible head wound. I called to all the men passing on the road, but no one took any notice until I cried that he was alive and was my husband. Then Sergeant Strickland came and helped me and carried the man to a wagon. And after we had arrived back in Brussels and a surgeon had tended him, the sergeant found these men with their stretcher and asked me where they could bring the wounded man. I could think of nowhere but here. I am so sorry. I—'

'He is *not* your man, missus?' Sergeant Strickland asked, eyeing Bridget with suspicious fascination.

The two private soldiers were leering and grinning.

'Did you find anything on him?' Bridget asked, looking at Rachel from her grotesquely mismatched eyes.

'Nothing.' Rachel felt horribly guilty then. Not only had she not collected any loot, but she had also burdened her friends with another mouth to feed – *if* he ever regained consciousness to eat, that was. 'He had been stripped.'

'Of everything?' Bridget stepped closer to the stretcher and lifted one corner of the blanket. 'Oh, my.'

'You look as if you are about to pass out yourself, Sergeant,' Phyllis said, wiping floury hands on her large apron.

He had lost an eye. For the first time Rachel looked closely at him, ashamed that she had virtually ignored

26

his plight in her anxiety over the other man. He was indeed looking pasty.

'That is not *blood* on your bandage by any chance, is it?' Phyllis asked. 'If it is, I am about to faint.'

'Where are we to put 'im, Sarge?' one of the private soldiers asked.

'You did the right thing, Rachel, my love,' Bridget said. 'Now where *shall* we put him, poor man? He looks more than half dead.'

Apart from a few small attic rooms designed for servants, there were no spare bedchambers – Rachel had been given the last one just the day before.

'My room,' she said. 'We will put him in there, and I shall sleep in the attic.'

The private soldiers carried the stretcher upstairs while Rachel led the way to her room to fold back the bedcovers so that the wounded man could be lifted straight onto the bed she had never yet slept on herself. She could hear Phyllis behind her in the hallway.

'If you don't have anywhere else to go, Sergeant,' she was saying, 'and I daresay you do not, we will put you to bed in one of the attic rooms. I'll make you some tea and some broth. No, you must not argue. You look dead on your feet. Just don't ever ask me to change that bandage. That's all I ask.'

'What exactly *is* this place?' Rachel heard the sergeant ask. 'Is it by any chance—'

'Lord love us,' Phyllis said. 'You must be more than half blind if you have to ask that question. Of *course* it is.'

Once Sergeant Strickland gave in to Phyllis's insistence that he lie down and allow himself to be nursed,

27

he became really very ill indeed, with a crashing headache and a mounting fever. Despite his feeble protests, Phyllis and Rachel went up and down stairs to him several times for the rest of the day, as did Bridget after her appointment with Mr. Hawkins was over.

It surprised Rachel to realize that she felt nothing at all – no shock, no embarrassment, no revulsion – to know that she was sharing a house with a whore who was in the very act of plying her trade. There were more important things to think about.

She spent most of the afternoon and evening in her own room, seated at the bedside of the unknown man, whose identity she might never know, she realized. He had shown no flicker of returning consciousness since the first moment she saw him. He was deathly pale – almost as white as the bandage in which his head was swathed and the large nightshirt that Bridget had found for him and that she and Phyllis had dressed him in after shooing Rachel from the room. That fact would have amused Rachel if she had been in the mood to feel amused. She was the one who had found him naked, yet her old nurse now thought that her modesty needed preserving.

A few times Rachel felt the pulse in his neck to assure herself that he still lived.

Flossie and Geraldine returned early in the evening – empty-handed.

'We went all the way to the village of Waterloo and out beyond it to where the battle was fought yesterday,' Flossie told them when they all gathered in the sitting room, which was set up for cards later in the evening – this was a working night, Rachel gathered. 'You can't imagine the sight, Bridge. Poor Phyll

28

would have been in a dead faint from the first moment.'

'There were plentiful pickings out there,' Geraldine said. 'We could have been as rich as Croesus by now if we had not run into a couple of greedy women. The very first dead body we came across was that of a young officer who couldn't have been a day over seventeen, could he, Floss? And he was being stripped of all his precious finery by two women who had all the tender sensibilities of two blocks of wood. I gave them the length of my tongue, I can tell you.'

'She made the air turn blue,' Flossie said admiringly. 'Then one of the women made the mistake of sneering. I punched her senseless. Look, Bridge, my knuckles are still red. It will be *days* before I have the hands of a lady again. And one of my precious nails broke off. Now I'll have to cut the others to match. I *hate* having short nails.'

'I sat guard over the boy,' Geraldine told them, 'while Floss went in search of a burial party that would treat him with the proper respect. Poor lamb. I shed more than one tear over him, I don't mind telling you.'

'After that,' Flossie explained rather sheepishly, 'we didn't have the heart to raid any of the other bodies, did we, Gerry? We couldn't help remembering that all those men had mothers.'

'I like you both the better for it,' Phyllis assured them.

'So do I,' Bridget said. 'I didn't say so at the time, but I was glad young Hawkins was coming this afternoon and I had an excuse not to go out myself. It didn't seem right somehow. I would rather end up in

29

the poorhouse than make my fortune off the deaths of brave boys.'

'We will have to discover another way,' Geraldine said. 'There is no chance that I am going to get philosophical about this, Bridge, and return meekly to earning my living on my back for another ten years or so. I may have to do it, of course, but only after finding that man and giving him what for. Then I won't find the whoring so bad even if we don't recover a penny of our money. But how did you do, Rache? Did you find anything?'

They both looked at her hopefully.

'No treasures, I am afraid,' she said with a grimace. 'Only liabilities.'

'Rachel came across a wounded, unconscious man in the forest,' Phyllis explained, 'and brought him home with her. He was naked.'

'That must have been a thrill,' Flossie said, looking interested. '*Was* it, Rachel? Was he worth looking at?'

'He certainly was that, Floss,' Phyllis said, 'especially in the part that matters most. *Very* impressive. He is up in Rachel's bed, still unconscious.'

'There is a sergeant up in the attic too,' Bridget said. 'He helped Rachel bring the other man here, but he was half dead himself. He lost an eye in the battle. We put him to bed.'

'And so now, since yesterday morning,' Rachel said, 'you have acquired three more mouths to feed, all courtesy of me. But if your young officer had been alive, would you have been able to leave him there to die any more than I could with this man?'

'We would be fighting over whose bed we were going to put him in – Flossie's or mine,' Geraldine said. 'Don't feel bad, Rache. We'll find a way to run that villain to earth and get our money back – yours too. In the meantime we get to play the part of merciful angels. I fancy it.'

'We had better go look the patients over, Gerry, while we have time,' Flossie said, getting to her feet. 'We are going to have to get ready for work soon. We still have to earn our daily bread.'

They all discussed the mystery of the unconscious man's identity as they stood about his bed a few minutes later, gazing down at him. There was no knowing who he was, of course. But they all agreed that he was probably a gentleman – an officer. For one thing, it appeared that he must have had a horse. The cut and lump on his head suggested that he had done more than slip and fall as he walked through the forest. The wounds were more consistent with a fall from horseback. Then there were the facts, pointed out by Flossie, that his hands were not callused and his fingernails were well manicured. His body showed no sign of abuse either, apart from the recent wounds – there were no whip marks on his back, Bridget reported, to suggest that he was a private soldier. His dark hair was short and fashionably cut, Rachel could recall even though it was now almost completely covered by the bandage. He had a prominent nose – an aristocratic nose, according to Geraldine, though that in itself was inconclusive evidence of his social status.

Rachel sat up with him all night though there was nothing to do but gaze at him and occasionally feel his cheeks and his forehead for telltale signs of fever and his neck for the beat of his pulse – and listen to the sounds of merriment from downstairs and later to different sounds from the other bedchambers.

This time they *did* cause Rachel discomfort. But she could feel no moral superiority over her friends and no disapproval of the way in which they had chosen to earn their living – if they had had any choice in the matter. Not for a moment had they blamed her for what had happened, though they had ranted and raved against Mr. Crawley, with whom she had left Brussels a few days before. They were housing and feeding her with the little money that was left them and would continue to do so, she did not doubt, with the money they were now earning and the money they would earn in the nights and days to come.

In the meanwhile, she was living the life of an idle lady and was doing nothing to contribute.

Perhaps she ought to put that matter right, she thought.

It was a prospect upon which she did not care to dwell, though there was very little to distract her during that night of vigil except the man on the bed. She imagined that he must be rather handsome under more normal circumstances. She tried to picture him with his eyes open and color and animation in his face and the bandage gone from his head. She tried to imagine what he would say, what he would tell her about himself.

She did make a few trips up to the attic to make sure that Sergeant Strickland did not need anything, but each time he was sleeping.

How very unpredictable life was, she thought. After a precarious childhood and girlhood with a father who constantly gambled and was more often than not only half a step ahead of his creditors, and

32

after taking a position as companion to Lady Flatley following his death, a dreary existence to say the least, she had thought just a few days ago that finally she had found security and possible happiness as the bride of a man worthy of her utmost respect and loyalty, even affection. Yet now here she was, as single as the day she was born and living in a brothel, watching over an anonymous wounded man, and wondering whatever was to happen to her.

She yawned and dozed in her chair.

Chapter Three

Alleyne became aware of pain and tried to escape
from it by sinking back into the blessed darkness of
oblivion. But it was not to be ignored. Indeed, there
was so much of it that he could not even analyze its
source clearly, except that a great deal of it seemed to
be concentrated in his head. It seemed to him not so
much that he was in pain as that he was pain. There
was light beyond his closed eyelids, turning them
uncomfortably orange. There was too much light. He
turned his head to escape from it, and pain shot at him
like a bullet entering his brain and shattering into a
thousand shards of metal. Only some blind instinct of
self-preservation stopped him from screaming and
making matters even worse.

'He is coming around,' a voice said. A female
voice.

'Should I fetch some burnt feathers, do you think,
Bridge, and hold them under his nose?' another
female voice asked.

'No,' the first voice replied. 'We don't want to jolt
him awake, Phyll. He is going to have a giant of a
headache as it is.'

There was nothing future about it, Alleyne thought. And a giant would look like a pygmy if it were to stand beside his headache.

'Is he going to live, then?' a third female voice asked. 'All last night and today I have expected him to die. He is as pale as the pillow. Even his lips are white.'

'Only time will tell, Rache,' a fourth voice, husky and sultry, said. 'He must have lost a lot of blood with that head wound. They are always the worst for bleeding. It is amazing he survived at all.'

'Less talk about blood, if you please, Gerry,' one of them said.

He was close to death? Alleyne thought in some surprise. Even now he was in danger of *dying*? Were they really talking about *him*?

He opened his eyes.

The room was flooded with light painful enough to make him wince and then squint. The space above his head was rimmed by four heads bent over him and examining him closely. Hovering closest to him, a foot or so above him, was a heavily painted face, the lips and cheeks brightly rouged, the eyes outlined with some black substance that also made the eyelashes spiky, the eyelids shaded sky blue. It was the face of a woman trying to appear ten years younger than she was and failing dismally. The face was framed with elaborate curls of burnished copper highlighted with dashes of scarlet and orange.

He moved his gaze to another woman, a Latin beauty vivid in emerald green silk, her black hair swept into lavish swirls, her eyes black and bold in a handsome face made more alluring with subtly applied cosmetics. She wore an old-fashioned black patch in the shape of a heart to the right side of her mouth. Beside her was a smaller, voluptuously shaped woman with a heart-shaped face surrounded by luxurious masses of short blond ringlets. She gazed frankly back at him from large, pure-blue eyes enhanced slightly with paint. The fourth face, plump and pretty and also sporting cosmetics, was rimmed by shining light brown hair. He was half aware that someone else was standing at the foot of his bed, holding onto the bedpost, but he dared not move his head to bring her into focus. Besides, he had seen enough to have been able to draw a startling conclusion.

'I have died and gone to heaven,' he muttered, closing his eyes again. 'And heaven is a brothel. Or is it really a cruel hell since, sadly, I seem to find myself incapable of taking advantage of my good fortune?'

The sound of appreciative feminine laughter was such excruciating agony that he retreated thankfully into unconsciousness again.

They had been right – he really *was* a gentleman, Rachel thought as she sat by the unknown man's bedside again during the night, having slept for much of the day at Bridget's insistence before helping in the kitchen and then assisting Geraldine in changing Sergeant Strickland's bandages. It had not been for the squeamish, that task. The sergeant kept wanting to get up, but as Geraldine had explained to him, he was not with his men now, able to get his way over every little thing by barking and blustering. He had five women to deal with, and they were far more formidable than a company of soldiers. The sergeant had lain meekly – and probably gratefully – back on his pillows.

During his brief spell of consciousness, the mystery man had spoken with the refined accents of a gentleman. He must be an officer, then, who had been wounded in battle. Perhaps he had family members right here in Brussels who were anxiously awaiting news of his fate. How frustrating not to be able to inform them that he was safe – though that was not by any means a foregone conclusion, Rachel thought, getting to her feet for the dozenth time to feel his forehead, which was surely warmer than it had been an hour ago. He might yet die of his ghastly head wound – a truly nasty cut that ought to have been stitched but had not been, and a lump the size of a large egg. He might very easily die if he became fevered, as so many men did after submitting to a surgeon's knife. At least his leg had not had to be amputated.

She ought to tiptoe up to the attic to look in on Sergeant Strickland again, she thought. She had heard the sounds of two men leaving the house within the past hour, but two of the ladies must still be entertaining. Perhaps she ought to go down to the kitchen to make some tea for them all. They must be weary and thirsty after a night's work.

It was truly amazing how quickly she was adapting to being where she was.

She ought to do *something* or she would be nodding in her chair again.

But she became suddenly aware of a slight stirring from the direction of the bed. She sat very still and willed him to live, to recover from his wounds, to open his eyes. She felt very responsible for him in some curious way. If only he could survive, she thought, perhaps she could forgive herself for having been in the forest on such a sordid mission. If she had not been there, after all, she would not have found him. No one would, and he would surely have died.

Just when she thought she must have imagined his movements, he opened his eyes and gazed blankly upward. Rachel got hurriedly to her feet and leaned over the bed so that he would not have to turn his head in order to see her. His eyes turned in her direction and focused on her in the candlelight. They were dark eyes and convinced her that she had been right about something else – he was a handsome man.

'I dreamed I was in heaven and it was a brothel,' he said. 'Now I dream that I am in heaven with a golden angel. I believe I like this version better.' His eyes fluttered closed and his lips curved upward at the corners. He was a man with some sense of humor, then.

'Alas,' she said, 'it is a very earthly paradise. Are you still in great pain?'

'Did I drink a barrel of rum dry?' he asked. 'Or did I do something else to my head?'

'You fell and hit it,' she said. 'I think you fell from a horse.'

'Unpardonably clumsy of me,' he said. 'And deuced embarrassing too if it is true. I have never fallen off a horse in my life.'

'You had been shot in the leg,' she said. 'Riding must have been very difficult and excruciatingly painful.'

'Shot in the leg?' He frowned and opened his eyes again. He moved both legs and swore most foully before apologizing. 'Who shot me?'

'I believe,' she said, 'it must have been a French soldier. I hope it was not one of your own.'

His eyes focused more sharply on her then. 'This is not England, is it?' he said. 'I am in Belgium. There was a battle.'

She saw that his cheeks were now noticeably flushed with fever. It was in his eyes too – they seemed unnaturally bright in the light of the single candle. She turned to the bowl of water that was on a table beside the bed, squeezed out the cloth that was soaking in it, and held it to his cheeks one at a time and then to his brow. He sighed his appreciation.

'It is best not even to think of it now,' she said. 'But the battle was won, you will be pleased to know. I daresay it was still being fought when you left the battlefield.'

He stared up at her, a crease between his brows for a moment before he closed his eyes again.

'I am afraid,' she said, 'that you have a slight fever. The musket ball was still lodged in your thigh and had to be removed by a surgeon, you see. Fortunately, that happened while you were unconscious. You really ought to drink some water. Let me help you sit up high enough to sip from this glass. It will not be easy for you – you have a nasty lump on your head. And a cut.'

'It feels as if the lump must be the size of a cricket ball,' he said. 'Am I in Brussels?'

'Yes,' she said. 'We brought you back here.'

'The battle. I remember now,' he said, frowning. But he did not say any more about it. Rachel was not sure she wanted to hear any of the gory details anyway.

He drank a little water, though she knew that the

pain of lifting his head was almost unbearable for him. She lowered him carefully to the pillow again, wiped up some of the water that had run down over his chin, and then pressed the cool cloth to his forehead once more.

'Do you have any family here?' she asked him. 'Or any friends? Anyone who will be anxiously awaiting news of your fate?'

'I ...' He frowned at her again. 'I ... am not sure. *Do* I?'

'We really would like to inform them that you are safe and that you are here in Brussels,' she said. 'Or perhaps your family is all in England. I will write a letter to them tomorrow if you wish.'

She was quite unprepared for what he said next.

'Who the devil am I?' he asked her, though she had the feeling it was a rhetorical question.

It chilled her to the bone.

He appeared to have lapsed into unconsciousness again.

It was daytime when Alleyne awoke again. Not that he had been entirely unconscious through the night. He was aware that he had been alternately burning up with heat and shivering with cold, that he had dreamed and had strange hallucinations – none of which he could now remember – and that he had called out several times. He was aware that someone had hovered over him all night long, cooling his hot face with wet cloths, tucking warm blankets about him, coaxing water between his lips, and crooning comforting words to him.

But he awoke feeling totally disoriented. Where the devil *was* he?

40

He had been shot in the leg, he reminded himself, and knocked from his horse, jarring every bone in his body as he landed and giving himself a massive concussion. He had been picked up and brought to a brothel, which was inhabited by at least four painted whores and one golden angel. He had contracted a fever and had been having hallucinations through the night. Perhaps it was all a strange, bizarre dream.

He opened his eyes.

He had not imagined the angel. She was rising to her feet from a chair beside his bed and coming to lean over him. She set a cool hand against his brow. Her hair was pure, shining gold, her complexion roses and cream. Her eyes, hazel in color, were large and thickly fringed with lashes several shades darker than her hair. Her mouth was wide and generous, her nose straight. She was neither slender nor plump. She was beautifully proportioned and all woman. She smelled sweet, though of no discernible perfume.

She was surely the most lovely woman he had ever seen.

He was in love, he thought, only half in humor.

'Are you feeling any better?' she asked him.

She was also, if his guess earlier had been correct, living in a brothel. Did that make her ...

'I have the monarch of all headaches,' he told her, giving his attention to his physical condition – not difficult to do when it was clamoring to be noticed. 'I feel as if every bone in my body has been wrenched none too gently into a new position, and I dare not even try moving my left leg. I am uncomfortably warm, yet I am shivering too. My eyes are sensitive to the light. Apart from those minor complaints, I am, I believe, in the best of health.' He tried to grin at her

41

and felt a sharp pull from somewhere to the side of his head – that must be where the wound was. 'Have I been a troublesome patient? I believe I have.'

She smiled down into his eyes. She had white, even teeth. The expression warmed her eyes and made her purely pretty as well as beautiful. It also gave her sparkle and a look of mischief.

He was in love indeed. He was a hopeless case. Terminally besotted.

But she had bathed his brow and murmured soft nothings to him all through a fevered night. What red-blooded male would not be infatuated, especially when she really did look like an angel?

Of course, he was at least partially delirious.

'Not at all,' she said in answer to his question, 'except that you do have a nasty habit of inviting me to go to the devil whenever I try to lift your head so that you may drink.'

'No! Have I really been behaving with such dastardly lack of gallantry?' he asked her. 'I do beg your pardon. I am still not convinced that I have not died and gone to heaven and been assigned my very own guardian angel. If I am wrong, you could try kissing me to wake me up.'

She laughed softly enough not to jar his headache, but she did not, alas, accept his invitation.

Someone else came into the room at that point – the black-haired, bold-eyed Latin charmer he had seen the first time he regained consciousness. She set down a fresh bowl of water, set her hands on her shapely hips, struck a pose that displayed both hips and bosom to best advantage, and looked him up and down slowly – it seemed to Alleyne that her eyes stripped away bedcovers as she did so.

42

'Well, you are a handsome devil now that your eyes are open and there is some color in your cheeks,' she said, 'though I daresay you will look even more gorgeous once you have shed the white bonnet. Gone to heaven and discovered that it is a brothel, indeed – you should be so lucky! It's time you went to bed, Rache, and got some beauty rest. Bridget says you have been up all night again. I'll take over in here. Does his thigh need rebandaging, by any happy chance?'

Her eyes met Alleyne's with frank appreciation and she pursed her lips. She was not wearing cosmetics this morning, but there was a raw sensuality about her that proclaimed her profession.

He chuckled and then winced and wished he had not acknowledged her bold flirtation by committing such violence to his own head.

'I'll just bathe his face once more to reduce the fever, Geraldine,' the golden angel said. She was Rache – Rachel? 'And then I will lie down. I *am* tired, I must confess. But so must you be.'

The dark-haired beauty – Geraldine – shrugged, winked boldly at Alleyne, and withdrew with the bowl of stale water.

'*Is* this a brothel?' Alleyne asked. It must be, but he ought not to have asked the question aloud, he realized as Rachel flushed.

'We will not charge you for the use of the bed,' she told him, a slight edge to her voice.

It was her way of saying yes, he supposed. Which fact made her ...

His eyes swiveled about the room. It was pleasantly, respectably decorated and furnished in various shades of fawn and gold – not a sign of scarlet

43

anywhere. The bed was relatively narrow – but then it was quite wide enough, he supposed, to serve its appointed function. The room was normally inhabited by a woman. There were brushes and bottles and a book on the dressing table.

'Is this *your* room?' he asked her.

'Not while you are in it.' She raised her eyebrows and looked very directly at him. Was she angry? 'And, yes, I *do* live here.'

'I beg your pardon,' he said. 'I have taken your bed.'

'You need not apologize,' she told him. 'You did not demand it, did you? Or even ask for it. I had you brought here after I found you in the forest. The sergeant who helped me – and you – is here too, in a bed in the attic. He lost an eye in the battle and is suffering a great deal more than he will admit to. The loss of his eye is particularly unfortunate because he has been summarily discharged from the army. Yet he has known no other life since he was thirteen years old.'

'You found me in the forest? The Forest of Soignés?' What the devil had he been doing there? He had a confused memory of the sound of heavy guns, but try as he would he could not recall any other detail of the battle. It had been against Napoléon Bonaparte and had been brewing for months – he knew that much. He must have been fighting in it. But why had he ridden into the forest? And why had his men abandoned him there? Or had he been alone? But if he had been wounded in battle, why had he not sought medical attention on the field?

'I thought you were dead,' she said, dipping the cloth in the fresh water and pressing its blessed coolness to his brow. 'If I had not stooped down to touch you, I would not have realized that you still lived. You would indeed have died out there.'

'Then I am eternally in your debt,' he said, 'and in that of the sergeant, whom I must thank in person as soon as I am able.' He thought of something suddenly and felt a flood of relief considering the fact that there was a detail far more important than the battle itself that he could not recall. 'What did you do with my belongings?'

He watched her squeeze out the cloth and dip and squeeze it again before answering.

'You had been robbed,' she said. 'Of everything.'

'Of ... ' He stared at her, aghast. 'Of *everything*? All my clothes too?'

She nodded.

Good Lord! She had found him naked? But it was not embarrassment that caused him to shut his eyes tightly and clench his teeth, heedless for the moment of the pain the tension caused him. He could feel panic welling up inside him and threatening to burst forth. He wanted to throw back the bedcovers, leap from the bed, and run from the room. But where would he go? And for what purpose?

In search of his identity?

There was nothing left to help him remember.

Calm down, he told himself. *Calm down*. He had fallen from his horse and banged his head hard enough to give himself a concussion. He had the headache to prove it. He was fortunate to be alive. There probably really was a lump the size of a cricket ball on the side of his head. He must give his brain a chance to reorganize itself. He must give the swelling time to go down and his head wounds time to heal.

45

He must give his fever time to recede completely. There was no hurry. Later today or tomorrow or the next day he would remember.

'What is your name?' she asked him as she pressed the cloth to one warm cheek.

'Go to the devil!' he exclaimed, and then snapped his eyes open to gaze up at her in instant remorse. Her teeth were sunk into her lower lip, and her eyes were wide with dismay.

'I am so sorry ... '

'I do beg your pardon ... '

They spoke simultaneously.

'I cannot remember,' he admitted curtly, deliberately quelling the panic he felt.

'You must not worry about it.' She smiled at him. 'You will remember soon.'

'Deuce take it, I do not even know my own name.'

The horror of it grabbed at his stomach like a giant hand squeezing tightly. He fought a wave of nausea as he grasped her wrist with one hand and her other arm with the other. He was aware of pain in both his arms. He could see black and purple bruises all along his right arm.

'You are alive,' she said, leaning a little closer, 'and you are conscious again. Your fever seems to have gone down considerably. By some miracle you did not break any bones in your fall. Bridget says you are going to live, and I trust her judgment. Just give yourself some time. Everything will come back to you. Until it does, let your mind rest along with your body.'

If he drew her any closer, he thought, he would be able to kiss her after all. What a stupid thought when there was not a bone in his body that did not feel sorely abused! Probably he would discover if he *did* kiss her that even his lips hurt.

'I owe you my life,' he said. 'Thank you. And how inadequate words can be sometimes.'

She drew gently away from his grasp and swilled out the cloth again.

'Are you one of them?' he asked abruptly, closing his eyes and fighting nausea again. 'Are you a ... Do you *work* here?'

For a few moments all he heard was the trickling of water. He wished he could recall the question.

'I am here, am I not?' she said, the edge back in her voice.

'You do not look ... You look different from the others,' he said.

'Meaning that they look like whores and I do not?' she asked him. He could tell from the tone of her voice that he had offended her.

'I suppose so,' he said. 'I beg your pardon. I ought not to have asked. It is none of my business.'

She laughed softly – it was somehow not a pleasant sound.

'That is my main appeal,' she said, 'that I look like an innocent, like a lady, like an angel, as you remarked earlier. It takes all types to run a successful brothel. Men have vastly different tastes when it comes to the women for whose favors they will pay. I cater to the taste for refinement and the illusion of innocence. I do innocence very well, would you not agree?'

Very well.

He opened his eyes to find her smiling at him as she dried her hands on a towel. It was a smile that matched the voice she was using – not quite pleasant.

47

'I do beg your pardon – again,' he said. 'I seem to have done nothing but insult you ever since I regained consciousness. I hope such unmannerly behavior is not habitual with me. Forgive me, please?'

His head was feeling like a balloon that was expanding to the point of bursting. His leg was throbbing like a giant drumbeat. There were other assorted ills clamoring only slightly less insistently for his attention too.

'Of course,' she told him. 'But I do not find this profession shameful or degrading or my fellow ... whores less human or less precious than other women of my acquaintance. I will see you later. Geraldine will look after you in the meanwhile. Are you hungry?'

'Not really,' he said.

He *had* offended her, he thought after she had gone. And she had every right to be annoyed with him. If it were not for her, he would probably be dead by now. And she and her friends had opened their home to him. She had given up her room for him. They were giving him twenty-four-hour care. He might have fared a great deal worse if he had been found by a respectable lady. Indeed, any lady would probably have screamed and run and then swooned after seeing his naked body and left him to die.

He chuckled softly at the mental image of such a scene but then felt a return of the nausea. And the panic.

What if his memory never returned?

Chapter Four

The kitchen was filled with delicious smells when Rachel went down there after her sleep to see if there was anything she could do to help. Phyllis was stirring a large pot of soup. One counter was covered with freshly baked bread and currant cakes. The lid was off the big teapot and the kettle was boiling on the hearth.

'Did you have a good sleep?' Phyllis asked. 'Everyone is up in William's room. Make the tea if you would be so good, Rachel, and we will take it up there. Is the other poor man still sleeping?'

Rachel had not looked in on him on her way down. She still felt somewhat embarrassed at what she had led him to believe – that she belonged here, that she worked with Bridget and Phyllis and the other two. At the same time, she felt annoyed by her own embarrassment – and by his questions. These ladies had taken her in when she had nowhere else to go. They had taken him in too. What did it matter that they were whores? They were also good people.

Sergeant Strickland had become a general favorite. Although he had lost an eye as well as his livelihood, he had refused from the start to wallow in self-pity. It had taken the combined willpower of them all to persuade him that he must remain in bed for at least a few days in order to give his wounds a chance to heal properly. Rachel was especially fond of him. He had come to the rescue of a stranger who was more severely wounded than himself.

'You won't look so bad once the eye socket has healed up and you have a patch to wear over it,' Bridget was saying as Rachel came into the small attic room carrying the tea tray while Phyllis came behind her with a plate of thickly sliced bread generously buttered. Bridget had been cleansing the wound and was winding a clean bandage about the sergeant's head.

'I just lost my appetite,' Phyllis said.

'You will look like a pirate, Will,' Geraldine told him, 'though I don't suppose you ever were a beauty anyway, were you?'

'That I were not, lass,' he agreed with a hearty laugh. 'But at least I had two eyes to go a-soldiering with. It is what I have done since I were a nipper. I don't know ought else. But I'll find something to earn my daily victuals with, I daresay. I'll survive.'

'Of course you will,' she said, leaning forward to pat his big hand. 'But you are to stay in that bed for at least another day or two. That is an order. I'll put you back there with my own two hands if you try to move.'

'I don't think you would have much success at that, lass,' he said, 'though I daresay you would give it a good try. I feel silly lying here when all I done is got an eye knocked out. But when I got up a while ago to go see that feller we brought here, I found I was swaying like a leaf in a breeze on the stairs and had to turn back. It's all this lying around that's doing it.'

'Ah, fresh bread,' Flossie said. 'There is no better cook in this world than our Phyll. She is wasting her talents being a whore.'

'I should be carrying that heavy tray, missy,' the sergeant said to Rachel. 'Except that I would probably walk into the table with it and shower everyone with boiling tea. But I will be better by tomorrow, I daresay. Would you ladies by any chance have need of the services of a hefty feller who looked ferocious even before he had to wear a black patch over his eye socket and would now make even the devil himself turn and run? To watch the door while you are busy at your work, perhaps, and to toss out any impertinent gent who forgets his manners?'

'You wish to be promoted from army sergeant to doorman at a brothel, William?' Bridget asked, biting into a slice of bread and butter.

'I wouldn't mind it until I get my feet under me, so to speak, ma'am,' he said. 'I wouldn't expect no more than my victuals and this bed here in return.'

'The point is, though, Will,' Geraldine said, 'that we don't intend to stay here longer than we have to. Now that the armies have gone as well as most of the people who came to keep them company, business is not brisk. We need to go home, and the sooner the better. We have a villain to catch and take apart piece by piece, and we mean to pursue him until we find him.'

'He took all the money we worked hard for four years to save,' Bridget explained. 'And we want it back.'

'More important than that, though,' Geraldine said, 'we want *him*, the lying, smiling toad.'

51

'Someone took off with your money?' The sergeant frowned ferociously as he took a plate with two hefty slices of bread and butter from Phyllis's hand. 'And you are going after him? I'll come with you. One look at me will wipe any smile from his face, you mark my words. And I'll give him more than a look to remember me by. Where did he go?'

'That is the trouble,' Bridget said with a sigh. 'We are almost sure he has gone to England, William, but apart from that we do not know. England is rather a large place.'

'Bridget and Flossie have written to all our sisterhood who can read,' Geraldine said. 'One of them will spot him, and even if they don't, we'll find him somehow – even if it takes a year. Or longer. What we need is a plan.'

'What we need, Gerry,' Flossie said dryly as Rachel handed about the tea, 'is money. If we are to go jaunting about England, we are going to need plenty of it. And if we are jaunting about, we won't be able to work at the same time.'

'Perhaps,' Phyllis said, 'we will go running after him and never find him and never recover our money. And in the meantime we will have spent a great deal more money and earned almost nothing. Perhaps it would be more sensible just to give up and go home and start to build our savings again.'

'But there is the principle of the thing, Phyll,' Geraldine said. 'I for one am not willing to let him get away with it. He thinks he *can* simply because we are whores. He was not nearly as contemptuous about his thieving with everyone else. He took money from Lady Flatley and other ladies, according to Rache, but he told them it was for his charities. They may never

52

even realize that their money went into his pockets instead and stayed there. But he never so much as mentioned charities to us. He just took everything, including our thanks. *That* is the point that has my blood boiling over. He made fools of us.'

'Yes,' Phyllis agreed. 'We do need to teach him a lesson even if we end up making beggars of ourselves.'

'What we need is money,' Flossie said again, tapping her fingernails against the edge of her plate, 'and plenty of it. How are we going to get our hands on it, though – apart from the obvious way, of course.'

'I wish,' Rachel said fervently, 'I had access to some of my fortune.'

The finger-tapping stopped and everyone looked at her with interest.

'You have a fortune, Rache?' Geraldine asked.

'She is Baron Weston's niece on her mother's side,' Bridget reminded them.

'My mother left me her jewels,' Rachel said. 'But they will not come into my possession for another three years, until I am twenty-five. I am sorry I even mentioned them, since they can be of no earthly use to us now. For the next three years I am going to be the poorest of any of us.'

'Where are they kept?' Flossie asked. 'Are they somewhere where we can go and get them? It would not be theft, would it? They *are* yours.'

'With black cloaks and masks and daggers shoved behind our ears as we climb ivy-covered walls in the dead of a moonless night?' Geraldine said. 'I fancy it. Do tell, Rache.'

But Rachel shook her head, laughing. 'I do not

53

even know,' she said. 'My uncle has charge of them, but I have no idea where he keeps them.'

There was, of course, a way in which she could acquire her jewels before she was twenty-five, but that was not relevant to the current situation.

'What about the man downstairs?' Sergeant Strickland asked. 'I were right about him, were I? He is a nob?'

'He is indeed a gentleman,' Rachel told him.

'Who is he, missy?' he asked.

'He does not remember,' she said.

He chuckled. 'Knocked his memory clean out of his head, did he?' he said. 'Poor devil. But if he is a nob, there will be plenty looking for him to claim him, mark my words. He may even have family right here in Brussels if they did not all run away before the fighting started as most of them did. They will be very willing to pay you all a sizable reward for saving him and caring for him, I daresay.'

'But what if he never remembers who he is?' Phyllis asked.

'We could put an advertisement with his description in all the Belgian and London papers,' Bridget suggested. 'But that would take time and money and even then his people may not pay up.'

'What we could do,' Geraldine said, 'is conceal his whereabouts when we *do* advertise, and hold him for ransom. We could demand more that way than if we merely asked for a reward. Keeping him won't be a problem, after all, will it? He does not possess a stitch of clothing apart from the nightshirt Bridge found for him. He can't run away unless he wants to be seen dashing naked down the street. And he won't be able to dash anywhere for a long time – not with that leg

54

wound of his. Where would he go anyway? He does not even know his own name.'

'I could make sure he don't run nowhere,' the sergeant said.

'How much could we demand?' Bridget asked. 'A hundred guineas?'

'Three,' Phyllis suggested.

'Five,' Geraldine said, sawing the air with one hand and slopping some of her tea into her saucer.

'I would not take a penny less than a thousand,' Flossie said. 'Plus expenses.'

They all burst out into hearty laughter then, Rachel included. She knew, of course, that none of them was serious about the kidnapping scheme. Tough as they appeared to be, these ladies were soft at heart. Their inability to rob the dead out on the battlefield proved that.

'In the meantime,' Phyllis said, 'we will have to take his nightshirt away from him so that he can't escape so easily.'

'And tie him to the bedposts,' Flossie added. 'All four of them.'

'Ah, be still, my palpitating heart,' Geraldine said, fanning her face briskly with the hand that had been waving in the air. 'We won't be able to allow him any bedsheets either, will we? He might knot them together and escape out the window with them and then wear them like a Roman toga. I'll volunteer for double guard duty every day – and night.'

'I'll stay after all,' the sergeant said. 'You will need my hefty muscles to carry in all the heavy bags of ransom money.'

'We will be *rich*, William,' Flossie said, tossing her head and setting all her curls to bouncing.

They all dissolved into laughter again.

'Seriously, though,' Rachel said when their mirth had subsided, 'his loss of memory could prove to be a serious problem, especially since it is going to be some time before he can walk again. He will have nowhere to go. But I know you are all eager to return to England soon, and so am I.'

'We'll toss him out on the street when we are ready to leave, Rache,' Geraldine said.

She was not serious, of course. They all knew that none of them would have the heart simply to abandon him.

If she could only gain access to her fortune, Rachel thought, she would be able to do far more than finance the search for Nigel Crawley, which she was not sure was such a practical idea anyway. She would be able to repay her friends all they had lost and restore their dream. She would be able to make it possible for them to retire and live the respectable lives they longed for. She would be able to salve her conscience for having caused their loss in the first place. And, of course, she would gain a welcome independence for herself.

But there was no real point in dreaming, she thought with a sigh.

'I am going down to check on the patient,' she said, getting to her feet and setting her cup and saucer on the tray. 'He may be awake and needing something.'

When Alleyne awoke again late in the afternoon, he was alone. He felt considerably better, though he dared not move either his head or his left leg. He guessed that his fever had subsided. He tried to be cheerfully nonchalant and practiced what he would say when one of the women came into his room.

'Ah, good afternoon,' he would say. 'Allow me to introduce myself, if I may. I am ... ' But although his mind remained alert and he smiled at the empty room and made a slow circling motion with one hand, the elusive name would not come.

How ridiculous to have forgotten his own name! What was the point of having survived by the skin of his teeth if he was to live the rest of his life as an anonymous nobody? Though it was foolish to start thinking that way yet, he decided, touching the bandage that was still about his head, trying gingerly to find the lump and feel how large it still was.

The door to his room opened and the golden angel – she was Rachel, though he could not call her that – came inside.

'Ah, you are awake,' she said. 'You were sleeping when I looked in earlier.'

He smiled back at her and found that the expression no longer caused him agony. He spoke before he could think about it and lose his nerve.

'I just awoke,' he said. 'Good afternoon. Allow me to present myself, if I may. I am ... '

But of course he ended up gaping foolishly at her, like a fish that had been removed from its pond and dangled in the air. His right hand, resting on the outside of the bedcovers, formed a tight fist.

'I am pleased to make your acquaintance, Mr. Smith,' she said with a light laugh, coming toward him with her right hand extended. 'Mr. *Jonathan* Smith, did you say?'

'Perhaps,' he said, forcing himself to chuckle with her, 'it is *Lord* Smith. Or Jonathan Smith, the Earl of Wherever, or Jonathan Smith, the *Duke* of Somewhere.'

'I should call you *your* grace, then, should I?' she asked him, her eyes twinkling at him as he took her hand in his and felt its slim smoothness at the same time as he became aware of the sweet, clean smell of her.

He appreciated the fact that she was encouraging him to laugh at himself. And why not? What was the alternative, after all? He closed his hand more firmly about hers and raised it to his lips. Her eyes slid from his for a moment, and he watched as her teeth sank into her lower lip. Ah, yes, she played the part of innocence consummately well. And no woman had any right to be this beautiful.

'Perhaps you had better not,' he said. 'It would be humbling to discover later that I am no duke after all, but a mere mister. I do not believe I am a Jonathan or a Smith, either.'

'Shall I address you merely as mister, then?' she asked him, smiling again as she repossessed her hand and leaned over him to unwind the bandage from his head. She examined the damage he had done to himself without touching him. 'The cut is no longer bleeding at all, mister. I believe it will be safe to leave off the bandage. If that suits you, of course, mister.'

There was laughter in her eyes as she straightened up.

It felt good to feel the air against his head. He lifted one hand to run his fingers through his hair and realized ruefully that it was matted and badly in need of a wash.

'I must be Mr. *Someone*, though, must I not?' he said. 'It would be eccentric not to be. What mother would christen her son *Mister*? But I really cannot be

58

anyone as exalted as a duke or an earl. I would not have been fighting in that battle if I were. I must be a younger son.'

'But the Duke of Wellington was fighting,' she said.

Her eyes looked more green than hazel today, perhaps reflecting the color of her dress. She was looking down very directly into his eyes, humor twinkling in her own, though it seemed to him that he could see the warmth of sympathy there too. It was absurd to be feeling slightly breathless at her closeness, he thought, and wondered if he was normally such a mooncalf in his attitude to beautiful strangers. It was very stupid too. He still felt as if his body had been abandoned in the wake of a herd of stampeding elephants.

'Ah, yes, of course,' he said, snapping the fingers of one hand. 'Perhaps that is who I am. Mystery solved. I certainly have the nose for it.'

'Except,' she said, and he noticed for the first time the ultimate perfection of her face – a small dimple to the left side of her mouth, 'that he would surely have been reported missing before now. You remember the Battle of Waterloo, then? That is what the battle is being called, I understand.'

She had rolled up the bandage and set it down beside the bowl of water. She sat down, though she leaned a little forward in her chair so that he could still feel her nearness. It struck him that perhaps she was very expert indeed at her profession and was deliberately trying to enslave him. If so, she was succeeding.

'I do.' He frowned and tried to concentrate upon

59

some memory – *any* memory. But it was no good. 'At least, I know that the battle was fought. I can remember the guns. They were deafening. No – actually they were worse than that.'

'Yes, I know,' she said. 'We heard them from here. How do you know you have a nose like the Duke of Wellington's?'

He stared at her, arrested.

'*Do* I?' he asked her.

She nodded. 'Geraldine called it an aristocratic nose.'

She got to her feet and crossed the room to a chest of drawers while he watched her. Her very feminine figure had alluring curves and was far lovelier than that of many overslender girls who were considered fashionably beautiful – though she was not much more than a girl herself, at a guess. She opened one of the drawers and then turned back toward him, a small looking glass in one hand. He glanced warily at it and licked his lips nervously.

'You do not have to look,' she said, nevertheless holding it out toward him.

'Yes, I do.' He reached out a hand and took it warily from her. What if he did not recognize the face he saw? It would somehow be more terrifying than not remembering his name. But he had known that he had a big nose, and she had confirmed that he was right.

He raised the mirror and looked. His face was pasty pale. It was surely longer and narrower than the one he was accustomed to seeing. His nose seemed correspondingly more prominent. His dark hair was disheveled and oily. The dark stubble on his cheeks and chin would almost qualify as a beard. His eyes

60

were slightly bloodshot. There were dark smudges beneath them. He looked unwell and he looked rough, but he knew the face. It was his own. He could have wept with relief. But as he gazed into his eyes, searching for answers in their depths, he could see nothing but blankness and an impenetrable barrier of anonymity.

It was like looking at himself and a complete stranger at the same time.

'I wonder you do not dash screaming from the room,' he said as she seated herself again – he noticed that she sat like a lady, her spine not quite touching the back of her chair. 'I look like a ruffian and a cutthroat – of the unwashed variety.'

'You would need a pistol in one hand and a knife in the other to be really convincing, though,' she said, tipping her head to one side and regarding him with smiling eyes again. 'Thank heaven we have no guns in the house and Phyllis guards the kitchen knives with her life. Is it the face you expected to see?'

'More or less,' he said, handing back the looking glass, 'though I believe I usually look somewhat less disreputable. It is a face without a name, though, and so I had better take whatever is available. Jonathan Smith at your service, ma'am. That is *Mister* Jonathan Smith, by the way.'

'Mr. Smith.' She laughed lightly. 'I am Rachel York.'

'Miss York.' He inclined his head in her direction and then wished he had not moved it. 'I am delighted to make your acquaintance.'

They stared at each other for a time, and then she got to her feet again and surprised him by seating herself on the side of his bed and reaching up a hand to touch his wound. He was very aware of the bare, creamy flesh above the low, square neckline of her dress and the beginnings of cleavage, most of which was hidden from sight below a lacy frill. He was aware of the faint fragrance of soap, and of her hair like a golden halo against the late afternoon sunshine beyond the window. He held his breath until he realized he could not do so indefinitely.

She was not just impersonally beautiful. She had him thinking of tumbled sheets and tangled limbs and sweat-soaked bodies. Trust his luck to land himself in a brothel without a penny to bless himself with.

'The cut is healing nicely,' she said, her fingers cool against it and causing no unnecessary pain, 'even though the surgeon did not stitch you up. The lump is going down, but it is still there.' He could feel her touch it, her fingers feather-light.

And then she was looking, not at his wounds, but directly into his eyes from only a few inches away. The laughter was gone from her own, and he could see in them only warm sympathy.

'Give yourself time to heal,' she said. 'Everything will come back to you. I promise.'

It was an absurd promise, since it concerned something quite outside her power to grant. But it comforted him, nevertheless. She gazed down at him and moistened her upper lip, corner to corner, with her tongue. Then she blushed rosily and got to her feet.

For a moment he wondered if his fever had come back.

He no longer wondered if she had set about deliberate enslavement. It was true that her manner of flirtation was more subtle than that employed by her colleagues, who were far more blatant and risqué in their dealings with him. But it was flirtation nevertheless. He was badly wounded and could scarcely move without giving himself excruciating pain. But he was not dead. He could react sexually even if he could not act on his desires. She would have to be a fool not to know it.

He did not believe she was a fool.

'I'll leave you to rest,' she said without looking at him. 'I'll come back later if there is not too much work to do. Someone will bring you dinner. You must be hungry.'

He closed his eyes after she had left the room. But sleep could no longer be summoned at will. He felt dirty and uncomfortable and restless and hungry and . . .

Deuce take it, he felt half aroused.

He needed a wash and a shave. But it struck him suddenly that he did not possess even as much as a razor or a comb. Somehow the absence of just those two small items brought crashing home to him the ghastly extent of his dilemma. And he had no money with which to buy either one. Not a single farthing.

What the devil was he going to do if his memory did not come back? Wander naked about the streets of Brussels until someone claimed him? Find some military headquarters in the hope that someone would know him there? Or that some officer had been reported missing in action? Ridiculous – there must be dozens at the very least missing in action and unaccounted for. Find an embassy, then, and set them to doing a search for a gently born family that was missing one male son or brother – probably a younger one? *Was* there an embassy in Brussels? He seemed to recall that there was one at the Hague, but when he paused over the memory, he could draw nothing personal out of it.

What was his regiment? And rank? Was he a cavalryman or an infantryman? Or perhaps he belonged to the artillery? He tried to picture himself riding into a cavalry charge with his men or leading an infantry advance. But it was no use – his imaginings could trigger no real memories.

She would come back, Rachel York had said, *if there was not too much work to do*. He grimaced. Where did she ply her trade, he wondered, now that he was occupying her room?

It was none of his business. Neither was she.

Except that he was deeply in her debt and had no idea how he was going to be able to repay her. And except that she was plain gorgeous, and he was behaving like a schoolboy dizzy and randy with his first infatuation.

Starting tomorrow, he told himself sternly, he was going to have to make a concerted effort to set his feet – figuratively even if not literally – on the road to recovery. He was already tired of this helplessness.

And tomorrow he was going to remember.

Of course he was.

Chapter Five

Rachel did not go back to the room that day. She had realized anew the uncomfortable power she had over men.

She knew that she was considered beautiful even though she would have been quite happy to be only passably good- looking. Her glass told her that it must be true, though. More than that, men had been looking at her with thinly veiled – or sometimes quite unveiled – admiration for a number of years. She had never chosen to use her power. Quite the contrary, in fact. Although she had had a strange upbringing with a father who had always lived on the edge of danger and poverty, with occasional periods of heady affluence when he had been lucky at the tables, she had been raised as a lady, and ladies did not flaunt their beauty. Besides, the sort of gentlemen she had met before her father's death, the men with whom he consorted, were certainly not the sort with whom she would wish to make any sort of alliance. And since then, since she had taken a position as Lady Flatley's companion, she had been very careful to draw as little attention as possible to her looks. One thing she had thought she liked about Nigel Crawley was that he had never made much reference to her beauty. He had seemed to admire her as a person.

She had not intended to arouse the admiration of the wounded man. She had merely wanted to show her concern and sympathy. But she had sensed his physical reaction to her and had felt the tension sizzling between them as she leaned over him.

What a foolish thing to have done. The very thought of being alone with a man in a bedchamber should have shocked her. But to have sat on the side of his bed, leaning over him, touching his head and then looking down into his eyes ...

Well, it had been remarkably unwise.

And, of course, if she was strictly truthful with herself, she would have to admit that he was not the only one to react as he had. She had felt severely discomposed. He might be wounded and helpless, but he was still a young and good-looking man. And he positively exuded masculinity – a thought that made her cheeks grow warm.

She stayed away from his room until the following morning when it seemed safer to go inside – it was full of people.

The ladies had taken the night off from work, as they claimed they did once each week, and were consequently up early and in high spirits. Phyllis took Mr. Smith his breakfast and stayed for a chat. Bridget and Flossie followed twenty minutes later, armed with a clean nightshirt, clean bandages, hot water, wash-cloths, and towels. Geraldine took Sergeant Strickland's breakfast up to the attic. At the same time she intended to ask him if he would lend his shaving gear to Mr. Smith – they had all decided to call the mystery man by that name.

By the time Rachel had washed the dishes and cleaned and tidied the kitchen, they were all in his room, including the sergeant. She stood just outside the doorway watching and listening.

'I must say,' Mr. Smith was saying, 'that I feel five pounds lighter – no, six. The grease in my hair alone must have weighed a good pound.'

'I told you I would be as gentle as your own mother, my love,' Bridget told him boldly as she folded up the towel.

'I suppose, Bridget,' he said, 'you tell them all that, do you?'

'Only the very young ones,' she said. 'I wouldn't tell *you* that under normal circumstances.'

'Actually,' he said, and Rachel could see that he was smiling and enjoying himself, 'my memory came back to me last night and I remembered that I am a monk. Poverty, chastity, and obedience are my guiding principles.'

'With *that* body?' Geraldine said in her tragedy-queen voice, setting her hands on her hips. 'What a mortal waste.'

'I don't mind the obedience part,' Phyllis said.

'A gorgeous, penniless monk in a brothel,' Flossie added. 'It is enough to make a poor girl weep.'

'He will be more gorgeous without the scrubby beard,' Geraldine said. 'I went for Will's shaving gear but he insisted on coming with it.'

'A rival?' Mr. Smith said, clapping one hand over his chest. 'My heart is broken.'

They were all enjoying themselves immensely, Rachel could see. They were all flirting. She wished she could be as blasé. Her friends were all dressed for morning, without cosmetics or elaborate coiffures or flashy clothes. They were all pretty women and looked much younger this way.

'This is Sergeant William Strickland,' Geraldine said. 'He was wounded in battle.'

'I lost an eye, sir,' the sergeant said. 'I haven't quite got the hang of seeing out of only the one yet, but it will come in time.'

'Ah,' Mr. Smith said, extending his right hand, 'so you are the sergeant who helped Miss York save my life, are you? I am deeply indebted to you.'

The sergeant eyed the hand in obvious embarrassment and took it very briefly while at the same time delivering an awkward, bobbing bow.

'We were asking for the loan of your razor, not for the loan of *you*, William,' Flossie said. 'You ought to be in bed.'

'Don't scold, lass,' he said. 'I can't lie in bed every minute of the mortal day. I would go back to my men, but the army won't have me no more on account of my eye is gone.'

'Yes, well,' she said, 'your men would go marching off west, you see, William, while you were marching briskly off east because they were on your blind side. You would be no good to them, would you? So you are going to slice Mr. Smith's throat instead, are you? It would be a dreadful waste of a lovely man, I must say. I could think of much better things to do with him.' She bent a deliberately lascivious glance upon Mr. Smith.

'I believe,' he said, 'that I will shave *myself* if someone would be good enough to help me sit up higher in the bed.'

68

'Anything to do with beds is my department,' Geraldine said. 'Out of my way, Will.'

'If in my usual life I *am* a duke, of course,' Mr. Smith said, grimacing slightly as Geraldine hauled him upward and stuffed the pillows behind his back, 'I have probably never done this before in my life and am about to slash my own throat as surely as Sergeant Strickland would have done.'

'Lord love us,' Phyllis said, elbowing her way past Geraldine, 'no more talk of blood if it is all the same to you, Mr. Smith. I'll do it. I have shaved a thousand men in my time, give or take a hundred or so here and there.'

'Did they all survive?' he asked, grinning at her.

'Give or take a hundred or so here and there,' she told him. 'But they all agreed it was a lovely way to go. Look at this jawline, Gerry. Have you seen any more firm and masterful? Lord love us but he's a beauty!'

It was the moment at which Mr. Smith's laughing eyes alit upon Rachel just beyond the doorway. They did not stop smiling, but there was an arrested look in them for a moment, and she knew that his awareness of her was different from the way he felt about her friends. She felt suddenly breathless and horribly self-conscious. He was pale, and she knew that the wash and all this fuss were tiring him and probably causing his head to ache, but even so, with his clean nightshirt and damp, clean hair and roguish smile, he looked quite devastatingly handsome.

She had given the wrong impression yesterday, she thought as Phyllis brushed soap over the stubble of his beard and waved the open razor with a flourish in the air. She really ought not to have sat so boldly on his bed.

But when everyone left the room ten minutes or so later, all still in high spirits and talking and laughing, it was Rachel who stayed to pull the curtains closed across the window to cut out some of the bright sunlight. She approached the bed and straightened the bedcovers, though Bridget had just done it before leaving.

He was looking at her, a guarded smile still lurking in his eyes.

'Good morning,' he said.

'Good morning.' She felt somewhat tongue-tied. 'I can see that you are tired. And that you have a headache.'

'I am exhausted from doing nothing.' The smile had disappeared to be replaced with a somewhat bleaker look. 'I awoke in a panic this morning, searching my nonexistent pockets for the letter.'

'What letter?' She leaned over him slightly and frowned.

'I have no idea.' He raised one hand and set the back of it over his eyes. 'Was it just a meaningless dream, or was it some fragment trying to detach itself from the pervading fog?'

'Was it a letter *to* you or *from* you?' she asked him.

He sighed after a few silent moments and removed his hand. 'I have no idea,' he said again, and his smile was back. 'But I am not entirely without memory, you know. You are Miss York – Miss *Rachel* York. And I am Jonathan Smith – mister. You see how perfectly my memory works provided you ask it to perform its tricks only upon events of the past few days?'

He made a joke of it, but she realized suddenly that his loss of memory was a more devastating injury to him than any of the more obvious ones.

She had not intended to stay, but she sat down anyway, pulling the chair closer to the bed as she did so. She guessed that terror probably lurked behind his cheerful manner this morning.

'Let us discover what we *do* know about you, shall we?' she suggested. 'We know that you are English. We know that you are a gentleman. We know that you are an officer. We know that you fought in the Battle of Waterloo.' She was counting the points off on her fingers. She tapped her thumb. 'What else?'

'We know that I am a poor rider,' he said. 'I fell off my horse. Does that mean I am not a cavalryman? Perhaps I had never ridden before in my life. Perhaps I stole the horse.'

'But you had been shot in the thigh,' she reminded him. 'The musket ball was still embedded there. You would have been in great pain, and you were losing blood. And you had already ridden some distance from the battlefield. You are not necessarily a poor rider.'

'Kind of you,' he said with a faint smile. 'But when I was wounded why the devil – I beg your pardon – *why* did my men not carry me off the field to the nearest surgeon? Why was I alone? Why was I on the way to Brussels? I assume that is where I was going. Was I deserting?'

'Perhaps,' she said, 'you have family members here and were coming to them.'

'Perhaps I have a wife,' he said. 'And six children.'

She had not thought of that possibility since discovering that he was alive. But of course there was no reason in the world to feel disappointed at the very

71

real possibility that he was married. Perhaps he was *happily* married. And perhaps there really were children.

'She would not have brought children to Brussels,' she said. 'She would have stayed in England with them. How old are you?'

'Trying to trick me into remembering another detail, are you, Miss York?' he asked her. 'How old do I look? Twenty? Thirty?'

'Somewhere in between, I would guess,' she said.

'We will say for the sake of argument that I am twenty-five, then,' he said. 'I would have to have been a busy man to produce six children already.' He grinned and looked suddenly boyish and vital despite his pallor.

'Three sets of twins,' she suggested.

'Or two sets of triplets.' He laughed. 'But I surely could not have forgotten a wife, could I? Or children? On the other hand, perhaps they are the very reason my memory has decided to take a leave of absence.'

'We also know,' she said, 'that you have a sense of humor. All this is very distressing for you, is it not? But you can still joke and laugh about it.'

'Ah, now we are getting somewhere,' he said. 'I have a sense of humor. A key piece of evidence. Now we must be able to work out exactly who I am. But, no, perhaps not – there are no such persons as court jesters these days, are there? So much for that apparently promising clue.'

He set an arm over his eyes and sighed.

Rachel gazed at him with sympathy. Her life had not been filled with a great deal of happiness, but even so she would hate to wake up one day and find

72

that everything she had ever been or known was erased from memory. What would be left?

It seemed almost as if he had read her mind.

'I am perhaps the most fortunate of men, Miss York,' he said. 'We are frequently encouraged, are we not, to look on the bright side of every event, even the worst disaster? With the loss of my memory I find myself quite unencumbered by my past and all its burdens. I can be whoever I want to be. I can create myself anew and shape my future without any restraining influence from my past. What should I become, do you suppose? Or, perhaps more to the point, *who* should I become? What sort of person shall Jonathan Smith be?'

She closed her eyes and swallowed. He spoke lightly still, as if he found his words amusing. She found them terrifying.

'Only you can decide that,' she said softly.

'Naked I was born into that other life I cannot remember,' he said, 'and naked I have been born into this new life. I wonder if, when we are born the first time, we forget all that has gone before? William Wordsworth would have us believe it is so. Have you read any of his poetry, Miss York? His Immortality Ode? 'Our birth is but a sleep and a forgetting'?'

'Now we know something else about you,' she said. 'You read poetry.'

'Perhaps I write it too,' he said. 'Perhaps I go about declaiming bad verse wherever I go. Perhaps this demise and rebirth is the greatest favor I have ever done my contemporaries.'

Rachel laughed aloud, and he removed his arm and laughed with her.

'You, of course,' he said, 'fell out of heaven

73

through a hole in a cloud. I have decided that it is the only explanation.'

She laughed again and looked down to brush an invisible speck from the skirt of her dress. Here she was again, alone with him, feeling the unwilling pull of his masculinity. But he was an *invalid*. She was his *nurse*.

'And so,' he said, 'I have been fortunate enough to enjoy two births in the course of one lifetime. Except that this time I do not have a mother to nourish and nurture me. I am on my own.'

'Oh, no, do not speak that way,' she said, leaning forward in her chair. 'We will support and help you, Mr. Smith. We will not abandon you.'

Their eyes met and held. Neither spoke for what seemed a long time, but the air fairly crackled between them. Rachel wondered again if she was responsible and looked away.

'Thank you,' he said. 'You are extraordinarily kind. All of you are. But I have no intention of being a burden to you for longer than I absolutely must. I am already overmuch in your debt.'

The conversation was threatening to become personal.

'I'll leave you alone,' she said. 'I am sure you must need to rest.'

'Stay.' He reached an arm across the bed toward her but lowered it to the bedcovers before she could begin to wonder if he expected her to take his hand in hers. 'If you may, that is, and if you feel so inclined. I find your presence soothing.' He chuckled softly. 'At least, sometimes I do.'

He fell asleep almost instantly. She might have tiptoed from the room then. But she stayed where she was instead, gazing at him, wondering who he was, wondering what he would do when he had recovered sufficiently to leave the house.

Wondering if it was normal to feel such a – such a *physical* attraction to a man one had saved from death.

Over the next week Alleyne's head wounds healed sufficiently that he could move his head freely provided he did not jerk it suddenly in any direction. And he could sit up for increasingly lengthy spells without feeling dizzy. The worst of his bruises faded and his other aches and pains were gradually easing. His leg was healing more slowly, since the musket ball appeared to have done some damage to muscles or tendons in the thigh. Certainly he could not yet put any weight on it, and Geraldine had threatened to tie him to the bed if he so much as tried.

'*Naked*,' she had added as she swept from the room, provoking a guffaw of laughter from him.

He was horribly restless. He could not lie in bed forever, growing weaker and weaker every hour. He moved the leg and flexed his foot and ankle as much as he could beneath the bedcovers. Often when he was alone, he sat on the side of the bed, exercising the leg in any way he could devise that did not involve him in actually putting weight on it or that did not cause him to black out from the pain. What he needed, he realized, was crutches. But how could he ask for them when he had no means of paying for them?

He felt rather like a prisoner. Apart from the fact that he had only one working leg, he possessed nothing at all, not even the nightshirts he wore. How could he acquire other clothes? But how could he leave the house, or even this room, unless he did? He was itching to be out, searching for some clue to his identity, even though Phyllis had told him that most of the British had gone back home by now.

He wondered why she and the others were still here, since it seemed logical to assume that they had come to do business at a time when Brussels was bustling with army personnel and British visitors. And then it struck him that perhaps it was his presence here that was delaying them. He winced, as if with pain.

Of course, they still were doing some business. Almost every night he heard the noise of revelries downstairs and then the more intimate sounds of private pleasures from closer at hand. It was all very frustrating.

It was Rachel York whom he saw most often. She sat with him several times a day, even though constant vigilance at his bedside was no longer necessary. Usually she brought some sewing with her and kept her head bent over her work while they talked or sat in companionable silence until he dozed. Sometimes she read to him from the book he had seen on her dressing table – a copy of Fielding's *Joseph Andrews*. It was interesting to realize that she could read – a whore with an education.

He tried his best not to use that word when thinking of her. It was strange really – he liked the other four ladies none the less for their profession. It made him uncomfortable to know that she was one of them. Perhaps it was because no gentleman liked to admit that he was besotted with a whore.

He looked forward to Rachel's visits. He liked to look at her and listen to her voice. He liked her

76

silences. He liked the way she quickened his blood and made him feel more full of life and energy. Not that she had flirted with him again as overtly as she had done that afternoon when she had sat on his bed and touched the lump on his head. Perhaps he had misunderstood after all, he thought. Perhaps the sexual tension on that occasion was something he alone had felt, occasioned by her beauty and her proximity and her sympathy.

Sergeant William Strickland had taken to coming to his room once or twice a day to see if there was anything he could do for him.

'It's like this, sir,' he said unbidden one day. 'I am well enough to leave here. I wasn't bad enough to stay here in the first place, though the ladies treated me as if I was about to draw my last breath, so to speak. But now that I am here, I can't seem to get up the courage to leave. Where am I supposed to go? All I know is soldiering.'

'I can sympathize with you,' Alleyne assured him.

'I have thought of going with the ladies when they return to England,' Strickland said, 'as a sort of body-guard, sir, which they ought to have on account of they are ladies without a gent even though there are some what would not call them ladies. But I'm not sure they really need me or want me.'

He brought shaving water and his razor with him once a day and always offered to do the shaving himself, though Alleyne always declined and did it himself. The sergeant spoke up one morning while watching him.

'I don't suppose you are in need of a valet, are you, sir?' he asked with a pathetic sigh. 'There are more than enough women to tend your needs but no man.

A gentleman ought to have a man of his own.'

'Sergeant Strickland,' Alleyne said with a rueful chuckle, 'you at least own a shaving kit and probably one or two other belongings in addition to your uniform and your boots. You may even have a few coins to rattle around in your pockets. At the moment I own the skin I was born in but nothing else – absolutely nothing.'

The sergeant sighed again. 'Well, if you change your mind, sir,' he said, 'I daresay I'll be here a few days longer. We could come to some arrangement.'

The blind leading the blind, Alleyne thought after Strickland had returned to his own attic room. Or the half blind leading the lame might be a more accurate image.

He had begun to fear – it was a deep, bowel-churning, knee-weakening, soul-dizzying terror actually – that his memory was not going to return at all.

Did he exist if he had no past?

Did he have any human validity if he was nobody?

Of what value or significance was anything he might have done during his life if it could be so totally wiped out with one fall from the back of a horse?

Whom had he left behind after losing his memory as effectively as if he had died?

Who mourned for him?

Foolishly, foolishly he wished for Rachel York – as if, like a mother, she could kiss his hurt and make it all better.

Though he certainly did not think of her as a mother.

Somehow, he decided, he was going to have to get his hands on some crutches and some clothes. He was going to have to get out of here.

Chapter Six

The ladies were restless and impatient to go home. They were desperate to pick up the trail of the Reverend Nigel Crawley. Their determination to confront him, to punish him, and to get back their money had not diminished by one iota. He was simply not going to be allowed to get away with such a crime, they declared – or with making fools of them when they had thought it impossible for any man to deceive them. Flossie and Bridget had written to as many of their literate acquaintances as they could think of, but they had specified that any replies should be sent to London, not having expected to be delayed in Brussels for so long. They were eager to discover if there had been any.

They held a meeting in the kitchen one afternoon while Sergeant Strickland was with Mr. Smith.

There were some minor matters to discuss first. All of the women except Rachel had numerous acquaintances among the male population of Brussels. And Flossie and Geraldine were both adept at sizing up a man – literally sizing him up – without having to go at him with a measuring tape. They discussed what

79

clothes Mr. Smith would need to enable him to move more freely about the house and eventually to leave it. They all undertook to wheedle the requisite garments out of various sources. And Phyllis knew someone who could donate, or at least loan, a pair of crutches.

But there was a far larger problem to be solved, of course, before they could feel free to leave at last.

'He still can't remember a blessed thing that happened before he woke up here in Rache's bed, can he?' Geraldine said. 'And so we have nowhere to send him, and he has nowhere to go.'

'Anyway,' Phyllis said, 'he can't even walk yet.'

'And he will be as weak as a baby after more than a week in bed,' Bridget added.

'He is a lovely, lovely man,' Flossie said with a sigh. 'But there are times when I could wish him to perdition.'

'If I could just go back and do things differently,' Rachel said, 'I would leave him at the Namur Gates. He would have been looked after by someone. He would have been recognized as an officer as soon as he regained consciousness, and someone would have undertaken to discover who he was.'

Except that she could not have borne to abandon him. And now she could not bear to hear him spoken of as a burden.

'Lord love us but he is handsome,' Phyllis said with a sigh. 'I am a fair way to being in love with him.'

'We all are, Phyll, though it's not just his looks, is it?' Geraldine said. 'He has that roguish gleam in his eye. No, don't be sorry you brought him here, Rache. I don't begrudge him the last ten days – or Will Strickland either.'

80

'We are going to have to do something about them soon, though, Gerry,' Flossie said. 'We cannot stay here forever. I am so homesick for England I could scream.'

'Any suggestions about what we ought to do with Mr. Smith?' Bridget asked.

'We could all go out,' Phyllis suggested, 'and knock on every door up and down every street to see if anyone has mislaid a handsome gentleman with roguish eyes and an aristocratic nose.'

They all laughed.

'Some of us don't speak French, though, Phyll,' Flossie said.

'We could offer him a job with us in London,' Geraldine suggested, 'and he could work while we go off in pursuit of Crawley.'

'The ladies would be queued up down the street and around the corner,' Bridget said. 'Our gentlemen clients would not be able to get near the door when we got back to London.'

'We could charge him a percentage of his income for rent,' Flossie said. 'We would soon be rich enough to buy two boarding houses.'

It was a good thing they had a keen sense of humor, Rachel thought as they all laughed again. Their prospects were really rather bleak. The chances that they would ever find Nigel Crawley were slim, and even if they did, it was unlikely that they would recover any of their money. Yet she knew that indignation and pride would send them on the chase anyway. They would be doubly poor by the time they admitted defeat and returned to work. It was a very good thing that they could at least laugh at themselves.

If only she could think of some way to help them. But wealthy as she would be in three years' time, at present she was as poor as the proverbial church mouse.

'I think what we sometimes forget,' she said, 'is that Mr. Smith has lost his memory, not his intelligence. He is recovering from his wounds, and I do not believe he will be content to remain in bed or dependent upon us for much longer. Perhaps it is not up to us to decide what to do with him. Perhaps he has some ideas of his own.'

'The poor dear,' Phyllis said. 'Perhaps *he* will wander up one side of each street and down the other, knocking on doors.'

'He will be snatched up by the first woman to open a door,' Geraldine said with a sigh. 'I suppose we *should* ask him, though.'

'I will,' Rachel offered. 'I will sit with him for a while this evening while you are all entertaining. If he has no ideas, then we will all put our heads together again. If we can just solve the problem of Mr. Smith, then we can turn our attention to acquiring enough money to go after Mr. Crawley.'

She hated thinking of him as a *problem*. She also hated the thought of the day – surely soon now – when he would not need them any longer and would leave.

'My favorite idea is still the one about climbing the ivy on a dark night to get your jewels, Rache,' Geraldine said, provoking laughter.

Rachel got to her feet and carried their empty cups and saucers and plates to the bowl to wash.

Phyllis told Alleyne when she brought him his evening meal that he was going to have crutches by the following

82

morning. He could have kissed her and told her so.

She came toward the bed with saucily swaying hips and leaned over him, lips puckered, so that he could do just that. He laughed at her as he drew her head down with one hand against the back of it and pecked her lightly on the lips.

'And where are they coming from?' he asked her as she straightened up and fanned her face vigorously with one hand while batting her eyelids at him.

'Never you mind,' she told him. 'I know someone.'

It was almost exactly what Geraldine said later when she came to collect the tray and informed him that he would have some clothes soon – perhaps even by tomorrow.

'We know people,' she said, striking her usual hands-on-hips, bosom-thrust-forward pose and winking at him.

Later in the evening he could hear the outside door opening and closing downstairs and the rumble of male voices mingled with feminine laughter. There were card games at the house every evening, Strickland had told him, with the ladies holding the bank and acting as hostesses. But there was a strict curfew at one o'clock, when the ladies turned to the other part of their profession.

Since there was no point in dwelling constantly upon his plight, Alleyne chose to be amused yet again over the fact that he had taken refuge in a brothel and was in the nature of being a kept man. It was perfectly clear to him from whom his crutches and clothes were going to come. The ladies were certainly not going out to buy them. In a sense that was a relief, but even so it was an uncomfortable realization if he let his mind dwell upon it. He chose to laugh instead. One

83

day in the future, after his memory had returned and he had resumed his normal life, he was going to look back on this episode in his life and be enormously tickled by it.

At least by this time tomorrow he ought to be able to move around the room. If some clothes had arrived also, he might even be able to move beyond the room. Perhaps within a few days he would be able to go out at last in search of his identity. It was going to be a daunting task when he was in a foreign city and apparently most of the British visitors had left, either to follow the armies to Paris or to return to England. But at least he would finally be able to *do* something.

Perhaps then he would have more success at keeping the terror at bay.

He was bored and picked up *Joseph Andrews*, which Rachel York had left on the table beside the bed. But he found after a few minutes that he was staring at the same page, his brow furrowed in thought. He had woken again from an afternoon nap with that panicked concern for the letter. What letter?

Deuce take it, *what* letter?

He had the feeling that if only he could remember the answer to that question everything else would come flooding back. But nothing would come at the moment except the familiar throbbing of a headache. He closed the book, set it back on the table, and stared at the canopy over his head.

He was still staring upward when the door to his room opened.

It was Rachel York – and his breath caught in his throat.

She was wearing a simply designed evening dress of pale blue satin. But on her, of course, nothing elaborate was necessary. Its low neck and high waistline showed her fine bosom to best advantage. Soft, silken folds clung to her alluring curves and shapely legs. She had done something prettier than usual with her hair. There were narrow, looped braids and curls with a few wavy tendrils teasing her neck and temples. He was not sure whether the blush of color in her cheeks was natural or the result of carefully applied cosmetics. Either way she looked more alluring than ever.

He was seeing her for the first time in her working clothes, he thought. He really would rather not have done so. It had struck him just today that he called the other ladies by their given names whereas he always called her *Miss York*. He did not like to think of her as a whore.

'Good evening,' she said. 'Are you feeling neglected?'

'More like a beached whale actually,' he said. 'But I understand that I am to expect crutches and even clothes tomorrow. You cannot know how grateful I am to all of you.'

'We are happy to be of assistance.' She smiled at him.

'Are you not working?' he asked, and then wished he had not.

'Not tonight,' she said. 'I came to sit with you for a while. May I?'

He indicated the chair with one hand and she sat down in her usual graceful, ladylike way. Listening to a burst of laughter from downstairs, he was glad she was not there.

'You will be happy to be able to move about again,' she said, 'and to get your strength back.'

'More than you can possibly know,' he told her. 'I

will not be a burden to you for much longer, I promise. As soon as I am able to get about at a reasonable speed and as soon as I am decently clothed, I will be leaving here and finding out who I am and where I belong.'

'Will you?' she said. 'We were discussing just this afternoon how we might help you, but then it occurred to us that perhaps you would have some ideas of your own. What will you do? How will you go about discovering who you are?'

'There must be some military personnel still here,' he said, 'and some members of the British upper classes. Someone may recognize me or have a record of the fact that I am missing. Failing any answers here, I will find my way somehow to the Hague. There is a British embassy there. They will help. If nothing else they will probably get me back to England.'

'Ah, so you *do* have plans.' She gazed at him with her lovely hazel eyes. 'But there is no hurry. You must not feel that you have to rush away from here. This is your home for as long as you need it.'

He felt a sharp jolt of desire for her.

'On the contrary,' he said. 'I have been here for almost two weeks, with no sense of identity or belonging, while all sorts of people have probably been searching for me and thinking the worst. Perhaps even more important, you must all be eager to return to England. I have kept you here too long already.'

'It has not been one moment too long,' she said. 'We have all been happy to have you here. I will miss you when you are gone.'

We have been happy, but I will miss you. He did

not fail to notice the change in pronoun.

And he would miss her too.

Without thinking he stretched out a hand toward her. She looked at it for a few moments, and he would have withdrawn it if he could without making an issue of it. She leaned forward and set her hand in his. It was warm and smooth-skinned and slender. He closed his fingers about it.

'I will find you again one day,' he said, 'and find some way to repay at least a part of the debt I owe you. There is no way to repay you for my life, of course.'

'You owe me nothing,' she said, and he was aware suddenly that the brightness of her eyes was caused by unshed tears.

He ought to have released her hand then and turned the subject. There must be any number of topics on which they might safely converse. He might have asked her to read more of *Joseph Andrews*. Instead he squeezed her hand more tightly.

'Come here,' he said softly.

She looked rather startled for a moment, and he thought she would refuse – which would be just as well considering the level of tension in the room. But she got to her feet and came to sit on the side of the bed, all without relinquishing his hand.

She was far too close for comfort. There seemed to be less air in the room than there had been a short while ago. His nostrils were being teased by a fragrance that he realized he associated with her.

'Roses?' he asked.

'Gardenia.' She was gazing down into his eyes, her own wide. 'It is the only perfume I ever wear. My father used to give some to me every birthday.'

He inhaled slowly.

'Do you like it?' she asked him, and it occurred to him suddenly that she was flirting with him in her own very subtle manner. Had she orchestrated the whole of this scene?

'I do,' he told her.

He watched her lick her upper lip, her tongue moving deliberately from one corner to the other. He fixed his eyes on the movement. She had the softest, most kissable lips he had ever seen – at least, he thought she did, since it was something he could not be sure of.

'Miss York,' he said, 'I ought not to have invited you so close. I am about to take advantage of your kindness in coming to sit with me, I am afraid. I am about to kiss you. You had better scuttle back to your chair or even out through the door if you consider me impertinent or presumptuous.'

If it was possible, her lovely eyes grew wider. Her cheeks grew pinker. Her lips, which she had just moistened, parted. But she did not move.

I do innocence very well, would you not agree?

She had spoken those words to him some time ago and he had agreed with them even then. Now he agreed a hundred times more.

'I do not consider you presumptuous.' She spoke so softly that her words were a mere whisper of sound.

He released her hand and took her by the upper arms. They were covered with goose bumps, he could see. He rubbed his hands up and down them a few times and then drew her down. Her hands splayed across his chest as his lips touched hers.

He kissed her lightly, his lips moving over hers, at first closed and then parted. He licked her lips with

88

his tongue and pushed it through to caress the warm, moist flesh behind. But it was not, of course, enough, and she made no move to cut the embrace short, as he half expected she would, to smile teasingly at him, and whisk herself off back downstairs to the paying customers – perish the thought.

He allowed a little more of his control to slip and deepened the embrace, wrapping his arms about her, drawing her bosom down against his chest, and kissing her more hungrily, his tongue pressing deep into her mouth. He could feel one of her narrow braids sway and tap against the side of his face. She was every bit as gorgeous as he had ever thought her. Even in such a relatively chaste encounter she was all soft, shapely, enticing woman.

And yet she kissed like an innocent at first, he noticed, her lips closed and slightly pouted and opening only at the prodding of his tongue. She was very alluring. The illusion of innocence mingled with the reality of her hot sexuality made for an explosive mix. He was far more aroused than it was comfortable to be under the circumstances. But for a while he was past caring.

She drew back her head after several minutes and looked down at him with heavy-lidded, questioning eyes. When he drew her head down to his again, he kissed her more gently, ravishing her mouth with slow thoroughness.

He was the one who set her away from him at last, though he did so with the deepest reluctance.

'I am sorry,' he said. 'This is probably not very thrilling for you, is it, when you had expected a free night. And I cannot even pay your fee, whether it is sixpence or a hundred pounds. Besides, I like you and would not take advantage of your good nature.'

He saw what might have been bewilderment in her eyes and then something else. She dipped her head down to rest on his shoulder, and he allowed her to come down on top of his chest again. Her hair teased his cheek and his nose.

He was going to suffer for this foolishness, he thought. He had owed her better than this. He would be fortunate if their friendship – and there was a sort of friendship between them – survived this night's doings. But even before he could suffer tomorrow's regrets there was this evening's discomfort to deal with. He was hard with need for her.

He had no way of knowing how long he had been without a woman, but it felt altogether too long. Not that just any woman would do, he suspected. Deuce take it, but he had allowed himself to become too infatuated with Rachel York. He had had nothing better to do with his time and energies, he supposed.

'I was not thinking about any fee,' she said. 'And you were not taking advantage of me.'

'It must have been the other way around, then,' he said chuckling softly, trying to make light of the situation. '*You* were taking advantage of me.'

'Because you are weak from your injuries?' She lifted her head, supported herself with her hands on his chest again, and looked down at him with troubled eyes. 'Did I do that? I did not mean it. I will go away immediately.'

Damnation, he thought, he had *hurt* her. He ought not to have made mention of her profession. Clearly she was not plying it here. She knew he had nothing with which to pay her.

He grasped her by the arms when she would have got up.

90

'Rachel,' he said, 'don't go. Please don't go. I just wanted to know that I was not offending you – but I seem to have done it anyway. Forgive me?'

She nodded and he set one hand behind her head and drew her downward to kiss her again.

'Stay with me?' he asked against her lips.

He heard her swallow.

'Yes,' she said.

'Does that door lock?' he asked her.

'Yes.'

'Lock it, then,' he said. 'Let's be sure of privacy.'

'Yes,' she said again, and got to her feet to cross to the door.

She stood with her back to the room for a few moments after he heard the click of the lock. He was going to make love to her, he thought, and not feel guilty about it. She had just said she had not thought of a fee, meaning that she genuinely wanted to be with him. Very well, then. If she wanted him as he wanted her, they would enjoy themselves together and part amicably as soon as he was fit enough to leave. They would leave each other with pleasant memories.

But as she turned back toward him and he saw the color warm in her cheeks, it seemed to him that she looked like the innocent she sometimes pretended to be, and he felt ever so slightly sinful for wanting her so badly.

Chapter Seven

It was only as she stood at the door and turned the key that she realized fully what she had just done and what she was about to do.

He had warned her that he was going to kiss her, but she had not stopped him. She had not *wanted* to. Now he had asked her to stay and she had said yes even though she had been in no doubt of his meaning.

He was going to bed her.

And she had said yes.

Was she mad? Was she utterly, out-of-her-mind *insane*? She scarcely knew him. Indeed, she did not even know his real name. Soon he would be gone from her life, gone forever despite his promise to find her one day so that he could repay some of the debt he felt he owed her.

He believed her to be a whore. He thought this was nothing more to her than a pleasant little fling on the side with no money involved.

It was not too late. Even now she could tell him no, unlock the door, and flee up to her attic room.

But she was twenty-two years old and her life and been so barren of excitement, sensual or otherwise.

The men she had had a chance to meet, including certain gentlemen who had frequented Lady Flatley's and had thought she was easy pickings just because she was a sort of servant, had always given her the shudders. And when she had chosen very deliberately with her head and agreed to marry Mr. Crawley because she had thought he was very different from all the others, she had found him to be a coldhearted villain.

She wanted to do this. She longed for it – with him, with Jonathan Smith. There were no illusions, no promises involved. There was no future. Just tonight. She could not bear to unlock the door and go away. If she did, she was sure, she would congratulate herself for the rest of her life on her good sense and pretend that she did not regret that she had not found the courage to do what she wanted to do.

She was terribly attracted to him.

It took only a few seconds for these thoughts to tumble through her mind. Then she drew a slow breath and turned back into the room. Perhaps she would regret this tomorrow, but she would think of that when tomorrow came.

The trouble was, she thought as she looked at him and saw naked desire in his darkly handsome face, that she did not know how to go about this. If she had not left the bed, she would not have thought about her ignorance, but here she was stranded at the other side of the room, not knowing what to do next.

She smiled at him.

'You will have to help me out of my dress and stays,' she told him.

She went to sit on the side of the bed again, her back to him, and tipped her head forward.

He did not say anything, but she felt his fingers work at her buttons and pins and laces. She held her dress to her bosom as both it and her stays opened along the back and she felt the cool evening air against her bare flesh. He eased her dress off her shoulders, and she shivered as his hands caressed her back.

She stood up then and released her hold on her dress. It slithered down her body, taking her stays with it, and she stepped free of them. All that remained was her skimpy shift, which the stays had molded to her body, and her stockings. She sat down on the bed again and rolled them down and off her feet. At the same time she was aware that he was pulling off his nightshirt and tossing it onto the floor on top of her dress.

She turned and looked down at him. He looked very broad shouldered and well muscled and masculine despite the fact that he had been an invalid for almost two weeks. He was gazing back at her with dark, intense eyes. She was terribly afraid suddenly of the barely leashed passion that seemed to sizzle between them, but of course it was far too late now to change her mind.

Besides, there was a fascination, an overwhelming attraction all mixed in with the fear.

'Let your hair down,' he told her. But before she could lift her arms, he caught at her hands. 'No, let me take it down.'

Geraldine had dressed it for her since she had had time to spare before the evening's revelries and had come into Rachel's attic room for a chat and possessed herself of Rachel's brush without a by-your-leave. She had produced a work of art, which had pleased Rachel, as she had wanted to look pretty for the evening's visit to Jonathan's room.

He took his time about drawing out pins and unraveling braids. She dipped her head down so that their faces were close all the time he worked, and her freed hair fell about them like a curtain. A few times he interrupted his efforts by drawing her closer and kissing her softly – on her eyelids, on her nose, on her lips. Her breasts felt tight and almost sore. There was a heavy pulsing low in her abdomen and down between her thighs that she recognized as the physical effects of desire.

All this felt terribly sinful, she thought. It was also unbearably erotic. If he did not finish with her hair soon she would surely burn up with heat.

'I am afraid,' he said at last, combing his fingers through her loose hair and drawing her head downward once again so that his lips were touching hers, 'that my leg wound makes me less mobile than I would wish to be at this moment. You are going to have to come on top of me and do most of the work. Stand up for a moment.'

When she did so he turned back the covers so that she could join him on the bed. Her knees almost betrayed her then. She almost forgot to breathe. She set one knee on the bed, and he grasped the hem of her shift with both hands. She lifted her arms as he peeled it off and sent it to join their other garments on the floor.

She was startlingly aware of the candle burning on the table beside the bed.

He was gazing at her with narrowed gaze and pursed lips.

'In fairness to other women,' he said, 'there ought

95

to be some imperfection in your person. But, if there is, I fail to see it. Come.'

She was twenty-two years old. She was not entirely ignorant of what happened. But he would surely expect experience and skill. She *had* told him once, though, that she was the one who catered to the taste for demure innocence.

'You must instruct me,' she told him. 'I am new to this, remember?'

He laughed softly. 'Come astride me,' he said, 'and I will give you a lesson in love – though I daresay I will end up as more pupil than teacher.'

She blessed his bandaged thigh at that moment. Having to move across him and settle herself above him in such a way that she did not jolt him or inadvertently touch the wound somehow alleviated the awkwardness and intense embarrassment she might otherwise have felt at being above him. She could feel his body heat beneath her spread thighs.

A weakness that was almost painful spiraled up inside her until even her throat ached. She set her hands on his shoulders and leaned over him, her eyes on his.

He took over at that point, cupping one hand behind her head and kissing her openmouthed again, his tongue plundering her mouth so that she was soon consumed by needs her body had never before dreamed of.

He touched every inch of her over the next several minutes – with his hands, his palms, his fingers, his fingertips, his thumbs, his lips, his tongue, his teeth. He touched her in ways she had not known there were ways. He suckled her breasts, moistened her nipples with his tongue, nipped them lightly with his teeth

96

until they were hardened and almost unbearably sensitive. He set one hand flat over her throbbing private place, almost startling her into madness, and then probed the folds, exploring, caressing, teasing, scratching lightly – and sliding one finger and then two slowly up inside her. She was wet there, she realized, as muscles she had not known she possessed clenched hard about him.

She was not idle while he gave her an education in foreplay. Her hands roamed over him too, marveling at the solid maleness of him and by very instinct knowing where to pause and caress. After he had suckled her breasts she lowered her head and licked one of his male nipples, startling a gasp and an exclamation from him. She raised her head and smiled into his eyes.

'Does that feel good?'

'Witch!' he said.

She moved her mouth to the other one.

'If you do not mount me soon,' he said at last, 'I am going to disgrace myself.'

But he did not wait for her to take the initiative. He set his hands on her hips and brought her down until she could feel him hard against her entrance, which was pulsing and aching with raw need. And then he pressed down firmly on her hips and she felt herself being penetrated and stretched until there was increasing discomfort, a sharp pain, and then no more as he came deeper than she could ever have imagined.

For a few moments her mind could not grasp at any coherent thought. There was only the pure physical shock of lost innocence. Her teeth clamped onto her lower lip at the same moment as she heard his muffled exclamation.

'Deuce take it ...'

For several moments neither of them moved. And then he did things to her that numbed her with shock again. He half lifted her off him and pumped swift and deep in and out of her, over and over again until he drew her down hard and held her there while she felt a hot rush in her depths and knew that it must be over.

There was a curious feeling of disappointment. It was all over so soon after the slow building of pleasure that had gone before it. The actual act had seemed almost anticlimactic.

But she would not regret it tomorrow. She *would* not. She had wanted it and she had had it, and it was her fault if she had found the last part of it less than earth-shattering. It had still been lovely to exercise her womanhood freely and to lie with a man for whom she had been feeling a growing attraction for the last two weeks.

She lowered her forehead to his shoulder while she brought her breathing under control. She hoped she had not disappointed him dreadfully.

'It is going to be quite intriguing,' he said after a minute or two of stillness and silence, his voice sounding startlingly normal, 'to hear your explanation for this, Miss York. Pardon me if I am too exhausted to hear it just at the moment.'

Rachel shut her eyes very tightly. How humiliating! She had not fooled him for a moment.

Alleyne's leg was throbbing like the very devil. He ignored the pain and concentrated upon his irritation. He had given in to the temptation to dally with what he thought was an experienced woman, but instead he had found himself debauching innocence. He should have listened to his instincts, he told himself now that it was too late. He had always thought of her as a lady. He had always called her *Miss York*.

Why the deuce had she allowed it?

He felt like a rapist, for God's sake.

And he ought not to have done it anyway, even if she had been a whore of twenty years' experience. She had saved his life. She had nursed him tirelessly ever since. And he had thanked her by lusting after her and taking her . . . Well, he had taken her virginity.

But not by force, damn it.

She might have stopped him at almost any moment along the way.

He was annoyed with her, more than annoyed with himself. Good God, he had not even tried to make their actual copulation a pleasurable experience for her. He had been so shocked . . .

She had removed herself from his body and from the bed moments after he had spoken to her and had disappeared behind the screen in the corner of the room, taking her clothes with her – a rather pointless display of modesty after what they had just done together.

At the risk of adding even more to the pain in his leg he reached over the side of the bed and pulled his nightshirt back on. He laced his fingers behind his head, stared up at the plain canopy over the bed, and waited.

She came tiptoeing around the screen eventually – perhaps she was hoping he had fallen asleep. She had forgotten to take the hairpins back there with her. She had pushed her hair behind her ears, but it lay along her back in thick, disheveled golden curls. She looked more gorgeous than ever, he thought resentfully.

'I thought you were asleep,' she said after darting him a quick glance.

'Did you?' he said. 'Sit down, Miss York, and tell me what the deuce that was all about.'

She sat on the chair and gazed blankly at him.

'Why,' he asked her, 'did you not tell me? Did you feel coerced? Did I say or do anything to suggest that you had no choice?'

Her cheeks flamed and her teeth sank into her lower lip. She clasped her hands in her lap and looked down at them for a few moments while he regarded her with something that felt very like loathing. Perhaps it ought not to have mattered whether she was a whore or a virgin, but it did. It mattered a great deal. He was not the sort of man – surely he was not – who went about deflowering virgins. Was he the sort of man who went about sleeping with whores, then? He did not know, though suddenly he hoped not.

Good God, they were women. They were *people*. He thought of Geraldine and the others. Yes, they were people.

'Has it occurred to you, Mr. Smith,' she asked him, 'that there has to be a first time for every woman?'

'And for a *respectable* woman,' he retorted, 'for a *lady*, that ought to be in a marriage bed. I cannot even offer you marriage. Did you realize that? I may already be married.'

She bit her lip again – but he had stopped finding the sight enchanting.

100

'I would not marry you even if you were as free as a bird,' she said, 'and went down on one knee and made me a pretty speech. I am not a fool, Mr. Smith, even if I *was* a virgin until a short while ago. I did this for the same reason you did it – because I wanted to, because I *fancied* you. It makes no difference to anything except that what might have been a pleasant memory has now been spoiled by your anger. Why are you angry? Was I so terribly disappointing? So were you if you want to know the truth.'

He looked at her, arrested, and despite himself felt a smile tug at the corners of his mouth.

'No! Was I?' he asked her. 'I *did* go off like an inexperienced schoolboy, I must admit. You took me so completely by surprise.'

She stared back at him, looking rather mulish.

'I can hardly wait,' he said, 'to hear your story, Miss York. You are a lady and you *were* a virgin until a short while ago, and yet you live in a brothel with four whores and obviously care so deeply for them that you will even claim to be one of them rather than seem to set yourself above them morally. Perhaps now you even believe you *are* one of them. How long have you been here?'

'Since June the fifteenth,' she said. 'Since the day of the Battle of Waterloo.'

'The same day I came here?' He looked at her with narrowed eyes.

'The day before,' she said. 'But we were up all night and so I never actually slept in this room.'

He shifted position slightly to try to ease the burning in his leg. He ought to send her on her way. Doubtless she was eager to be gone from here – she had found him disappointing, by God. A few minutes

101

ago he had been eager to see the back of her too. But this whole experience at the brothel had been somewhat bizarre. He had the feeling it would become more so if he heard her story. And he was not going to sleep anytime soon even if she went away.

'What brought you here?' he asked her. 'Am I permitted to know the details?'

She looked down at her hands.

'My mother died when I was six years old,' she told him. 'My father hired a nurse to care for me. She was Bridget Clover and became a second mother to me, though I realize now that she must have been very young at the time. I loved her dearly. I had little contact with any other children – or adults, for that matter. We lived in London, and my father was rarely at home. My heart was broken when I was twelve years old and Bridget had to leave. I no longer needed a nurse at that age, my father told me, but I knew it was an excuse. He could no longer afford to pay her. He was forever winning and losing fortunes at the gaming tables, but at that time he had suffered a whole series of losses. It was ten years before I saw Bridget again – on a street here in Brussels a couple of months or so ago.'

'That must have been quite a shock for you,' he said.

'Because of her appearance, you mean?' she asked him. 'Her hair was bright red, of course, and she was somewhat flamboyantly dressed, though she was not wearing cosmetics. But the thing was that I recognized her instantly and did not really notice how her appearance had changed. She was just my beloved Bridget.'

He watched her hands twist in her lap.

'When you love someone,' she said, 'you no longer see that person objectively. You see with your heart. I wondered why she evaded my questions about what she was doing here and where she was employed. I wondered why she kept glancing around at the other people on the street as though she were embarrassed and seemed eager to get away from me. I was hurt.'

'But you would not be so easily shrugged off?' he asked her.

'No.' She sighed. 'It would have been better for Bridget and the others if I had stuck my nose in the air as soon as I realized the truth – and I *did* realize it after a few minutes – and had gone on my way. I did her no great favor by insisting upon visiting her here in this house. She allowed me to come only after I had told her that I was employed too, as companion to Lady Flatley, and that I was lonely and homesick. My father died over a year ago, leaving nothing but debts behind him.'

'And so you visited the brothel,' he said. What an innocent she must have been. But rather a brave one, he conceded, and one who lived by principle rather than by social convention.

'Yes.' She looked at him and smiled suddenly at the memory. 'They were all gathered in the sitting room the afternoon I came, and they were all dressed with almost dreary respectability and were on their very best behavior. I liked them instantly. They were ... I am not even sure I know what word I am searching for. They were *genuine*. They were real people, unlike Lady Flatley and all her brittle friends.'

He waited for her to continue, to describe the events that had led her to coming here to live.

'I met the Reverend Nigel Crawley at Lady

103

Flatley's,' she said. 'He used to come there often, sometimes alone, sometimes with his sister. He was very charming. All the ladies were enchanted with him. He did not have a church of his own in England. He wished to be free, he explained, to devote himself to charitable works and to raising money for worthy causes. He had come to Brussels because he thought he could bring some comfort to all the thousands of men who would soon be facing death in battle.'

'There *are* regimental chaplains,' Alleyne said.

'I know,' she said. 'But he claimed that they devoted their time to the officers and neglected the needs of the enlisted men.'

'I suppose,' he said dryly, 'you fell instantly in love with him. Was he handsome?'

'Oh, gloriously so,' she told him. 'He was tall and blond and had a charming smile. But I merely admired him at first. He did not even notice me. I was little more than a servant.'

Perhaps, Alleyne thought cynically, it was because she had no money with which to fill the man's charitable coffers.

'Do I begin to smell a rat?' he asked.

She frowned. 'When he *did* notice me,' she said, 'and began paying court to me, I found him irresistible. *Not* because of his looks or because I fell in love with him, but because he was full of zeal for his work and for his faith. And because he was a principled, steady, generous, dependable man. I have not known many such men in my life. I was undeniably dazzled. Miss Crawley became my friend too.'

'Definitely a rat,' Alleyne said. 'But it must have been your looks rather than your fortune that attracted him. You are penniless, I suppose?'

104

He noticed the flush of color in her cheeks, but she was looking down at her hands again.

'He started to speak to me whenever he came to Lady Flatley's,' she said. 'He took me walking whenever I had an hour free. Miss Crawley invited me for tea. How long ago it seems already and how naive I was then! When he asked me to marry him, I accepted without hesitation. Perhaps the thing I admired most about him was the fact that when we came upon Geraldine and Bridget while we were out walking one afternoon, he asked for an introduction even though it must have been very obvious to him what they were. He spoke kindly to them, and somehow – I still do not know how it happened – we were invited here for tea.'

From her silence and several audible swallows, he guessed that the narrative was becoming painful to her. But he said nothing. He tried again to ease his leg into a more comfortable position.

She laced her fingers into her palms and then closed her hands about them.

'He was very skilled at worming information out of people,' she said. 'Without realizing I had done it, I had told him about my inheritance even before he started to court me in earnest. And Geraldine or Bridget – I do not remember which – told him about their dream of saving enough money to buy a guesthouse somewhere in England so that they could retire from their profession. I believe they must even have told him that they were close to achieving their goal but had never trusted any bank to keep their money safe.'

If she was an heiress, Alleyne thought in surprise, why the devil had she taken employment as a lady's companion and then come to live in a brothel? But he would not interrupt her narrative by asking the questions aloud.

'I was pathetically grateful to him for treating my friends with such respect and kindness,' she said.

Alleyne grimaced. 'And he took all their money?' he asked her. 'He must be very clever indeed. Whores are notoriously difficult to dupe.'

'He was so very courteous and kind with them,' she said. 'He even worked into the conversation one day the fact that he felt a particular reverence for prostitutes since our Lord himself treated them with respect. He persuaded them that being in a foreign country during uncertain times made them unusually vulnerable to theft. He persuaded them to put the money into his safekeeping since he was about to leave Belgium. He promised to take it back to London and deposit it at a bank, where it would earn interest.'

'Poor ladies,' he said with genuine sympathy. He had grown to like them all.

'And so he left,' she said, 'with what had taken them years of hard work to earn. He also left with sizable donations for his various charities from Lady Flatley and half the other ladies here in Brussels. Lady Flatley was leaving for England too, but she was vexed with me when I told her I was going to marry Mr. Crawley and dismissed me out of hand. I left with the Crawleys. We were to marry in England and were then to go to my uncle's to claim my inheritance. But quite by chance I overheard Mr. and Miss Crawley talking together while we were waiting for passage to England – I had followed them down to breakfast at the inn instead of staying in my room to write a final letter to Bridget as I had planned. They were talking about what they would do with all the money, and they were laughing. They both sounded very much unlike their usual selves.'

She frowned down at her hands, and for a few moments Alleyne wondered if she was going to be able to continue. But finally she looked up at him with troubled, unseeing eyes.

'I confronted them immediately,' she said. 'It did not occur to me to dissemble. I demanded that they give me my friends' money and my own, which I had given Mr. Crawley for safekeeping, though it was not a vast sum. But they both protested their innocence and tried to assure me that they had been *joking*. I ran upstairs with them both on my heels and tried to find the money, but of course I could not find it in either his room or hers. I knew anyway that he would never let me take it. If I went for a constable, what would I say? Flossie had given him the money voluntarily with the full approval of the others. I had given him my money – I was his *betrothed*. I remembered that he carried pistols as a precaution against highwaymen and thieves. I gave in to cowardly fear, apologized for my silly doubts, returned to my room, which was mercifully on the ground floor, and then fled out through the window. I made my way back here to tell Bridget and the others how they had been deceived and how I had unwittingly been responsible for their loss.'

'That took some courage,' he said.

She continued to stare blankly at him. 'They did not utter one word of reproach for the part I had played in their loss,' she said. 'They fumed and swore quite horribly about *him* and his villainy, but Bridget just hugged me tightly and wept over me. All she seemed

107

able to think about was that I had been hurt, that I must be devastated to know how he had deceived me.'

'And were you?' Alleyne asked.

'Perhaps my last shred of trust in men was shattered,' she said, hunching her shoulders, 'and that was certainly painful. But my feelings had not been deeply engaged. I had agreed to the marriage for other reasons than romantic ones. Now I can feel only embarrassment and incredulity that I did not see him for what he was.'

'It would be best not to be too hard on yourself,' he told her. 'Flossie and Geraldine and the others did not suspect him of villainy either, and they are hardened, experienced women of the world. But I suppose you feel yourself deeply in their debt for all the money your former fiancé stole from them.'

'Yes.' She nodded. 'But there is little I can do to help them. Our first plan to raise money to go after Mr. Crawley failed when I found you, and Flossie and Geraldine found a poor boy whose body was being plundered.' She blushed and bit her lip. 'We went out there to see what valuables we could find in the aftermath of the battle, but we came back with nothing.'

'No!' He could not stop himself from laughing out loud. 'I can just see it – three women striding off in search of plunder, only to discover that their hearts were too soft for the task. And so you found my naked body instead of treasure. Poor Miss York.'

'I would *rather* have found you than treasure,' she said, looking mortified.

'Thank you,' he said, and grinned at her. Though he sobered somewhat when he remembered the cause of her disheveled, tumbled appearance.

Damn it, it ought never to have happened. What had possessed him? It was a rhetorical question if ever he had heard one, of course. It was obvious what had possessed him – lust.

'I wish I could pay them back *everything*,' she said passionately. 'I wish I could restore their dream. But I cannot. I will not inherit my jewels until I am twenty-five. Three years is an awfully long time to wait. I could have them before then, of course, if I were to marry with my uncle's approval, but I do not believe that is going to happen. It will be a long, long time before I trust any other man.'

'Ah,' he said, 'Crawley's motive becomes clear. I suppose you told him about this condition of your inheritance?'

'Yes.' She looked at him with a frown. 'It was dreadfully stupid and gullible of me, was it not?'

'Dreadfully,' he agreed, shifting position again.

'You are in pain,' she said, frowning and focusing fully on him.

'A little discomfort,' he admitted. 'I have been engaging in the wrong sort of sport for my physical condition, I suppose. One might say that I am being served my just deserts.'

'Your leg is hurting?' She jumped to her feet. 'I will go and fetch fresh water and cleanse it and apply more salve and clean bandages. Let me see. Is it bleeding?'

But he held up a firm staying hand as she approached the bed.

'I think it would be altogether better for my peace of mind if you kept your distance, Miss York,' he said. 'Since we both seem agreed that what happened here between us tonight was a great mistake, and

109

since it would appear that we were a disappointment to each other, it would be as well if we avoided any possibility of a repetition.'

She stared at him wide-eyed for a few moments while color mounted in her cheeks. Then she turned and made for the door with almost ungainly haste, fumbled clumsily with the lock before it scraped back, and dashed from the room, closing the door none too quietly behind her.

Well, deuce take it, that had not been a very gentlemanly speech, had it? He had just informed a lady after her first sexual encounter that it had been a great mistake and that she had been a disappointment to him.

He was going to have some humble pie to eat tomorrow.

He dreaded the very thought of tomorrow.

Chapter Eight

Alleyne might have thought he had not slept all night if he had not woken in a panic early in the morning and tried to get out of bed before he remembered that he could not.

He had to reach the Namur Gates. She was waiting for him there, and he was terrified that she might be in grave danger.

Pain served the dual function of banishing the remnants of sleep and cutting off the dream – if it had been just a dream. He lay very still, one hand cupped over the throbbing wound in his thigh, the other gripping the bedcovers, and tried desperately to recapture it. *Who* was waiting for him? And why? What was the danger?

Was it just a dream?

Or was it a memory?

He gave up after a few minutes and tried for perhaps the hundredth time to piece together what had happened to him before he regained consciousness here in this house. He had been riding away from the Battle of Waterloo toward Brussels. At least, that was the direction he must assume he had been taking, since it must have been at the battle where he had been shot. There had been a letter. And there had been a woman waiting for him at the city gates.

But try as he would – and he tried until his face was wet with perspiration and his head began to throb – he could bring nothing more into focus. And there seemed no connection among the random details that might be real memories or might just as likely be mere dreams. If he had been fighting in the Battle of Waterloo, why would he have been riding north to keep a rendezvous with some woman? And why was the letter so important? Was it something she had written to him, summoning him to protect her from some danger? *In the middle of a battle?*

No, it made no sense whatsoever.

It was a relief to hear a knock on his door, though he did turn his head warily as it opened, half expecting that it would be Rachel York. He was not ready to face her yet. But it was Sergeant Strickland instead, shaving gear in his hands, a pair of crutches tucked under one arm, a broad grin on his face despite the bandages that still swathed one side of it.

'You are going to be up and mobile today, sir,' he said after bidding Alleyne a cheerful good morning. He set down the shaving gear and propped the crutches against the foot of the bed. 'Those will cheer you up. I'll give you a hand with them later.'

'I will be even happier when I get some clothes,' Alleyne told him. 'I have been helpless and dependent for too long. I am eager to get out and about. I need to find out who I am and reclaim my old life.'

'If it is all the same to you, sir,' Strickland was saying, 'I'm going to shave you myself today. I'm getting used to seeing things one-eyed.'

Alleyne looked at him dubiously.

'You really do have ambitions to be a valet, then, do you?' he asked.

'I've got to do something,' the other man said, rubbing soap on the shaving brush. 'I've only ever known soldiering. I took the king's shilling when I was little more than a nipper. It were either that or take to thieving and as like as not hang for it. I never did fancy thieving – or a hanging. I have to find something other than soldiering now, though. And why not valeting? I been taking orders from gentlemen and humoring their whims for six years since I made sergeant. I can dress you and shave you and look after your clothes with one eye the same as two.'

'There is still the problem of my total poverty, though,' Alleyne reminded him. But he let the sergeant soap his face and prepared to have his throat cut.

'I do have a bit of money, though, you see, sir,' Strickland told him. 'Not much to a gentleman's way of looking at things, I reckon, but enough to keep me going for a while. It's not so much money I need, sir, as a sense of belonging and being useful, at least for a little while till I get my feet under me.'

'I know exactly how you feel,' Alleyne said ruefully. 'But you might do better than me, you know. We cannot even be sure that I am a gentleman, can we?'

'Oh, we certainly can be that,' the sergeant assured him. 'Never doubt it for a moment, sir. I have known men what are gentlemen and men what are not and men what pretend to be. You are one of the first kind and no doubt about it. I don't know *who* you are – you weren't in my regiment and I never set eyes on

113

you till I saw you in the forest. But I know *what* you are.'

Alleyne lay still as the razor scraped away stubble and the sergeant's face hovered over his own, bandaged and bruised and fierce as he frowned in concentration.

'Do you ever feel frightened, Strickland?' he asked.

'I reckon you are the one what should be feeling that,' the sergeant said, grinning and revealing large, widely spaced teeth. 'This is the first time I ever shaved another man. And I only got one eye to see out of so's I get it right.'

'Frightened at losing your old way of life so abruptly, I mean,' Alleyne explained, 'and having to create a new one for yourself.'

Sergeant Strickland straightened up, having completed one side of Alleyne's face.

'Frightened?' he said. 'I never been frightened in my life, sir. Leastways I've never called it fright. It seems unmanly, don't it? Or maybe it's not the fright so much as what a fellow does with it. P'raps I do feel some fear, sir, but there's no point in letting it get a grip on, is there? There's a whole other world out there apart from the army. I'll go and find what there is. Maybe I'll like it better than what went before. Or maybe I won't. But if I don't, then I'll go looking for something else again. There's nothing to stop me, only my death, which will come when it comes whatever I do in the meanwhile.'

He bent over Alleyne to tackle the other side of his face.

'In actual, honest fact,' he continued, 'it's not cowardly to be frightened. It's what I always said to

114

my boys before a battle, especially the raw recruits fresh from England and their mothers' sides. If you was never frightened, sir, you would never find out what you was made of and what you was capable of doing. You would never become a better man than what you started out being. P'raps that is what *you* will discover – what you are made of and what you are capable of. And when you finally *do* remember who you are, p'raps you will find that you have become a better man than he ever was. P'raps he was a man who never ever grew any more once he reached manhood. P'raps he needed to do something drastic like losing his memory so that he could get his life unstuck. Begging your pardon for saying so, sir. Sometimes I talk too much.'

'I perceive that you are a philosopher, Strickland,' Alleyne said. 'I wonder if I will have the strength of character to fulfill your expectations of me. Have you cut me yet?'

'That I have not,' the sergeant said, straightening up again and examining his finished handiwork before wiping Alleyne's face with a clean towel. 'I figure you lost enough blood for one month.'

'Thank you,' Alleyne said, running a hand over the smoothness of his jaw and thinking about the sergeant's words. He was, of course, desperately frightened, though it seemed shameful to admit it. It was surely one of the most dreadful of fates – to lose oneself, to have no memory of any of the twenty-five years or so of one's life. Did he have the courage and strength of character to build a new identity and a new life, perhaps better than the ones that went before them?

But even the sergeant was not quite as courageous

115

as his words suggested. He was still at the brothel, even though he was mobile enough to have left anytime during the past several days. And he was willing to attach himself to a man who had not a penny with which to pay him – just so that he would not have to step out into the world alone just yet.

Stepping out into the world alone – it was a truly terrifying thought. Eager as he was to leave here, Alleyne realized suddenly, he was just as anxious to stay, to find some excuse to postpone the inevitable moment.

Sergeant Strickland was taking his time over washing out the brush and razor in the washbowl. He cleared his throat and spoke without looking at Alleyne.

'I like the ladies here, sir,' he said. 'I even manned the door for them last night so they would be free to entertain their gentlemen and feel safe if any of the gents decided to get rough. It don't matter to me what they do to earn their victuals. But I do wonder what Miss York is doing living here with them. She ain't one of them. Is she?'

Alleyne looked sharply at him.

'My understanding,' he said, 'is that she is a lady.'

'I knew it, sir,' the sergeant said. 'From the first moment, when she was yelling out that you was her man and you was hurt bad, I knew she was a lady. But there is always the danger that her good name might be soiled on account of she is living in a brothel. We don't want to make it worse for her, if you get my drift, sir, do we? What do you want me to do with them hairpins on the table here? I wouldn't want the other ladies to see them there when they bring your breakfast, and get the wrong idea.'

For a moment Alleyne felt like a private soldier cringing under the sergeant's gentle but unmistakable tongue lashing. Deuce take it, he had forgotten about the hairpins. He fervently wished that that had all been a dream. But there were the hairpins as incontrovertible proof that it had not been.

'Gather them up if you will, Strickland,' he said, 'and put them in the top drawer of the chest over there. She had a headache when she was sitting in here last evening keeping me company and removed the pins to reduce some of the tension.'

What a purely asinine explanation!

'Quite so, sir,' the sergeant said agreeably, scooping the pins into one large hand. 'I would protect that little lady with my life if anyone tried to harm her – as I am sure you would yourself, sir. I'll always remember the way she was sobbing over you even though as it turned out you was not her man. A tenderhearted lady she is, sir.'

'I am well aware that I owe her my life, sergeant, and a great deal more even than that,' Alleyne assured him.

Sergeant Strickland did not labor the point. He picked up the shaving things and took them from the room. Without even waiting for his breakfast to arrive, Alleyne flung back the bedcovers, swung his legs carefully over the side of the bed, and drew the crutches toward him.

He was feeling restless, weak, irritable, guilty – and downright sinful. He could do something to alleviate the first two conditions, at least. And the others? He was going to have to think of some way of making his peace with Rachel York. But a simple apology would not do it, he sensed.

117

He would have to think of something.

He tucked the crutches firmly beneath his arms and hoisted himself up onto his right foot.

Rachel busied herself in the kitchen for much of the morning, helping Phyllis bake bread and cakes and peel potatoes and chop vegetables. The other ladies did not leave their beds until late, a fact for which she was very thankful. She was amazed that Phyllis appeared to notice no difference in her. She felt as if last night's activities must be written all over her face and person.

She was also very thankful that Sergeant Strickland had firmly established himself as Mr. Smith's valet and catered to all his needs during the morning.

Before noon she volunteered to do some shopping and hurried away from the house. She had avoided going out much following her return to Brussels, lest she be seen by some of Lady Flatley's acquaintances and be accused of being Mr. Crawley's accomplice, even though she realized that it was unlikely any of them would be aware of his villainy yet. Indeed, it was possible that most of them never would unless they checked up on the charities to which they thought they had contributed. But today she was desperate for air and exercise and did not much care whom she met. It did not even occur to her that in London before her father's death she had not been allowed to set foot outdoors unchaperoned.

She walked farther than her errand made necessary. She even strolled for a while in the Parc de Bruxelles and watched the swans on the lake and soaked up sunshine and warmth. It was the middle of the afternoon before she returned to the house, and even then she dreaded doing so. She was going to have to confront Mr. Smith again, and she shrank from the prospect. How ever would she be able even to look at him after what had happened between them last night? She would take a cup of tea into the sitting room and compose herself first, she decided, hearing the sound of voices and laughter coming from that direction.

She opened the door gingerly and peered around it, fearful that perhaps her friends were entertaining clients, though they did not often do so during the daytime. And indeed she almost jerked back her head when she saw that there was indeed a gentleman in the room with them – an extraordinarily handsome gentleman. For a split second she did not recognize him. But there was a pair of crutches propped against the chair beside him.

'Rachel!' Bridget called. 'Come in, my love, and meet our gentleman caller.'

'Isn't he gorgeous?' Phyllis asked gleefully.

Geraldine was standing by the window, her hands on her hips. 'He dresses up well enough, I must admit,' she said. 'It's just a pity those pockets are empty.'

'I am not sure I care, Gerry,' Phyllis said.

'We will be putting the poor man to the blush,' Flossie said as Rachel came unwillingly into the room and shut the door behind her. 'But he is enough to make any self-respecting girl squabble with her closest friends.'

They were all joking and flirting as usual, and Mr. Smith was grinning and taking it all in good part. But he busied himself with his crutches and hauled himself out of his chair at the sight of Rachel. He made her a surprisingly graceful bow.

'Miss York,' he said.

He looked very directly at her, some of the laughter gone from his eyes. Rachel hoped fervently that she was not blushing. It was almost impossible, seeing him now, to realize that less than twenty-four hours ago they had been naked and intimate together. But since it was not *quite* impossible, she felt she could cheerfully die of mortification.

... since it would appear that we were a disappointment to each other ...

She could hear him speak those words as clearly as if he were saying them now.

She had not realized quite how tall he was. His clothes had not been fashioned by the most exclusive of tailors, she guessed, but his shirt was dazzling white, his cravat crisp and neatly knotted about his neck, his blue coat well fitting enough to show off the breadth of his shoulders and chest, and his gray pantaloons tight and creaseless about shapely, well-muscled legs – if one discounted the outline of the bandage about his left thigh. He wore leather shoes rather than the Hessian boots that might have been more usual with such an outfit, but altogether Phyllis was quite right. He looked gorgeous. His hair had even been freshly washed. One dark lock had fallen forward invitingly over his right eyebrow.

'Your new clothes all fit well, then, Mr. Smith?' she asked him, concentrating hard upon keeping her manner casual and amiable.

'All except for one coat,' he said. 'And, alas, it is the one I most fancy. But even with all of Sergeant Strickland's strength thrown into the effort, I could not be squeezed inside it.'

'We miscalculated, Floss,' Geraldine said mournfully.

'That chest is even broader than we supposed.'

'The shoulders too, Gerry,' Flossie said, looking him over frankly. 'We paid too much attention to that handsome face and the roguish smile that goes with it. I would not make the same mistake again.'

'You might have asked for my measurements, ladies,' Mr. Smith said, lowering himself carefully to his chair again after Rachel had seated herself.

'But they were afraid you would not remember and I would have all the pleasure of going at you with my measuring tape,' Phyllis said. 'This will teach them never to leave home again without theirs.'

And so the conversation proceeded for the next ten minutes or so to the accompaniment of much laughter while Rachel tried to compose herself and rehearse what she would say when she was finally alone with him, as she inevitably would be sooner or later.

It was sooner rather than later.

'In my bobbing progress about the house,' Mr. Smith said, 'I have seen that you have a pretty garden at the back, ladies, and that someone has even been considerate enough to place a wooden seat beneath the willow tree overhanging the lily pond. If you will excuse me, I am going to convey myself out there and take a turn about the paved paths before sitting for a while, breathing in the air of the outdoors.'

'Just be careful not to overdo the exercise,' Bridget warned him. 'Remember that this is the first day you have been up.'

'We would hate to have to carry you back to your bed,' Phyllis told him.

'No, we wouldn't, Phyll,' Geraldine said.

'I'll be careful,' he promised. 'Miss York, would you care to accompany me?'

121

Bridget smiled and nodded her consent in Rachel's direction just as if she were still her nurse. Rachel set down her empty cup and saucer and got to her feet. She would have given a great deal to be able to avoid this encounter, she thought. She was not ready for it yet. But would she ever be? And since she could not now go back and change last night, she could only go forward and deal with the embarrassment of being alone with him. She opened the sitting room door and held it back while Mr. Smith moved past her on his crutches.

He made slow but quite steady progress on them, she noticed as they proceeded outside. She fell into step beside him after closing the back door. She clasped her hands behind her.

'Well, Miss York,' he said, the amused, flirtatious tone he had used in the sitting room gone from his voice, 'we need to talk.'

'Do we?' she asked, concentrating her attention on the flagstones over which they walked. Like a child, she avoided stepping on the cracks. 'I would really rather not. What is done is done. It was not of any great significance, was it?'

'What a blow to my masculine pride!' he exclaimed. 'Of no great significance, indeed. I am well aware that under normal circumstances I should now be making you an offer of marriage.'

She felt more mortified than ever.

'I would not accept it,' she said. 'What a foolish idea!'

'I am glad you think so,' he said. 'I cannot, of course, make any such offer – not yet, at least. I would have no legal name to write on the license or marriage register. And I may already be married to someone else.'

She had forgotten that possibility. She felt a slight churning in her stomach.

'Not *ever*,' she said firmly. 'Not even if you discover after you know your identity that you are still unwed. I have been involved in one unconsidered betrothal this year, Mr. Smith. I have no intention of engaging in another anytime soon.'

'What *are* you planning to do?' he asked her.

She felt at a disadvantage now that he was on his feet. She was accustomed to looking down at him. Even last night while they were ... But really, she preferred not to think about that.

'I have not decided,' she told him. 'I will take employment again, I suppose.'

'And I daresay,' he said, 'you would need a character reference from Lady Flatley. Would she give you one?'

Rachel grimaced.

'The ladies here want to go in search of Mr. Crawley as soon as they return to England,' she said, 'if they can raise enough money to cover their traveling expenses, that is. I have thought of going with them. I do not suppose he will be easy to find, and there is very little chance that any of their money can be recovered, but I feel the need to help them as much as I can.'

'Those ladies,' he said, 'do not need your help, Miss York. They are hardened women of the world. They will survive.'

'Yes,' she said, stopping on the path and turning to face him, anger sparking from her eyes, 'of course they will. They will survive. It does not matter that they will do nothing more than that, that they can never expect freedom or happiness or bounty. They are only *whores*, after all.'

123

He sighed out loud. 'My meaning was only,' he said, 'that you are not responsible for them any more than you are responsible for me – or than I am responsible for you. Sometimes one simply has to allow others to live their own lives even if it is painful to watch.'

She frowned at him. She had been in the mood for a good quarrel. But he had refused to take up his cue.

'Perhaps,' he suggested, 'we ought to sit down before we continue this conversation. I would hate to totter and fall at your feet and perhaps give the wrong impression.'

She went ahead of him, but she waited until he had seated himself with slow care and propped his crutches against the wrought iron arm of the seat before perching on the other end. She wished it were a little longer.

'Tell me about your uncle,' he said.

'He is Baron Weston of Chesbury Park in Wiltshire,' she said. 'There is not much else to tell. He was my mother's brother, but he disowned her after she eloped at the age of seventeen to marry my father. The only time I saw him was after her death, when he came to London for her funeral and stayed for a few days.'

'He is your only living relative?' he asked her.

'As far as I know, yes,' she said.

'Perhaps,' he said, 'you ought to go to him. He would hardly turn you away, would he?'

She turned her head to look at him incredulously.

'I have heard from him *twice* since I was six years old,' she said, 'once when he refused my request for my jewels when I was eighteen and once when I asked for them again last year after my father died. On that occasion he wrote that I might not have them but that

124

if I was destitute I could come to live with him and he would find me a husband.'

'And so it is possible for you to go there,' he said.

'Mr. Smith,' she said, her anger returning, 'if you were in my place, would *you* go? To someone who had cut your mother's acquaintance when she married and who had ignored you all your life except for a few days when you were six? And someone who was so eager to see you again that he informed you that you could come *if you were destitute* and threatened to marry you off to someone of his choosing if you did so. *Would* you go?'

His nearness was disconcerting. Even more so was that she still had to look up at him. He seemed to loom over her, far larger and more imposing than he had appeared to be when lying in bed.

'I suppose not,' he said. 'No, that is an inadequate answer. I would probably tell the bastard to go and boil his head in oil.'

She was so surprised and so shocked that she burst into laughter. He smiled slowly, and she could see that his eyes had focused upon her dimple, which she always thought such a childish feature.

'Tell me about the jewels,' he said.

'I have never even seen them,' she told him, gazing into the lily pond, 'though I *do* know that they are really quite valuable. My grandmother left them to my mother under the condition that they remain in my uncle's care until she married with his approval or reached the age of twenty-five. She married without his approval, and she died when she was twenty-four. But she must have had some communication with my uncle before she died. She left the jewels to me under exactly the same conditions.'

'Perhaps,' he said, 'she thought they would be safer with him than with your father.'

She had thought of that humiliating possibility. Poor Papa – he would have gambled the whole fortune away and then wept with remorse and gone back to the tables in an attempt to win it all back.

'Perhaps,' she said, 'he thinks they are safer with him than with *me*. My father was dead when I asked for them last year. Yet they are mine. If I were a man, there would be no question of withholding my inheritance when I am already of age. I *wish* it were already mine. I would give everything back to these ladies that they lost and restore their dream. How happy they would be. How happy *I* would be.'

She bit her lower lip as she felt tears well into her eyes.

'There is a way you can get your hands on your inheritance early, though, is there not?' he said.

She laughed scornfully and turned her head to look at him again. He was gazing back with an arrested look in his eyes.

'I would have to be *married*,' she said.

He lifted one eyebrow.

'And win his *approval*,' she added.

The other eyebrow went up and his eyes filled with the sort of laughter he usually reserved for his bantering exchanges with her friends.

'Mr. Smith,' she said curtly, 'I cannot marry *you*. You have said so yourself, and besides, I would not marry anyone just for the sake of getting my hands on my jewels.'

'Admirable,' he murmured, and grinned.

'And how could you possibly win his approval anyway?' she asked him. 'You do not even know your *name*.'

126

He waggled his eyebrows at her and suddenly looked boyish and roguish – and really rather irresistible.

'Have you never heard, Miss York – or dare I call you *Rachel*,' he said, 'of a masquerade?'

'What?' She stared at him wide-eyed.

'I will *pretend* to be your husband,' he said, 'and go to Chesbury Park with you to wrest your fortune from the clutches of this tight-fisted, hard-hearted rogue of an uncle of yours. Then you can do whatever you wish with it, though I would warn you that you may find it extremely difficult to persuade these ladies to take so much as a penny from you.'

'But you are eager to be on your way from here,' she said. 'You want to find your people and your home.'

He grimaced and some of the laughter faded from his eyes.

'Yes, I am and I do,' he agreed, 'but you cannot know how much I dread doing so at the same time. What if I get out there and find no clues to my identity? Worse, what if I find a large family and a whole host of friends and discover that they are total strangers to me? Can you understand the terror inherent in such a thought? Perhaps if I postpone my journey of self-discovery for a while, my memory will come back on its own.'

'But,' she said, thoughts tumbling so chaotically through her brain that she could not think straight at all, 'I cannot ask you to do this for me.'

'You did not ask me.' He grinned at her again, and suddenly she wanted to reach out to touch his warmth and vitality. 'I offered. Save me from the terror of having nothing to do but step out into the vast

127

unknown, Miss York. Let's do this.'

There must be a million arguments against it – at least a million. But all she could see in her mind was the image of herself handing over to Flossie the exact sum of money she had seen Flossie hand to Nigel Crawley while she had stood by, smiling happily. She would be able to do it in reality. And she need not feel guilty about the masquerade, need she? It was *her* money, and Uncle Richard had always been quite horrid to her. She owed him nothing.

'Very well,' she said, and smiled.

He rested one forearm over the back of the seat and continued to grin at her like a mischievous schoolboy – except that he looked disconcertingly gorgeous in the process.

'I just hope you do not now expect me to go down on one knee to propose to you,' he said. 'I fear I might never get up again.'

Chapter Eight

Alleyne lay on his bed for longer than an hour after coming in from the garden, though he did not sleep. He ached in every bone and joint, and he suspected that his left leg was slightly swollen. It dismayed him to discover just how weak he was, but at the same time it was satisfying to know that he could now move about and begin to build up his strength and stamina again.

He was a dreadful coward, though. He wondered if he always had been. For almost two weeks he had been chafing at the bit, longing to be on his feet again so that he could get out of this house and begin discovering who the devil he was. But when it had come to the point today, when that moment had seemed imminent, he had found himself consumed by terror. He had spoken the truth to Rachel York.

And, good Lord, what sort of a scrape had he found himself in instead?

He had wanted to help her. Annoyed as he had been with her last night for not warning him of what he was about to do and not therefore giving him a chance to leave her virtue intact, he had also wanted to do something positive for her. She had, after all, saved his life. There was no doubt in his mind that he would have died in the Forest of Soignés if she had not come along and found help for him. And she had nursed him for well over a week since then. He had grown fond of her. Correction – he had been besotted with her from the first moment his eyes had alit on her.

He had wanted to do something for her. He had invited her into the garden so that he could find out something about her uncle and see if it was possible for her to go to live with him. He had been planning to offer to escort her there. It would not have been much in comparison with what she had done for him, but it would have been something.

Something sane, sensible, and honorable.

And if he *did* discover that he was a single man, he had decided, then he would be able to go back to her there and make her the marriage offer that honor dictated he make.

But look what he had done instead!

The thing was, though, that the terror that had been hovering over him all day had fallen away as soon as he had made his suggestion, and all he had been able to feel was the exhilaration of a mad challenge.

What did *that* say about his character? Did he usually behave like this? Like a twenty-five-year-old boy who was up to any madcap scheme? If he *was* twenty-five, that was. He might be thirty.

He grimaced.

But it was too late now to change his mind about this particular madcap venture even if he wanted to – and he was not sure he did. He was to assume a whole new identity, and he was to acquire a new wife in the process – presumably in a love match. Yes, definitely a love match. He was to convince Baron Weston of his eminent respectability and steadiness of character.

He chuckled softly. A challenge was just what he needed, and this was a colossal one. He felt ... surely he felt like his old self again.

But that thought threatened to bring on a fit of melancholy again. He closed his eyes and set the back of one hand over them.

He expected to spend the rest of the day in bed, or at least in his room, but Sergeant Strickland appeared in the doorway late in the afternoon to inform him that this was the ladies' night off and that he had been sent to invite Mr. Smith to join them for dinner if he felt up to it.

'I would warn you, though, sir,' he added, 'that they have invited me too.'

'And I may not think it proper to dine with a sergeant?' Alleyne asked him, his eyebrows raised. 'I do not know how high in the instep my usual self is, Strickland, but this self will be delighted to dine with one – and with four ladies of the night too.'

He would be glad of the company, he decided, as Strickland helped him back into his coat and brushed his hair for him while Alleyne tweaked his cravat back to some semblance of smartness. And then his hands fell suddenly still as it occurred to him on a wave of amusement that someone would be horrified indeed to see him now.

Except that the thought, vivid as it was, failed to provide either a face or a name.

Who would be horrified?

For a moment he thought he was going to be able to pull a name out of the depths of his memory. It was as if a curtain fluttered before the blankness of his mind, threatening at any moment to be blown aside by a gust of wind to reveal everything that was behind it.

But the curtain remained stubbornly in place.

He tried to salvage at least something. Was it a man or a woman? Who the deuce *was* it who had flashed into his mind when he had not even been trying to remember anything?

But it was no use.

'More pain, sir?' the sergeant asked.

'No, nothing,' Alleyne said.

At first when he entered the dining room, he thought that Sergeant Strickland must have been mistaken about its not being a working night. The ladies were dressed in full regalia, including brightly colored silks and satins, bosoms dangerously close to spilling out of bodices above tightly laced stays, elaborately curled coiffures, towering hair plumes, strong floral perfumes, and facial paint. He was reminded of his very first sight of them and made them as deep and courtly a bow as his crutches would allow.

'I am still convinced,' he said, 'that I have died and gone to heaven.'

He noticed that the small heart-shaped black patch that Geraldine sometimes wore close to her mouth had been placed to the left side of her cleavage tonight.

They had dressed up for *him*, he thought – because he was dining with them. He could have chuckled at the realization, but he would not risk giving offense. He really did like them all immensely.

Rachel York was dressed as she had been last night except that her hair had been styled more simply tonight and shone like pure gold in the light from the candelabrum in the middle of the table. He shook his head mentally at the sight of her. He really must have lost his wits as well as his memory to have believed that she belonged in this brothel and was a working member of it. Now that his eyes had been opened, it was blindingly clear to him that she was a refined, elegant lady.

He still felt somewhat out of charity with her – or perhaps with himself for his stupidity.

It was a strange meal. They had no servants, as he had realized before. Apparently it was Phyllis who did most of the cooking. Fortunately, she seemed to have a considerable talent for it. But all the ladies – all five of them – helped serve the food, carrying hot dishes into the dining room and empty dishes out. And the conversation was intelligent and lively. They talked about Brussels, about the contrast between the city as it had been just a few weeks ago when it had been bustling with all the glittering entertainments of the visiting *ton* and the city as it was now when almost all foreigners had left. They talked about the war and its aftermath, about the prospects for a peaceful and prosperous Europe now that Napoléon Bonaparte had been taken captive again. They asked Sergeant Strickland for his observations on the battle strategy that had been used. They talked about London and its theaters and art galleries.

It was only as they ate their dessert that Rachel York, who had been rather quiet during the evening, spoke up at last, looking directly at Alleyne as she began and blushing rosily.

'I do believe,' she said, 'that I am going to be able to get my hands on my jewels after all.'

'You are going to let me climb the ivy, Rache,' Geraldine said.

'Mr. Smith is going to come to Chesbury with me,'

133

Rachel explained, 'and pose as my husband. We will win my uncle's approval for our marriage, and he will turn over my inheritance to me. Then I will be able to sell a piece or two and we can go in search of Mr. Crawley if you still wish to do so while Mr. Smith finds his family and home.'

There was a loud clamor as four excited voices all tried to talk at once. Bridget won the contest.

'*Pose* as your husband, my love?' she said. 'Why does he not *be* your husband?'

'I shall go into deep mourning if he does, Bridge,' Geraldine said, 'on behalf of all the rest of the women in the world. I look good in black.'

'But this is a *splendid* idea,' Flossie said. 'I cannot understand why we did not think of it before. It is bound to work.'

'It cannot be a real marriage,' Rachel explained. 'Mr. Smith does not yet know who he is. Besides, I have decided that if I ever marry, it will be a love match. I was foolish to settle for less with Mr. Crawley. Thank *heaven* I realized my mistake in time.'

'It will work like a dream,' Phyllis said, clasping her hands to her bosom. 'One look at you, Mr. Smith, and the baron will rush to fetch the jewels.'

'I don't think we can assume, though, Phyll,' Flossie said, 'that the baron will fall for him the way we have. He will have to use his charm in a different way, but I daresay he is up to it. He has a roguish gleam in his eye that tells me he will enjoy something like this and excel at it.'

'And he has that air about him,' Geraldine said, 'that speaks of lineage and money and power. Ah, be still, my heart! Do you think your uncle would be

134

fooled if *I* impersonated *you*, Rache, and pretended to be Mrs. Smith?'

'Not for a moment, Gerry,' Phyllis said. 'But think how romantic this is. I daresay Mr. Smith will fall in love with Rachel and she with him, and they will marry and live happily ever after.'

'It would not at all surprise me,' Sergeant Strickland said, 'if you will forgive me for saying so when no one asked me my opinion, missy. And if *you* will forgive me, sir. I sometimes talk too much.'

Alleyne grinned about the table. Rachel, he could see, was looking decidedly uncomfortable.

'But the next step,' Bridget said, bringing order back to the gathering, 'is to decide on a story for Mr. Smith to tell. We must work out a whole life history for him and leave nothing to chance. Then he will need to learn his part, and Rachel will need to learn hers.'

There was a flurry of suggestions, most of them quite preposterous – and most of them provoking a great deal of laughter. Alleyne let them talk for a while before holding up one hand and drawing everyone's attention.

'I will definitely not be a chimney sweep who has discovered he is a prince,' he said, 'or a duke who is the king's natural son by his favorite mistress, though both were brilliant and tempting suggestions. I will perhaps be a baronet with an estate in the north of England. But it would be best if Miss York and I decided upon the details between ourselves and reported back to all of you for approval.'

'*Miss York*!' Phyllis exclaimed. 'You must call her Rachel now, Mr. Smith, and she must call you *Jonathan* – unless you choose to become *Orlando*, as

135

I suggested a moment ago, since it is a far more romantic name.'

'There is a bottle of wine,' Flossie said. 'It is in the pantry on the floor under the bottom shelf, if you would be so good as to fetch it, William. We have been keeping it for a special occasion. I do believe this is it. We have a pretend marriage to celebrate.'

Rachel York was subdued, Alleyne noticed as toasts were drunk a few minutes later just as if they had really celebrated their nuptials today. Everyone else made merry.

But an already mad scheme was about to become considerably more outrageous.

'You can't turn up on the baron's doorstep without a valet to your name, sir,' Sergeant Strickland told Alleyne as he set down his empty glass. 'I'm not the best-looking gentleman's gentleman you ever set eyes upon, on account of I am big and talk rough and have only ever known soldiering, but I'm better than nothing. I'll go with you, sir. There is no need to worry about paying me no wages. Like I told you before, I got enough for my own passage to England and for my needs for the next month or so, and this will give me something to do while I get my feet under me, so to speak.'

Alleyne looked at him with raised eyebrows. But really, the man was right. How impressive would he look if he turned up at Chesbury Park as Rachel's husband without a valet? And without baggage and money? With little more than the clothes on his back, in fact. He suddenly realized that there was going to have to be a great deal of careful planning for this scheme before they could rush off to Wiltshire.

But before he could give the sergeant any answer, Bridget spoke up.

'And Rachel ought not to arrive at the house with no one but Mr. Smith for company,' she said, 'even if she is supposedly married to him. It is only a recent marriage, after all, and Baron Weston must be shown that she was in Brussels with a decent companion. I'll be she, and I'll go with you, my love. Besides which, since Mr. Smith and Rachel are not really married, it would not be right for them to travel together without a chaperon, would it?'

'Except that with that hair, Bridge,' Flossie told her, 'Baron Weston would spot you for a whore even if he's blind in both eyes.'

'I can dye it,' Bridget said. 'I'll dye it back to my own color, a nice, respectable mousy brown.'

'We can't let you have all the fun, though, Bridge,' Geraldine said. 'If you are going to have a holiday for a week or two, then I don't see why we all can't. I for one don't feel like going back to work in London before we have dealt with that Crawley toad, and we can't do that until we have heard from one of the sisters about his whereabouts, can we? If we have to sit around twiddling our thumbs, we might as well have fun at the same time. I fancy myself as a lady's maid. I have a gift for dressing hair – you have all said so – and picking out what a woman ought to wear so she can show to best advantage. I'll come along as your personal maid, Rache. It would appear peculiar if you did not have one. With any luck I'll discover that Baron Weston employs a houseful of tall, handsome footmen and a stableful of rugged, handsome grooms and a parkful of bronzed, handsome gardeners. You won't have to worry about me disgracing

137

you, though. I know how to be respectable when I have to be.'

Alleyne, looking about the table, caught between hilarity and dismay, wondered if Rachel was feeling as out of control of the situation as he was. Her silence suggested that she was.

'What about us?' Phyllis asked, sounding aggrieved. 'What are Flossie and I supposed to do while the two of you are enjoying yourselves at Chesbury Park?'

'Use our imaginations, Phyll, that's what,' Flossie said. She batted her eyelids over her big blue eyes and touched one hand coquettishly to her blond curls. 'Ladies, gentlemen, meet Mrs. Flora Streat, respectable and respected widow of the late Captain Streat, and dear friend of Miss Rachel York, who was recently married from my home. And you, my precious,' she added, smiling graciously at Phyllis, 'are my dear departed husband's sister, if I do not mistake, whose own husband, Captain Leavey, is at present on active duty in Paris.'

'What, Floss?' Phyllis replied, draining her glass of wine. 'You have trouble being sure that you recognize your own sister-in-law? When we came out from England together and are going to return there together?'

'Making a detour on the way to our own home,' Flossie said, 'in order to accompany our young friend, the new Lady Smith, to Chesbury Park in Wiltshire with her husband.'

'Now,' Geraldine said, 'I am mortally sorry that I have condemned myself to the kitchen. Though perhaps not. At least I'll have all those footmen and grooms and gardeners to myself when I am not busy brushing Rache's hair. And I'll have Will to gossip with.'

Alleyne cleared his throat, and four sets of hair plumes nodded in unison as the ladies gave him their attention.

'We must all remember, though,' he said, 'that this is not just a lark we are kicking up. Our main concern must be to see to it that Miss York – that *Rachel* and I make a good enough impression on her uncle that she is granted what would be hers anyway at the age of twenty-five.'

They had all sobered and were gazing earnestly at him.

'But it *will* be a lark too,' Geraldine said after a short pause.

They all launched into merry chatter again.

'We will have to wait at least a week or so longer before leaving, though,' Rachel said, speaking up at last. 'We must wait until Mr. Smith has more of his strength back and until Sergeant Strickland is free of his bandages.'

'*Jonathan*, Rachel,' Phyllis reminded her. 'You are going to have to start calling him *Jonathan*. Or Orlando. Don't you think he looks like an Orlando?'

'I got an eye patch,' the sergeant said. 'But I haven't worn it yet on account of all the bruises haven't quite gone away. I don't want to scare you ladies.'

'I think you will look rather dashing, Sergeant, bruises notwithstanding,' Phyllis told him. 'As long as there is no blood.'

'There is no need to wait upon my account,' Alleyne assured them. 'We might as well get this charade started as soon as possible.'

He – a man without money or possessions or identity – was fated, it seemed, to travel to England with a fake bride, surrounded by an entourage consisting of a piratical ex-military valet and four flamboyant whores masquerading as servants and ladies. And they were going there in order to trick a perfectly respectable gentleman out of a fortune in jewelry.

And it had all started with his impulsive suggestion in the garden this afternoon.

'You are in pain, Mr. Smith,' Rachel York told him suddenly, 'and desperately tired. I daresay you have overtaxed your strength today. You must be more careful tomorrow.'

She was quite right, of course. He had been ignoring the symptoms for some time. But he hardly knew how to sit upright at the table. His leg throbbed unceasingly. A headache niggled at him from somewhere behind his eyes.

She got to her feet.

'Come,' she said, 'I will take you to your room.'

He raised his eyebrows again. *Take* him there? He was incapable of going alone? But he did not argue.

'Yes, you go with him, Rache,' Geraldine told her. 'And you tuck him up warm for the night.'

'Just don't tuck yourself up with him, though, there's a good girl,' Flossie added. 'This is a respectable establishment, and you are only pretend married.'

'And don't stay too long, my love,' Bridget said, just as if her former charge had not spent hours of each day in his room for the past two weeks. 'Leave the door ajar.'

'Ah, but I do love a bit of romance,' Phyllis said with a sigh. 'Even if it is only a pretend one.'

140

'There is one thing about a lie,' Alleyne said to Rachel when they were out of earshot of the others. 'It grows like a rolling snowball as soon as it has seen the light of day. Are you alarmed by what you have just heard?'

'I have been alarmed by everything I have heard since this afternoon,' Rachel told him as she closed the door of his bedchamber but did not latch it behind them. 'But I will not stop either you or them. You are going to help me make them happy, and they need a break from this way of life that has been theirs for years past. Despite appearances, they are not really vulgar creatures. They are my friends, Mr. Smith. And even if they are found out, even if *you* are, so what? I will be no worse off than I am now, will I? My uncle will be unable to deny me my inheritance after my twenty-fifth birthday.'

'We had better follow their advice,' he said. 'You had better call me Jonathan, and I had better call you Rachel from this moment on. We are presumably going to be deeply in love and not the sort of couple who address each other with distant formality.'

She regarded him with a frown.

'Very well, then,' she said. 'But one thing must be clear from the start, Mr. Jonathan. There must be no repetition of last night and no flirtation – on either of our parts. You may be already married, and even if you are not, you would not want to be saddled with a wife even before you have remembered your usual life. And I am not in search of a husband. I thought perhaps I was when I met Mr. Crawley, but I have realized since I got away from him that my independence is altogether too valuable to me to give up easily.'

141

'Besides all of which,' he added, not to be outdone, 'we were both disappointed last night.'

'Y-yes.' She had the grace to blush.

'There will be no private dalliance despite the public display of genteel affection we will need to show, then,' he agreed as her eyes slipped from his.

He was rather enjoying himself, he discovered – except that he was weary to the point of exhaustion and felt like one giant ache from the crown of his head to his toenails.

He lowered himself to the side of the bed and propped his crutches against the headboard – and held up a staying hand when she would have dashed toward him.

'Rachel,' he said, 'there is no need for you to wait on me hand and foot and other body parts any longer. Indeed, I would be altogether happier in my mind if you were to keep a permanent distance from me from this moment on.'

The color fled from her face.

'Very well, then,' she said. 'I will send Sergeant Strickland.'

And she turned and exited the room without another word. Alleyne rather suspected that far from being a whore, she was really quite a dangerous innocent. She had not even understood him just now. She had thought he could not bear to have her touch him. She was right, of course, but not for the reason she was probably imagining.

He might be still annoyed with her, and he might have taken leave of his senses today – indeed there was no might about it – but he was still not dead. And she was still the most beautiful, most alluring creature he could remember setting eyes upon.

Now that it was too late, it struck him that devising a scheme that would keep him close to her – very close, in fact – was perhaps the most stupid thing he had done in his life. And that was probably saying something!

Who would have thought that one fall from a horse's back could cause such havoc with one's life?

He was in the process of trying to lift his left leg up onto the bed when Sergeant Strickland arrived to help him.

'You done the right thing, sir, begging your pardon for giving my opinion when you did not ask for it,' Sergeant Strickland said as he removed Alleyne's coat and then swung his legs onto the bed.

'Thank you, Strickland,' Alleyne said. 'But since I suspect you are accustomed to expressing your opinion whether asked for it or not, you need not apologize every time you do it.'

'Thank you, sir,' the sergeant said, helping Alleyne off with his pantaloons. 'This bandage has worked a bit loose. Shall I rewrap it for you?'

'Please,' Alleyne said. 'But you understand, do you not, that my marriage to Miss York is an entirely fictitious one?'

'What I understand, sir,' Strickland said, 'is that you have undertaken to be the lady's husband and protector, whether for real or not, and that since you are a gentleman and a gentleman don't end connections like that unless the lady does it for him, it is not really just pretend at all. You've done what is right and proper after she got a headache here last night and took out all her hairpins. The next step is up to her now, isn't it? About whether she wants it to be real or not once your memory comes back and you

143

know you are not a married man, I mean.'

'Thank you, Sergeant,' Alleyne said curtly, noting as his new valet removed the bandage and prepared to wrap it more securely about his thigh that despite some swelling and the pain it had caused, the wound itself was healing quite nicely. 'I really needed that lecture on my gentlemanly obligations.'

'No, you did not, sir,' Strickland said. 'I just talk too much. No putridity here, is there? You will be as right as rain in another week or two, though I daresay there is more to heal up on the inside than shows on the outside.'

Alleyne looked consideringly at the sergeant as the man straightened up, his task completed. 'How willing would you be, Strickland, to lend me half of the money you have?' he asked.

The sergeant stood smartly to attention and spoke without hesitation.

'I been trying to think of a way of offering you some of it, sir, without offending you, though it isn't so much,' he said. 'A gentleman ought to have funds, oughtn't he? It wouldn't be right for him to be waiting for the ladies to open their purses for every glass of ale he fancies to slake his thirst. But it don't need to be a loan. You can have some and welcome to it. I got plenty.'

'But a loan it will be nevertheless,' Alleyne said firmly. 'And a very temporary one, I hope. What do you know of Brussels? Were you posted here before the Battle of Waterloo? Do you know the establishments a man would go to in order to play deep? Apart from here, I mean.'

'Cards?' The sergeant was helping Alleyne out of the rest of his clothes and then helping him on with his nightshirt. 'I know one or two places, sir, though they are not the ones the real nobs like you would go to.'

'It does not matter,' Alleyne said. The chance that he might be recognized if he went somewhere frequented by the upper classes, though appealing in one way, might only complicate matters now that he had agreed to go to England with Rachel York. 'Just direct me to one you know.'

'You are going to play, sir?' Strickland asked, sliding a spare pillow beneath Alleyne's knee and giving him instant ease. 'Are you sure you remember how?'

'Memory loss is a strange thing,' Alleyne said. 'At least my memory loss is. All appears to have remained to me except the details relating to my personal identity.'

'And you was lucky in cards, was you, sir?' the sergeant asked him.

'I have no idea,' Alleyne admitted. 'But I must hope so. If not, it is going to be a horribly impoverished gentleman and his wife who will be arriving at Chesbury Park a short while from now. And I am going to be embarrassingly deep in *your* debt as well as that of the ladies here.'

'You have been lucky in love, though,' the sergeant said cheerfully, apparently determined to believe that the marriage was soon to be real and a love match to boot. 'We will take that as a good omen, sir. I will find out which establishment is the best for you to go to. Things may have changed a bit since the battle. I'll even go with you if I may, sir. To keep an eye on you, like, in case anyone should try some rough stuff, which I don't in no way expect. And to try my own luck too.'

'Done,' Alleyne said. 'I am to be consigned to darkness and sleep this early, am I?'

The sergeant was blowing out the candles and preparing to leave the room.

'You are tired, sir,' Strickland told him. 'Miss York told me so, though I would have known it for myself.'

And so he was stranded in bed and in darkness at an hour when he supposed most of his peers were just sallying forth for an evening's revelries, Alleyne thought. He wished he could remember just one occasion when he had done so. He wished he could tease just one memory past that heavy curtain that hung so relentlessly in front of his mind. Just one – and then they would all come flooding out, he was sure.

But having no memories with which to regale himself while he sought sleep, he found his mind slipping back over the past few hours.

Soon he was chuckling softly to himself.

Chapter Ten

Rachel doubted she would recognize her uncle when she finally saw him again. She had not seen him since she was six years old. At the time he had seemed tall and broad and rock solid, dependable and good humored. But those memories had soon grown sour.

The carriage jolted through a rut in the road, sending up a spray of mud though the rain had stopped an hour ago, and one of her knees touched one of Jonathan Smith's across the small space between their seats. It was the knee of his good leg, fortunately, though the other one had healed rapidly during the two and a half weeks since he had acquired crutches. He was able to put some weight on it now, though he still made use of a stout cane when he walked.

She moved her own leg hastily, and her eyes met his before moving away on the pretense that she was interested in the scenery beyond the window. They had both lived up to the agreement they had made the evening after he had suggested this masquerade. They had scarcely touched each other, scarcely been alone together, scarcely exchanged a private word with each other.

As a result, far from being more comfortable in his presence, she was quite the opposite. She kept feeling incredulous about the events of that infamous evening. It could not possibly have happened. She must have dreamed it. But then she would have vivid and lurid images of herself, of him, of *them*, and she would want to go and jump into the nearest pond to hide herself and cool her cheeks.

It did not help that every day he was stronger and more healthy and more handsome and more masculine and more – oh, and more *everything*.

In a million years, she thought, catching hold of the leather strap above her shoulder as the carriage swayed over another rut, she could not have predicted that her life would take this turn. It was just too, too bizarre.

The jolting had woken Bridget from a doze. She sat up and straightened her bonnet.

'I almost fell asleep,' she said.

'I *do* like the way you look, Bridget,' Rachel told her.

'It's because I resemble a staid matron, my love,' Bridget said ruefully.

'It is because you look like my beloved nurse again.' Rachel squeezed her arm.

Flossie, Phyllis, and Geraldine were riding in the carriage behind with Sergeant Strickland. All four ladies had shed their bright plumage before leaving Brussels and were dressed with almost comical respectability. Bridget, her face shiny with cleanliness, her hair a suspiciously uniform shade of mouse, looked like her dear old self. She also looked younger, though she probably would not have admitted as much herself.

Jonathan was also looking smarter and more elegant than any gentleman had a right to look. He had expensive new clothes. He had *money*.

Where he had acquired it she did not know, though of course it did not take any great intellectual effort to guess *how* he had got it. He had gone out a couple of times with Sergeant Strickland, and the second time he had come back with a new trunk and new clothes and boots and a cane – as well as with lavish amounts of food for the house. He had even paid for his own passage to England and hers too, though she had every intention of paying him back once she had her jewels and had sold a few of them. And he was the one who had hired the carriages and horses here in England.

If he had been a gambler in his past life, he obviously had lost none of his touch. He must have won a vast sum.

If there was one class of gentleman Rachel despised more than any other, it was the gamer. Her father had been one. It was a very good thing she had not conceived a passion for Jonathan Smith and that their marriage was not a real one. Gamers did not make responsible husbands or providers – and that was a colossal understatement. There were moments of overflowing plenty and giddy extravagance, but there were weeks and months and even years of scrounging poverty and skulking debt.

He had other weaknesses of character too, of course. What other gentleman would have dreamed up and actually implemented a scheme like this? Or thrown himself into it with such enthusiasm? He had discussed details for *hours* with her and her friends, and he had always looked as if he were enjoying himself enormously.

His eyes were handsome enough as they were, she thought resentfully, without the twinkle and the roguish gleam that so often set them alight. She looked at those eyes now to find that they were focused upon her.

'We should be there soon,' he said.

At the last change of horses they had been assured that another would not be necessary. For a moment Rachel wished she were anywhere else on earth but close to Chesbury Park. Her stomach seemed intent upon turning a complete somersault inside her and she felt a few moments of raw panic.

What on earth was she *doing*?

But she was only going to get what was hers, what her mother had left for her. Anyway, it was too late to change the plan now, though from the way Jonathan was looking at her, she suspected that he knew she was very close to doing just that. His eyes smiled at her. And that was something else she resented. How could he make his eyes smile when the rest of his face did not? He must know how very attractive the expression made him look.

'Does the countryside look at all familiar to you?' she asked him.

'It is England,' he said with a shrug. 'I have not forgotten the country, Rachel, only my own place in it.'

But she scarcely heard his answer. The carriage was turning between high wrought iron gates, and she realized that they had arrived at Chesbury Park.

A gravel driveway beyond the gates wound its way

through a forest of old oak and chestnut trees. It all looked alarmingly huge and stately to Rachel. The audacity of what they were all doing struck her anew.

And then, gradually, there were glimpses through the trees of an imposing gray stone mansion, far grander than anything she had expected. *This* was where her mama had grown up? Where she had belonged? There were spacious, tree-dotted lawns about the house beyond the woods, she could see, and a large lake to the stable side of it. There was a long parterre garden stretching across the front of the house.

It was only as the carriage wheels crunched over the driveway while it proceeded along beside the lake and then turned sharply before the stable block and rumbled across the terrace that separated the house from the parterres that Rachel had the sudden thought that perhaps her uncle was from home.

What a dash to all their expectations that would be! She almost hoped that it would happen, except that they would all then find themselves stranded in the middle of Wiltshire, virtually penniless and without a plan.

Jonathan had leaned forward in his seat to set a hand on her knee.

'Steady,' he said. 'All will be well.'

But she jumped with awareness and felt anything but steady.

The carriage rolled to a halt at the foot of a wide flight of stone steps that led up to the double front doors. They were fast shut, and no one came running outside to investigate the arrival of two strange traveling carriages. No groom came running from the stables. The coachman jumped down from the box, opened the door, and set down the steps. Warm, fresh summer air flooded the rather stuffy interior. Jonathan descended carefully and then braced his weight on his cane as he handed Rachel down.

The others were alighting from the second carriage, she could see. Geraldine and Sergeant Strickland stayed back beside the conveyance. Despite her plain gray dress and cloak and the voluminous cap she wore beneath a plain bonnet, Geraldine still looked like a voluptuous Italian actress. She also looked like someone other female servants would resent on sight and all their male counterparts would come to fisticuffs over. Sergeant Strickland, a black patch covering his empty eye socket, his facial bruises faded to a motley blend of sickly yellow and a pale gray, did indeed look like the ferocious pirate of Geraldine's predictions.

The other two came forward along the terrace while Jonathan was helping Bridget to alight. Phyllis looked like a complacent young matron who had never in her life entertained a naughty thought. Flossie, her blond hair tamed beneath her neat black bonnet, her shapely person encased in decent black, looked fragile and pretty and as respectable as a parson's wife.

'I still can't accustom myself to not having to squint every time I look at your hair, Bridge,' Phyllis said.

'Pinch your cheeks, Rachel,' Flossie advised. 'You look as pale as a ghost.'

Jonathan made her jump again then by taking her hand in his and drawing it through his arm. He smiled at her, his eyes warm and adoring.

'Let the game begin,' he murmured.

'Yes.' She smiled dazzlingly back at him.

He led her up the steps and rapped on one of the

doors with the head of his cane. A whole minute passed – or so it seemed – before an elderly servant answered the knock. He looked from one to the other of them as if they had two heads apiece.

'Mrs. Streat, Mrs. Leavey, Miss Clover, and Sir Jonathan and Lady Smith, formerly Miss Rachel York, to wait upon Baron Weston,' Jonathan said briskly, handing the man a calling card. 'He is at home?'

'I will see, sir,' the servant said noncommittally. But he did stand aside to admit them to the house.

Jonathan had even remembered to have calling cards made.

Rows of tall fluted columns soared upward from a checkered floor to fan outward in support of the floor above. The celling was gilded and painted with what appeared to be angels and cherubs. Marble busts on stone pedestals gazed with stern, sightless eyes from their wall niches. A grand, wide staircase opposite the doors led upward and divided at the first landing into two curving branches. A great chandelier hung down over the staircase.

It was a hall designed to awe the visitor, Rachel thought. It certainly succeeded with her.

The servant disappeared up the stairs.

Rachel had always imagined Chesbury Park as a sizable manor surrounded by sizable gardens. She had not expected a great mansion or – despite its name – a vast park. For the first time she understood the enormity of her mother's defiance in insisting upon marrying Papa despite Uncle Richard's opposition. She had gone from this to the dark, crowded rooms they had usually rented in London.

'It is *enormous*,' Phyllis said in a whisper.

153

They were all gazing about them with open awe – except for Jonathan, Rachel noticed. There was a look of interest on his face, but he appeared to be perfectly at his ease. Did that mean he was accustomed to such surroundings?

After what seemed like forever, the servant returned and invited them to follow him. He led them up the left branch of the grand staircase to the second landing, from which wide corridors led in both directions. But they did not proceed along either one. Instead, they were ushered through the tall double doors directly ahead of them into a drawing room. Its wine-colored brocaded walls were hung with portraits and landscape paintings in heavy gilded frames, its coved ceiling was lavishly painted with scenes from classical mythology, and its long windows were hung with rich velvet. A Persian carpet covered most of the floor, and the heavy gilded furniture was arranged in conversation groupings, the dominant one being about the high, ornately carved marble fireplace and mantel.

There was a gentleman standing before the fireplace, his back to it. He was not very elderly, though he appeared to be at first glance. He was thin and gray – even his complexion seemed to be gray-tinged – and stoop-shouldered. But even had he stood upright, he would have been no taller than medium height. Rachel had not seen her uncle for sixteen years and looked intently at him now. He was very different from the man she remembered. Could it be he?

He looked back at her from keen eyes beneath bushy gray eyebrows as she stepped toward him ahead of the others and curtsied with deep formality. And she recognized him at last. She remembered those eyes, which had always looked very directly at her. So many adults did not really see children at all.

'Uncle Richard?' She wondered if she ought to close the rest of the distance between them and kiss his cheek, but she hesitated a moment too long, and then it was impossible to do. Besides, he was a stranger to her even if he *was* her only known relative.

'Rachel?' He kept his hands behind his back as he inclined his head courteously but quite impersonally. 'You resemble your mother. So you have married, have you?'

'I have,' she said. 'Just last week in Brussels, where I went before the Battle of Waterloo.' She turned her head and smiled warmly as Jonathan appeared at her side. 'May I present Sir Jonathan Smith to you, Uncle Richard? Baron Weston, Jonathan.'

The two men exchanged bows.

'I was living with dear friends in Brussels before my marriage,' Rachel said, 'and since they were also returning to England this week, they were kind enough to give us their company here. May I have the pleasure of introducing them? Mrs. Streat, Mrs. Leavey, her sister-in-law, and Miss Clover, who was kind enough to act as my chaperon after I left Lady Flatley's service.'

Bows and curtsies were exchanged.

'Phyllis and I positively insisted upon accompanying our young friend to your very door before proceeding on our way,' Flossie explained, 'though of course it was unnecessary to do so when she is now wed to Sir Jonathan and when she has dear Bridget to keep her company. But such is our fondness for her.'

Somehow she succeeded in looking both picturesque and weary to the bone, as if coming here had been a great ordeal and a noble sacrifice.

'We assured dear Rachel that Baron Weston would be vexed with us if we abandoned her as soon as we came to England's shores,' Phyllis added with a gracious smile, like a queen conferring her notice upon a commoner. 'Though I daresay you would not have been too vexed, since she is now a married lady. It is still hard even for us to believe, is it not, Floss Flora? Such a whirlwind courtship and such an affecting nuptial service.'

'Do have a seat, ladies,' Rachel's uncle offered. 'And you too, Smith. The tea tray will be arriving in a moment. I will have rooms made up for all of you. It is out of the question for you to continue on your way until you are well rested after your journey.'

'That is extraordinarily kind of you, my lord,' Flossie said. 'I am not a great traveler and confess to being quite exhausted after a few days of being on the move.'

'And I retch most miserably whenever only the flimsy boards of a ship stand between me and the deep blue depths,' Phyllis said. 'I suppose *vomit* would be a more genteel word, would it? But I am famous for my plain speaking, am I not, Flora?'

Rachel seated herself on a settee and Jonathan sat beside her. Their eyes met, a slight grimace in her own, a hint of laughter in his, though he had played the part of dignified gentleman very well so far. She hoped Flossie and Phyllis would not talk too much.

But she soon turned her attention back to her uncle. She gazed at him with troubled eyes. *This* was the tall, robust, laughing uncle of her childhood memory?

Even given the fact that she had been very young and had regarded him from a child's perspective, he had surely changed considerably in sixteen years. He seemed ill. No, there was no doubt about it. He was gaunt and weary-looking.

She had expected that she was coming here to pit her wits against a robust, blustering, stubborn man – against someone she would feel justified in deceiving and defying. She resented the fact that he looked frail.

She was also disturbed by it, even a little frightened by it.

He was, as far as she knew, her only living relative, the only person who kept her from being all alone in the world. It was an absurd concern when her only contacts with him in twenty-two years had been those few days when she was six, and two letters since then, both of them denying her what she had asked for.

But she felt upset.

Alleyne was happy to be in England. It felt like home, even though he had no idea to which specific part of it he belonged. He also felt perfectly comfortable in his present surroundings, though they looked quite unfamiliar to him. So did Lord Weston, though he had wondered if perhaps the baron would recognize him. Matters would have been hopelessly complicated if he *had*, of course.

Weston was not at all what he had expected – a bluff and boorish bully. But invalids could be petulant and quite unpleasant, and Weston was clearly an invalid. However it was, Alleyne was feeling exhilarated by the challenge now that they were finally putting it into effect. The last couple of weeks had seemed interminable as his leg had healed sufficiently for him to travel.

But he could see that Rachel was looking disconcerted. It was understandable. This was her uncle, her only relative. He took her hand in his and set it on his sleeve before holding it there. Flossie was commenting on the beauty of the house and informing the assembled company that it reminded her of her brother-in-law's house in Derbyshire – Phyllis's *brother's* house, she must have realized suddenly.

'Would you not agree, Phyllis?' she asked, smiling graciously.

'I was having the exact same thought, Flora,' Phyllis agreed.

'How *are* you, Uncle Richard?' Rachel asked, leaning forward slightly in her seat.

'I am well enough,' Weston said as he lowered himself into a chair by the fireplace, though he looked to Alleyne more like a man with one foot in the grave. 'This is all rather sudden, is it not, Rachel? You went to Brussels as Lady Flatley's companion. Did you already know Smith at that time?'

'I did,' she said. This was all a part of the story they had invented, of course. 'We met in London last year, not long after Papa's death. And then we met again in Brussels and Jonathan began to court me in earnest. When Lady Flatley decided to return to England before the Battle of Waterloo, Bridget offered me a home with herself and these ladies, her friends.'

'Bridget is our dearest friend,' Flossie said just in case Weston had not clearly understood that it was a particularly dear relationship.

'And she was my nurse for six years after Mama

died,' Rachel explained. 'I was more than delighted to discover her again in Brussels and gladly accepted her invitation, especially when it was kindly repeated by Flora and Phyllis. And then Jonathan persuaded me to marry him before we came home.'

Weston was looking consideringly at Alleyne, but before he could make any further comment the tea tray arrived. Phyllis settled herself behind it without a by-your-leave and proceeded to pour and hand around the cups and saucers.

'We all agreed, my lord,' Bridget told Weston, 'that I should accompany Lady Smith here since she is only very recently married. And then Flora and Phyllis could not resist coming too.'

It still amused Alleyne to look at Bridget and see a pleasant-looking, respectable-seeming, youngish woman who just happened to speak in the same voice as the Bridget Clover he had known in Brussels.

Weston meanwhile had fixed his gaze upon Alleyne again.

'And you, Smith?' he said. 'Who might you be exactly? Smith is a common enough name. There are some of good lineage in Gloucestershire. Are you one of them?'

'I doubt it, sir,' Alleyne said. 'I am from Northumberland, and most of my family has remained there for generations.'

Northumberland was the farthest north they had been able to place him without putting him in Scotland.

He went on to explain that he had inherited a sizable and prosperous estate from his father two years before – but neither *too* sizable nor *too* prosperous, though Geraldine and Phyllis would have

159

made him into a veritable nabob and Croesus all rolled into one if they had had their way. Alleyne, seconded by Rachel, had pointed out that he must be the sort of gentleman of whom Baron Weston would approve but not someone of whose existence even in remote Northumberland he would feel he ought to know.

He had gone to Brussels, he explained, because his cousin was stationed there with his regiment.

'And there I met Rachel again,' he said, turning his head to smile fondly at her and curling his fingers beneath her hand as it rested on his sleeve. 'I had not forgotten her. How could I? I fell head over ears in love as soon as I set eyes on her again.'

It was interesting to see her blush and bite her bottom lip.

'I was never more affected in my life than by the sweetness of the romance developing before the watchful chaperonage of our dear Bridget,' Phyllis said with a sigh, 'and before the benevolent eye of Flora and myself, my lord.'

'Sir Jonathan reminds me so very much of my beloved late husband, Colonel Streat,' Flossie said, a handkerchief materializing in one hand. 'He died a hero's death in the Peninsula two years ago.'

Streat had been promoted to dizzying heights, Alleyne thought. He had started out two weeks or so ago as a captain, had he not? He hoped the ladies did not plan to be too expansive with their lies – not unless they had very good memories.

The baron set aside his empty cup and saucer.

'I am disappointed, I must confess,' he said, 'that Rachel saw fit to marry without first coming to me. I am well aware that she is of age and could marry whomsoever she chose for the past year and more. She certainly did not need my permission. But I would have liked to be asked for my blessing. And if I felt that I could give it, I would have liked to host the wedding here at Chesbury. But I was not consulted.'

And so, Alleyne thought, he was starting at a disadvantage. He was being seen as a man whose passions had led him into an indiscretion. He had not brought Rachel home to England to marry, he had not taken her to introduce to his family in Northumberland, and he had not brought her here to Chesbury Park to seek a blessing from her uncle. Any sane person would wonder why he had done none of those things.

But then, Weston had never shown any real interest in his niece. His concern now was hypocritical, to say the least.

'Sir Jonathan is wondrously romantic and impulsive,' Phyllis said, her hands clasped to her bosom. 'Nothing would do for it, my lord, but there had to be a nuptial service in Brussels so that he could bring Rachel home with him as his bride. My dear Colonel Leavey is much the same.'

'So was Colonel Streat,' Flossie added. 'He insisted that I follow the drum all about the Peninsula with him, summer and winter.'

Ah, *another* colonel. And had not Flossie just claimed to be a poor traveler?

'And so you have come here now,' Weston said, his attention still on Alleyne and Rachel. 'I suppose it is not difficult to guess why.'

Rachel was looking steadily back at her uncle, Alleyne saw, her chin up.

'I have married a gentleman of whom you cannot

possibly disapprove,' she said, 'even if you *do* believe we married with unnecessary haste. But why would I have come here to marry? You have never shown any interest in me. You have never wanted to know me. Even after Papa died and you invited me to come and live here, it was only so that you could marry me off as soon as possible and be done with me. Well, I have done the deed for you. I have come for my jewels, for my inheritance from Mama. You can have no ground for refusing me this time.'

Her belligerent words and hostile manner were very definitely unwise and not a part of any plan they had discussed together. But Alleyne could only admire her for not fawning upon her uncle. At least she had decided to be honest about her feelings even if everything else was a lie. He squeezed her hand more tightly.

'I am not aware,' Weston said, 'that I have to have a *ground*, Rachel.'

She drew breath sharply. But Alleyne patted her hand and spoke first.

'Your caution on behalf of your niece and your reservations about me are understandable, even commendable, sir,' he said. 'I would not expect you to be delighted at being presented with this fait accompli quite without warning, and at finding that it is followed immediately by a request that you release jewels entrusted to your care and judgment by the late Mrs. York. All I ask, sir, is that you give me a little time to prove to you that I am indeed worthy of your niece's hand, that she has chosen with her head as well as her heart, that I am not a fortune hunter, and that neither of us will squander her inheritance. I ask that you allow us to remain here for as long as you deem to be a suitable probationary period, in fact. I am, of course, eager to take my bride home, but I will do what makes her happy. And winning your trust and confidence will make her happy.'

The trouble with playing a part, he was discovering, was that one could easily become immersed in it. He spoke with firm conviction. And yet almost every word was a lie. Of course, he really did want to see her happy.

'Very well,' Weston said, nodding curtly after looking broodingly at Alleyne for several unnerving moments. 'We will see how I feel after a month, Smith. In the meantime I have been neglecting my other guests. For how long were you in the Peninsula with your husband, ma'am?' he asked Flossie.

A month?

Flossie launched into a bold and colorful description of her years there while Alleyne observed the baron more closely. That the man was ill had been clear from the start. But his complexion had surely turned grayer in the past few minutes. Was it the effect of being faced with five unexpected guests? Or emotion over seeing Rachel again and feeling her hostility?

Or was it something else?

Alleyne turned his gaze on Rachel, and because she too was looking rather pale, he first grinned at her and then winked. For better or for worse, he was her devoted husband for the next *month*. Deuce take it, he had expected that a few days would do it, or a week at the longest. But they could only press onward now.

He raised their clasped hands and held the back of hers to his lips for a few moments while he smiled warmly into her eyes, well aware that his gesture

163

must be visible to the other occupants of the room. In fact, he hoped it was. He had scarcely touched her in two and a half weeks and already realized that it had been very wise to keep away from her.

She was altogether too beautiful and too attractive for his peace of mind. He had better be careful to keep these displays of affection to the minimum.

Good Lord, a month.

A whole month.

But he had no one but himself to blame, had he?

Chapter Eleven

All the footmen look like frogs and all the grooms look like weasels,' Geraldine said. 'I have not met any of the gardeners yet, so there is still hope, though there don't appear to be very many of them. The cook is sulking because there are so many extra mouths to feed.'

'Oh, Geraldine,' Rachel said, laughing, 'how can you judge so quickly? There is no need to do my hair. I can do it myself.'

But Geraldine took the brush firmly in her own hand and flourished it in the air.

'If I am going to be earning my fortune as a lady's maid,' she said, 'I'll be doing your hair for you, Rache, and lacing your laces and buttoning and pinning your dresses and tucking you into your bed at night. There will be precious little else to do. Mr. Edwards, the butler who opened the door to you, has been telling everyone belowstairs what grand ladies Floss and Phyll are, which shows you what a great judge of character *he* is. I couldn't even *look* at Will. I would have burst out laughing.'

'Really, though,' Rachel said, 'this is not a joke.

My uncle is ill, and the welcome he gave us was cool at best, though he was perfectly civil, especially to Flossie and Phyllis. He disapproves of my marriage, or at least the *manner* of my marriage. It is going to take us forever now to convince him that we belong together, that ours will be a perfectly steady and prosperous marriage, and that my jewels belong in my own hands rather than his. It is beginning to look as if we will *never* be able to go after Mr. Crawley.'

'Never you mind about that,' Geraldine said, pulling the brush through the length of her hair. 'A man like Crawley will be up to his tricks forever and a day until someone stops him. We will find him, and we will deal with him even if we have to wait a year. Floss has written to London to have any letters from the sisters redirected here. It's not up to you to finance us anyway, Rache, and even if you do we will pay you back every penny. To tell the truth, we are here only because we couldn't resist either the holiday or the adventure. So never you mind about us.'

One thing Rachel was very aware of as she sat still for Geraldine to style her hair was that her dressing room and Jonathan's were separated only by an arch but no door, and that each dressing room was open to the bedchamber beyond it. It was a good thing that neither of them wanted to get any closer to the other than their charade dictated. It was horribly embarrassing, though, to discover that they had a connecting suite of rooms without even a door separating them, just as if they really were husband and wife. And Jonathan was in his rooms now with Sergeant Strickland, dressing for dinner. Rachel could hear the murmur of their voices.

'Ooh, don't *you* look gorgeous!' Geraldine

exclaimed as she finished styling Rachel's hair a few minutes later. 'Pardon me while I swoon.'

Rachel looked up, startled. But Geraldine was not addressing her. Jonathan was standing in the archway. And Geraldine had not exaggerated. He was dressed with elegant formality in ivory-colored knee breeches with white stockings and black shoes. He wore a dull gold waistcoat, a black tailed evening coat, and white linen. He must have tied his neckcloth himself – Sergeant Strickland could not possibly be capable of such artistry. His dark hair, which had grown longer in the past month, had been brushed to a shine, though the one lock had fallen, as it often did, over his right brow.

Rachel might have submitted to being broken on the rack rather than admit it, but she was glad she was sitting down. Her knees had turned weak. Even his cane looked elegant.

'What a perfectly genteel comment from my lady's maid,' he said with a grin. Then he turned his eyes upon Rachel and looked her over from head to toe. She was wearing a pale green evening gown that was three years old and yet was almost new because she rarely had a chance to wear it. 'We will keep you on, though, Geraldine. You have done exquisite things with Lady Smith's hair. Or perhaps it is the woman beneath the hair who is making my heart thump against my ribs.'

There was really no call for such talk when her uncle was not even present to hear him. But he was winking at Geraldine and having a fine time at her expense, Rachel could see. She got to her feet, twisting the wedding ring that he had remembered to buy for her after they landed in England.

'It is both,' Geraldine said. 'That golden hair is part of the woman and sometimes makes me sorry that my mother was Italian. I had better go and talk to Will and see what he thinks of this place.'

She disappeared through the archway.

'Well, Rachel,' Jonathan said, clasping his hands behind his back, 'what do you think?'

'I *think*,' she said, lifting her chin, 'that we ought to pretend that archway is a solid wall.'

Even knowing that Geraldine and Sergeant Strickland were probably just a few feet away, this situation felt altogether too intimate to her.

He raised one eyebrow and looked both arrogant and impossibly handsome.

'Shall we go down, my lady?' He made her an elegant bow and offered his arm.

'I keep thinking,' she said as she took it and they proceeded from the room, 'that this was my mother's home until she was seventeen and ran away with my father. This is where she grew up. Under different circumstances I would be very familiar with it. I would have come here often with her. I would have spent Christmases and other holidays here both before her death and after. I would have known my uncle well. I would have had another relative in addition to Papa.'

'But Weston never forgave your mother,' he said.

'How I longed for brothers and sisters and cousins and uncles and aunts as I was growing up – or even just for one uncle,' she said with a sigh and then felt foolish for having opened her heart to him like this.

'I hope,' he said, 'you are not going to have regrets about doing this, Rachel. It is too late for those now, is it not? And so on with the masquerade.'

'I have no regrets,' she said. 'My uncle pretended that he wished we had come here before marrying so that he could host our wedding. And then he told us that he would see after one whole month. He has no love for me. My only regret is that he is ill. Do you think he is dying?'

The very real possibility still upset her though she did not know why. He could mean nothing to her – by his own choice.

Jonathan patted her hand on his arm.

Flossie and Phyllis were already in the drawing room, conversing with Rachel's uncle. Bridget was there too. They all looked neat and genteel. How easy it was to deceive, Rachel thought – except that they were going to have to keep it up for a whole month. Would they all stay so long?

Her uncle was dressed immaculately, though he still looked gaunt and stooped. Rachel felt a twinge of guilt and resented the feeling. If he were in the best of health she would surely not care at all that she was deceiving him. What difference did illness make? He still did not love her – his niece, his closest relative.

Dinner was a far less strained occasion than Rachel had feared it might be. Everyone made an effort to converse, and no one commented on the fact that the food was ill prepared and almost cold. Jonathan expressed an interest in the estate toward the end of the meal.

'I will have my steward take you about,' Uncle Richard said. 'I have been somewhat indisposed lately and have not been outdoors a great deal. Drummond will show you whatever you wish to see – Rachel too if she is interested, though I daresay she is not. Most ladies have other interests.'

'I *am* interested, Uncle Richard,' Rachel said, annoyed. 'My ignorance is vast since I have lived all my life except the past few months in London. But I am eager to learn more now that I am married to Jonathan and will be living in the country.'

She would have been familiar with the country if he had only invited her here a few times when she was growing up.

'I for one am not particularly interested in cows and pigs and hay crops,' Flossie said. 'But I do look forward to exploring the park during the coming days. With your permission, of course, my lord.'

'I will be disappointed,' he said, 'if you do not make yourself at home while you are at Chesbury, ma'am.'

'Do you keep a large stable, sir?' Jonathan asked. 'Perhaps I may make use of one of the horses?'

'Is it wise, Sir Jonathan?' Bridget asked him. 'Your leg has not fully healed yet.'

They had explained to Rachel's uncle earlier that Jonathan had been wounded while bringing a runaway horse under control in the streets of Brussels.

'I need the exercise,' he explained.

'I do not keep quite the stable I used to keep,' Uncle Richard said, 'but you are welcome to ride any of the horses that are there.'

Rachel smiled at Jonathan and reached out to touch his hand. She was finding it more difficult to play her part than the others. But she must get used to showing some public signs of affection for the man who was supposed to be her new husband.

'Do be careful, then, Jonathan,' she said.

'And you must ride with me, my love,' he said, smiling back into her eyes with such warmth that she

170

had to stop herself from leaning back to put more distance between them.

'I do not ride,' she told him. 'Remember?'

There was a flicker of surprise in his eyes.

'Neither do I, Rachel,' Bridget said. 'Don't feel bad about it.'

'I did nothing *but* ride when I was in the Peninsula with Colonel Streat,' Flossie announced. 'I grew rather fond of the beasts.'

Jonathan covered Rachel's hand on the table between them.

'Of course I remember, my love,' he said. 'But we must rectify the situation without delay if we are to spend most of our days together. You will learn to ride. I will teach you.' She could see the familiar gleam of mischief in his eyes.

'But I have no wish to learn,' she assured him, trying to slide her hand free. He curled his fingers about it and his smile spread to his lips.

'You are not a coward by any chance, are you, my love?' he asked her. He raised their clasped hands to his lips as he had done earlier in the drawing room. 'If you are to be my wife and live in the country with me, you must be able to ride with me. I will give you your first lesson in the morning.'

'Jonathan,' she said, wishing that this subject had arisen when they were alone together so that she could say an emphatic no and mean it, 'I would really rather not.'

'But you will.' He was still smiling that smile filled with warmth and admiration and affection – and roguery.

She sighed out loud.

So did Phyllis. 'Ah,' she said, 'I do love to see a

171

good romance develop before my very eyes. It comforts me somehow for my separation from my dear Colonel Leavey, who was obliged to march to Paris with his company.'

Rachel winced. A colonel with no more than a *company* of men under his command?

But her uncle appeared not to have noticed.

'You *have* ridden on horseback, Rachel,' he said. 'You rode up with me when I went to London for your mother's funeral.'

She had forgotten that particular detail of his visit, but she remembered as soon as he reminded her. Her six-year-old self must have understood that her mother was dead. She could even remember crying inconsolably at the graveside and clinging to her father's hand and hiding her face against his breeches. But conversely, or perhaps in the nature of children, she had been wildly happy during the following days when Uncle Richard had taken her about with him from morning until bedtime, showing her places she had never seen before – or since in some cases. He had taken her to see the animals at the Tower of London and the horse show at Astley's Amphitheatre. He had bought her ices at Gunter's. He had bought her a porcelain doll, which one of her father's cronies had lurched against not long after while in his cups and smashed beyond repair. Best and most exhilarating of all, he had let her ride before him on his horse.

But she did not want to remember. He had abandoned her after that. She had not heard from him again until after she had written to him when she was eighteen because for months Papa had been deep in debt and even the meager food on their table had been

172

bought on credit and she had desperately needed her jewels.

'That was a long time ago,' she said stiffly.

'Yes,' he agreed. 'A long time.'

He looked gray and gaunt and infinitely weary. She resented his bringing up the past. She resented his frailty. And she wanted to wrap her arms about his neck and sob out her grief for she knew not what.

'I have not entertained or accepted any invitations for quite a while past,' he said. 'But I must make amends. I will invite my neighbors to come and meet my niece and her new husband and my other guests. I will arrange some sort of celebration for your marriage, Rachel, since it is too late to hold the nuptials here. I will give a ball perhaps.'

Rachel's eyes widened in dismay. It had not occurred to her that they need play out their masquerade before anyone else but her uncle. But then, she had not expected to be here for longer than a few days. He was going to invite guests? He was going to celebrate their wedding?

She looked at Jonathan, but he was no help. He was smiling back at her, his eyes filled with . . . adoration.

'This will be splendid, my love,' he said. 'We will not even have to wait until we return to Northumberland in order to dance together.'

Dancing. Uncle Richard had spoken of a ball. Rachel had never been to a ball even though she had learned to dance. Attending one had been one of the enduring dreams of her girlhood and early adulthood. For a moment a great welling of longing replaced the dismay. There might be a ball here at Chesbury. She would be the guest of honor. She would *dance*.

173

With Jonathan.

'Uncle Richard, no!' she said, coming back to reality. 'You really must not make any fuss. We did not expect any such thing. And Jonathan cannot dance. He still has to use a cane merely to walk.'

'But my leg improves daily,' he protested.

'A ball?' Flossie said in transports of joy. 'I will help you organize it, my lord.'

'And I too,' Phyllis offered. 'Oh, how I *wish* my dear Colonel Leavey were here to dance with me.' She sighed soulfully.

'Indeed, Rachel,' Uncle Richard said, 'I believe I really ought to make a fuss. I have no children of my own – my wife died without issue eight years ago. And my only sister had but the one daughter – you. Yes, yes, I will make a fuss.' He looked positively cheerful.

But Rachel's attention had been distracted. Uncle Richard had been *married*? She had had an *aunt*? She felt bereft, mourning for someone of whose very existence she had not known until now. And she felt angry that she had never known, that no one had ever told her. Yet Uncle Richard now talked of making a fuss of her because she was the only daughter of his only sister?

Rachel got abruptly to her feet, drawing her hand from beneath Jonathan's and pushing her chair away with the backs of her knees.

'Flora, Phyllis, Bridget,' she said, 'we will leave my uncle and Jonathan together and retire to the drawing room.'

But when she looked at her uncle, not even trying to hide her anger, she could see again that he was looking drawn and gray-complexioned.

174

'Uncle Richard,' she said, 'I fear we have over-taxed your strength. You look weary. Please do not feel you must come and entertain us afterward.'

He had stood up when she had, as had Jonathan.

'Perhaps I *will* retire early,' he said. 'Now, in fact. Smith, perhaps you would escort the ladies to the drawing room. Tea will be brought to you there. I will bid you all a good night and see you in the morning.'

She just had not expected anything like this, Rachel thought as she led the way to the drawing room a minute or two later. She had not expected this emotional pull to a man she had resented for years or to the ancestral home she had never before set foot in. When she had agreed to Jonathan's mad suggestion that they come here to acquire her jewels through deception, she had not even considered the possibility that she might have *feelings* about a past she had not even been a part of.

She had not realized how deep were the wounds of her own childhood.

'There are going to be social calls,' Flossie said when they reached the drawing room, plopping herself down on a chair and looking both pleased and gratified. 'And some grand wedding celebration – probably a ball. *Now* we can expect to hear Gerry complain!'

'That man is ill,' Bridget said.

'That cook should be paid her wages and sent packing,' Phyllis said. 'She should not be allowed to set one toe inside a kitchen for the rest of her life.'

'That is part of his problem, I daresay, Phyll,' Bridget said. 'He needs to be fattened up with whole-some, appetizing foods, properly prepared.'

'This is absolutely intolerable,' Rachel said, standing in the middle of the room and curling her hands into impotent fists at her sides. 'We cannot have neighbors coming here to be presented to Jonathan and me as if we really were husband and wife. We cannot allow a ball to be held in our honor. We have to *do* something. What can we do? Jonathan, do remove that odious grin from your face. You got us into this. Get us out of it.'

He went suddenly and suspiciously poker-faced as he possessed himself of both her hands.

'Rachel, my love,' he said, 'this is exactly what we planned, is it not? Your uncle has accepted you as his niece and he has acknowledged our marriage, even if he is not too pleased at the haste with which it was solemnized. He is offering us the perfect opportunity to shine, to show ourselves to both him and this rural world as the perfect couple. What more could we ask for?'

'He is right, Rachel,' Bridget said. 'I am more delighted with Baron Weston than I ever expected to be. He seems perfectly willing to acknowledge you and make much of you as his closest relative.'

'But can't you see that that is the whole trouble?' Rachel tried to withdraw her hands from Jonathan's, but he tightened his hold on them. 'His affection, if indeed he feels any, is the very *last* thing I want or need. I am here to *deceive* him, to trick him into giving me my jewels.'

'You could tell him the truth,' Bridget suggested. 'Indeed, it would probably be best, my love. You need your uncle as much as he needs you.'

'Tell the truth *now*?' Rachel asked, aghast. 'It is impossible.'

'And Baron Weston would probably cancel the ball if she did, Bridge,' Flossie pointed out. 'That would be a terrible pity, wouldn't it? Though I daresay Gerry would be glad.'

Jonathan raised Rachel's hands and set them flat against his chest, covering them with his own.

'Rachel,' he said, 'we are here at my suggestion and it is altogether possible that I miscalculated – both your feelings and Weston's. Do you wish me to go to him now and confess all? I will if you wish.'

She gazed into his eyes, horribly aware that they were serious – that *he* was serious. The decision was hers. She could end the charade now, this evening, if she wished. They could be on their way to somewhere else tonight or early in the morning if she just said the word.

She was very aware of dark eyes gazing questioningly into her own – and of her three friends sitting watching her, as if with bated breath.

If the truth was told tonight, if she left here tomorrow, she would never see her uncle again. There was no doubt in her mind of that.

'It is too late,' she said. She lifted her chin. 'And it is clear that all his plans have nothing to do with any affection for me. He still feels that he has the right to withhold what is mine. He plans to keep us waiting for a whole month just because he is annoyed that we did not consult him before marrying. Why *should* we have? He is not my guardian. And he means nothing else to me either.'

Jonathan was smiling at her, but just when she needed to see a spark of mischief in his eyes there was not the slightest sign of it.

'The tea tray has still not arrived,' Phyllis said. 'I

177

would be willing to wager that it never does. I do not have friendly feelings toward the cook and her minions.'

'This has been a busy day,' Jonathan said, not releasing either Rachel's hands or her eyes. 'Perhaps we should all follow Weston's example and have an early night.'

'A good idea,' Bridget said, getting to her feet.

'Besides,' Jonathan added, grinning at Rachel and looking more reassuringly normal again, 'you will need to be up early in the morning, my love. It is the best time for riding.'

She pulled her hands firmly away from his.

'I have no intention whatsoever of learning to ride,' she told him. 'I have lived quite happily through twenty-two years with my feet firmly on the ground and feel no ambition to become a famous whip – or an infamous one, for that matter.'

'You *are* a coward,' he said, his eyes twinkling merrily at her.

'Riding *is* something all ladies ought to be able to do, Rachel,' Bridget said. 'and now you have a chance to learn at last.'

'Just think what a favorable impression you will both make upon Lord Weston if he can see you engaged in a riding lesson when he gets up in the morning,' Flossie added. 'If you will not let Sir Jonathan teach *you*, Rachel, he is quite welcome to teach me instead.'

'But you are an accomplished horsewoman already, Flossie,' Jonathan reminded her with a grin. 'You have ridden all over the Peninsula with Colonel Streat.'

'Well, you cannot blame a girl for trying,' she said,

batting her eyelids at him.

'You and Sir Jonathan will look wonderfully romantic riding side by side in the early morning sunshine, Rachel,' Phyllis said.

'Don't make me call you a coward in earnest, my love,' Jonathan said.

'She will be up early, never fear,' Flossie promised him as she rose from her chair. 'I'll send Gerry up to throw a pitcher of cold water over her if she refuses to come out from under the bedcovers of her own accord.'

'And if Geraldine fails to do it,' Jonathan said, 'I will.'

'You may all force me out to the stables if you choose,' Rachel said, looking indignantly from one merry face to the other, 'but you will not get me onto a horse's back. That I can promise.'

They all ignored her protests as they bade one another a cheerful good night and proceeded on their way to their various rooms.

Rachel would have given a good deal to be back in her small attic room on the Rue d'Aremberg in Brussels. But instead she was at *Chesbury Park*, her mother's home, her own ancestral home.

Chapter Twelve

Alleyne was up at first light. He had had a disturbed night, at first due to the fact that though there were all of two small rooms separating his bedchamber from Rachel's, there was not one single door. And she had looked particularly lovely during the evening in her pale green gown and with her hair styled by Geraldine. It annoyed him somewhat that he found her so powerfully attractive when he was quite determined to avoid any emotional entanglement with her. But it was hardly surprising, he supposed, especially given the fact that he had once possessed her – an event he would prefer to forget if it were only possible to do so. But there were not many other memories to help him block it from his mind.

When he did finally fall asleep, his rest was disturbed by confused dreams that seemed vivid until he tried to recall them upon awakening. There were the familiar ones about the letter and the woman waiting for him at the Namur Gates. But now there was another one too. All he could remember of it during his waking spells, though, was a fountain shooting water thirty feet or more into the air from its marble basin in the midst of a circular flower garden. The water caught the sunlight, which turned the droplets into a sparkling rainbow. Try as he would, he could not place the fountain and garden into any wider setting. At first he thought that perhaps it was the front of Chesbury that he was remembering, but then he recalled that there was only a long parterre garden there.

But if it *was* a remembered scene, he supposed that coming into the country might have provoked it.

What a stupid and pointless dream it had been, he thought as he made his way out to the stables, using his cane though he tried not to lean too heavily on it. But then so were the other dreams, or fragments of memory or whatever the devil they were.

He was early, but he wanted to look over the horses before Rachel came and pick out suitable mounts for them both. More important, he wanted to discover if it was going to be possible to get himself onto a horse's back. His left leg was still not fully back to normal. Reluctantly he had asked Sergeant Strickland to come out here to join him.

There was only one groom up, and he was doing nothing more energetic than standing in the doorway of one of the stalls, staring vacantly off into the distance and scratching himself when Alleyne and the sergeant stepped into the cobbled stable yard. He looked at them and yawned before ducking out of sight within the stall.

'There is the same sort of look about the stables as there is about the kitchen,' the sergeant said. 'It is like there is no one to crack the whip, sir.'

It certainly seemed that no one had been cracking any whip in the vicinity of the stables for some time,

Alleyne agreed. It looked to him as he explored that the horses had been kept fed and watered, though none of them was looking particularly well groomed except for one sleek black stallion that he discovered later belonged to Chesbury's steward, Mr. Drummond. And the stalls looked and smelled as if they had not been properly cleaned out for several days at the least.

'Have these two horses saddled and brought out into the yard,' he instructed the groom, who had ambled into sight as soon as it became obvious to him that they were not about to leave him alone to his reveries and his scratching. 'This one with a sidesaddle.'

'And have the stalls properly mucked out and covered with fresh straw by the time they come back,' Strickland added.

'I takes my orders from Mr. Renny,' the boy said cheekily.

Alleyne's valet was suddenly transformed into the army sergeant he had once been before the boy's surprised eyes.

'Do you, lad?' he said. 'And if Mr. Renny is still asleep on account of he was working so hard yesterday, you will take your orders from whoever will set you to doing your proper work what earns your wages from the baron here. Stop worrying your flea bites now and stand to attention.'

Amazingly, the boy did, just like a private soldier under the critical eye of his sergeant.

'Look lively now, lad,' Strickland said amiably, 'and find them saddles.'

Alleyne chuckled, though he sobered almost instantly. It must be Weston's whip that had stopped cracking, he thought. The man's illness had caused a slacking off in the stables and apparently in the kitchen too. He could well believe it, judging by the quality of the dinner last evening – a meal that Weston had merely pecked at, he had noticed. It was doubtful he had always run a sloppy estate. There was no air of long neglect about the place.

Mounting the horse five minutes later proved every bit as difficult as he had anticipated. After a few abortive attempts and a refusal to allow the sergeant to hoist him up, he solved the problem by mounting awkwardly from the right side of the horse and therefore having to do little more with his left leg than swing it over the horse's back. Fortunately, once he was mounted, the leg felt almost comfortable.

'Do you realize, Strickland,' he asked as he gathered the reins into his hands, 'that this must have been the very last thing I was doing before I fell off in the Forest of Soignés and knocked my wits and my memory clear out of my head?'

'But it is clear to see that you was born in the saddle, sir,' Strickland said, standing back as the horse, which doubtless had not been ridden for a while, pranced and sidled and snorted skittishly.

Alleyne had not even really noticed that the animal was not standing still and docile. It was true, he thought, cheered immensely. He had responded to the horse and controlled it without conscious thought, as if he had reached deep into long familiar skills acquired during his other life.

'Wait here,' he said. 'I'll just take a turn outside the yard.'

It felt so astonishingly good to be on horseback that he knew riding was something he had been doing all his life. He took the horse out behind the stables and cantered across a wide lawn there, trying to picture himself riding with other people, racing with them, jumping fences and hedges with them, hunting with them. He tried to picture himself riding into battle – at the head of a cavalry charge or directing an infantry advance. He tried to recapture those final moments in the forest, when his leg would have been hurting like a thousand devils, when he would have been worried both about the letter and about the woman waiting for him at the Namur Gates. He tried to picture what it was that had caused him to fall off and bang his head hard enough to dislodge everything that was inside it.

But all he had succeeded in doing, he thought as he made his way back to the stables, was give himself a faint headache.

Rachel was there, talking with Sergeant Strickland and eyeing the other horse with obvious apprehension. She was wearing a serviceable blue carriage dress and a hat that was tipped pertly forward over her swept-up golden hair. She was standing in a patch of sunlight, and without the hat she would again have looked like his golden angel.

He felt a twinge of discomfort. Yesterday had not proceeded quite as he had visualized it. He had a nasty suspicion that Weston was not the cold monster Rachel had described and that she was not as indifferent to him as she pretended to be – or as perhaps she really thought she was.

'Good morning.' He doffed his hat and nodded to her.

'Good morning,' she said. But as he rode closer and his horse loomed over her, he could see her eyes widen and her face turn pale. 'Oh, no, I could not. I really could not. It is no good. If I had learned as a child, I might have been a tolerably accomplished horsewoman by now. But I cannot start learning at the age of twenty-two. Anyway, it is time you got down from there before you hurt your leg again.'

Incredible as it seemed to him that she could have lived her whole life without riding, he realized that he could not simply expect her to hop up into the sidesaddle on the other horse and ride off into the sunrise. She might not even get up onto that horse alone today. But she would ride. By Jove she would.

He discovered a stubborn streak in himself.

'You need to see life from the perspective of a horse's back,' he said. 'And then you will feel such exhilaration that you will know there is nothing to compare with it.'

'I believe you without feeling the need to prove it,' she said. 'Now I am going back to the house.'

He sidled his mount to block her way.

'Not until you have proved to me that you are no coward,' he said. 'You will ride up with me first. You will be quite safe. Despite what I did to myself in Belgium, I will not let you fall. I promise.'

'Ride up with *you*?' She tipped back her head and their eyes met and held.

Ah, yes, he could see her point though she had not put it into words. Holding her hands against his chest last evening had raised his temperature a notch. Knowing that she was sleeping in a room separated from his own by three doorways but no doors had kept him awake half the night. And now he was inviting her to ride up with him? Actually he had gone beyond inviting her, though. He had challenged her.

Well, so be it. He had decided that she was going

185

to learn to ride, and so learn to ride she must.

'Normally I would suggest that you set your foot on my left boot so that I could lift you up here,' he said. 'But, alas, I am unable to display such manly strength for your admiration today. Strickland, do you feel able to lift Lady Smith up here?'

She uttered something that seemed like a strange combination of a shriek and a squawk.

'I do, sir,' the sergeant said. 'If you will forgive me the liberty, missy. Mr. Smith – Sir Jonathan, I should remember to say, just as I ought to have remembered to call you Lady Smith. Sir Jonathan will keep you safe once you are up there. It is plain to see that he was born in the saddle, as I just told him a while ago. And I daresay you will enjoy it once you are up.'

Since Sergeant Strickland himself regarded her in something of the nature of an angel, it was doubtful he would have proceeded further against her express wishes. But fortunately – or perhaps unfortunately – he acted fast, and even while she was opening her mouth, doubtless to protest, he was hoisting her upward with two large hands splayed on either side of her waist, and depositing her on the horse's back before the saddle. Alleyne's arms closed about her to steady her.

'Oh,' she said. 'Oh.' And she clutched at him in panic.

'Relax,' he said, tightening his hold on her. 'The only danger can come from your fighting me. Relax, my love.' He grinned into her wide, dazed eyes.

'There you go, missy – Lady Smith,' Sergeant Strickland said. 'You don't look like you was born in the saddle, but you do look like you was born to be in Sir Jonathan's arms.'

He was chuckling over his own witticism as he turned away and disappeared inside the stable building – probably to harass the grooms and whip them into shape, Alleyne guessed.

In the meantime some of the tension had gone out of Rachel's body, though she sat very still indeed. Even her head did not move as she stared straight ahead.

'You are probably pretending,' he said, 'that you are sitting in a parlor, trying to decide whether to pick up your embroidery or a book.'

'I will never forgive you for this,' she said, her voice prim and tense.

He chuckled as he turned the horse out of the stable yard again.

He might never forgive himself either. He could feel her body heat all along his front. He could smell gardenia.

When one looked up with one's feet firmly planted on mother earth, a rider did not look so very far off the ground. But when one *was* that rider, or at least sitting up before the rider, which was more or less the same thing, the ground looked alarmingly distant.

Rachel was horribly aware of empty space ahead of her and below her, and also of the same amount of empty space at her back. If the horse had stayed very, very still, she might have gathered her wits about her after a few moments, but of course it was not in the nature of horses to stand still. It sidestepped and pranced and snorted.

And then it moved even more. It swiveled about with much clopping of hooves on the cobbles, and proceeded on its way out of the stable yard.

At any moment, she was convinced she was going to pitch forward or topple backward, and someone was going to have to come and scrape up her mortal remains. Or perhaps she would wake up somewhere several days hence with a lump the size of an egg on the side of her head and no memory – not even of this, her first ride in sixteen years.

Jonathan's chest looked reassuringly solid, she thought, seeing it with her peripheral vision only a few inches from her left arm. She could lean against him if she chose and feel relatively safe. But she disdained to show such weakness. She consciously straightened her spine. One of his arms was wrapped about her waist, she realized for the first time. Even if she leaned back, he would stop her from falling off. His other arm was holding the reins, but it touched her at the waist in front and felt like a solid enough barrier between her and the ground below.

In fact, she could feel his body heat and smell his cologne or his soap or his shaving soap.

And there was something else preventing her from slipping backward. It was his right thigh, she understood suddenly, pressed to her derriere. The inside of his left thigh was pressed against her knees.

It was strange how she became aware of the man long after the horse and the danger. Though not so very long, actually. They were only just outside the stable yard, and they were turning again, away from the front of the house, along beside the lake, and onto a long back lawn that stretched to a line of trees in the distance.

'This is all quite pointless,' she told him. 'You will never make a rider of me.'

'Yes, I will,' he said. 'I have decided that you will learn, and I have also decided that I must be a stubborn man who imposes his will on all around him. I must have been a general, or a colonel at the very least. Perhaps I was a close comrade of Colonel Leavey and Colonel Streat.'

She did not turn her head – she dared not – but she knew he was grinning. He was enjoying himself, just as he had yesterday, with not a care in the world.

'I daresay all your men hated you,' she said nastily.

He laughed. 'You cannot live in the country and not ride,' he told her. 'It would be an utter absurdity.'

'I have lived all my life except for the last few months in London,' she said, 'and I will live the rest of my life there after this is all over.'

'What do you plan to do there?' he asked her.

'I will find employment again,' she said. 'Or, if I have my inheritance, I will live on the proceeds of my jewels after I have paid my friends back what they are owed. *What are you doing*?'

'Urging this mount from a slow crawl to a sedate walk,' he said.

'And you seriously believe,' she asked him, 'that you are going to persuade me to do this myself one day, all alone on my own horse?'

'I was hoping it would be today,' he said. 'But I can see that I was overoptimistic in having a horse saddled for you. It will have to wait until tomorrow.'

'*What are you doing*?' she asked him again.

'Moving into a *brisk* walk.' He chuckled. 'Rachel, relax. I am not going to ride neck or nothing with you, and I am not going to jump any gates or hedges. We are merely going to trot across this grassy stretch and back so that you can get a feel for riding. I am

189

not going to let you come to any harm.'

'*Trot*?' Even to her own ears her voice sounded mournful.

The morning air was refreshingly cool, she realized suddenly. She had noticed it as soon as she set foot outside the house, but now she could feel it moving against her face, and as she got up the courage to unknot her neck muscles and turn her head to look about, she could see how lovely the lake was to one side of the lawn, its waters still and dark green from the reflections of the trees on the far bank. And this lawn was lovely too even though the grass had not been cut very recently. Daisies and buttercups and clover carpeted it, making it more meadow than lawn. The horse disturbed butterflies and other insects as it passed. Colorful butterfly wings fluttered above the green and white and yellow carpet of the ground. Birds flew overhead. The horse's hooves thudded rhythmically on the turf.

Rachel had a sudden surging memory of her six-year-old self riding up before Uncle Richard on the streets of London, and once in Hyde Park, when she had believed that riding must surely be the most exciting activity on this earth. Her childhood self had surely been right, she thought now at the same moment as she realized that they were indeed trotting – or perhaps cantering was the more appropriate word.

She heard herself laugh, and she turned her head to share her exuberance with the man beside her. He gazed back at her with very dark, unsmiling eyes.

She did not say anything – her stomach was too busy performing some sort of somersault. Neither did he.

She turned her head away again in some confusion and looked about her once more. Her exuberance had not diminished, but added to it now was an acute physical awareness of Jonathan Smith. She wondered briefly if she would have had the nerve to do what she had done with him in Brussels if she had seen him dressed and on his feet or on horseback first and had realized what a very virile, vital man he was when he was not laid low by injuries.

She surely would have dashed from his room and never returned. Though perhaps not. She had not lain with him because he seemed weak and puny, after all, had she?

She had simply been mad, that was all. Irresponsibly insane. Insanely irresponsible.

And then she had agreed to this wild charade.

Once upon a time she had considered herself an almost drearily sensible girl. She had had to be in order to hold together her father's household.

But she did not dwell upon such thoughts. She was, against all the odds, enjoying herself. The distant trees were moving up far too fast. Soon they would be turning back to the stables, and her first lesson – if it could be called that – would be over. She was reluctant to admit even to herself that she would be sorry.

'Well?' he asked, breaking a lengthy silence as they drew near to the trees. He eased the horse to a walk.

'The ride is quite pleasant, I must confess,' she said as primly as she could. 'But I know beyond any doubt that I could not do this alone.'

'Yes, you could and will,' he said.

But he did not immediately turn back, as she had expected. He rode closer to the trees and then slowly among them, bending his head as she did when they seemed uncomfortably close to a branch. At the edge of the wood the grass was long, but then most of it disappeared, discouraged from growing, no doubt, by the thickness of leaves and branches overhead.

They did not proceed very far, but they could both hear the sound of running water when they stopped.

'Ah, I suspected as much,' he said. 'I believe there must be a river flowing through these woods to feed the lake. Shall we investigate?'

'The trees grow rather thickly here,' she pointed out.

'Then we must go on foot,' he told her. 'Stay there. You will be quite safe for a moment.'

And he swung down to the ground before wincing noticeably.

'You forgot about your wound, did you not?' she scolded while feeling very unsafe herself. 'And you do not even have your cane with you.'

But he was grinning again when he reached up and lifted her down, though she could see from his gritted teeth that the effort was causing him considerable pain.

'I am mortally sick of my infirmity, Rachel,' he said, 'and of propelling myself about with a cane as if I were an octogenarian with gout.' He was tethering the horse to a tree as he spoke. 'Let us find this river.'

It was not far away, which was a fortunate thing, as Jonathan was limping. The view was well worth the short trek, though. The river was not very wide, but it was flowing downhill here, down a slope of land to their right. The slope was not steep enough to cause a waterfall, but nevertheless the water was cascading down over stones of varying sizes and foamed white in places. With trees growing to the bank on either side, it was a breathtakingly lovely sight. But there was more than sight. There was the rushing, bubbling sound of the water and the smell of it and of the greenery surrounding it. There was the sound of birds, hundreds of them, it seemed, though they were all hidden from view among the branches of the trees.

To Rachel, who had lived all of her life in a city, it was like a piece of heaven. She was dazzled. She felt rather as if a large fist had collided with her stomach, robbing her of breath.

'Shall we sit down?' he suggested.

They were standing, she realized, on a large rock, around which the water flowed fast – and it was flat on top. She could also see that his left hand was pressed against the top of his thigh.

'Foolish man,' she said. 'You should still be in bed.'

'Indeed?' He favored her with his haughty look – his eyebrows raised, his eyes appearing to be staring along the length of his prominent nose. 'With you as my nurse, Rachel? I do believe the innocence of those days is gone forever. Don't fuss at me. The leg is healing and I will not coddle it.'

He lowered himself carefully to the rock, his left leg stretched out before him, his right bent at the knee. He draped one arm over it while he propped the other behind him. Rachel sat down beside him, as far away from him as the rock allowed, and hugged her raised knees with both arms. Sometimes he seemed to be so full of laughter and mischief that she almost forgot he was also a man who felt the constant threat of terror.

He was *not* Sir Jonathan Smith. She did not know his name. Neither did he.

'But how are you going to get back onto the horse?' she asked him.

'I have been wondering that myself.' He laughed softly. 'I will think of a way when the time comes. This is a pretty spot and a secluded one too. It is perfect for dalliance if one were so inclined.'

'But one is not,' she said hastily.

'No,' he said, 'one is certainly not.'

Contrarily, she felt insulted. Did he have to make it so obvious that her gaucherie that night had rendered her totally unattractive in his eyes? He had found her disappointing. How horribly humiliating!

She rested her chin on her knees and gazed about her. A scene like this, she thought, could restore one's soul. She did not believe she had ever been so affected by natural beauty. She had always imagined that she would not even like the country.

'One misses a great deal,' she said, 'by living all of one's life in a city.'

'It *is* beautiful,' he agreed.

'Did you grow up in the country?' she asked.

'A trick question, Rachel?' he said after a short pause. 'But I believe I can answer it. I must have, or at the very least I must have spent a great deal of my life on a country estate. None of this looks familiar. I do not believe I have ever been here before, and your uncle showed no recognition of me, did he? But I feel comfortable here. I feel that I belong here, in this type of setting even if not in this specific place.'

She turned her head to look at him, her cheek against her knee.

'You are developing a stronger sense of yourself,

194

then?' she asked him. 'Are there any specific memories, no matter how small?'

He shook his head. He was squinting into the cascading water, upon which the light from the morning sun was sparkling.

'Not really,' he said. 'Only the persistent dreams, which I am not even sure are anything more than dreams. If I focus too much attention upon them, perhaps they will lead me astray. Perhaps they will lead me to create a reality that in no way resembles the truth. There is the letter, about which I always feel a sense of urgency whenever I dream of it. And the woman waiting for me at the Namur Gates. Was there a woman there when you and Strickland brought me into the city?'

'Dozens,' she said, 'and hundreds, even thousands of men. It was utter chaos, though there were people who were trying to keep some semblance of order. No one came to claim you, though there were several women frantically looking into every face in the hope of seeing a familiar one, I suppose.'

'Then perhaps she is a dream woman,' he said. 'But if she is not, who was she? Who is she?'

She could think of no answer with which to console him. She hugged her knees more tightly.

'And last night there was a new dream,' he said. 'It was of a fountain, its water shooting high into the sky, its basin set in the middle of a large circular flower garden. Nothing else. None of its surroundings. I believe when I heard the water from this river I thought I might discover the source of my dream. But that was man-made and very carefully cultivated. The light was shining on its waters as it is on these, but it was creating a rainbow of color. Some people deny that we dream in color. But I saw that rainbow in all its glory. Is that proof, I wonder, that the fountain really exists somewhere? But of what significance is it to me?'

'Perhaps it is at the home where you grew up,' she said. 'Your *country* home.'

He did not speak for a while, and Rachel became aware again of the sounds of water and birds, of the peace one could find in such a place. She wondered if her mother had come here to just this spot – to play as a child, to think and dream as a girl. Had she come here to consider her fateful decision of whether to give up Papa or defy Uncle Richard and elope with him anyway?

There was a time – a distant time, perhaps even before her mother's death – when Papa had been far more dashing and charming and full of laughter than he had been in later years, when his addictions to gaming and, to a lesser degree, to drinking had soured him and made his moods far more volatile and unpredictable. It was easy to understand why Mama had thrown away everything for his sake. Though, of course, had she lived another year she would have had access to the very jewels that were now still out of Rachel's reach. They would have been far more affluent – until Papa gambled it all away, as he surely would have done.

'I think I must always have loved the land,' Jonathan said. 'I wonder if that ever saddened me, given the fact that I must have been a younger son and therefore was fated to be shipped off to the army. Or perhaps I denied my love because I knew I could never inherit and live close to the land after I grew up.'

'You talk about the danger of putting too much

196

trust in your dreams,' she said. 'Have you considered the fact that even your assumptions about yourself are not real memories? Can you be sure that you were a military officer?'

He turned his head to look directly at her, his eyebrows raised. He stared for many moments, during which she found it impossible to look away.

'No,' he said at last. He laughed, though he did not sound amused. 'I cannot even be sure about that, can I? But why had I been at the battlefront if I was not with the armies? Getting shot at for the sheer fun of it? I do seem to be a rather reckless man, don't I? My being a civilian would explain why I was alone and why I had ridden away from the battlefield, though.'

'It is only a suggestion,' she said. 'I do not know any more than you do. I have just thought of something else, though. If you are twenty-five or thereabouts, you would probably have had your commission for five or six or seven years. But apart from the wounds you sustained no more than a day before I found you, there were no others anywhere on your body. No old wounds from old battles, I mean. Would that not be unlikely, even unbelievable?'

'Perhaps I was always extraordinarily fortunate,' he said. 'Or perhaps I always ducked behind some burly sergeant or private soldier when trouble came along carrying a musket or a sword along with it. Or perhaps until Waterloo I was always stationed at home.'

Rachel sighed and returned her chin to her knees. If only she could do something to help him remember, she thought, she would be able to feel that she had done more than merely save his life. She would be able to see him restored to his former self and the people who loved him. She would be able to have good memories of him after he had gone, confident that he had been restored to himself.

Was there anything she could do? she wondered. Could she make some inquiries of her own? She had a few friends in London. Could she write to them and ask if they knew of any gentleman of high social rank who had been missing since the Battle of Waterloo? It would surely be absurd even to ask. There must be hundreds of men missing. Most officers would have been accounted for, though, would they not? None of her friends moved in the highest circles. But should she at least try?

He had come here to try to help her.

'I suppose,' he said, cutting into her thoughts after several more minutes had passed in silence, 'I have kept you out long enough to convince your uncle that I am willing to spend time on your education and am passionate enough about you to steal some private time for ourselves.'

She looked into his face again. He was smiling lazily, his seriousness apparently forgotten or pushed beneath the surface again.

He leaned closer to her suddenly, and before she could realize his intent, he set his lips against hers.

It would have been the easiest thing in the world to pull away from him, to get to her feet, brush out her dress, and make her way back through the trees to the horse. He was not touching her anywhere else but on the lips.

But she did not think of that at the time. She sat, riveted by surprise and some other emotion far more seductive.

It was a soft, lingering kiss in which their tongues moistened each other's lips and briefly touched. It was not really lascivious and not at all in danger of leading into a deeper embrace. But it was not the kiss of brother and sister or of casual friends either. There was something definitely sexual about it.

It got all mixed up in Rachel's mind and emotions with the beauty of their natural surroundings, with the rushing of the water and the rustling of the trees and the trilling of the birds. It was all what her heart must have yearned for all her life, she thought – though in truth she was not really thinking at all, and it would have seemed a strange thought if she had been.

When he drew back she looked at him with dreamy eyes and parted lips and utterly defenseless sensibilities.

'There,' he said. 'Now you look rosy and just kissed, Rache, as you ought to look when we return from here.' He grinned.

She felt utterly foolish. It was all part of the charade, nothing else. She got hastily to her feet and brushed her hands over her skirt.

'I do not recall that I have ever given you permission to call me *Rache*,' she said foolishly.

He laughed. 'Now you have waved the proverbial red flag before the proverbial bull,' he said. 'Rache it is from now on. You may retaliate if you wish and call me Jon.'

She made her way back through the trees without waiting for him, though prudence kept her some distance away from the horse. Then she noticed, of course, that Jonathan was limping quite heavily. Sitting on the rock after riding had no doubt stiffened his leg considerably.

'I had better walk back to the stables,' she said, 'and see if there is a gig or a wagon that can be sent here for you.'

'If you take even one step in that direction, Rache,' he said, 'I will forget that I have ever even heard the word *jewel*, and I will walk off into the proverbial sunset – or rather I will hobble off into it on my trusty cane – and leave you to explain to Weston why he should give you your inheritance even as much as one minute before you turn twenty-five, when you have just been abandoned by your new husband.'

'You might simply have said no,' she said.

He had moved around to the right side of the horse and thus looked very awkward as he mounted. But mount he did, and entirely for her benefit, she believed, he did no more than grit his teeth against the obvious pain and then pretend that it was a smile as he looked down at her.

'You had better come around to this side too, Rache,' he said, 'though you will end up facing the wrong way.'

'I'll walk back,' she said.

'It is a pity we cannot be sure your uncle will be gazing out a back window,' he said. 'I would wield my whip at your back if I *could* be certain and thus assure him that you have acquired a husband who knows how to keep his wife in her place. Set your foot on my right boot or I will come down there and sling you across the horse facedown.'

Despite the fact that she felt indignant and wished to be on her dignity, she found his final words funny and laughed as she complied with his demands. It was not a performance that either of them would have liked to enact before an audience, but with an inelegant amount of scrambling and hauling and panting and laughter – on both sides – she was finally up before him again, though facing to the right rather than the left.

'But I will have exactly the same view going back as I had coming,' she said.

'Are you complaining?' he asked her. 'I could get the horse to walk backward to the stables if you wish, though I doubt he will like it. Or you could swing your legs over his neck and face the way you ought to be facing after all.'

They were still both laughing – like a couple of foolish children, she thought afterward. And why she should take his ridiculous – and not seriously intended – suggestion as a dare, she did not know. She still felt as if she were miles above the safety of the ground. There was, though, a branch conveniently close to give her both the illusion of safety and a measure of bravado as she steadied a hand against it.

She swung her legs over one at a time, exposing first her left ankle and then her left leg up to the knee and then the same parts of her right leg. They were both somehow still on the horse's back by the time she wriggled into position with her legs dangling over its left side and he bracketed her with his arms as he had done on the outer ride. They were also both almost wheezing with laughter.

It was about the most undignified scene of which Rachel had ever been a part.

'And if I were to suggest that you stand on the horse's back – on one leg – twirling hoops about your waist and neck and arms and raised leg?' Jonathan asked.

Rachel shrieked.

'You could earn your fortune at Astley's Amphitheatre,' he said, maneuvering the horse out of the trees and taking it to a walk and then a canter back across the lawn in the direction of the house and stables.

'And then I could enjoy it after I had broken every bone in my body,' she said. 'I would not even need my jewels.'

She had watched the lake and the land surrounding it on the way out. This time she looked across the wide expanse of grass to hilly land beyond, partially covered with trees. It still amazed her to realize that *this* was Chesbury Park, her mother's childhood home, which she had always imagined as far smaller and more modest.

'And to think,' Jonathan said, 'that there are only thirty days to go. There *are* thirty-one in the month, I believe, whether one considers this month of July or next month's August. Thirty-one days apiece.'

'It will take you every one of those days,' she said, turning her head to look into his face, 'to coax me up into that sidesaddle and back out onto this lawn.'

'Ah!' he exclaimed. 'I have made a convert, then, have I?'

Actually he had. She did not want this ride to end. She could scarcely wait for the next. Of course, the next time was going to have to be on her own, and she did not doubt she would be terrified. But she had missed so much in her life, she realized, caught up in Papa's hand-to-mouth existence in London. Perhaps it was not too late to do some catching up.

'Not really,' she said. 'But I do not intend to sit around for thirty-one days, twiddling my thumbs.'

'Just as I thought,' he said. 'I have made a convert.'

And he threw back his head and laughed.

Chapter Thirteen

Alleyne breakfasted alone – on slimy, cold bacon, sausages that were pink in the center, toast that was burned, and coffee that was weak and lukewarm. He passed over the eggs, which were congealed in the warming dish on the sideboard.

Rachel had gone straight up to her room from the stables – to write a letter, she had explained.

He found two of the other ladies out in the parterre gardens when he stepped outside later to look around. They were sitting on a long seat there, on either side of the baron. Flossie was dressed in black even to her lacy parasol, while Phyllis was all in pink. They made a pretty, eminently respectable picture. Alleyne suppressed a wave of amusement as he went to join them, making a conscious effort to put as little weight as possible on his cane. His leg was holding up well after the ride.

'Ah, here comes Sir Jonathan,' Flossie said, giving her parasol a twirl.

'Good morning.' Weston inclined his head as Alleyne bowed to all three of them.

'We saw you earlier through the window, Sir

Jonathan,' Phyllis cried, 'did we not, Flora? And we persuaded dear Lord Weston to come and take a look too. You were keeping Rachel as safe as can be up on your horse. You made a very handsome and romantic-looking couple, I must say.'

Alleyne acknowledged her words with a grin. 'We found the cascades among the trees, sir,' he said, 'and sat there for a while. It is a lovely part of the park.'

Weston nodded. He did not look much better for a night's sleep.

'I have had a complaint from my head groom,' he said, 'that your *valet* of all people, Smith, has been interfering in the running of the stables.'

When Alleyne and Rachel had left there earlier, Strickland had been stripped to the waist, mucking out stalls. And a few grooms had been busy right alongside him. Alleyne had declined his offer to return to the house to help him change out of his riding clothes.

'I beg your pardon, sir,' he said. 'My valet was an infantry sergeant until he lost an eye at the Battle of Waterloo. He is accustomed to working hard and ordering other men to do likewise when there is work to be done.'

'And there was work to be done in the stables?' the baron asked with a frown.

Alleyne hesitated. Allowing his valet to give orders to the Chesbury grooms in order to set the stables to rights was a breach of etiquette that was not likely to endear him to Baron Weston's heart.

'It was early morning, sir,' he explained, 'and Strickland came out to the stables with me to help me mount, as this was my first time in the saddle since I injured my leg. There was only one groom there and much to be done to care for the horses and clean their

204

stalls. I daresay it would all have been done or at least underway if we had arrived there an hour or so later. I will instruct my man to confine his services to my person in future.'

Weston was still frowning.

'I have not been out there since my last heart seizure several months ago,' he said. 'Perhaps standards have slipped. I will look into the matter.'

Alleyne was amused to see Flossie lay a solicitous hand on his arm.

'But you must not overexert yourself, my lord,' she said. 'Not in any way at all – not even to entertain us. We are quite capable of amusing ourselves. And we will even do our best to see to your greater comfort, will we not, Phyll?'

'You are kind, ma'am,' the baron said. But he was still frowning and looked distracted. 'The flower beds are full of weeds.'

There was also grass pushing up through the graveled paths in places.

'But even weeds can be lovely,' Flossie said. 'Indeed, I never understand why some plants are approvingly called flowers while others, equally pretty, are disparagingly called weeds.'

'You are attempting to make me feel better, Mrs. Streat,' Lord Weston said with a smile, 'and succeeding. Even so, I must have a word with the head gardener.'

'The person I would like to have a word with,' Phyllis said, dipping her opened parasol so that the long tip rested on the path, 'is your cook, my lord. I do not mean to be offensive, but she would appear to be in need of some advice.'

Alleyne winced inwardly. They were all going to

find themselves back on the road today, turned away from Chesbury Park with a boot at their rear end, if they were not very careful.

Flossie laughed, a demure titter in total contrast to her usual hearty mirth when she was amused.

'You do not need to have a long acquaintance with my sister-in-law,' she said, 'in order to learn that she has a passion for cooking, my lord. Colonel Leavey keeps his own cook when he is at home, but the poor woman usually ends up idle. Phyllis cannot resist spending her days in the kitchen. She is quite intolerant of anyone else's cooking but her own. And it certainly is superior, I must say.'

The baron sighed.

'I have been somewhat off my food lately,' he told them, 'but even so I have realized that the food with which my cook presents me leaves much to be desired. Finding a replacement for her here in the country might prove difficult, though. But I cannot have a guest of mine working in my kitchen, ma'am.'

'Believe me, my lord,' Phyllis said, 'it will give me the greatest pleasure. I shall go there immediately and look over the menus for today. I daresay I will wish to make some changes.'

She got to her feet, looking pleased and eager and pretty.

Flossie got up too and gazed down at the baron as she twirled her parasol over her head. 'It was kind of you to bring us out here, my lord,' she said, 'but you really ought to go inside to rest now, especially if there are to be visitors to entertain this afternoon. I will walk back to the house with you. I have some letters to write if you would be so good as to direct me to paper, pen, and ink.'

She took Weston's arm when he stood and the two of them moved off along the path in perfect amicable accord with each other.

Phyllis hung back.

'Poor, dear gentleman,' she said when he was out of earshot. 'He is being taken advantage of quite shamefully, Mr. Smith. It sounds as if the stables are in bad shape, and the gardens certainly are. Gerry says that the cook is into the gin, and that the house-keeper is into the gin and the port and scarcely comes out of her room. And the butler is one of those doddering old fools who has no control whatsoever over his staff.'

'I have no doubt,' Alleyne said with a grin, 'that between you and Geraldine, you will put at least some matters right in the kitchen, Phyllis. My stomach, I must confess, has protested the fare that has been served here so far, though a guest ought not to complain.'

'You can expect a tasty luncheon,' she promised. 'Heads are going to roll when I step into the kitchen, Mr. Smith. I have all the weight of the colonel's authority behind my name.' Her laughter was full of mischief.

Alleyne chuckled to himself as he watched her go. Flossie was already assisting the baron up the steps. They were a priceless pair and were apparently enjoying themselves immensely. And there were to be visitors during the afternoon, were there? They were all to be drawn deeper and deeper into deception, then. Well, there was no point in regretting any of it now. They were in deep, and as someone in literature had once said – Macbeth? – going back would be as difficult now as moving onward.

He sat down on the vacated seat. He had intended to find the steward and request a tour of the home farm, but perhaps he would wait until another day and be with Rachel when the visitors arrived. Besides, Strickland was already making his mark on the stables and Phyllis was invading the kitchen. He must be careful that his own interest in the estate could not be construed as interference.

But he *was* interested. He could not help remembering what he had said to Rachel earlier – he must have grown up on a country estate. This sort of life seemed bred into his bones. And he must surely have loved the land. Gazing about him now, he felt that he could almost weep at the pull of it all on his emotions after the few weeks he had spent in Brussels and then on the journey here.

Was he a younger son? Was he a military officer? How disconnected he must surely have felt, unable even to consider remaining on the land that was not his, but his father's and then an elder brother's. How had he dealt with his feelings? Had he been sullen, ungracious, resentful? He could not quite picture himself that way, but how could he know? Might memory loss entail personality change too? Had he suppressed his feelings, then, been restless and unfulfilled? Had he hated the army? Or pretended to himself that he loved it? Or simply made the best of it? Or – if indeed he had never been an officer – had he wandered through life aimlessly? Had he been able to afford to do so?

Perhaps, if his memory never returned and he could never find his family, he would take employment as a steward. Perhaps he *had been* a steward. It was a gentleman's position, after all, and though he was sure he must be a gentleman, he did not know how high on the social scale he had been. Perhaps employment had always been an imperative for him. But what would a steward have been doing wandering about the Forest of Soignés while the Battle of Waterloo was in progress, a musket ball in his thigh?

He envied Rachel and Flossie their letter-writing activity this morning. Letter writing was perhaps not something he usually enjoyed, but perversely he wished now that there were someone – *anyone* – to whom he could write. Was he the one who had written that letter that kept appearing in his dreams? he wondered. Or had someone written it to him? Or – a possibility he had not yet considered – had it been written neither by nor to him? Perhaps he had been merely a messenger.

He closed his eyes and tried to picture the scenario. By *whom*? To whom? And what was his involvement?

The familiar headache niggled behind his eyes.

He was almost thankful to see Bridget and Rachel out in the garden when he opened his eyes again. He got to his feet to greet their approach.

Rachel had changed into a light sprigged-muslin day dress. Alleyne remembered with some discomfort that he had kissed her again out at the cascades. He had promised himself that he would not do anything like that again. He had covered up his mistake with a reasonable-sounding excuse, of course, but really he had not intended to do it at all. It was just that she seemed to shine more brightly than ever in this country setting. And – deuce take it! – they had laughed together over her antics on the horse like a couple of carefree children, and she had seemed well nigh irresistible.

209

He had not suggested bringing her here to Chesbury in order to find her irresistible. He wanted to be free when he left here. He had no way of knowing what sort of baggage and emotional tangles he had left behind him when his memory went and that he would rediscover when it came back. He certainly did not need any new entanglement.

She was not wearing a bonnet, he noticed. Her hair was gleaming like pure gold in the sunlight. Bridget had a long, shallow basket over one arm. She looked very much younger than she had appeared in Brussels, with her brown hair and her straw bonnet and relaxed smile. She really was pleasantly good-looking, though she must be well past thirty.

'I am going to cut some blooms to brighten up the house, Mr. Smith,' she called when they came within earshot. 'Do sit back down and Rachel will join you. You really ought to keep off that leg as much as possible.'

'Yes, ma'am,' he said, grinning at her and waiting for Rachel to seat herself before taking his place beside her. 'Are you sure you can distinguish between the flowers and the weeds?'

'There *are* rather a lot of weeds,' she said, looking critically along the parterres. 'What I ought to have brought out with me was a hoe. I would love to have a good go at this garden. It is a disgrace.'

'It looks perfectly fine to me, Bridget,' Rachel said.

'That is because you grew up in town, my love,' Bridget told her.

'And you did not?' Alleyne asked her.

'I did not,' she said. 'I grew up in a parsonage, Mr. Smith. My father was a parson, but as poor as could be. And there were seven of us. I was the eldest. I loved nothing better than helping my mother in the garden – the flowers in the front, the vegetables in the back. There is no lovelier feeling in this life than to have one's fingers in the soil. I think I might have married Charlie Perrie if his house had had a garden and a few chickens and maybe a pig, even though he did not have a humorous or a generous bone in his body. But he didn't and so I went to London to seek my fortune when I was sixteen. I was the happiest girl in the world when Mr. York took me on as nurse to Rachel, and the job lasted six whole years. I am not complaining about my life since then, but having a garden is my idea of heaven. If we ladies can ever afford our boarding house, it is going to have to have a big garden. And a big kitchen for Phyll. But I am talking too much. I am going to cut some flowers now.'

She moved farther along the parterre before bending to cut some.

'Was it Bridget who taught you to read?' he asked Rachel.

'I think it must have been my mother who did that,' she said. 'Or perhaps my father. He liked to read and was a very well-educated man. He used to read to me when I was very young.'

'What was your life like?' he asked her.

She thought for a while. 'I think I must have been very close to my mother,' she said. 'I know that I had terrible tantrums for a while after poor Bridget came – to take her place, as I thought. But I soon grew to love her like a mother – such is the fickleness of childhood. I was unhappy after she left, and gradually things grew worse with my father's gaming and

211

drinking. I did like being the lady in charge, though, responsible for the running of our household, and I believe I did well at it. I learned to be frugal and to put things away during the good times to help us through the bad. But for the last few years the bad times were almost constant. I loved my father, and I will always treasure the memories of the times when he loved me cheerfully and generously and when he allowed himself to be loved. Those times too grew sparse toward the end of his life.'

'You never went to school?' he asked her.

'No.' She shook her head.

'You had friends?' he asked.

'A few.' She looked down at her hands. 'We had some good neighbors who have remained my friends to this day.'

She had been a lonely, deprived child, Alleyne thought, gazing at her profile through narrowed eyes. And for many years after Bridget left she had been starved for love, he guessed. And for friends. But she had made the best of her situation. She was not a whiner.

He had done the wrong thing, he thought. Instead of jumping into this lark like a gleeful schoolboy, he ought to have pressed his first idea on her more force-fully. This was where she ought to be living permanently – Miss York of Chesbury Park. He was beginning to have serious doubts about her assessment of Weston.

She turned her head to look at him.

'It was not a bad life,' she said. 'I do not want to give the impression that my father was cruel to me or even neglectful, or that I hated him. He was not and I did not. He was sick, I believe. He could not stop

212

himself from ruining us both. And then he caught a seemingly harmless chill and died within three days.'

'I am sorry,' he said.

'I am not.' She smiled rather tightly. 'His life had become something of a torment to him. And to me.'

But she bit her upper lip even as she said it and looked down sharply to hide her tears from his eyes. He saw one plop onto the back of her hand. He resisted the impulse to set an arm about her shoulders. She would not thank him for his pity.

'And now you believe that your jewels can solve all your problems,' he said, 'and enable you to live happily ever after.'

She looked up sharply at him, tears still swimming in her eyes.

'No, of course I do not!' she cried, and she jumped to her feet and glared down at him. 'Money will not bring back Papa and make him the way he used to be or the way he must have been when Mama first met and fell in love with him. Money will not make me happy. I am not stupid, Jonathan. But it is only people who have plenty of money who can despise it. To the rest of us it is important. It can at least put food in our stomachs and clothes on our back, and it can at least feed our dreams. You must be from a wealthy background or you would never have said what you just did say. And you are very like my father, I believe. You are a gamer. It just so happened that the last time you played, when we were in Brussels, luck was on your side and gave you enough money that at the moment you can be careless about it. Next time you may not be so fortunate.'

'Rachel,' he said, leaning forward and trying to

possess himself of one of her hands, 'I did not mean my words quite like that.'

She snatched her hand away.

'Oh, yes, you did,' she said. 'People always say they did not mean it when they know they have offended someone. How else could you have meant your words? I come of an improvident father and have always lived off my wits – that is what you think. And if I can only get my hands on my jewels, you think, I will squander the whole fortune as my father always squandered his winnings and will soon be a pauper again. Besides, I am only a woman. That is what you are thinking, is it not? What can women know about planning and spending wisely?'

'Rachel,' he said, 'you presume to know a great deal about my thoughts. But I am sorry I spoke so carelessly. I really am sorry.'

What he had meant was that she needed far more than money. She needed family and friends. She needed to belong somewhere. She needed to find love, or to let love find her. Not sexual love, necessarily, though she would doubtless find that too in time. She needed a home. She needed Chesbury and Weston, except that she had been too stubborn after her father's death to see it, and now she had got herself into a nasty situation that might make any real reconciliation with her uncle nearly impossible.

That was his fault, of course, damn it.

What he had *meant* was that there was probably a greater treasure here for her than her jewels. And Weston was as lonely and as much in need of family as she was.

But he had, Alleyne admitted to himself, expressed himself clumsily. And he *was* the one who had thought of this underhand scheme to get her jewels early.

'No,' she said, 'you are not sorry. Men never are. They rule the world, and women are merely foolish creatures and quite incapable of knowing what will bring them happiness. I *know* you do not want to be here even though you were the one who suggested we come like this, pretending to be what we are not. Well, now you are stuck with being here for a whole month. I do not care a fig what you think of me or my continued wish to have my own fortune in my own keeping. I do not *care*.'

He got to his feet without the aid of his cane. She was very upset, he could see – far more so than his provocation would account for. His guess was that the reality of being here at Chesbury Park was far different than what she had imagined. And he was feeling devilishly guilty over that.

'Perhaps,' he said, not for the first time, 'we should put an end to this whole charade, Rachel. I'll explain things to your uncle, the ladies can go off to reorganize their lives in their own way, and you can stay here to live.'

'Oh, yes!' she cried. 'It is just what you *would* suggest now that the novelty of this lark has worn off. You would leave me here where I am not wanted and where I do not want to be, and you would force me to abandon my dearest friends to a life that is insufferable even to think of. Well, it is not going to happen, and that is that.'

She reached out a hand and shoved him in the chest. It was not a hard shove, but she caught him off balance as he held some of the weight off his left leg. He toppled awkwardly and inelegantly backward and crashed down onto the seat.

He raised his eyebrows.

'And *now* look what you have made me do,' she said crossly. 'I have never in my life knocked anyone over.'

'I daresay I have never *been* knocked over,' he said. 'But I suppose I deserved it. I did not choose my words with care, something I will remember the next time I want to be kind to you when you are as prickly as a hedgehog.'

'Kind!' she said scornfully. 'And I am *not* prickly.'

But before she could quarrel more with him, Bridget came dashing up, her basket laden with blooms.

'Whatever happened?' she asked. 'Did you *fall*, Mr. Smith? I warned you—'

'Merely a lovers' tiff, Bridget,' Alleyne said, grinning and feeling rather foolish. 'Our first. It was entirely my fault, of course. Rachel knocked me over.'

'This all seemed such a brilliant idea back in Brussels,' Rachel said. 'Everyone thought it would be great good fun. And so it is, and so it will continue to be. I think Uncle Richard is dying.'

She caught up her flimsy skirt after uttering this apparent non sequitur, whisked herself about, and half ran along the path back to the house. Alleyne would have gone after her, but Bridget set a hand on his sleeve.

'Let her go,' she said. 'I can remember the time when she used to cry inconsolably for her mother every night. And I can remember when her lovely porcelain doll was smashed to pieces by one of Mr. York's doltish friends. She wrapped up the pieces in an old blanket and cried over them every night. But it was her uncle she wept for. He had come like a ray of sunlight into her life after her mother died, and he had bought her that doll. Then he disappeared as abruptly as he had come. She got over it all within that first year, and after that she was a girl of remarkable spirit and resilience. But now I wonder if she got over it at all. She hates Lord Weston. But what I think is that she won't admit to herself that she still wants desperately to love him. He is her mama's *brother* – her only link with her roots.'

'Oh, Lord,' Alleyne said with a sigh, 'it is what I think too, Bridget. And look at the scrape I have got her into.'

'Never you mind,' she said. 'It will all work out, you just wait and see.'

Alleyne wished he felt her confidence.

Chapter Fourteen

Half an hour later, almost before Rachel had properly composed herself after the quarrel, which had seemed to come out of nowhere and had provoked her into a physical attack upon another human being, there was a tap on her door, and Geraldine came inside without waiting for a summons.

'Such a to-do, Rache,' she said. 'Phyll is in the kitchen doing battle. She has taken command of the kitchen maids and the food and the ovens, but the cook has only retreated to recoup her forces for a counterattack. She and the housekeeper are fortifying themselves on gin. Then the pots and the language are going to fly, let me tell you. I wouldn't miss it for worlds, so I'll hurry with my message. The baron wants to see you in his private rooms. You had better go. Maybe you can discover where he keeps your jewels and I can don my black cloak and mask, stick a knife between my teeth, and find a stretch of ivy to climb tonight when the moon is down.'

Rachel laughed despite herself, but as she hurried along to her uncle's apartments she really wished she were anywhere else on earth. Suddenly all the lies and deceptions seemed despicable. But what could she do now but forge ahead with the plan? She was not the only one involved in the trickery, after all. She could not expose her friends as frauds.

She hated Jonathan. She *hated* him. He must have been wealthy, arrogant, insensitive, and heartless in his other life. She ignored the fact that he had not shoved her back but had apologized instead.

'Come in and have a seat, Rachel,' her uncle said after his valet had admitted her.

He did not rise from his chair. His feet were resting on a padded stool. He looked weary, and yet his eyes watched her keenly from beneath his bushy brows as she crossed the room and took the offered chair. They both sat facing a low window, which looked out onto the parterre gardens and the lawns beyond.

'Uncle Richard,' she asked him, 'how are you? I mean *really*, how *are* you?'

'It is my heart,' he told her. 'It is giving out on me slowly – or rapidly. Who knows? I have had a few seizures over the past three years, the most recent last February. I was recovering well enough, but then something happened to upset me. And then yesterday you arrived here.'

And she was being lumped in with whatever it was that had upset him recently? Well, she could hardly complain. She had invited herself here after refusing his invitation last year. She had not even written to warn him that she was coming. And she had brought a whole crowd of other people with her.

It had not really occurred to her that he would have aged in sixteen years. She had certainly never considered the possibility that his health might be gone. She had expected him to be the same robust, confident man –

219

except that she would be armed against him this time.

'We will leave tomorrow if you wish,' she said. 'Or even today.'

'That was not my meaning,' he said. 'How well do you know Smith, Rachel? How much do you know of him? He is handsome and charming, I will confess – at least, he is charming when it suits him to be. Did you marry him, perhaps, because you were a lady's companion and your choices seemed few? But that would have been foolish of you. You will be a wealthy woman one day. You could have been wealthy anytime during the past year if you had married with my approval.'

'I love Jonathan,' she said. 'And I know he is a man with whom I can live happily and securely for the rest of my life. You could not have chosen more wisely for me than I have done for myself, Uncle Richard.'

'And yet,' he said, 'you have quarreled quite violently with each other this morning. He insulted you, I suppose, and you pushed him over.'

Rachel closed her eyes briefly. Of course! He would have had a bird's-eye view of their altercation out of this window. She could see the seat on which they had been sitting without even having to stretch her neck. All she could be thankful for was that the window was closed and therefore he could not have heard a word of what they had said.

'It was nothing,' she said. 'A sharp exchange, soon made up. That is all.'

'But you did not make up your quarrel,' he said. 'You left him when you were still angry, and he let you go.'

'It was not serious,' she insisted. She spread her hands across her lap.

220

'I sincerely hope you have not made the mistake your mother made, Rachel,' he said.

She looked up sharply at him.

'How do you know it was a mistake?' she asked him. 'You disapproved of her marriage and then, after she had eloped, you cut her off and never saw her again until after she was dead. How do you know she was not deliriously happy all those years? How do you know she would not have remained happy until Papa died last year?'

He sighed. 'I would not speak ill of York,' he said. 'He was your father, Rachel, and I daresay you were fond of him. It would be unnatural if you had not been.'

'I *adored* him,' she said fiercely, though she was aware, of course, that she was protesting too much. She had loved her father to the end, but it had not been easy to do so. Sometimes she had hated him.

'What gives you the right to stand in judgment?' she asked him. 'To cut off all contact with your only sister because you disapproved of her choice of husband and then to come and gloat over her grave when she died? What gave you the right to win a child's affection – to *buy* it with ices and a doll and rides on your horse – and then to disappear from her life and leave her with the growing conviction that she must have proved unlovable? I was your own niece. I could not help it that you disapproved of my paternity. I was still your sister's child. And I was still a person in my own right.'

'Rachel.' He closed his eyes and set his head back against the cushions of his chair and one hand over his heart. 'Rachel.'

She stood up on shaky legs.

'I am sorry,' she said. 'I am so very sorry, Uncle

221

Richard. Please forgive me. I never quarrel – but I have done so twice this morning, with two different people. I came to Chesbury of my own free will. It is unpardonable of me to rip into you as if it were *you* who had invaded *my* home. All that happened was a very long time ago, and you *did* offer me a home here after Papa died, even if you did tie it to a threat to marry me off to someone of your choosing.'

'A threat.' He laughed softly. 'Rachel, you were twenty-one years old and had been given no chance, as far as I knew, to meet any eligible suitors. Your father had not arranged any sort of come-out for you. I thought to do you a kindness.'

'Well,' she said, 'I did not get that impression from your letter. But perhaps that was because I was not feeling kindly disposed toward you anyway. You offered no condolences for my loss of Papa.'

'Because I was glad,' he said wearily. 'I thought his passing would finally give you a chance in life while you were still young enough to grasp it. But it was thoughtless of me not to understand that *you* would be grieving.'

'It does not matter,' she said. 'I *have* grasped my chance for happiness, but not blindly, Uncle Richard. I chose a man who was both eligible and personable. I chose someone I could love and someone who loved me.'

For the moment she was so caught up in the part she played that she believed utterly that she *adored* Jonathan.

'May I fetch you something?' she asked. 'A drink, perhaps?'

'No.' He shook his head.

'I did not know you were ill,' she said. 'I have upset you by coming here. I ought to have stayed away.'

'It is twenty-three years since your mother left here,' he said. 'She was fifteen years younger than I, more like my child than my sister. I loved her dearly. But she was impulsive and stubborn and hopelessly romantic. I mismanaged the situation with York, and though I had a good marriage of my own, there has been an emptiness in my life ever since your mother left. I am glad you have come.' He closed his eyes.

It was an emptiness he might have filled anytime during the years following her mother's death, Rachel thought, torn between a terrible grief and a rising anger. But she would not quarrel anymore with him. She really had been an even-tempered person all her life until now. Only so, she believed, had she been able to cope with her father and his friends and all the turmoil of their life.

'Uncle Richard,' she said, 'let me have the jewels. I will treasure them and so will Jonathan. We will stay for a few days longer and then leave you in peace. I will write to you. I will come to visit.'

She *would* write to him, she vowed to herself. She would confess all to him. And if he would forgive her, she would come to see him whenever she could. She would try not to hold the past against him. Perhaps they could somehow become uncle and niece to each other.

'I am not in any hurry for you to leave,' he said. 'It is a long time since there were young people in this house, Rachel. And I like your friends. They are charming ladies. It is a long time since I entertained or indeed saw my neighbors except at church. It must be twenty years since there was a ball at Chesbury. There will be one here within the next month. Stay so that we can get to know each other and so that I can get to know your husband.'

223

Rachel bit her lip. The enormity of her deception was becoming more obvious and more painful to her with every passing hour, it seemed.

'And my jewels?' she asked.

He took his time answering.

'I will not promise those to you, Rachel, even at the end of the month,' he said. 'We will see. Smith is well able to support you if he has represented himself accurately, and so you cannot need the jewels to sell. And as for wearing them – well, they are old, heavy pieces not suited to a very young woman. They are heirlooms and were entrusted to my care – first by my mother and then by yours.'

And so all this was to be for nothing, she thought – with only the tiny hope offered by his *we will see*.

She might have argued. But she noticed that his hand had come up to cover his heart once more and that his complexion again looked gray-tinged. He had not opened his eyes. She looked down at him, alarmed. But though she leaned toward him, she could not bring herself to touch him.

'I have overtired you, Uncle Richard,' she said. 'May I send your valet to you?'

She hurried from the room without waiting for his answer, but his valet was pacing outside the door and so she did not have to go in search of him.

What a strange morning it had been, she thought as she went downstairs. It had seemed longer than a normal day – or even a week. She felt emotionally drained. There had been so little passion in her life before now, either positive or negative. Now there was a superabundance of it.

The cook and the housekeeper fought back by taking

their case in person to Baron Weston. The house-keeper played her trump card immediately. If his lordship could not trust her to hire the best possible employees for each position in the house, she declared, then she would resign on the spot. But she would not tolerate ladies she did not know from Adam – or Eve – invading her kitchen and upsetting her cook to such a degree that the poor woman doubted she would be able to produce a decent meal as long as Mrs. Leavey remained at Chesbury.

Baron Weston dismissed the cook and accepted the housekeeper's resignation.

'I did not fully realize,' he said in the drawing room during the evening, following dinner, 'just how unappetizing our meals had become here. I thank you, ma'am. Carlton House cannot have served more delicious fare than you served here tonight. I thought I was off my food, but I have eaten heartily enough this evening.'

Phyllis blushed.

'And the cakes at tea this afternoon were as light as air,' he said. 'All my neighbors will be trying to steal away my cook.' He chuckled and suddenly looked better than he had in a day and a half, Alleyne thought.

Mr. and Mrs. Rothe had called during the afternoon with their son and two daughters and had taken tea. So had Mrs. Johnson, her sister, Miss Twigge, and the Reverend and Mrs. Crowell. They had all expressed great delight at making the acquaintance of the baron's niece and her new husband. All had seemed enchanted by Flossie and Phyllis, who had given herself an hour off from her duties in the kitchen. Mrs. Crowell had enjoyed a comfortable coze with Bridget. They had talked about flowers and vegetables and hedgerows and other related topics, from what Alleyne had overheard of their conversation.

'But I cannot, of course, expect you to continue working in my kitchens, ma'am,' the baron said with a sigh. 'I will have to see what my steward can suggest tomorrow.'

'But nothing would give me greater pleasure, my lord,' Phyllis assured him. 'I like to keep busy – as Colonel Leavey would explain to you if he were here. Cooking is my great love, as embroidery or painting is to other ladies.'

'With your permission, my lord,' Flossie said, 'I will step down to the housekeeper's room in the morning and look over the accounts and organize the household duties of the servants for the day. It will be no trouble at all. Although Colonel Streat employed a full complement of servants whenever we were at home, I always insisted upon keeping a close eye on them myself.'

'That is a remarkably kind offer, ma'am,' Lord Weston said, looking understandably taken aback. 'I am overwhelmed.'

While he was speaking, Bridget was fetching a cushion to set behind his head and a stool for his feet. She had already told him, while they still dined, that she would mix a special tea for him at bedtime that was good for the heart.

It amazed Alleyne that they had not all been sent packing long ago for stirring up so many proverbial sleeping dogs so soon after their arrival. But the meals had certainly improved immeasurably. And the stables, Strickland had reported while dressing him for dinner, had had at least a month's worth of muck raked out of them while the head groom busied himself giving orders and seeing that they were carried out.

'I told him,' the sergeant had explained, 'that he might be depressed on account of the baron has let most of his hunters go and don't ride no more and don't even take the carriage out most days. But that is no excuse for losing his pride in a job well done or for not doing his duty for which he gets paid and housed and fed. I told him that if he was a soldier he would be expected to keep his gun cleaned and loaded and his gear in order and his stomach free of too much rum even when he wasn't in the thick of a war on account of one never knows when our nobs are going to pick a quarrel with the nobs from another country and the guns will be firing again.'

But they had not been sent packing. Indeed, Weston seemed to be almost enjoying their company. He did watch Rachel much of the time, though, a somewhat brooding expression on his face. Yet Rachel was the only one among them who made little or no attempt to beguile the baron – or to act the part of happy new wife that she had come here to act.

She was still out of charity with *him*, of course, Alleyne realized.

They all went to bed early, as they had done the night before. Bridget commented – out of earshot of Weston – that early nights were a luxury of which she would never tire, and Phyllis heartily agreed, especially as she would need to be up early in order to prepare breakfast.

Alleyne was not so sure that these country hours suited him. He was restless. He did think of going back downstairs and outside to take a walk, but clouds must have moved over sometime during the evening, he saw from the window of his bedchamber. It was black out there, and he did not know the park well enough to venture out without some light overhead. Besides, if Weston heard him, he would wonder why his niece's husband had abandoned her bed when their marriage was still in the honeymoon stage.

Alleyne allowed Strickland to help him off with his tight-fitting evening coat and to chatter for a few minutes, but he dismissed him before undressing entirely. He was aware of silence as he stood at the window. Geraldine must have left too – he had heard her talking and laughing with Rachel a short while ago.

He walked into his dressing room. There was no light in hers, but from beyond it he could see the faint shifting glow of a candle. She was still up, then. He hesitated for some time. One of their bedchambers late at night was probably not the wisest setting for a tête-à-tête, but at least they could be assured of some privacy.

'I am coming through,' he said aloud. 'If you have modesty to preserve, do it now.'

She was at her window, as he had been at his a minute or two ago, dressed in a plain, serviceable cotton nightgown in which, of course, she looked quite as alluring as any other woman might look in sheer lace. Geraldine had brushed her hair to a smooth gloss. It hung loose halfway down her back. Her feet were bare. There was a look of surprise and dawning outrage on her face. She was hugging her bare arms with her hands.

'Don't worry,' he told her. 'I have not come to assert my conjugal rights.'

'Why *have* you come?' she asked him, her eyes taking in his shirt and breeches and stockinged feet –

228

he had come without his cane. 'You have no business being in here. Go away.'

'We are supposed to be bride and groom, Rache,' he said. 'Ours is supposed to be a love match. We are supposed to be glowing with the newfound dimension of our love that nightly beddings have brought to us. Instead we are silent and tight-lipped with each other and barely civil. Is this the way to convince your uncle that ours is a match made in heaven?'

She turned away and looked out into blackness again while he propped one shoulder against the empty door frame between her dressing room and bedchamber.

'The one thing we forgot when we agreed to this,' she said, 'was that we were going to have to do it together. You are a far better actor than I am.'

'Do you hold me in such aversion, then?' He sighed and looked at her in some exasperation. 'There was a time not so long ago when the mere sight of you coming into my room brightened my days. I was besotted with you from the moment my eyes first alit on you. Did you know that? And there was a time when you chose my company, coming to sit with me and talk with me and read to me when there was no medical necessity for you to be there. Is it possible for us to forget what happened to change all that?'

'No,' she said after a lengthy silence. 'It is not possible. Things like that cannot be put from mind by a simple act of will. I was gauche and totally unskilled and gave you a disgust of me.'

'Deuce take it, Rachel,' he said, exasperated anew, 'do you think I care about gaucherie and inexperience? It is the fact that you did not warn me that I resented. But that is all in the past. It is time we put it behind us.'

229

'It is impossible to forget it,' she said. 'It is foolish even to suggest that we try.'

'Good Lord, Rachel,' he said, 'it is just a bedding we are talking about. It was not an earth-shattering experience, perhaps, for a few different reasons, but it was not all bad either. It was just *sex*.'

'Exactly,' she said.

Women, of course, were very different from men in their attitudes to such matters. He knew that, though he did not know how he knew. It had been a foolish thing to say. The fact that it had been sex was the worst thing about it as far as she was concerned. For her, he knew, it had been earth-shattering, though not in a pleasant way.

Deuce take it, he could be hobbling about the streets of Brussels or London now, uncovering relatives and friends beneath every stone. What on earth had put this madcap idea into his head? But he knew what. Rachel had wanted to help her friends, and he had wanted to help Rachel because he owed her his life and perhaps because he had still been just a little besotted with her.

'Well,' he said, 'you are going to have to try to do a better acting job tomorrow, Rache. You are going to have to pretend you are in love with me and let it show through every pore in your body. Otherwise we will have come here in vain and will be leaving here in one month's time no better off than we are now.'

She turned to look at him.

'My uncle has a bad heart,' she said. 'He could die at any moment. He says he is glad I have come, and he wants us to stay so that he can get to know both of us – even though he observed our quarrel through his window this morning. He says that there has been an

230

emptiness in his life since my mother eloped with my father. He is determined to give a ball in our honor. But he might have done all this years ago. He might have had me here visiting frequently for the past sixteen years. He might have forgiven Mama before that and had her visit here with me. And now he is dying.'

She covered her mouth with her hand, but he could see that behind it she was biting her upper lip to control her emotions.

'Perhaps, Rachel,' he said, 'it is time you simply forgave him.'

'How can I?' she asked him. 'How *can* I? My life has been empty too. Sometimes I used to think that I was more like a mother than a daughter to my father. Taking care of him was too great a burden.'

He stared broodingly at her. What heavy baggage people carried with them from their past. Was it one advantage of losing one's memory completely? What sort of unfinished business had he been hauling about with him before he fell and hit his head?

'I hate this,' she said suddenly, walking abruptly to the bed and folding back the bedcovers. 'I hate this self-pity and this doom and gloom. This is not what I am like. This is not me. I never used to go about proclaiming that my life was burdensome and empty. I just lived it. Why should it appear to me now that it was both?'

'Perhaps because you have come here and opened the book of your past,' he said. 'And perhaps the strength of your negative emotions is a result of coming here in the wrong way – for which I am entirely to blame.'

'Don't start offering again to confess the truth to

Uncle Richard.' She sat on the bed, her hands grasping the mattress beside her, apparently quite oblivious to the message she might be thought to be sending. 'It is too late for that.'

'I wonder if you realize,' he said, 'that even if you do gain possession of your fortune, these four ladies will refuse to take a penny of it in compensation for what they lost to Crawley.'

'Of course they won't.' Her eyes widened. 'It was my fault. And their dream is all they have to sustain them.'

'I doubt it,' he said. 'They are tough women, Rachel. They have survived some of life's hardest buffetings, and they will continue to survive in their own way. They are not your responsibility – or mine. They would not wish to be.'

'I will find a way of persuading them,' she said. 'I *must*. But first I have to persuade Uncle Richard. He said this morning that he will be in no hurry to give me the jewels. You are able to support me, he said, and so I do not really *need* them. It is so unfair. I ought not to have to beg and plead. If he cares for me, he ought to give me freely what is mine.'

What she needed more than anything in her life, he thought suddenly, was some laughter. There seemed to have been precious little of it through her life. And yet she had been completely transformed by it this morning when she had scrambled about on the horse's back, getting her legs hopelessly tangled in her skirts and revealing shocking lengths of leg.

He had got her into this mess, and it was now up to him to get her out again. But at the same time perhaps he could think of ways to make her laugh again – and again.

It was something he could do for her.

'Tomorrow, Rachel,' he said, 'we are going to have to act as if we had spent all night on that bed making love. We are going to have to commit ourselves – both of us – to this charade, since you will not permit me to end it. Smile at me.'

'What?' She stared blankly at him.

'*Smile* at me,' he said again. 'It is not so difficult to do, surely. You have done it before. Smile.'

'What nonsense!'

'Smile.'

She did. She stretched her lips and looked defiant and embarrassed.

He grinned at her.

'Try again,' he told her. 'Imagine that you love me more than life. Imagine that I have just tumbled you and am on my way back for more. Smile at me.'

He was glad then that he had remained where he was, his shoulder still against the doorpost, his legs crossed at the ankles. When she smiled, the whole of his insides seemed to jostle to take up a new position. He felt a stirring in his groin but fought it, well aware that he was still wearing his very revealing evening knee breeches.

He smiled slowly back at her and was aware of her knuckles whitening as she tightened her grip on the mattress.

'I'll see you in the stables at the same time tomorrow morning,' he said softly. 'Good night, my love.'

She did not answer him. Silence followed him back to his bedchamber, where he paid the penalty for his little experiment in a full hour or more of restless heat.

Chapter Fifteen

The morning's riding lesson had to be canceled because last night's clouds had brought rain with them, and it continued to drizzle down halfheartedly until almost the middle of the morning.

As soon as it cleared Alleyne went in search of Paul Drummond, Chesbury's steward, who had agreed to show him the home farm. He was soon even more sure than he had been yesterday that he belonged on a country estate. The sights and sounds and smells of the park and the stables were all as familiar to him as the air he breathed.

He found the whole tour fascinating – the waving green sea of the crops as the breeze rippled through them, the soil of the fallow fields rich and dark brown after the rain, the cows and sheep grazing in their meadows, the pigs in their pen, the chickens and ducks roaming free in the large farmyard, the huge plot of the vegetable gardens, the orchards, the hay- and manure-smelling barn with its inevitable cow and sickly calf, the hay wagons, the plows, the rakes.

'It is a prosperous-looking estate,' Alleyne said when they were on their way back to the stables.

'It is that, sir,' Drummond agreed. 'It could be even more prosperous with a few developments and improvements, of course, but his lordship has lost some of his interest in the land since his illness. He lets me run things, but he does not want to hear about change.'

Alleyne did not probe. It was not his business. But he could sympathize with the frustration of the steward. Having energy and enthusiasm but no real outlet for either could sap a man's love of life.

Was that what had happened to him at some time in the past? Had he been a man without purpose? Without direction?

He remembered suddenly something Sergeant Strickland had said to him in Brussels.

When you finally do remember who you are, p'raps you will find that you have become a better man than he ever was. P'raps he was a man who never ever grew anymore once he reached manhood. P'raps he needed to do something drastic like losing his memory so that he could get his life unstuck.

One thing he knew with certainty. He belonged in the countryside. He belonged on the land. If he discovered after this month was over that he was indeed a military officer, he was going to sell out. If he was indeed a younger son with no fortune and no independent income, he was going to seek employment as a steward even if his family – whoever they were – considered such a step demeaning to their pride.

He could not know for certain what sort of man he had been. But *this* man was very ready to take up the reins of his own life and do exactly what he wanted to do with it.

His reveries were interrupted when Drummond

asked him some questions about his own estate in Northumberland. The ease with which he invented a property convinced Alleyne anew that at least he had the knowledge with which to make the lies convincing.

By the time he had returned his horse to the stables and walked back to the house early in the afternoon he was feeling invigorated and more cheerful than he had felt since early the morning before.

Bridget was digging out weeds at one end of the parterres. Two gardeners were doing the same thing, one in the middle, and one at the other end. Four others were strung out in a line across the lawn beyond the parterres, cutting the grass with scythes, while two lads were raking it up into heaps. The smell of freshly cut, slightly damp grass was heavy on the air.

Rachel was standing on the graveled path, watching, but she turned at the sound of his approach and smiled dazzlingly. Alleyne wondered what he had done to ingratiate himself with her until he remembered her mentioning last night that her uncle's sitting room looked down over the parterres. He smiled back at her, slid an arm about her waist, and kissed her on the lips. He made the embrace neither too long – it would have been vulgar since they were within sight of both Bridget and several servants – nor too short. But when he lifted his head, he smiled again and kept his arm about her waist.

'I have been gone for two hours,' he said, 'and it has seemed like an eternity away from you, my love.'

'All morning,' she said, 'I have been regretting that I did not go with you. The hours have seemed interminable.'

Alleyne wondered if actors onstage ever found themselves in a state of continuous semiarousal. He grinned and hugged her closer to his side for a moment before looking away from her.

'This, I suppose,' he said, nodding in the direction of the busy industry proceeding before their eyes, 'is Bridget's doing?'

'Flossie called a meeting of all the servants,' Rachel explained, 'and Bridget attended too. From the account I had from Geraldine, it sounds as if Flossie had them all ankle-deep in their own sentimental tears as she aroused their loyalty to a master who has always treated them with kindness and generosity but who is now too ill to understand that they have been slacking off. *This* was the response of the gardeners. Bridget, of course, could not resist joining them.'

Alleyne laughed, and Rachel, looking up at him, laughed too.

She was wearing pale lemon this morning, he noticed, and yet again Geraldine had done pretty things with her hair, making of it a golden halo of curls and ringlets. Of course, one did not need to notice the details of Rachel's appearance. She was always beauty personified – even when clad in a plain cotton nightgown with her hair down her back.

Purely for the benefit of her possibly watching uncle, he kissed the tip of her nose.

'Do you see the difference, Rachel?' Bridget called, straightening up and passing the back of one gloved hand over her glistening brow.

'I do,' Rachel admitted, looking along the part of the flower bed that had already been weeded. 'How brilliantly colorful the flowers look now. And how *glorious* the grass smells.'

She closed her eyes and inhaled, looking endearingly happy while Alleyne gazed down at her.

'We will make a countrywoman of her yet, Bridget,' he said.

Bridget looked from one to the other of them and smiled.

'I hope so,' she said. 'For both your sakes I do hope so, Sir Jonathan.'

Rachel had lain awake through much of that night when Jonathan had come to her room, a thousand thoughts crowding through her mind, none of them pleasant. But she had come to the conclusion that all she could do for the next month was continue what she had started and play her part to the best of her ability. She would even, she had decided, put aside her prejudices as much as she was able and give herself a chance to get to know her uncle. After all, she might never have another chance. He might not recover from another heart seizure. Anyway, she was not here to rob him exactly.

She would throw off her gloom, she had decided, and her guilt too. She was mortally sick of both. One thing was sure – she could never go back to change the past. All she could do was live the present and shape the future to the best of her ability.

And so for the next week she learned to ride – slowly, painstakingly, diligently – and was rewarded by a sense of accomplishment and an exhilaration she had rarely known before. She spent time with her uncle, often deliberately seeking him out instead of just not avoiding him when she had little choice. She participated in the numerous visits of neighbors and returned several of the calls with Jonathan and Bridget and sometimes Flossie too – though Flossie spent much of her time poring over the household books and trying to bring them from chaos to order or else bending over the estate books with Mr. Drummond while he patiently interpreted the columns and figures for her. Rachel attended church. She helped Flossie and Bridget write invitations to the ball from a list her uncle had provided.

And she let love of Jonathan flow out of every pore of her body, as he had put it, smiling at him, laughing with him, riding and walking with him, visiting the home farm with him and listening to his explanations, holding his hand, lacing her fingers with his, allowing him to kiss her hand and even her lips at every flimsy excuse, sitting beside him, talking with him, gazing at him with admiration and devotion, and generally behaving like a bride in the early days of a love match. Sometimes she almost forgot that it was all an act – on both their parts.

Her glass told her that her eyes were brighter and there was more color in her cheeks than there had been since she was a girl. Much as she longed to have the ordeal of this month over with, and much as she remembered that her friends must be eager to be on their way with sufficient funds to begin their long-postponed search for Nigel Crawley, a part of her dreaded having to leave Chesbury and return to London to seek employment again if her uncle proved obstinate about her jewels.

One day they were all eating a delicious and wholesome luncheon of vegetable soup, freshly baked bread, and cheese followed by apple pudding and custard, all prepared by Phyllis, when Rachel noticed how much her uncle's appearance had changed for the better during the past week. He had surely put on some weight. His face looked fuller and had lost its gray tinge. Sometimes he still looked gaunt and brooding, particularly when he was looking at her, but he had found the energy to do some entertaining, and he seemed altogether more cheerful. He appeared to be fond of Flossie and Bridget and Phyllis.

Rachel smiled at him.

'The rector and his wife are calling again this afternoon,' he said. 'But the rector needs to discuss some matter with me, and Mrs. Crowell will wish to discuss gardening with Miss Clover, I daresay. Drummond is taking Mrs. Streat to see the smithy, and Mrs. Leavey as usual insists upon preparing our tea and dinner. Why do not you and Sir Jonathan slip away together for the afternoon, Rachel? The last few days have been cloudy and cool, but today is sunny and warm. It would be a pity to waste such a day by remaining indoors.'

But apart from the morning riding lessons, almost all of the time Rachel had spent with Jonathan had been in company with others. She was not at all sure she wished to be alone with him when there were no horses on which to fix her attention.

She turned toward Jonathan, her face bright with inquiry, and willed him to make some excuse. And she was not the only one whose looks had changed as a result of the country air, she thought. He was sunbronzed despite the cloudy nature of the last few days, and more incredibly handsome than ever.

He smiled back at her, his eyes fairly worshiping her, and set a hand over hers on the table.

'A brilliant idea,' he said. 'Where would you suggest we go, sir?'

'The lake, perhaps,' Uncle Richard said. 'You have not been out on it yet, have you? Take one of the

240

boats out to the island. I daresay it may be somewhat overgrown this year, but it has always been a quiet retreat. There is a folly there and a pleasing prospect over the park.'

'Oh, do take Rachel over to the island, Sir Jonathan,' Flossie said. 'I daresay it is a wondrously picturesque setting. And you will be all alone there.'

There was sheer mischief in her eyes when she glanced at Rachel.

'Take a parasol to shield your complexion, Rachel,' Bridget advised.

'I am afraid of water,' Rachel said.

'Nonsense, my love!' Jonathan grinned at her and squeezed her hand. 'You stood at the ship's rail every moment when we were coming from Ostend and enjoyed yourself immensely.'

'But that was a large ship,' she protested. 'This would be a small boat right down on the water.'

'Do you not trust me to keep you safe?' He moved his head closer to hers.

Rachel sighed. 'Oh, you know I would trust you with my life, Jonathan,' she said.

'Well, then.' He raised her hand to his lips. 'The matter is settled. Thank you, sir, for excusing us from this afternoon's visit. I must confess that the prospect of a whole afternoon alone with my bride is enticing.'

'I will pack a picnic tea for you,' Phyllis said, clasping her hands to her bosom.

And so it was that less than an hour later Jonathan was stowing a picnic basket in the boat the head gardener had pointed out as the most sturdy, and Rachel was eyeing both the boat and the water with an uneasy eye. The lake had always appeared large to her. Now it looked enormous, almost like an inland sea. She could not swim, a fact that had not seemed to matter too much when crossing from England to Belgium and back. She had reasoned on those occasions that if the ship sank, the ability to swim would not greatly help a survivor anyway.

'Was this really necessary?' she asked.

'When your uncle himself suggested it?' he said. 'I would have to say yes. Besides, would you rather sit through another visit with the worthy rector and his wife?'

Rachel assumed the question was rhetorical, but she was not at all sure she would have given the expected answer if called upon. He was reaching out his hand to help her into the boat, looking quite sturdy on his feet even though he had finally abandoned his cane only a couple of days before.

The boat rocked alarmingly when she stepped into it, but Rachel sat down quickly on one of the cross benches and resigned herself to her fate. Jonathan took off his coat before seating himself on the bench opposite, and set it in the bottom of the boat with the basket. His hat soon joined them, and the breeze ruffled his longish hair. He looked healthy and virile.

'You look remarkably cheerful,' she said, opening her parasol to shield the back of her neck from the sun's rays as he took up the oars.

'Why would I not be?' he asked as he maneuvered the craft out into the water and Rachel clung to the side of the boat with her free hand. 'The sunshine is enough to fill anyone with a sense of well-being.'

'I thought,' she said, 'we were both eager to avoid being alone together.'

She glanced at his left leg, which was flexing and stretching as he rowed. It was hard to believe that this

242

was the same man who had lain on her bed in the brothel looking closer to death than life not so long ago. Who was he? she wondered. Sometimes she forgot that he was not Jonathan Smith. How strange not even to know his real name.

It must be stranger still to him.

'We are not children, though, are we, Rache,' he asked her, 'to be scrapping with each other at every opportunity? Can we agree simply to enjoy an unexpectedly free afternoon together?'

'I suppose so,' she said, turning her head to look about her. The lake water was sparkling in the sunshine. The trees on the opposite bank looked a brighter green than usual. Somehow the water seemed less frightening now that she was out on it. Or perhaps that was because he obviously knew what he was doing at the oars. 'Do you swim?'

'One of your trick questions?' he asked. 'Shall I dive overboard and see? But what would you do if the answer proved to be no and the last you saw of me was a bubble on the surface? You might be stranded out here for the rest of your widowed life. Yes, Rachel, I can swim. It is strange, is it not, that I know certain impersonal things like that about myself? Do *you* swim?'

'No.' She shook her head and trailed her free hand in the water. It was cool but not really cold. 'I never had the chance.'

'That is another thing we are going to have to put right, then,' he said.

She did not argue. She had always thought it must be lovely to swim, to be able to move through a different medium, buoyed up mysteriously by the apparent fragility of water. Now more than ever she craved to know all that she had missed by growing up

243

in London and never venturing into the country even for a short visit.

'What did you do for fun when you were a girl?' he asked.

She had hardly known the word had any meaning that could apply to her.

'I read,' she said, 'and I sewed and embroidered. Sometimes I painted. When Bridget was still with me, and I think while my mother was still alive too, I used to go for walks in Hyde Park and other places. We sometimes took a ball with us.'

'And after Bridget left?' he asked.

'I was not allowed out without a maid,' she said. 'Sometimes, when we *had* a maid, I used to go to the library. A few times I went shopping with our neighbors.'

'Going to Brussels must have seemed like an enormous adventure to you,' he said.

'In a way.' She smiled. 'But I was an employee, if you will recall, and I was kept busy with my duties.'

'Did Lady Flatley take you about with her?' he asked. 'To balls and soirees and routs?'

'No.' She shook her head. 'She was in Brussels because her son was a cavalry officer. Miss Donovan, his betrothed, was there too with her parents. I was not really needed at all except during the mornings. Or to pour the tea and run and fetch if Lady Flatley was entertaining.'

'Ah,' he said. 'Then there is no chance that you saw me anywhere.'

'None,' she said. 'The closest I came to going to any entertainment was on the evening of a moonlit picnic in the Forest of Soignés. Lady Flatley wanted me to carry her wraps for her in case the night grew colder. But Mr. Donovan decided at the last moment that he would accompany his wife and daughter after all, and there was no room for me in the carriage.'

She had been bitterly disappointed.

He was looking at her and blinking rapidly. He had stopped rowing.

'What is it?' She leaned forward. 'Were you *there*? At that picnic?'

She could see the strain on his face, the effort he was making to remember. Beads of perspiration broke out on his forehead. But after what might have been a full minute, he shook his head.

'Who hosted it?' he asked.

'I cannot remember,' she said after thinking for a few moments. 'An earl, I believe. He did not have a very good reputation, and there was talk about him afterward because he came near to compromising a young lady who was foolish enough, I suppose, to fall prey to his charm. No, his name escapes my mind. He was no one who ever came to Lady Flatley's.'

'Sometimes,' he said with a sigh, 'it is as if a heavy curtain before my memory sways and threatens to drop away altogether. But each time it falls still again and remains firmly in place. If I was in Belgium at that time, it is altogether possible that I was there at that picnic. For a moment I was sure I was. But I grow tedious with these endless references to the lamentable state of my mind. I brought you out here so that we might enjoy the afternoon. Are you enjoying it?'

'Yes,' she said.

And it was true. She was, in fact, becoming more and more intoxicated with the country. Riding, exploring the park, visiting, strolling in the lovely parterre gardens, and now boating on the lake – it all seemed like one long idyll. That was, of course, if she ignored all the negative aspects of her stay here that could rob her of joy the moment she dwelled upon any one of them. But these days she was firmly ignoring them.

Jonathan had started rowing again and was maneuvering the boat alongside a small jetty on the island. He tied the boat securely to a post and handed Rachel out.

The island seemed larger than it had from the mainland. It rose upward from the water's edge, and they climbed to the top, though they could have taken one of the overgrown paths to the left or right that apparently led around the perimeter. Jonathan carried the picnic basket, though Rachel had offered to do so out of deference to his weakened left leg, which he still favored slightly as he walked.

There were bushes and a few trees on the slope, but the crown of the hill was covered only by somewhat overlong grass and a folly at the peak. It was a ruined stone hermitage and had obviously been built that way. There was a sturdy wooden bench beneath the slope of the slate roof that offered both protection from the elements and a splendid view back across the lake to the stables and house.

But it was a lovely, sunny day with a very slight warm breeze, and the shade of the hermitage did not invite them. After Jonathan had set down the basket and Rachel had propped her parasol beside it, they strolled about the open area, looking at the views in every direction. The loveliest view was of the river water cascading over rocks into the lake some distance away.

Rachel could feel the sun warm on her bare arms and

her whole body. The sky above was a deep, clear blue. She could smell grass and flowers and water. She could not remember any other time when she had experienced a feeling of such utter well-being. Even that morning at the cascades did not really compare to this.

She tipped back her head so that she could feel light and heat on her face, stretched her arms to the sides, and turned once about.

'Is the world not a beautiful, beautiful place?' she said.

Jonathan had already moved back to the basket. He was down on one knee beside it, taking out the thin blanket Phyllis had put inside to spread on the grass. He had left his coat and hat in the boat. His shirt was moving in the breeze. So was his hair. He looked up at her, his eyes squinted against the sunlight.

'It most certainly is,' he agreed. 'And the woman standing on top of it is not its least attraction.'

She felt a rush of almost debilitating awareness. Her arms fell to her sides, and she felt foolish for her show of exuberance. The island seemed suddenly very secluded indeed. And there he was, more vital, more attractive, than any man had a right to be.

He stayed very still for several long moments, and the air fairly crackled between them. He was the one who looked away first. He got to his feet after snapping the lid of the basket closed and spread the blanket over the grass.

'The thing is, Rachel,' he said, his voice sounding testy, 'that whenever we look at each other for longer than a few seconds at a time, we feel an attraction to each other, but the image intrudes of the ugly episode that spoiled what we had together. One impulse of pure lust on my part and temptation on yours, and our friendship was gone. Nothing has been the same since.'

247

All the brightness, all the joy, had gone from the day. It felt as if heavy clouds had moved over the face of the sun, though in fact the sky remained cloudless. She clasped her hands about her forearms, as if to ward off the chill.

Lust.

Temptation.

Had there been a friendship between them? Yes, of course there had. And a certain tenderness, perhaps on both their parts.

'Take me back to the house,' she said, 'and pack your things and leave. I will explain to Uncle Richard. You need not worry anymore. You do not owe me anything.'

'That was not my meaning,' he said with a sigh. 'I just mourn for that lost relationship and wonder if you do too.'

'We do not *have* a relationship,' she told him.

'Of course we do,' he said, his voice impatient. 'I do not doubt that after the turmoil of the past you are looking forward to having the means with which to take command of your own life before you settle to marriage and motherhood. I am looking forward to discovering my past and somehow bringing my present and my future in line with it. We will go our separate ways when this month is over and very probably never meet again. But there will always be some sort of relationship between us. We will always remember each other whether we wish to do so or not. I will never forget the woman who saved my life, and I daresay you will never forget the man whose life you saved. Is *this* how we are going to remember each other? The month since that night has not been a comfortable or a happy one for us, has it?'

She had been happy during the past week. He had always seemed full of laughter and vitality. They had behaved like a couple of infatuated newlyweds in company. But he was right. With the possible exception of the mornings when they rode together, they were not comfortable in each other's company. They had been during those two weeks in Brussels before they had ended up in bed together.

'What do you suggest, then?' she asked him. 'That we shake hands and make up?'

She turned her head away to look back along the lake to the cascades. She felt like weeping. She had been a little in love with him before that night. She had been only attracted to him since – physically attracted – and it was not nearly as heartwarming a feeling.

And they had been friends too. She had lost a friend on that evening.

'What we need to do, Rachel,' he said, 'is to go back somehow and make different memories to take with us into our separate futures. Better memories.'

'What?' She looked back over her shoulder at him.

He was standing on the far side of the blanket, his booted feet apart, his hands on his lean hips, his shirt fluttering in the breeze.

'We need to make love,' he said, 'but with more pleasure, more joy, more togetherness, this time. We need to take it to a full and happy conclusion. Here in the outdoors, in the sunlight, in the summer heat. We *need* to, Rachel.'

Chapter Sixteen

The idea came to him only as he looked at her and spoke with her. But though it struck him that he might regret his words when he had the chance to consider them in a more reasonable frame of mind – he knew by now that he must always have been an impulsive sort of person – he was not sorry he had spoken. It was not her beauty alone that had put the idea into his mind, or this perfect opportunity of being alone together on the island. And it certainly was not just lust, even though he knew that he wanted her badly – that he always wanted her.

But he had spoken the truth to her. He could scarcely look at her without remembering that night. If what they had done together had seemed slightly sinful at the time, it had seemed overpoweringly so since. And it really had changed their relationship, and therefore their future memories of each other, for the worse. There had been something sweet between them – a friendship and perhaps a little more – before that, and he very much wanted to remember her as he had seen and felt about her then. He wanted her to remember him as the man she had liked well enough to sit with even when his wounds did not need tending.

They *had* to make amends for that night in Brussels.

She was gazing at him, wide-eyed, her head turned back over her shoulder.

'Are you *mad*?' she asked him.

'To believe that two wrongs will make a right?' he asked her. 'Perhaps. But although liking was all mixed up with the lust on that last occasion, basically I was a man consorting with a whore. I hate even *thinking* about that, but it is true. It says terrible things about me morally. And then I resented you after discovering the truth because you had not told me. And this was after I had *disappointed* you. It was your first time and I made it a ghastly experience for you.'

'You were not entirely to blame,' she said. 'You did not seduce me. If anything, it was the other way around. I let you believe that I worked there and that I was available that night. And then I was so gauche that ... Well, never mind.'

It struck him suddenly, looking at her, that she was the perfect lady of breeding, dressed daintily and fashionably in muslin, her hair neat and shining beneath a small-brimmed straw bonnet, her frilly parasol on the grass beside the basket. He ought to be paying gentle court to her, not inviting her to lie with him here on the grass. But her life had not developed along typical lines. Neither had his since the fifteenth of June.

She continued to look back at him across the space of perhaps twenty feet that separated them. But the thread of their conversation had broken, and there were several moments of silence during which he felt a heightened awareness of the sun beating down on them, the water sparkling below them, insects whirring in the long grass, and a single unseen bird trilling from one of the trees.

Her gaze slipped to somewhere on the grass between them.

'I will not touch you without your permission,' he told her. 'If you would prefer, we will forget everything that has just been spoken and sit down on this blanket to eat the picnic tea Phyllis has prepared for us before I row you back to the house. We will go back to the pretense and make the best of the situation until the time comes when we can part and try to forget we ever met. The last thing I wanted to do was make things worse between us.'

She opened her mouth to say something, but then closed it again and looked down at her hands, which she spread at waist level, palms down. Her face was lost to view beneath the brim of her straw bonnet.

'I do not know anything about ... making love,' she said. 'I lived a very sheltered existence with my father and a restricted life with Lady Flatley – until I met Nigel Crawley. But even he never so much as kissed my hand. I did not know what I was doing that night in Brussels with you. I do not know how to make it ... pleasant.'

He closed his eyes briefly as it struck him that his feelings were perhaps more deeply engaged with Rachel York than he cared to admit to himself.

'You do not need to know,' he said. 'I *do* know. I want to leave you with happier memories of me. I want to take away with me happier memories of you. Just tell me something, Rachel. Have there been consequences of that night? It was a month ago. You must know by now.'

That brought her eyes up to his again and turned her cheeks rosy.

'No,' she said.

'And there will not today either,' he said. 'I promise you that. Let me make love to you.'

She lifted her chin slightly and kept her eyes on his.

'Very well, then,' she said.

She came toward him then. She did not stop when she reached the other side of the blanket but walked right across it to stop a foot away from him. He untied the ribbon bow beneath her chin and tossed her bonnet to the ground, cupped her face with both hands, and set his mouth to hers.

This was, of course, no clinical, dispassionate exercise to set matters right between them. There had been an attraction between Rachel York and himself from the first moment, and it had not weakened with time even though their relationship had taken a wrong turn. It was more than an attraction, in fact – and always had been. It was a deep need, a raging passion.

On both sides – he was instantly aware of that.

They wanted each other, and now that they had mutually decided to have each other, there was no barrier of manners or propriety to cool the heat that flared between them and had nothing to do with the sun beaming down on their heads. She twined her arms about his neck and leaned into him. He wrapped one arm tightly about her waist and spread the other hand over her buttocks, drawing her even more firmly against him.

The kiss deepened. He ravished her mouth with his

tongue, and she sucked on it, driving him close to distraction. But he wanted more than urgent, mindless lust between them.

He drew back his head and gazed into her eyes, his own squinted against the sunlight and her nearness. She gazed back at him, her lips moist and parted, her eyelids heavy with a desire that matched his own. She was Rachel. She was his golden angel.

He smiled at her, and she smiled back.

He kissed her forehead and then her eyelids one at a time, her temples, her cheeks. He gentled their passion. When he returned his attention to her mouth, he kissed her more softly, tasting her lips with his tongue, nipping them lightly with his teeth. She did the same to him with soft, untutored sensuality.

He burned for her.

Lovemaking should always be done in the outdoors, he thought, feeling the coolness of the breeze and the warmth of the sun, seeing its brightness through his closed eyelids, hearing the droning and chirping of insects in the grass, aware of it soft and green beneath his feet. And holding a golden woman in his arms.

But he remembered suddenly that from where they now stood he had been able to see the house. That meant that anyone looking across here from the house would be able to see them. It would not matter – they were believed to be husband and wife, after all. On the other hand, when he had knelt on the grass a few minutes ago, both the lake and the house had been hidden from view by bushes and trees.

'We had better lie down,' he said against her lips.

'Yes.'

She lay down on the blanket, arranging her skirts neatly about her as if to preserve her modesty, and

254

looking a little self-conscious again. He went down on one knee beside her and leaned over her to kiss her softly on the lips. He touched one of her breasts through her dress, cupped it in his hand, ran his thumb over the nipple until he could feel it harden beneath his touch and could see it press against the thin muslin that covered it. He moved his hand to the other breast and then down her body, over her flat, softly feminine abdomen to pause at the apex of her thighs. He curled his fingers between to cup her and kissed her again before raising his head far enough to watch her face.

She smiled at him – a slow, almost lazy, utterly sensual smile.

His hand continued the journey downward, feeling the shapely outline of her legs. Then with both hands he raised her skirt until it was well above her knees but not so high that she might feel uncomfortably exposed. There was all the time in the world, he thought, for her to grow comfortable. He eased off her shoes and then rolled down her stockings one at a time before tossing them to the grass. He lowered his head to kiss her feet, her ankles, the insides of her knees, her inner thighs. He did not move higher. She was a woman of inexperience, and he was bound upon giving her pleasure – giving them *both* pleasure. He would not risk shocking her.

He eased the square-necked bodice of her dress off her shoulders and down her arms until she could slide her hands free of it. He suckled first one breast and then the other while her fingers stroked through his hair and then reached down to pull his shirt free of his pantaloons. Her hands came beneath it and roamed along the bare flesh of his back, raising goose bumps and catching at his breathing.

But it was almost languid foreplay in which they indulged, the heat of passion licking below the surface until the moment should come to unleash it. There was no hurry.

Passion and intense pleasure.

'Mmm,' he said, covering her mouth with his own again.

'Mmm,' she agreed.

He lifted her skirt higher and slipped his hand beneath to caress her as he kissed her. He rubbed her lightly, feeling her heat and growing moistness – *hearing* it and feeling the growing tautness of his erection. And then he felt her hand against it, lightly rubbing, though she made no attempt to unbutton his pantaloons. He parted folds with two fingers and slid them up inside her. She was slick with wetness, and he knew that the desire pulsing through him was no longer to be denied – and no longer *needed* to be denied. She was ready for him.

'Hot and wet,' he said, nipping her lips with his teeth. 'Do you know what a delicious combination that is for a man who has been invited to the feast?'

'It is not embarrassing?' she asked with a soft, breathless laugh.

He found her naïveté strangely touching. *How* could he have failed to detect it that other time? But that other time no longer mattered. This was all. This was everything.

He slid his fingers in and out.

'Infinitely enticing,' he told her. 'A woman's body ready for sex. Your body ready for mine.'

'Oh,' she said against his mouth as he lowered it to hers again.

He unbuttoned the flap of his pantaloons to release himself and then slid the blanket up beneath her as he lifted himself over her at last and lowered his weight onto her, pressing her legs wide with his knees as he did so.

'Rachel,' he said against her mouth, sliding his hands beneath her and half lifting her from the ground as he positioned himself for his mount, '*this* is the intimacy with you that I will always remember and that I would have you remember. The other memory is healed and gone – forever.'

Her lips curved into a smile beneath his.

He lifted his head as he entered her slowly but firmly, and watched the smile, though her teeth sank into her lower lip and her eyes drifted closed as he penetrated deep. He held still in her while she bent her knees and braced her feet against the ground and then tightened her inner muscles about him. He drew his hands free and lifted some of his weight onto his forearms.

Even now, when instinct urged him onward to climax and ease, he concentrated upon the pleasure of it. She was beautiful beyond belief – both his eyes and his body were fully aware of that. And the summer day was perfect, as were their surroundings. He was glad this was happening here and not on a bed somewhere indoors. He felt strangely as though they had nature's blessing, as though they were a part of it.

Part of its beauty and light and warmth. Part of its bounty.

He held still in her for as long as he could, reveling in the feel of her, the look of her, the smell of her. And reveling too in her opening eyes, heavy with desire, and her dreamy, sensual smile. They were long moments of pleasure that was very close to pain but made glorious by the knowledge that soon – very soon – it would bring them both to ease and to peace.

Maybe even to bliss.

And then her inner muscles closed slowly and tightly about him again and her eyes closed and he knew that for her there would be no more rest until he had driven her past pain.

He lowered his head to rest beside hers as he began to move in her, withdrawing to the brink of her and entering over and over again with slow, firm strokes, reading the responses of her body with his own while at the same time keeping his needs in careful check lest he finish too quickly and leave her unsatisfied and disappointed again.

She must be satisfied. Only so could he earn pardon and peace for himself.

It was warm work. After a few minutes they were both heated and damp and panting from the sun and their exertions. But she did not lie passive – not even at the beginning, when her movements were awkward and untutored. Strangely, her very lack of skill inflamed him more. But soon she used her inner muscles to match his rhythm and her feet to raise herself sufficiently from the ground that she could rock and rotate her hips to increase friction and pleasure.

Pleasuring her was sweet agony. In the end it was only agony.

But he waited for her until his body knew beyond any doubt that she was close to climaxing. He broke rhythm deliberately then, throwing her off stride before driving fast and hard into her. She gasped and moaned beneath him, tensed, strained upward against him, and then shuddered into release at the same moment as she cried out.

For all his continued pain, it was a blessed moment of redemption. He felt strangely as if he had been dirty and had suddenly been cleansed.

Her arms were tight about him as she shivered into relaxation. Female orgasms were rare, he knew. He did not know if he was normally a man who was careful of giving as well as receiving pleasure in sex, but if he had not been, then his new self had discovered a secret. Sex was an unsurpassable pleasure when it was an experience shared with his partner.

When she lay quiet beneath him, he took his own final pleasure of her, moving swift and hard and deep in her until he could hold back no longer and then withdrawing to spend his passion into the grass.

His redemption would have been of little value to him, after all, if he had impregnated her in the process.

He lay heavy on her for a few moments, savoring the pleasure, knowing from the total relaxation of her body that she was doing the same thing, and then he moved off her and lay at her side, one arm thrown over his eyes to protect them from the sunlight, his breathing and his heartbeat gradually returning to normal. The breeze felt blessedly cool against his face.

He found Rachel's hand with his own and clasped it, lacing their fingers together.

And now what? he wondered. Had he healed one wound only to open another? He remembered how he had been in love with her before that night but how he had attributed his feelings to his physical weakness. What he had just done with her had felt very like lovemaking – *love* making. But he would think of that problem later.

He drifted off into a doze, lulled by his exhaustion and the droning of insects.

She could feel the soft grass tickling her bare legs and feet. The sun had made her dress warm to the touch. Sunlight bathed her face, which was unprotected by either bonnet or parasol. Along her right side she could feel the extra heat radiating from his body. Her hand, clasped in his, their fingers laced, was sweaty. A pair of birds flew overhead to some unknown destination.

Rachel did not believe she had ever been happier in her life. No, that was not it. She *knew* she had never come even close to being as happy.

She knew too, of course, that she was in love with him, that she probably had been for a long time. But she would not allow that complication to mar her contentment in this moment. He was from a different world than her own. He was far above her socially, she suspected, even if her mother *had* been a baron's daughter. Of more significance, there was a whole life hidden somewhere in his lost memories, and even if that life did not include a wife or a betrothed, it was doubtless rich with people and experiences in which she could have no part. It was Jonathan Smith she loved. She did not even *know* the man he had been before she found him, not even his name.

She loved a mirage, an illusion, which just happened to have the flesh-and-blood body of a real man.

She was in love, but it was not and could never be a possessive thing. It was fleeting and temporary, and she was content to let it be so. She would not allow herself to suffer heartbreak when he was gone. Instead, she would simply remember him. And now she had this most wonderful, this most perfect, of all possible memories to take with her into the future she must live without him.

How precious a gift was memory.

And he had lost his!

The enormity of it struck her anew, and she turned her head to look at him. He was gazing back at her with lazy, squinted eyes, the back of his hand, which had been over his eyes a few moments ago, resting against his forehead.

'I don't know about you, Rache,' he said, 'but I feel like a sweat bath from head to toe.'

Had she expected soft, romantic sentiments?

She laughed softly. 'Did you not know,' she asked him, 'that ladies do not *sweat*, Jonathan?'

'I'll leave you here with your ladylike perfection, then, shall I,' he said, 'while I swim alone?'

She had been enjoying the heat of the sun, but as she turned slightly toward him, she could feel the muslin of her dress clinging damply to her back. When she raised her free hand to put back an errant lock of hair that was tickling her cheek, she found that it was damp. So was her forehead. The sunshine, in which she had basked a few moments ago, now felt almost oppressively hot.

'The water is probably too deep for me anyway,' she said wistfully. 'I cannot swim.'

'The water is quite shallow in the area around the jetty,' he said. 'And even if you cannot swim, you can *frolic*.'

She laughed again. 'I have never frolicked in my life,' she said. And yet she felt a strange surge of longing to do just that, to behave like a child, to have fun for the simple ... *fun* of it.

261

He sat up, releasing her hand as he did so, and pulled his shirt off over his head. Then he hauled off his Hessian boots one at a time and stood to remove his pantaloons. He grinned down at her, clad only in his drawers. The only imperfection Rachel could see on his whole person was the fading scar of the wound on his left thigh. He had a body that was perfectly sculpted, perfectly proportioned.

She remembered suddenly that he had once told her that if there was any imperfection in her person, he failed to see it.

'You are not embarrassed, are you?' he asked her with a grin, holding out his hands to his sides. 'You have seen me in less.'

'I am not embarrassed,' she said. Why should she be? He had just been inside her body. She still felt tender and pleasantly sore where he had been.

'If we are going to frolic,' he told her, 'that dress is going to have to go, Rache.'

She stood and undressed down to her shift. Far from being embarrassed, she felt light and exuberant and free. For the first time in her life she was going to bathe in the outdoors. She pulled the pins from her hair and shook it loose before turning to him and laughing again – for no particular reason except that she was happy.

He was looking at her with narrowed eyes.

'I am ready to frolic,' she told him.

'Immerse me in cold water quickly,' he said, 'before I explode.'

Still laughing, Rachel ran down the slope ahead of him toward the lake. She shrieked a few times when her bare feet encountered sharp stones, but she kept going.

Chapter Seventeen

Perhaps one of the most attractive things about Rachel York, Alleyne concluded as he caught up to her, passed her, and splashed into the water ahead of her, was that she seemed largely unaware of her extraordinary beauty. She was nothing short of dazzling.

He did not know what sort of life he would discover once he left here and found the missing part of himself. He did not know what sorts of relationships, commitments, devotions, were woven into the fabric of that man's life he had somehow left behind on the ground in the Forest of Soignés. And there must, of course, be some caution about immersing himself too deeply into the new life he had found since then.

But now, at this moment, he was in love with Rachel. And he was going to enjoy the moment. Simply that. The past was hidden behind that curtain in his mind, and the future was even more unknown than it must be to most people. But today was pretty wonderful.

And so was she – both pretty and wonderful.

She set one foot in the water, laughed, and withdrew

it. Her legs were long and shapely.

The water was chest-high where he stood a short distance into the lake. Another few steps backward and it would be shoulder-high and then over his head. But there was a sufficient area shallow enough to accommodate someone who could not swim.

She tried the other foot and withdrew it too.

He dipped his hands deep and heaved two mighty handfuls of water at her. She shrieked. And then she jumped in up to her waist and disappeared until only her hair floated dark gold on the surface. She came up sputtering and gasping and clawing at her tightly closed eyes.

While he was still grinning at her, his guard totally down, a great wall of water collided with his face and had him coughing and sputtering too.

She might not be a swimmer, but she was a worthy water warrior.

'Oh,' she cried to him after immersing herself again, 'this is wonderful. The water is actually warm.' She pushed back her hair, which lay sleek over her head and down her back to the water, where it floated on the surface. 'How do I swim?'

'After several lessons and much practice,' he said. 'Were you thinking of challenging me to a race to the opposite bank and back?'

'Teach me,' she demanded.

Her timidity with horses – which she was overcoming with great grit and determination – did not extend to water, it seemed.

He taught her how to float, a skill she learned surprisingly fast despite a few sinkings and sputterings that called for some hearty pounding on the back. And even after she had learned the trick of it she

264

could stay on the surface for only a few seconds before sinking gradually from view. But she had made an impressive start.

'I will have you swimming on both your front and your back before the summer is over,' he told her before remembering that they were going to be gone from here long before the summer was over.

He left her in the shallow water and struck out into the lake with powerful strokes, reveling in his returned strength and in the cool buoyancy of the water.

There was a tree growing on the bank not far from the jetty, a few of its branches stretching obligingly over the lake. Alleyne swam toward it and noted that at this particular spot the water was deep. And one at least of the branches looked sturdy.

'Where are you going?' Rachel called as he pulled himself up onto the bank, which fell off sharply just here, and water streamed from his body.

'Diving,' he said, grinning back at her.

Climbing a tree when one was almost naked was not comfortable going, of course. But he knew it was something he had done many times before. He sat down on the branch and inched out along it, careful not to be taken unawares if it should prove to be weaker than it looked. But it held his weight without either bowing or breaking.

'Do be careful,' Rachel called from some distance away. She was standing up in the water and shading her eyes with one hand.

He grinned down at her and stood up slowly on the branch, using his arms for balance. It still held. He had to show off for her, of course. He walked out to the very end of the branch, struck a pose, his body straight, his arms out ahead of him. And then he bent his knees and launched himself off into space, his arms straight above his head, his chin tucked in, his legs together, his feet pointed back.

He cleaved the water and streaked through it, arcing upward a moment before he would have crashed against the bottom. There was the familiar surge of exuberance at having done something daring and dangerous and long-forbidden during his growing years, and then he broke the surface, shook the water clear of his eyes, and grinned toward his equally daring, reckless coconspirators and partners in crime.

But only Rachel York was there, her hand pressed over her mouth and then dropping away as she smiled in obvious relief.

There was a feeling of deep, stomach-churning disorientation.

Who was it he had expected to see?

Who *was* it? It was more than one person actually. Let him remember just one of them, though. Just one. Please? Please let him remember just one.

Rachel was wading in his direction, a look of concern on her face, but she stopped when she was shoulder-deep and the floor of the lake was still falling away beneath her feet.

'What is it?' she asked him. 'You hurt yourself, did you not, you foolish man. Did you hit your head? Come here.'

He was treading water. He gazed back at her, but he did not go to her. He swam to the bank instead, pulled himself out, and made his way up the slope without looking back.

There was no reason why he should not remember, was there? His head wound must have healed by now both inside and out. The headaches had gone away except when he strained too much to remember. He had *been* prepared to be patient. He had been patient. But sometimes panic attacked him like a thief in the night.

He sat cross-legged on the blanket, draped his wrists over his knees, and bowed his head. He tried to concentrate upon deep, even breathing. He tried to bring his consciousness to a place below his chattering, frightened mind.

He did not hear her coming. He knew she was there only when one cool arm came about his shoulders and the other slid beneath his arms to circle his waist. Her head came to rest against his shoulder, facing away from him. Her wet hair fell down over his arm. She was kneeling beside him, he realized. She did not say a word.

'Sometimes,' he said after a while, 'I feel completely unmanned.'

'I know,' she said. 'Oh, Jonathan.'

'That is not my name,' he said. 'I have been robbed even of my *name*. I do not know who or what I am, Rachel. I am more of a stranger to myself than you are or Geraldine or Sergeant Strickland. At least you can tell me stories about yourself and I can form impressions of you as a person who is a product of her upbringing, though you have brought your own unique character to bear upon it. I have no such stories of myself. My oldest story is of waking up in the house on the Rue d'Aremberg to see four painted ladies looking down at me. That was not much longer than a month ago.'

'I know who you are,' she said. 'I do not know the *what* of your life. I do not know any of your stories except the ones in which I have shared. But I know you as a man of laughter and vitality and generosity and daring. I do not believe you can have changed in essential qualities. You are still *you*. And I have seen your courage in the weeks since I have known you. You may believe at moments like this that you will collapse and let life slip away from you as something meaningless that you no longer value. But you will overcome such moments. I know it because I know *you*. I do. I wish I could call you by name because a name is important – it becomes part of a person's identity. But even without a name I *know* you.'

He listened to his breathing again, but after a couple of minutes he noticed that he had tipped his head to one side to rest against the top of hers.

'Do you know why I suggested this charade?' he asked her. 'I did not even realize it myself until this moment. It was not entirely for your sake, though I did believe at the time that it would be best for you to wrest your fortune from a tyrant who cared nothing for you. It was for my sake so that I would not have to go in search of my identity.'

'You were afraid you would not find out who you are?' she asked him.

'No!' He pressed his cheek more firmly against her damp hair. 'I was afraid I *would*. I was afraid I would discover my father and my mother and not know them. Or brothers and sisters. Or a wife and children. I was afraid I might look at them and see only strangers. I might see a *child*, Rachel, a child I begot and loved, and that child might be a stranger to me. And so I gave myself a reason for not going yet. Perhaps my memory would come back naturally if I waited, I thought. Or I *suppose* that is what I thought. It was not conscious.'

'Jonathan,' she said softly, and held him for long minutes while he grappled silently with the blackness of despair.

'I suppose,' he said at last, lifting his head, 'Phyllis will be mortally offended if we do not eat every last crumb of the tea she sent with us.'

'Yes,' she said.

'Are you hungry?'

'A little,' she admitted. 'Yes, actually, I am ravenous.'

'I could eat the proverbial horse,' he said, realizing in some surprise that it was true, even if not quite literally. 'And should we be amazed when we have indulged in a bout of vigorous lovemaking and a brisk swim?'

She did not answer him. She moved instead to the picnic basket, which she opened and began rummaging inside. Her drying hair hung about her face like a dark gold curtain, so that he could not see her expression. She seemed to have forgotten to dress before eating.

He gazed at her, though not with lascivious intent. What would he have done without her all these weeks?

What would he do without her when the month was over?

Life at Chesbury Park settled into something of a pattern after that day on the island. And despite the fact that she had got herself deep into a tangle and could not see any way of getting herself out of it, Rachel was almost happy.

269

She loved living in the country. Strolling in the parterres or through the park beyond them, riding with Jonathan with increasing ease and skill, learning to swim and row on the lake, picnicking in various beauty spots, sitting in the drawing room window watching the rain come down on wet days, visiting various parts of the farm with Jonathan and Flossie and Mr. Drummond, calling upon the laborers with baskets of food supplied by Phyllis, riding in the carriage to call upon neighbors, exploring the village shops and being shown around the church and the churchyard by Mr. Crowell – she could never have enough of it all, she believed.

She could be happy here for a lifetime without ever craving the busier activities of London. There was somehow a feeling of rightness about it all, as if she belonged here.

She was enjoying her uncle's company too, unwillingly at first but then with a kind of gratitude and joy. She had taken to visiting him most mornings in his sitting room while he rested. Sometimes they sat looking out the window, scarcely talking at all, though their silences were never awkward – sometimes he even dozed. Sometimes he told her stories about her grandparents and about her mother. She felt as if she were gradually regaining a heritage of which she had been almost totally unaware.

He took her and Jonathan to the portrait gallery on the upper floor one rainy afternoon when there were no visitors. It was a room that was not kept locked, though she had avoided going there until then. He explained her relationship to a whole host of ancestors pictured there, and she felt a welling of emotion as the emptiness, the loneliness, of her life began to fall away from her. She *did* belong.

The only portrait of her mother was a family group, painted when she was three and Uncle Richard was a slender, good-looking, golden-haired young man. Rachel almost feared to look at first, but then she peered hungrily at the little girl with her rosy, round cheeks and mass of blond ringlets. She could not fit that child's face to the very vague memory she had of her mother's, though.

'She looked like you when she was older,' Uncle Richard said.

'Papa always regretted that he had not had her portrait painted,' Rachel told him. 'Sometimes I try and I try, but I cannot bring her face to mind.'

Her hand was in Jonathan's, she realized at that moment, and he was lacing his fingers with hers and tightening his grip. He was comforting her, and yet at least she knew who her mother had been. She could remember her father clearly. Uncle Richard was still alive. This was her ancestral home, and here were the portraits of her ancestors.

She turned her head to smile at Jonathan. There had been a certain quiet tenderness to their relationship since that afternoon on the island, though they had both been careful not to invite a repetition of what they had done together there. Neither had breached the open doorways between their rooms since then. And yet there was that tenderness, which was not an act on either of their parts, though it was winning Uncle Richard over to approving their supposed marriage, Rachel sensed, even more than their earlier attempts to look like a couple in love had done.

She was glad she would be able to remember him this way – though there was an ache of almost

271

unbearable pain about her heart at the thought that the day of their parting was drawing closer.

It seemed to her that Jonathan had found some contentment during these weeks too. It was very obvious to her that he loved the farm. He spent a great deal of time out there or talking with Mr. Drummond. He also spent a great deal of time with Uncle Richard, and she knew that they talked about farming, that sometimes Jonathan worked into the conversation ideas for developments or innovations that Mr. Drummond had suggested to him or that he had thought of for himself.

Uncle Richard even gave the nod of approval for a few of the suggested changes. He liked Jonathan, she thought. He respected him.

She *wished* there were an easy and painless way out of the tangle they had got themselves into, but she could not see it. And so she would not dwell upon it. After this was all over, she would confess the truth and beg forgiveness, and then it would be up to her uncle whether to grant it or not.

Her four friends, she sensed, were happier than they had been all their lives.

Apart from the fact that she could not keep the household accounts because she could not read or write, Geraldine had assumed most of the duties of the housekeeper. She was busily and happily organizing the indoor servants, even the menservants, since the butler was elderly and seemed not even to notice that he had lost control, and she had everyone engaged in conducting a full inventory of linens and china and crystal ware and silver and other household items of any value. The house had begun to gleam under her rule. She still insisted upon being Rachel's maid, but during her spare time she sat in the house-keeper's parlor, working at mending jobs.

She was quite unlike the Geraldine Rachel had known in Brussels, but she seemed somehow to be in her element. She fussed over Sergeant Strickland until he – not unwillingly in Rachel's estimation – took over much of the leadership role with the menservants and became unofficially the butler, though Mr. Edwards still held the title.

Phyllis was happily cooking and ruling her new domain, the kitchen at Chesbury Park. And since she was such a superb cook and good-natured to boot, no one seemed to resent her intrusion.

Flossie, in addition to keeping the household books with meticulous care, was busy being courted by Mr. Drummond.

'You do not have to worry, any of you,' she assured them all one night when they were gathered in Rachel's dressing room and Sergeant Strickland was standing in the archway between the two dressing rooms, his massive arms crossed over his massive chest. 'I have told Mr. Drummond the truth about myself without implicating any of you. He knows who I am, and he still wants to step out with me, the foolish man.'

'Lord love us, Floss,' Phyllis said, clasping her hands to her bosom, 'how romantic! I think I am going to weep. Or swoon.'

'Don't do that, Phyll,' Bridget advised. 'You would knock your head against the edge of the washstand – and then you would swoon again over the sight of your own blood.'

'Are you going to have him?' Geraldine asked Flossie. 'I would offer to be your bridesmaid, Floss, but it would look strange when I am Rache's maid, wouldn't it?'

'He is a *gentleman*,' Flossie said, looking rather tragic.

'So?' Geraldine planted her hands on her hips and looked belligerent.

Flossie did not answer.

Bridget walked back and forth to the rectory every few days, visiting Mrs. Crowell and her garden. She also kept disappearing into the park at every opportunity with various garden implements and a large apron and her wide-brimmed straw hat.

None of them seemed overly impatient to be off on the trail of the villain who had stolen both their money and their dream. And Jonathan had described his reluctance to begin his own search.

And so Rachel relaxed into an enjoyment of the weeks that preceded the ball Uncle Richard had insisted upon hosting.

Much preparation had gone into making it an impressive entertainment, and the neighborhood was buzzing with the happy prospect. No one else for miles around had a ballroom, and even though there were occasional assemblies in the rooms above the village inn, there was apparently a special sense of awe surrounding a private ball in a private ballroom.

What she would do, Rachel had decided, was enjoy the event to the fullest, and then, after it was over, do something decisive about the future. She would ask Uncle Richard once more for her jewels, and if by chance he gave them to her, then she would go away, sell at least some of them, and do with the proceeds what she had planned to do. If he did not agree, she would give up trying to persuade him and simply go away.

Her friends would be on their own. So would Jonathan.

She had tried to do something for him. She had written to three of her acquaintances in London, and she had had replies from two. Neither had knowledge of any gentleman who had been missing since the Battle of Waterloo. She had not expected that they would. But she was disappointed nonetheless, she had to admit to herself. She would have liked to help him recover what he had lost in that fall outside Brussels.

She would never see him again after they left here, she supposed. It was altogether possible that she would never hear of him again either, that she would never know if he had found his people and his past. There was something quite devastating in the thought. But she would not let herself dwell upon it.

Neither would she allow herself to wonder what she would do after she had left here. Much would depend, of course, upon whether she had her jewels with her or not.

And what about her uncle? How would he feel when he learned how much he had been deceived? Again, she supposed, much would depend upon whether he had given her the jewels or not.

She still did not know how deeply he cared.

Despite everything she looked forward to the ball with almost feverish excitement. She had never attended any entertainment nearly so grand, and never a ball. She could dance only because her father had liked to dance and had taught her during his brighter, more carefree moments, humming the tunes himself and teaching her to be both precise and graceful in her steps.

But to dance with other gentlemen in a ballroom with a real orchestra . . .

To dance with Jonathan ...

There were no words with which to express her sentiments.

Uncle Richard had summoned the village seamstress and commissioned her to remain at Chesbury for a few days to make the ladies' gowns if they so desired. Rachel was given no choice. She was to have a new ball gown, and no expense was to be spared. There was a brief argument with Jonathan about who would pay for it, but Uncle Richard would brook no opposition to his will.

'Rachel is my niece, Smith,' he said, holding up one hand, palm out. 'If I had had my way, she would have had a come-out in London when she was eighteen and I would have footed the bill for the whole Season. As it stands, *this* is her come-out ball as well as her wedding ball, and I am not to be denied the pleasure of clothing her for the occasion.'

His strange words might have upset Rachel a little, but who was she to be indignant over a lie? Anyway, she was touched more deeply than she cared to admit over her uncle's obvious eagerness to make amends.

'Thank you, Uncle Richard,' she said, very close to tears. 'You are generous and kind.'

Jonathan merely bowed to him and did not argue further. Would he have been able to pay for the gown anyway? Rachel wondered. How much did he have left from his winnings in Brussels?

The last few days before the ball passed happily and rather as if they had wings. And finally the day of the ball itself arrived. Morning slipped into afternoon as servants, including numerous extras hired especially for the occasion, hurried about in order to get all ready in time. And the afternoon slipped away

276

until it was finally time to retire to their rooms to dress for the evening.

It was only when Rachel entered her dressing room and saw all her finery laid out and Geraldine waiting with a steaming hip bath that reality struck her. She was almost sick with anticipation – this was, after all, her first ball. But it was also the beginning of the end.

Tomorrow ...

But she would not think of tomorrow yet.

There was tonight to live through first.

Chapter Eighteen

Oh, Lord, Rache, I could weep,' Geraldine said. 'But instead I'll find a quiet corner and dance the night away with Will, whether he wants to or not.'

Rachel felt rather as if she could weep too. She had never looked even half so magnificent before.

Her gown was of white lace over a white satin petticoat, the high-waisted skirt very full even though it clung in soft folds about her figure when she stood still. The deep lace flounce at the hem was trimmed with a green leaf design and embroidered with delicate sprigs of greenery. The sparse bodice was of spring green satin, the short, puffed sleeves striped green and white. Her satin slippers were green, her long kid gloves white. Geraldine had dressed her hair high on her head, though curls had been allowed to soften the outline of her face at the temples and along the back of her neck. She wore two white hair plumes, which had been woven into the back of her coiffure and curled invitingly over the top of her head.

'You have done wonders for me, Geraldine,' she said with a sigh as she stood before the pier glass in her dressing room.

'I do believe nature did that,' another voice said. 'Geraldine has merely added the finishing touches.'

Jonathan stood in the archway between their dressing rooms. Rachel spun about to face him. He looked as magnificent as ever in his evening clothes, which she had first seen the evening they arrived at Chesbury. But he himself had changed since then. He was sun-bronzed and looked fitter. He had had his hair cut, though one lock of it still fell invitingly over his right eyebrow.

Even if she were being impartial, Rachel did not believe she had ever seen a more handsome man.

'My, my, my,' Geraldine said to him. 'Don't you look gorgeous? I wish now we had tied you naked to the bedposts in Brussels while we had the chance.'

He grinned and wagged a finger at her and looked doubly handsome. His teeth looked dazzlingly white in his bronzed face.

'Among the four of you, though, Geraldine,' he said, 'you would have worn me out and I would be a mere shadow of my former self by today.'

'Even your shadow would be something to sigh over, though,' Geraldine told him. 'Is Will still in your rooms? I have to go teach him to dance.'

'He has fled belowstairs already,' Jonathan told her. 'To hide from his ghastly fate, I believe.'

'The poor love,' Geraldine said fondly as she swept from the room. 'He does not know when he is beaten.'

Jonathan smiled at Rachel and she realized that of course she could no longer see him impartially. For almost a month she had been playing the part of his devoted wife, and the pretense had had a definite effect on her emotions. And during that time there had been the afternoon on the island – neither

279

repeated nor referred to since, though it had certainly not been forgotten.

How could she *ever* forget?

'You really do look beautiful,' he said, stepping fully into the dressing room.

'Thank you.' She smiled wistfully at him. 'I am going to enjoy myself tonight more than I ever have before. It is my first ball and perhaps my last. This is the end, Jonathan. You do realize that, do you not? Tomorrow we will go to my uncle and ask again for my jewels. But if he says no, I am not going to continue the fight. The day after tomorrow we will leave here no matter what. And then you will be free.'

'Will I?' he asked her softly. 'Rachel, we need to—'

But a knock at her dressing room door interrupted him. He strode toward it and opened it. Rachel's uncle stepped inside and then stopped abruptly.

'Ah, Rachel,' he said, his eyes roaming over her, 'you cannot know how I have longed to see you just so. Or how I longed to see your mother decked out for her first ball.'

She did not want to quarrel with him on this of all nights, but the question was out of her mouth before she could stop it.

'Why did you say,' she asked him, 'that I would have had a come-out Season at the age of eighteen if you had had your way?'

He waved away the chair that Jonathan offered him.

'Your father would not hear of it,' he said, 'just as he would not allow me to have you here for holidays as you grew up and just as he would not allow me to send you to a good girls' school. From what you have said in the last few weeks, I gather that he never allowed

280

you to have any of the gifts I sent for Christmas and your birthday each year. He would allow your mother no communication with me after their marriage – until she was on her deathbed. I no longer blame him entirely. I mismanaged the business of their courtship. I was young and dictatorial and quite unyielding. I drove them to elope. But how can I be sorry it happened when their union produced you?'

It was strange how simple the truth was. And how quickly it could cut through sixteen years of misunderstanding. Uncle Richard had *not* neglected her – or her mother. They had all suffered long years of separation and unhappiness because long ago two stubborn men had quarreled over one woman – one as her brother and guardian, the other as her lover.

'Uncle Richard,' she said, taking two steps toward him.

But he held up a staying hand.

'We will sit down and talk about it tomorrow, Rachel,' he said. 'You and I and your husband. There is much to say, but it can wait. Nothing is to threaten our pleasure tonight. Tonight I will finally see you dance at a ball I am hosting – with a husband who is worthy of you and capable, I believe, of giving you the lifelong happiness you deserve.'

Rachel felt rather as if a knife had been plunged into her stomach and twisted. Ah, the price of deception! Jonathan had clasped his hands behind him and was gazing intently at her.

'I have come with this,' Uncle Richard said, holding up a velvet box she had not noticed until now. 'They were your aunt's, Rachel, and will now be yours. I am glad you are wearing no other jewelry.'

He opened the box and Rachel found herself gazing

281

at a string of small pearls with an emerald set in diamonds pendant from it. At one end of the box were emerald and diamond earrings to match.

'My wedding gift to you,' he said.

Rachel thought her legs might well buckle under her. Then she felt Jonathan's arm firm about her waist.

'It is a beautiful set, sir,' he said. 'I have been silently lamenting the fact that I have not yet had a chance to buy jewels for my wife. But now I am almost glad. May I?'

It was Jonathan who took the necklace from the box and clasped it about Rachel's neck. It settled heavy and cold and magnificent against her bosom, the emerald nestling in just above her cleavage. He clipped the earrings to her ears. He smiled at her, still the consummate actor, just as if he did not feel the terrible tragedy of what was happening.

'Uncle Richard.' She closed the distance between them and touched him for the first time. She wrapped her arms about his neck and pressed her cheek to his. But there were no meaningful words to force past the painful lump in her throat. 'Uncle Richard.'

He patted her back. 'They are not needed to enhance your beauty, that is for sure,' he said. 'But they are where they belong nevertheless. To whom else would I give Sarah's jewels? There is only a distant cousin and his wife, and I never see them.'

She would have to give them back tomorrow, of course. The necklace felt like a chain of guilt about her neck. But she had promised herself tonight. More important, she owed her uncle tonight. Perhaps at some time in the future – pray God he lived so long – he would find it in his heart to forgive her for what she had done or at least remember this evening with less pain than he was bound to feel after learning the truth.

She stepped back and smiled and linked her arm through his.

'Shall we go down?' she suggested.

She turned her smile on Jonathan and linked her other arm through his. He pressed it reassuringly to his side, but really what consolation could he offer?

This scheme of theirs had seemed like *such* a lark when he had suggested it back in Brussels. She had agreed to it. And so she could not blame him for any of the consequences.

This was a country ball and nothing to compare with some of the grander *ton* squeezes of the Season in London that Alleyne was sure he must have attended. But what it lacked in numbers and glitter it more than made up for in enthusiasm.

All the guests, it seemed, had come to enjoy themselves. And enjoy themselves they did as the orchestra played and the dancers tramped out the lively and complex steps of one country dance after another.

But no one outshone Rachel. Or squeezed more enjoyment out of the evening. Alleyne was dazzled by her. So were many of the other guests, he could see.

He was more than dazzled. He was, of course, head over ears in love with her. He had known it without any doubt at all since their afternoon on the island. It had been mortal agony to keep aloof from her in private since then while engaged in the double deception of pretending to pretend deep love and devotion in public. The three empty doorways that stood between their bedchambers had been an invitation more and more difficult to resist.

But instead of drawing her deeper into an entanglement with him that might lead to nowhere but heartbreak for her once he recovered his past, he was determined to do something for her. It had been as clear as the nose on his face almost from the moment of their arrival at Chesbury that her uncle loved her and that she could be happy here. It had become even clearer since the brief explanation for his apparent neglect that Weston had made in Rachel's dressing room before the ball. This was where she belonged.

After they left here, Alleyne had decided, he was going to come back. He was going to confess the truth to Weston, take all the blame on himself – where it rightfully belonged – and plead her case. If Weston loved her as deeply as Alleyne believed he did – unconditionally, that was – then he would forgive her and bring her back home. In time she would marry and settle down and belong somewhere even after Weston died.

Perhaps if his own search led him to the discovery that he was not, in fact, a married man or a betrothed man . . .

But he dared not think of that yet.

They danced the opening set of country dances together. If they were at a London ball and this were her come-out, Alleyne thought, her manner would be severely censured by all the highest sticklers. It was fashionable for young ladies of the *ton* to wear an air of ennui, as if the transition from schoolroom to ballroom had necessitated a transformation from youthful gaiety to mature cynicism.

Rachel looked like joy personified.

She also knew the intricate steps of the dance and

performed them with careful precision for a few minutes until she laughed suddenly and kicked up her heels both figuratively and literally.

Alleyne laughed back at her.

'Perhaps you should save some energy for later in the evening,' he said.

'Why?' Her cheeks were already flushed and her eyes sparkling. 'Why do we always save everything of value for later? I want to live *now* Now is perhaps all I have.'

'Now is all we ever have,' he said, laughing again as he kicked up his heels with her. But it was a phrase that rang in his head long after he had spoken the words.

He caught sight of Weston, who was standing close to the double doors of the ballroom with one of his neighbors. He was watching Rachel, his head nodding in time to the music, a look of contentment on his face. He still did not look like a healthy man, but his complexion was no longer gray, and he was no longer thin to the point of gauntness. He no longer looked like a man with one foot in the grave.

If only he could live for a year or two longer – for Rachel's sake.

They both danced with other partners for the next several sets. Alleyne danced with Flossie and Bridget among others. He had long ago given up the hope – or fear – of being recognized in this neighborhood. Very few of the neighboring families, he had learned, visited London a great deal, and none of them moved in *tonnish* circles.

The dance before supper was a waltz – the only one of the evening. A number of couples took to the floor, but not as many as for the other sets. Rachel was standing with her uncle, her hand linked through his arm.

285

'You are not waltzing?' Alleyne asked her after strolling up to them.

'Alas,' she said, 'I do not know the steps.'

'Then it is time you did,' he said, offering her his hand.

'Here? Now? I think not,' she said, her eyes wide.

'A coward, my love?' He smiled at her. 'I'll teach you.'

'Go on, Rachel,' her uncle urged.

Alleyne thought she was going to refuse. But then she laughed and set her hand in his.

'Why not?' she said. 'If I make a great spectacle of myself, I daresay I will give amusement to the guests and provide them with a topic of conversation for the next week or so.'

It was not easy to teach someone to waltz when the music was playing and other couples were twirling about the floor and an audience looked on. But the members of the audience quickly understood what was happening and called out encouragement and laughed and applauded and generally seemed to be enjoying themselves more than ever.

And Rachel continued to sparkle even while she stumbled and stalled and laughed and determinedly tried to follow his instructions and his lead. And then suddenly, after a few minutes, she picked up the rhythm and the steps and laughed into his eyes instead of down at her feet.

'I am waltzing,' she said.

'You are waltzing,' he agreed. 'Relax now and let me lead.'

She did just that, and soon they were waltzing with tolerable skill, though he did not attempt any fancy steps or twirls. He watched her teeth sink into her lower lip and her smile fade as her eyes remained on his. His arm was about her waist. Her hand rested on his shoulder. Their other hands were clasped. There were only a few inches of space between their bodies. He could feel her body heat. He could smell gardenia.

He had ridden with her, walked with her, even swum with her since that afternoon on the island. But he had scarcely touched her since then and had avoided being close to her like this. She had avoided it too.

But what could they do now? They were waltzing together in the Chesbury ballroom, a few dozen eyes watching them and the other dancers. And yet somehow it seemed as if they were alone, twirling slowly through a magic world that was doomed to disappear soon. After two or three more days, he might never see her again.

Beautiful, beautiful Rachel. His golden angel.

'Well,' he asked her after they had danced for several minutes in silence, 'what is your verdict on your first ball?'

'It has been magical,' she said, echoing his own thought. 'It *is* magical – present tense. It is not over yet.'

But he could see her awareness that it almost was. This was a country ball. People in the country did not dance all night as they did in London during the Season, when most of them had nothing to do with themselves all the next day but sleep and get up to socialize again. The ball would end soon after supper – and supper would be served right after the waltz.

A certain light had gone out of her eyes as she gazed at him. And then they were bright again – with tears that she tried to hide by dipping her head sharply downward.

Fortunately they were close to the French windows

that opened onto a balcony. He waltzed her through them and stopped by the stone balustrade. The night air felt blessedly cool after the fragrant stuffiness of the ballroom.

'Jonathan,' she said, one hand closing about the emerald pendant of her necklace, 'I cannot do this any longer.'

He knew exactly what she meant and set one hand against the back of her neck.

'It never occurred to me,' she said, 'that perhaps I would love him. And that perhaps he loved me. It never occurred to me that perhaps there was an explanation for his apparent neglect.'

'You ought to have come here when he invited you,' he said.

'After my father's death?' She gazed away toward the lake, across which a band of moonlight shone. 'I felt bruised and battered. I thought that if he had had any vestiges of feeling left for me, he would have come in person as he did after my mother's death. It did not occur to me that he was ill and could not travel, and I suppose it did not occur to him to let me know. Perhaps he assumed that I already did. His letter seemed abrupt and imperious. It seemed cold.'

'If you had come then,' he said, 'you would not have gone to Brussels and become involved with Crawley. You would not have incurred this sense of deep obligation to your friends. You would not have become involved in this charade.'

'And I would not have met you,' she added.

'Now there is a thought.' He laughed softly. 'If you had come here last year when your uncle invited you, I would very probably be dead.'

'I think,' she said, 'I would hate that.'

'So would I,' he said fervently.

'Look,' she said, pointing downward.

There, in a paddock behind the stables, two people were dancing in the moonlight, the man large and somewhat ungainly, the woman tall and voluptuous. Geraldine and Strickland.

'Now there is a match made in heaven,' he said before turning to set his back against the balustrade so that he could look more closely into Rachel's face. 'So what is your plan?'

'Tomorrow,' she said, 'I am going to explain to the ladies that I cannot help them, though I will always consider myself in their debt and will repay them when I am able – in three years' time. We are all going to leave here the day after tomorrow without asking Uncle Richard for my jewels. And then, once I have returned to London, I will write to him to tell him the full truth. And I will return this jewelry. You will be free to do what you must do. You will be free to find your family. It has only recently occurred to me that I have wronged them by agreeing to your plan to help me and so keeping you from them a whole month longer than necessary. What pain they must have suffered.'

'Why wait until after you leave here?' he asked her. 'Your uncle loves you, Rachel. He always has.'

She shook her head.

'Let me go to him tomorrow,' he said, 'and tell him everything. I believe I can break it to him in such a way that he will forgive you. How can he not when he learns that this deception was my suggestion and that you agreed to it only because you love your friends and felt that you owed them a debt of honor? *And* because your father kept from you all knowledge of Weston's concern for you and his attempts to be an uncle to you. He will understand how intolerable your deception has become to you now that you have had a chance to get to know him and love him. Let me do this for you.'

She turned her head to look at him.

'No,' she said. 'I have got myself into this mess and I will get myself out. I did not have to agree to your suggestion. I am not a mindless puppet.'

'Then tell him yourself in person,' he said. 'Do it tomorrow, Rachel, and trust his love for you. He has loved you all your life.'

'It is too late,' she said, 'I do not deserve anyone's trust. Or anyone's love. I have forfeited both. The music is ending. We must go in to supper, and we must look bright and happy. *He* is looking happy tonight, is he not? And better than he looked when we first came? We must give him the rest of tonight at least. Or rather *I* must.'

If someone would only be obliging enough to put a gun to his head, Alleyne thought, he would gladly pull the trigger himself.

He offered her his arm.

One thing Rachel had not expected, though she knew that the ball was partly in honor of her marriage, was that there would be speeches and toasts during supper, and a large cake, which she and Jonathan cut and then took from table to table to serve to the guests.

She smiled and smiled and felt sick inside.

She really had used no imagination at all when she had thought this an excellent way of getting her hands on money so that her friends would be free to travel about England in pursuit of revenge.

But there was worse to come. When Rachel and

Jonathan finally sat down and there was a stir among the guests in preparation for a return to the ballroom and the final few sets of the evening, Uncle Richard got to his feet again and held up his hands for silence. It fell almost instantly.

'I think it appropriate,' he said, 'to make this announcement publicly, though I did originally intend to inform my niece and nephew-in-law privately of it tomorrow. It does in a sense concern the whole neighborhood after all. It is probably general knowledge that I am the last male of my line and that my title will die with me when the time comes. But fortunately my estate and fortune are mine to leave where I will, since they are unentailed. There is a distant cousin on my mother's side whom I have long considered, though he lives in Ireland and I have not met him above two or three times in my life. I always did intend to leave a sizable portion of my fortune to my niece, Rachel, Lady Jonathan Smith, of course, since she is my closest relative. But I have got to know her and have grown to love her dearly during the past few weeks, and I have got to know Sir Jonathan as a steady, dependable young man with an obvious and intelligent interest in the land. I have made arrangements to rewrite my will tomorrow. My niece will inherit everything after my days are done.'

Rachel did not hear the swell of interest and the applause that followed the announcement. She could hear only a buzzing in her ears as her head turned icy cold. She was about to faint, she realized. She bowed her head forward and covered her face with both hands while she felt Jonathan's hand against the back of her neck. She drew a few steadying breaths.

Her uncle was standing beside her when she lifted

291

her head again. She got to her feet and hugged him wordlessly while there was a murmur of approval from the guests and another smattering of applause.

'It is what will make me happy, Rachel,' he said, beaming at her as he set her at arm's length. 'Happier than anything in the world.'

'I don't want you to d-d-die,' she said before wrapping her arms about his neck and burying her face on his shoulder.

But *she* wanted to, she thought suddenly. She just wanted to die.

Rachel never afterward knew how she got through the rest of the evening. But she did, smiling and laughing with strangers, assiduously avoiding everyone she knew. She concentrated upon being the radiant bride, and – heaven help her – she succeeded.

She also succeeded in hurrying up to her room in the flurry of activity that followed the departure of all the guests. But she had reckoned without her friends' total lack of consideration for closed doors – and there were not even any of those between her bedchamber and Jonathan's. Within a few minutes of her arrival they were all there – Bridget, Flossie, Geraldine, and Phyllis crowded into her dressing room, Sergeant Strickland in the archway, his arms crossed over his great chest.

'Well, Rache,' Geraldine said, 'now you are in a pickle.'

'We did not even hear about it at the time on account of we were outside,' the sergeant said with what in a lesser man might have been construed as a blush. 'Geraldine and me, I mean. We was looking at the horses.'

'We were dancing, Will,' she said. 'And then we were kissing. And then we came inside and Phyll told us.'

'My love,' Bridget said, 'we had better go away from here.'

'Away?' Phyllis looked blank. '*Away*, Bridge? Who is going to cook for the baron?'

'I came here to ask for my inheritance,' Rachel said. 'It seemed so logical at the time to pretend I was married and to bring my supposed husband with me so that Uncle Richard would be persuaded that I could be trusted with my jewels. I wanted desperately to be able to help you all find Mr. Crawley and to repay you what he stole from you. Now I cannot do it – any of it. We are going—'

'Just a moment, Rachel.' Flossie held up a hand. 'What is this about repaying us? *You* were going to give back what he took? When he used you so ill and took everything you had too? Are you daft?'

'Without me,' Rachel said, 'you would not even have met him.'

'Rachel, my love,' Bridget said, 'we would not even think of taking a penny from you beyond what we planned to borrow for our journeys until we could pay it back.'

'I would think not,' Geraldine said, hands on hips. 'Do you have windmills in your head, Rache? You did not steal the money from us.'

Phyllis hurried across the small room and caught Rachel up in a tight hug.

'But the thought was beautiful, Rachel,' she said. 'Do you know how long it is since anyone had a beautiful thought about us girls? And *this* has been beautiful – this stay at Chesbury Park. I have been happier here than I have been anywhere else my whole life. I think we all have. And we have you to thank for such a splendid holiday. So don't you go adding guilt about us to your other woes.'

'But what woes they are, Rache,' Geraldine said.

'What you need to do, missy,' Sergeant Strickland said, 'not that you have asked me and not that it is my business to say anything anyway on account of I am only a one-eyed gentleman's gentleman and not a very good one yet into the bargain – but what you need to do, missy, and you too, sir, though you have gone into your bedchamber instead of coming to face the music out here. What you need to do is get married for real, and then everything will be solved.'

'It would be wonderfully romantic,' Phyllis said. 'You are quite right, Will.'

'No,' Rachel said firmly. 'That is not an option. I intend to put everything right in the next little while and then I am going to sort out my life. The last thing I need is a forced marriage. And it is the very last thing Jonathan needs. I will work things out.'

Though heaven knew how. Uncle Richard had looked so *happy*. She had not even known that his property and fortune were unentailed. She had not even given the matter a thought.

The ladies had plenty more to say, but Rachel did not listen. Sergeant Strickland retreated into the other dressing room, and finally the four ladies went on their way, all talking at once after hugging Rachel. And then Geraldine remembered that she was Rachel's maid and came back to undress her and brush out her hair.

It seemed like forever before Rachel was alone and able to crawl off to bed and pull the bedcovers up over her head.

Chapter Nineteen

An hour or so after Sergeant Strickland had finally left for the night, his silence loud with disapproval and unspoken advice, Alleyne was still standing at the window of his bedchamber, staring out into the moonlit park. He doubted Rachel was sleeping either.

He wondered if he should go to Weston in the morning without her knowledge. But he doubted he would. He had done enough to harm her without taking away her freedom to deal with this matter herself, as she clearly wished to do.

He felt rather than heard or saw movement and turned his head to see her standing in the doorway to his dressing room. There were no candles burning, but his eyes had grown accustomed to the darkness. She was wearing the same white nightgown she had worn the night he had walked into *her* bedchamber. Her hair was loose.

'I thought perhaps you would be sleeping,' she said.

'No.'

'Oh.'

'You had better come here,' he said when she stood

there mutely, apparently with nothing else to say.

She came, hurrying toward him before stopping abruptly two feet away.

'I want you to leave,' she told him. 'In the morning.'

'Ah,' he said.

'Yes,' she said. 'I am going to tell my uncle everything. I *have* to. I cannot have him changing his will in my favor, can I? But he will blame you as much as he blames me. He will accuse you of having compromised me and insist that you marry me. At least, that is what he *may* do if he does not just simply order us both off his property. But I have to think of all the possibilities and be prepared for them. I *will not* have you coerced into marrying me, Jonathan.'

'I cannot be,' he said. 'We have discussed this before, remember? Until I know my identity and until I know whether I am already married or not, I cannot marry you or anyone else – or even promise to marry you.'

'But you will find out who you are,' she said. 'And you may discover that you are single. I will not have anyone try to force you into marrying me. It would be grossly unfair to you. You did this for me, and I freely agreed to it. Besides, I do not want to marry you. It is altogether possible that I will never marry, but if I do, it will be because I have found the love of my life and the certainty of a lifetime of happiness – as much as one can be certain of any such thing. I am not insulting you, Jonathan. I know that you are as reluctant as I to be forced into any marriage, and therefore I can speak plainly so that you will not feel *obliged* to offer if the time should ever come. But I do not intend it to happen

296

anyway. You are to go away – early, before Uncle Richard is up.'

'This is good-bye, then?' he asked her.

'Y-yes.'

He took one of her hands in his. It was like a block of ice. He chafed it between both his own.

'I will not do it,' he said. 'We will face him together tomorrow.'

Honor as much as concern for Rachel dictated that he face Weston with her, if that was her intention. Weston had come to trust him. He must look the man in the eye as he admitted that that trust had been misplaced.

She shivered.

'We had better get to bed,' he said.

'Together?'

That had not been what he meant. But he could sense that she needed company and perhaps more than that. She needed to be held. And he, God help him, wanted to hold her.

'Is it what you wish?' He raised her hand to his lips.

She nodded. 'If it is what you wish.'

He laughed softly and drew her to him. She lifted her face to his and their mouths met – hungry with longing and need and the desire to give and to draw comfort.

What had Geraldine just called it? A pickle. They were in a pickle. Tomorrow, for better or worse, they would extricate themselves from it. In the meantime there was tonight.

He stooped down and lifted her into his arms for no other reason than that he *could* now that his leg was healed and strong again. He carried her to the bed and set her down in the middle of it before stripping off his clothes and joining her there.

They made love only once. They did it slowly, thoroughly, almost languorously. It was not just sex, Alleyne realized in the middle of it – at least, it was not sex in its rawest sense. Neither was it really love, since it appeared she did not love him, as she dreamed of one day loving a man. But it was something precious nevertheless. It was a warm sharing of human comfort. And there *was* comfort.

She was asleep almost before he had disengaged his body from hers and settled beside her, though she burrowed in against him first. He rested one cheek against the top of her head and followed her into oblivion.

Rachel pushed her breakfast plate away from her, her food almost untouched. She found it difficult even to look at Jonathan. She had gone to him in the middle of the night in order to persuade him to leave Chesbury early this morning, and she had stayed to sleep in his bed. Not just sleep there . . .

It was very mortifying.

But it was not Jonathan who had taken her appetite away. Uncle Richard was up, though he was breakfasting as usual in his own rooms. He had sent his valet down to ask her and Jonathan to wait upon him there at their earliest convenience.

Geraldine was upstairs, packing Rachel's trunk. They would all be gone by noon at the latest. Rachel tried to concentrate upon that thought. But there was this morning to live through first. And how would she be able to feel any relief even when they were finally on the road when she had thrown so much away and would be leaving her uncle behind, angry, upset, and betrayed? And then the final parting from Jonathan would be imminent.

Sometimes life seemed so bleak that the only consolation was that it could not possibly get worse.

She got to her feet and pushed away her chair with the backs of her knees. Jonathan got up at the same time. Uncharacteristically, neither Bridget nor Flossie said a word as they left the room.

Uncle Richard was seated in his usual chair, though it had been turned to face into the room this morning. He was looking ill again, Rachel noticed. Last night had been too much for him. And now this morning . . .

'Sit down,' he said, his manner grave.

'Uncle Richard,' she said, 'there is something I must say. There is no point in delaying it. I will just—'

'Please, Rachel.' He held up a hand. 'There is something *I* must say first. I have been too cowardly to say it before now, but the time has come. Sit down, please. And you too, Smith.'

Rachel perched unhappily on the edge of a chair while Jonathan sat back in another.

'I believe I would have made the decision I announced last night even without any other incentive,' her uncle said. 'I have always longed for you to be here, Rachel, and for you to discover that this is where you belong. And now I have seen it as well as the happy fact that you have a husband who loves and understands the land and who will always look after it even if the two of you will make your principal residence far away in the north of England.'

'Uncle Richard—'

'No.' He held up his hand again. 'Let me finish. I believe I would have made the decision anyway, though it may seem to you in a moment that I have simply bought you off in order to salve my conscience. I planned to tell you today that I would withhold your jewels until you are twenty-five, since that was basically your mother's wish. I reasoned that I would probably be dead by then.'

'Don't say that.' She leaned forward in her chair. 'I do not even *want* the jewels.'

He sighed and set his head back against the cushions. His complexion was gray-tinged again, she could see.

'They are gone, Rachel,' he said.

'Gone?'

'Stolen,' he said.

Jonathan got to his feet, poured a glass of water from a jug on the tray beside her uncle, and set it down close to his hand. Then he went to stand at the window, looking down on the parterre gardens.

'Stolen?' Rachel whispered the word.

'I am not even sure exactly when or how or by whom,' her uncle said. 'They just were not there when I went into the safe for something else a week or so before you arrived here. I found it impossible to suspect anyone who was employed here, even if their service *had* become slipshod over the past couple of years. And yet the only stranger who was in my library and could have seen where I keep my valuables was a *clergyman* – and a man of conscience and charity at that. It would make no sense to suspect him.'

Jonathan turned his head back over his shoulder, and his eyes met Rachel's.

'A clergyman,' she said. 'Nigel Crawley?'

'Nathan Crawford,' her uncle said.

'Tall, blond, and handsome?' she asked, her eyes widening. 'Very charming? Between thirty and forty years of age? Perhaps with a sister accompanying him?'

He stared at her. 'You *know* him?' he asked.

'I believe I sent him here.' She laughed rather shakily. 'I met him in Brussels when I worked for Lady Flatley. I was even betrothed to him. We were returning to England to marry and then come here to see you and persuade you to give me my jewels. But I overheard him talking with his sister, and they were laughing about what they would do with all the money they had been given for their charities. They also had with them a large sum of money from my friends who are with me here – all their life savings, in fact.'

Uncle Richard had closed his eyes. He looked deathly pale.

'A number of people here gave to his charities,' he said. 'I did too. I gave him the money when we were in the library together and did not even try to hide the safe from his eyes. He seemed eminently trustworthy. I suppose he came back for the jewels. Chesbury is not hard to break into, and my servants have not been vigilant of late. But however it is, Rachel, they are gone and I have done nothing to recover them. I have not known what to do or whom to suspect.'

Strangely, given the lengths to which she had been prepared to go to get her hands on the jewels, Rachel was far more concerned about her uncle at that moment than about them. They had caused her nothing but grief. Let them go and good riddance. She got to her feet, hurried over to his chair, knelt on the floor before him, and set one cheek on his knees.

'It does not matter, Uncle Richard,' she said. 'It does not. He did not hurt you, and that is all that matters. I have never even seen the jewels. I will not miss what I have never had. I am almost *glad* they are gone.'

'Perhaps you do not realize what a vast fortune was there,' he said, his hand resting on her head. 'How can I forgive myself for the deception I have perpetrated against you ever since you arrived here? I ought to have told you immediately. I ought to have sent in search of you as soon as I missed them.'

'Uncle Richard,' she said, 'you know *nothing* about deception.'

His hand smoothed over her hair. Jonathan at the window cleared his throat. Rachel's heart hammered against her ribs.

'If you were betrothed to Crawford or Crawley or whatever his name is,' her uncle said into the silence, 'then how—'

'Sir,' Jonathan said, 'it was Rachel who introduced Crawley to her friends. He took their life savings, with their blessing and hers, supposedly to invest the money safely for them at a London bank. Rachel blamed herself for their considerable loss and vowed to herself – without their knowledge – that she would pay them back every penny. To do that she needed her inheritance. She needed to sell a few pieces of the jewelry.'

Rachel had closed her eyes.

'And what is your part in this, Smith?' Uncle Richard asked.

'I owe Rachel my life,' Jonathan said. 'She found me abandoned and close to death after the Battle of

302

Waterloo and nursed me back to health. She needed a husband if she was to persuade you to allow her to have her inheritance early.'

'And you are *not* her real husband?' Uncle Richard asked.

'No, sir.'

It was unfair to allow him to do all the explaining after all, Rachel thought. She really had not intended for it to happen. But she kept her eyes closed. This whole ghastly morning seemed to have moved out of her control.

'Why not?' Her uncle's voice was low and stern.

'I regained consciousness to find myself without memory,' Jonathan explained. 'I know nothing about my past. I do not even know if I am married to someone else.'

'You are not Sir Jonathan Smith, then?' Uncle Richard asked.

'No, sir,' Jonathan said. 'I do not know my real name.'

'And you do not have an estate and fortune in Northumberland.'

'No, sir.'

'It was all my fault,' Rachel said. 'Jonathan felt he owed me his life, and he knew that I wanted to get my hands on my jewels more than anything else in life. And so he offered to help me. It is all my fault. Absolutely all of it. He is in no way to blame. But I could not keep up the deception, especially after last night. I never *ever* knew about the birthday gifts and the offer to send me to school and the offer to give me a Season. I thought you had completely forgotten about me. I thought you hated me. And I could not *bear* it when you gave me my aunt's necklace and

303

earrings and then told everyone that you had decided to leave everything to me because you loved me. I came here this morning to confess everything to you. Jonathan insisted upon coming with me.'

'Well, bless my soul,' her uncle said after a short silence.

Then he did something so unexpected that Rachel jumped in alarm.

He started to laugh. At first it was a mere tremor that might have been fury, then it was a low rumble of sound that might have been a death rattle, and then it was a hearty bellow that was unmistakably laughter.

She sat back on her heels and looked up warily at him. But she had always found laughter infectious even when she did not know its cause. She certainly did not know the cause of this. But her lips twitched, she felt a giggle bubble up inside, and then she covered her face with her hands as she dissolved into laughter.

'There *is* a truly marvelous absurdity about it all,' Jonathan said dryly.

And then they were all off into whoops of merriment over matters that had seemed enormously tragic just a short while ago – and surely would again when they had calmed down and thought everything through.

Sometimes, though, Rachel thought later, when she had a chance to think, farce merely breeds farce. Before any of them had quite sobered in order to face reality, the door crashed open without any heralding knock, and Flossie strode into the room, Geraldine, Phyllis, and Bridget on her heels. Flossie was waving a sheet of paper in one raised hand.

304

'He is in Bath, Rachel,' she announced. 'The villain is in Bath, charming all the old dowagers out of their pittances and going by the name of Nicholas Croyden. But it's him, right enough.'

'We are going after him, Rache,' Geraldine said. 'Will is going to hold him down while I pull out his toenails one by one.'

'I am going to batter in his nose until it is poking out the back of his head,' Phyllis added. Appropriately, her arms were liberally coated with flour and she was brandishing a rolling pin.

'I am going to pull out all his hair and stuff a pillow with it,' Bridget said, 'and then ram it down his throat.'

'This,' Flossie said, waving the letter, 'is from one of the sisters. She is going to keep a friendly eye on him until we get there. Are you coming with us, Rachel?'

Uncle Richard cleared his throat.

'Rachel,' he said, 'I think it is time you introduced me properly to your friends and, er, your maid.'

They all went to Bath. At first it seemed that Phyllis would remain behind, smitten at the prospect of leaving Lord Weston without proper food to restore his health and fatten his person. And then Rachel tried to insist that Alleyne go to London without further delay, since their masquerade was over. She would remain at Chesbury, she declared, if her uncle would have her. Bridget then announced her intention of staying with Rachel, since she was now officially an unmarried young lady again and needed a chaperon. Strickland, who had been hovering outside the door of Weston's sitting room from the beginning, explained at great and convoluted length that though he would like to go with the ladies to protect them and pound Crawley to a pulp on their behalf, he felt it his duty, at least until he got his feet properly under him, so to speak, to go with Mr. Smith as his valet. Then Geraldine recalled that she was Rachel's maid – until she remembered that with all explained and out in the open she no longer was so. Nevertheless, she was reluctant to leave just when she was bringing order belowstairs and was over halfway through the household inventory she was supervising. Flossie then turned all soft-eyed and mentioned the fact that Drummond had taken her out on the lake in the moonlight the night before and proposed marriage to her and that she had not said yes, though she had not said no, either. She had promised him an answer today or tomorrow.

And then it seemed as if no one would go.

But Weston spoke up.

'It is remarkably poor-spirited of everyone to choose to remain here when adventure beckons from Bath,' he said. 'I daresay I will have to go alone, then.'

'Oh, splendid!' Flossie exclaimed, crushing the letter to her bosom. 'You are a right good sport, my lord. Mr. Drummond can wait for his answer.'

And then all the clamor and confusion resumed as everyone suddenly found every reason to go to Bath and none to remain behind.

Rachel did not take her uncle's decision lightly, of course.

'You *must* remain quietly here, Uncle Richard,' she said. 'You are not strong enough to travel. I will remain with you and everyone else can go. Except Jonathan.'

'Rachel,' he said, 'I expected this morning to be one of the darkest of my life. Instead it has given me a new lease on life. Despite the loss of your jewels, which may well never be recovered, I have never been so diverted in my life. I would not for worlds miss the action in Bath.'

Alleyne's thoughts had been neither solicited nor offered. But he did find Rachel looking at him wide-eyed after her uncle had spoken – and of course all the ladies followed suit. So did Strickland – minus the wide eyes – from beyond the doorway.

'London can wait just as easily as Drummond can,' Alleyne said, grinning at them all. 'So can my memories and my former life. Strangely and somewhat alarmingly, though, I have the feeling that this present life is not so very different from the old one. Being involved with madcap people in madcap schemes appears to come naturally to me – and was not I the one who suggested the last one? I am off to Bath even if no one else is.'

'Good,' Geraldine said. 'Do you hear that, Will? You will be coming too.' And *very* interestingly, Alleyne noticed, she blushed.

But his attention was almost instantly diverted. Rachel was smiling at him, her eyes shining with pleasure and dancing with merriment.

'Bath may very well find,' she said, 'that it cannot contain us all.'

'I certainly hope so.' He winked at her.

No stranger spirited into the room at that moment would have known that almost all of them were the victims of recent and devastating thefts and that all had been involved in prolonged and complex deceptions until confession time just a few minutes ago.

They all launched into mirth at the prospect of what their arrival would do to staid and respectable Bath society.

It really was extraordinary, Alleyne decided. It was also a great relief not to have to pretend any longer, and to know that Rachel had found the home where she belonged and that she would be happy and safe here after this business was all over with – and after he had gone.

But he would think of their parting when the time came.

In the meanwhile Baron Weston saw his solicitor, as planned, and rewrote his will.

And early the next morning they all set out for Bath in a veritable cavalcade of carriages and baggage coaches with the avowed intention of making Nigel Crawley, alias Nathan Crawford, alias Nicholas Croyden, sorry that he had ever been born.

Chapter Twenty

Baron Weston took rooms for them all at the York House Hotel, the best that Bath had to offer, despite protests from the ladies that they could not pay for them – not, at least, until they had accosted Nigel Crawley and wrested their savings from him. He would pay the bill, Lord Weston told them all, and that was that. He did not want to hear another word on the matter. At his suggestion they were all to keep the identities they had assumed when they arrived at Chesbury, except for Rachel, who reverted to her real name, and Geraldine, who was elevated to the rank of Miss Geraldine Ness, sister of Mrs. Leavey, whom she resembled about as much as a horse resembles a rabbit.

Rachel's uncle took to his bed for the two days following their arrival, desperately weary after his journey and the excitement that had preceded it. Rachel sat with him much of the time, more worried about him than all the jewels and all the villains in the world. But she was cheered to learn from the physician who was summoned to attend him that it was indeed only exhaustion that ailed him and not any descernible recurrence of his heart problems.

She sat with him, in silence when he needed sleep or merely quiet, and talking to him when he had a little more energy. She even read to him on occasion. She was powerfully reminded of another sickroom she had haunted and another patient she had tended not so very long in the past – though it seemed an age ago.

She saw very little of Jonathan and resigned herself to the fact that this really was the beginning of the end. He would not return to Chesbury Park with her, she guessed, though that was where she would go. Uncle Richard had already invited her to live there, and she had accepted. There had been no cold duty involved in either the invitation or the acceptance, she knew. Incredibly, he loved her – he *still* did despite what she had done to him. And perhaps even more incredibly, she loved him. During those days, she bathed herself in the light of a love that was unconditional and made no demands on her.

He had even accepted her friends, though they had frankly confessed to him just who and what they were. He had done more than accept them, in fact. He actually *liked* them.

'Rachel,' he said one afternoon after waking from a nap, 'I did not feel any great degree of admiration for your father, but somehow he raised you well. Not many ladies would condescend to befriend four of society's most shunned members just because one of them had been her childhood nurse, and even fewer would recognize a debt of honor to them or go to such extreme lengths to pay it. But your actions have reaped certain rewards, I believe. They are as true friends to you as any you are like to make among your peers.'

'They are, Uncle Richard,' she agreed. 'They took

310

me in when I was destitute even though they had just lost almost everything they had saved for their retirement.'

'And Miss Leavey can cook like a dream,' he said with a sigh.

She was content, Rachel told herself. Whether they found Nigel Crawley or not, whether they recovered any of their property or not, this adventure had turned out far more happily than she had ever deserved.

And she was glad she saw so little of Jonathan.

She would be gladder still when he had left for good. Then her heart could begin to heal and perhaps she could look forward to happiness as well as contentment. And yet she dreaded the moment of his leaving. Once it was over, she told herself, she would be fine. It was just the moment itself. She mentally rehearsed what she would say to him, how she would look. How she would *smile*.

The ladies meanwhile spent the two days visiting the friends whom they called sisters and gathering more information about the clergyman, Nicholas Croyden, who had taken rooms with his sister on Sydney Place and was often to be seen charming all the widows and unattached ladies of uncertain age with whom the spa abounded. He was reputed to put in an appearance at the Pump Room each morning for the fashionable stroll and drinking of the waters, though none of the sisters consulted had ever set foot in that hallowed place.

'*We* will, though,' Flossie said when they were all gathered for dinner in the baron's private dining room on the second evening. 'It is an eminently respectable place for Mrs. Streat, widow of Colonel Streat, to go, and for her sister-in-law and *her* sister and their dear

311

friend Miss Clover. We will go there in the morning.'

'Yes, we will,' Jonathan agreed. And he turned his head and inclined it elegantly to Rachel before grinning at her. 'May I have the honor of escorting you there, Miss York? With your uncle's permission, of course, and under the chaperonage of Miss Clover, whose company is much in demand for the occasion.'

He was enjoying himself, Rachel thought. He really was a daredevil at heart. She guessed that he always had been and felt a pang of regret over the fact that she had never known him then and would not know him after he had returned to that other life.

'Thank you, Sir Jonathan,' she said. 'It would be my pleasure.'

'And mine too,' her uncle said. 'No one is leaving me behind. We must just hope, I suppose, that we will not be faced with the sad anticlimax of the gentleman sleeping in and failing to appear for the morning promenade.'

'Uncle Richard—' Rachel began. But he held up a staying hand.

'Most people come to Bath for one of two reasons, Rachel,' he said. 'Because they are on a repairing lease or a small pension and Bath is cheap, or because their health is not all it ought to be and they wish to take the waters. I am one of the latter. I will take the waters – in the Pump Room tomorrow morning.'

'And we,' Geraldine said, quite unabashed, 'are the former. Though not for long. I'll squeeze that villain when I get my hands on him until he spews money.'

'Very genteel language, Gerry,' Flossie said, clucking her tongue. 'Remember who you are, if you please. Ladies do not *spew* or cause to be spewed. You will squeeze him until he *ejects* our money. I'll help.'

312

'What I do not understand,' Rachel said, frowning as she cut into her pudding with her spoon, 'is why he would appear in a public place like Bath when there must be so many people in England now who will recognize him.'

'It is a calculated risk,' Jonathan told her. 'Remember that most people actually *gave* him the money for his charities. Far from pouncing on him with fury if they should happen to see him again, they would probably greet him gladly and make yet another contribution – though they might wonder about his changed name. However, it is unlikely that he meets many people a second time. The sort who were in Brussels during the spring are not the sort who frequent Bath. Next he will probably go somewhere like Harrogate, another spa, of course, but one that is far north of here and unlikely to attract the same clientele.'

'Well, *this* time,' Phyllis said, 'he has made a big mistake. He ought not to have tangled with us. Though we might not have found him, might we, if he had not used a name so similar to the one we knew him as. I wonder why he did that? If I were him, I would be Joe Bloggs this time.'

'Who would give a donation for some poor deprived orphans to a *Joe Bloggs*, though, Phyll?' Geraldine asked. 'Use your imagination.'

'I see your point,' Phyllis said.

Jonathan excused himself soon after that, and the rest of them retired early.

Baron Weston was recognized and greeted by a number of his acquaintances when he made an appearance in the Pump Room early the next morning. But it was his companions who aroused most interest since all of them, with the possible exception of Bridget, were young, and even she was a good twenty or thirty years younger than most of those who had come there to stroll and gossip and – in a few cases – drink the waters.

Flossie and Phyllis were soon borne off by a retired general, one on each of his arms, to walk about the room as he asked about their experiences with the armies and shared his own. Geraldine and Bridget were taken under the wing of a haughty dowager distinguished by a tall bonnet with a formidable array of plumes towering above it and a lorgnette that she used expansively as she talked, rather like a particularly flamboyant conductor of an orchestra with his baton. Rachel stood at the water table with her uncle and was made much of by a steady parade of fellow drinkers. Alleyne found himself in conversation with an elderly couple who claimed to know Smiths from Northumberland and persisted in trying to ascertain if they might be of the same family to which Sir Jonathan belonged.

Nigel Crawley did not put in an appearance. Not that Alleyne had ever met him to recognize him again. But he knew the man's description. A tall, blond, handsome youngish gentleman would not be difficult to spot amid the somewhat sparse crowd gathered in the Pump Room.

It *was* something of a disappointment given the feverish excitement of all the ladies as they had set out from the York House Hotel earlier. Once he had seen them back there for breakfast, Alleyne thought, he would walk over to Sydney Place to discover for himself if the man and his sister were still in residence there.

It was a lovely day and warm even so early in the morning. Those who had strolled in the Pump Room were in no hurry to return home. As if they had not conversed and gossiped enough indoors, many of them continued their conversations outside in the abbey yard. General Sugden was unwilling to relinquish the company of his two charming companions and regaled them with one more story of a battle in which he had figured as the conquering hero. The dowager trusted she would see Miss Ness and Miss Clover at the Upper Rooms one evening and invited them to take tea with her there. She hoped too that they would bring Baron Weston and his niece and Sir Jonathan Smith with them. Three ladies and two gentlemen detained the baron and Rachel, and the elderly couple who knew the Smiths from Northumberland suddenly recalled that they were actually *Joneses* – an understandable error on their part since for some reason Smith and Jones were names easily confused. They wanted to know if Sir Jonathan was acquainted with any of the Joneses from that county.

There must have been a morning service at the abbey. A small congregation of the faithful was spilling out into the yard and proceeding to do what the Pump Room crowd was doing – stand about in conversational groups. There was even some intermingling among the groups.

Included among the worshipers were a tall, blond, handsome gentleman and a fair-haired lady, whose hand was tucked beneath his elbow. With them was a group of four ladies of indeterminate age, all of whom were listening to what the blond gentleman was saying with identical looks of pious adoration.

Alleyne darted a quick glance at Rachel. But if he had felt any doubt at all, it disappeared when he saw the look on her face. Her eyes were riveted upon the man who had just stepped out of the church, and her face had paled. Alleyne looked quickly back at the man – at the very instant when his eyes alit on Rachel and perhaps on Weston too.

His smile vanished and he dipped his head forward and clutched the brim of his hat with his free hand, muttered something that must have been an excuse to the ladies, and turned sharply about, intent, no doubt, upon hurrying away.

'Leave me to handle this,' Baron Weston said as Alleyne closed the distance between himself and Rachel and drew her arm firmly through his own.

But it was too late for any discreet handling of the situation. Phyllis had spotted her prey, and with a shriek she dashed away from the general's side when he was still midsentence and launched herself upon Crawley's back, her arms about his neck, her legs about his waist.

'Got you at last!' she cried. 'You villain, you.'

Flossie was not far behind.

'Well, if it isn't the Reverend Creepy Crawley,' she said, and kicked him in the shin.

Geraldine had brought a parasol with her. She advanced upon him like an Amazonian warrior with a spear poised for action. She poked him in the ribs with the point of the parasol.

'Where is our money?' she demanded. 'You black-hearted cur, you – what have you done with it? Speak out, man. I can't hear you.'

'Oh, dear,' Bridget said, hurrying along to join the fray, 'you have dropped your hat, Mr. Crawley, and

316

someone has stepped on it and ruined it.' She knocked it from his head and jumped up and down on the fashionable, clearly expensive hat until its tall crown crumpled flat and was gray with dust.

For a few moments the numerous spectators to this spectacularly vulgar display formed a silent, motionless tableau about it. And then everyone moved and spoke at once.

The general advanced with his stout cane to the rescue of his ladies; the dowager with the lorgnette blessed her soul and looked about for acquaintances with whom to share the delicious scandal of the moment; strangers materialized, seemingly out of nowhere, to fill the yard; the fair-haired lady screeched for help; the four besotted churchgoers wailed and screamed and beseeched his four attackers to release their dear Mr. Croyden; the attackers paid them no attention; Alleyne and Rachel and the baron approached closer; and the victim of the attack went on the offensive.

'Far be it from me to condemn anyone, being a man of the cloth who loves *all* humanity as our Lord did,' he managed to say while trying to deflect the parasol point and dislodge Phyllis from his back – and while every member of the audience tried to shush every other member, 'but these four women ought not to come within a mile of so genteel a place. It is not seemly. They are all whores.'

The general's cane was obviously more effective than Geraldine's parasol. Crawley winced when it connected with his middle, and let out an inelegant grunt of pain.

'Such remarks as that, young man,' the general said sternly, 'invite pistols at dawn.'

317

The crowd had fallen silent, unwilling, no doubt, to miss a single word that passed lest they be unable to spread an accurate account of the incident among fellow citizens who were unfortunate enough to be absent.

'They *are*,' Crawley insisted. 'I am *almost* sorry now that I befriended them in Brussels, where they ran a brothel. But such is the nature of love of *all* mankind that our Lord taught us – and womankind too.'

'Where is our money, you rascal?'

'You lying, thieving toad, you.'

'You stole our money, and you are jolly well going to account for every penny of it.'

'And you stole Rachel's jewels. I'll scratch your eyes out!'

All four of the ladies spoke at once.

There was a swell of sound in the abbey yard, its nature shocked and indignant, its sympathy tending toward the handsome clergyman and against the ladies who were certainly not behaving like ladies.

And then Crawley's eyes alit upon Rachel again, and they filled with malice. He drew himself up, shedding Phyllis from his back as he did so, and stretched out one accusing arm, finger pointed.

'And her,' he said while half the crowd made shushing noises and the other half fell silent and all turned their eyes upon Rachel. 'She is one of them too. She is nothing but a whore.'

Although Rachel was neither the wife nor the widow of an army colonel, the general out of sheer gallantry might have subjected Crawley to another poke with his cane for the insult. But Alleyne elbowed him aside. He did not consider the fact that Crawley

318

was only an inch shorter than himself and probably weighed as much as he did. He gripped the lapels of the man's coat and hauled him upward and inward.

'I beg your pardon?' he asked through his teeth.

Crawley grappled with his hands and tried to return his heels to the ground, but to no avail.

'I did not hear your answer,' Alleyne told him. 'Speak up. To whom were you referring a moment ago?'

'I fail to see what business it is of—'

Alleyne shook him like the rat he was.

'To *whom* were you referring?' he asked again.

A pin might almost have been heard to drop in the abbey yard.

'To Rachel,' Crawley said.

'To *whom*?' Alleyne hauled him a little higher and a little closer.

'To Miss York,' Crawley said.

'And *what* did you say of her?'

'Nothing,' Crawley said, his voice higher pitched.

There was another murmur of sound, quickly hushed.

'*What* did you say?'

'I said she was one of them,' Crawley said.

'And that *is*?' Alleyne moved his head a little closer so that they were virtually eyeball to eyeball.

'A whore,' Crawley said.

Alleyne punched him squarely in the nose and had the satisfaction of seeing blood ooze from the man's nostrils.

The fair-haired lady screamed. So did the entourage of ladies who had exited the church with her and her brother.

'Perhaps,' Alleyne said, hauling Crawley closer

again, 'you would care to amend your statement. What is Miss York?'

Crawley mumbled something nasally as he tried in vain to get his hands close to his nose.

'I cannot hear you,' Alleyne barked at him.

'A lady,' Crawley muttered. 'She is a *lady*.'

'Ah,' Alleyne said. 'You lied, then. And Mrs. Streat, Mrs. Leavey, Miss Ness, and Miss Clover?'

'Ladies too.' Blood was dripping from Crawley's chin onto his snowy white cravat. 'They are all ladies.'

'Then they have a champion four times over,' Alleyne said, and hit him four more times, twice with each fist, two to his jaw, one more to his nose, and the final one to his chin.

Crawley went down without throwing a single punch in his own defense. He lay on the ground, propped on one elbow, cradling his nose with one hand and weeping noisily from the pain.

Most of the spectators were inclined to applaud, even to cheer. A few, most notably the ladies who had been with Crawley, were shocked and indignant on his behalf and called upon everyone else to bring a constable. No one took any notice, perhaps because no one wanted to miss a single moment of the show.

The audience had turned to him for the next move, Alleyne realized as his cold fury subsided somewhat and he became aware of his surroundings. He turned his head to look at Rachel. She was standing a short distance away, Weston's arm about her shoulders, pale and wide-eyed and gazing at him.

'Well done, Sir Jonathan,' Weston said. 'If I were twenty years younger, by God, I would have milled him down myself.'

320

'I believe this man is known in Bath as Nicholas Croyden,' Alleyne said, addressing the crowd and raising his voice so that everyone could hear him. 'He was known as Nigel Crawley in Brussels before the Battle of Waterloo and as Nathan Crawford when he visited Chesbury Park and its neighborhood in Wiltshire shortly after. But wherever he goes, he pretends to be a clergyman devoted to humanity and works of charity. He solicits donations for his nonexistent charities and, when opportunity presents itself, he robs his victims outright.'

'No!' the fair-haired lady cried. 'That is not true. My brother is the kindest, most loving man in the world.'

'Shame!' the lady next to her said, addressing Alleyne. 'I would trust my whole fortune and my very life with dear Mr. Croyden.'

'These ladies,' Alleyne said, indicating the four friends, who looked as if they were enjoying themselves enormously, 'were robbed of their life savings when Crawley promised to deposit the money at a London bank for them.'

'And I did it too,' Crawley protested, fumbling in a pocket for a handkerchief. 'I deposited every penny.'

'And he robbed Miss York of all her money,' Alleyne continued.

'She *gave* it to me for safekeeping,' Crawley said, 'and then she ran away back to those wh—, back to those ladies to spread her lies. I have it safely set aside to return to her.'

'These are serious accusations, Sir Jonathan,' the general said. 'Perhaps you ought to send to the bank in London where Croyden says he deposited the money.'

321

'Miss York trusted him enough at that time,' Alleyne continued, 'to inform him that she possessed a fortune in jewels, which were in her uncle's keeping until her twenty-fifth birthday. Crawley's first destination after landing in England was Chesbury Park, where he ingratiated himself with Baron Weston, accepted a donation from him for one of his charities, and then came back during the night to steal the jewels.'

There was a loud swell of outrage.

'If any of those jewels are discovered at Crawley's lodgings,' Alleyne said, 'then I believe it will be safe for everyone here to assume that he is the thief I say he is. I intend to accompany him to those rooms without further delay.'

Weston cleared his throat.

'Miss Crawford – or Crawley or Croyden – is wearing a brooch from the collection,' he said.

The lady slapped a hand to her bosom.

'I am not,' she cried. 'You lie, sir. This was a gift from my mother twenty years ago.'

'I will come with you, Sir Jonathan,' the general announced importantly. 'There ought to be an independent authority to confirm your findings. And since the brooch can no longer be used as irrefutable evidence since both Lord Weston and Miss Croyden claim ownership of it and one would not wish to call either a liar without due consideration, I would ask for a detailed description, Weston, of as many pieces as you can remember.'

There was a fresh flurry of excitement as Miss Crawley tried to slip away unnoticed and four ladies, headed by Geraldine, fell upon her with much wrath and name-calling – the most colorful and lurid of which came,

322

interestingly enough, from Miss Crawley's lips. But the spectacle was virtually at an end.

Lord Weston advised anyone who had made a donation to one of Crawley's charities to make a claim for its return without delay and anyone who was thinking of making a donation to think again.

One of the churchgoing ladies shrieked and swooned. Two others declared that they would defend the poor dear man to their dying day.

Rachel meanwhile had stepped forward and stood looking down at Nigel Crawley, who had still not got to his feet, perhaps out of fear that he would be knocked off them again.

'It is strange,' she said, 'how good can come out of both evil and seeming disaster. It is through you and your villainy, Mr. Crawley, that I discovered true friendship and love and compassion. I hope as much good can come out of this evil and this disaster for you.' She switched her attention to the lady. 'And for you too, Miss Crawley, though I feel compelled to say that I doubt it.'

Alleyne hauled Crawley to his feet and quick-marched him across the abbey yard and through the pillared arches at its entrance to one of the carriages that had been awaiting them ever since they stepped out of the Pump Room. The crowd fell back before them, and Miss Crawley with her four female guards plus Weston and Rachel fell in behind.

'That is the greatest excitement we have seen in Bath,' one gentleman was commenting to another as Alleyne passed, 'since Lady Freyja Bedwyn accused the Marquess of Hallmere right in the middle of the Pump Room of being a debaucher of innocence. Were you there?'

323

They were words that somehow lodged themselves in Alleyne's mind even though he had no opportunity to take them out again immediately to examine them. He was too busy loading Crawley into one of the carriages, climbing in right behind him, and then helping Weston and the general in to join them.

The ladies meanwhile – all six of them – were piling into the other carriage, all of them apparently intent upon coming to Sydney Place too.

Alleyne just hoped that no one would think of sending a constable there just yet.

Chapter Twenty-One

Rachel could hardly bear to look at Nigel Crawley. It was humiliating indeed to realize that she had once respected and admired him well enough to agree to marry him. How could she have been so gullible? As well as being a cheat and a thief, he was a cringing coward. He was almost the same size as Jonathan and no one had held him down in the abbey yard, but he had not even attempted to fight back. And after he had been knocked down, he had lain on the ground weeping. Now he sat on the chair in his rooms where Jonathan had deposited him, looking shriveled up and darting glances about the room as if seeking an avenue of escape.

It was doubtful he would find one. Geraldine, Flossie, and Phyllis stood triumphant guard over him while Bridget kept a firm eye on Miss Crawley, who was seated a short distance away from her brother.

Her one consolation, Rachel thought, was that many other women, and even some men, had been deceived by them too – not that any of those others had come close to marrying him, of course.

There was a huge amount of money in the rooms, as

well as the box of jewelry that had been taken from the safe in the library at Chesbury. Uncle Richard had identified all the pieces, and General Sugden had confirmed that they matched the descriptions that had been given him during the carriage ride to Sydney Place.

The general had taken charge from the moment of their arrival and was enjoying himself enormously, Rachel believed. He sat now at a cloth-covered table in the middle of the sitting room with paper, pen, and ink acquired from the landlady, making written lists of everything that had been discovered on the premises apart from the furnishings of the rooms and the personal effects of the two occupants.

There were significant omissions from his list, though. Before sitting down, he had counted out the exact sum Flossie had named to him as the combined life savings of the four friends and set the money in her hand with a magnificent military bow. And he had given Rachel the small sum she had deposited for safekeeping with Nigel Crawley when she left Brussels with him. He had offered Uncle Richard the sum he had donated to charity, but her uncle had refused it.

Only then had General Sugden asked the landlady to send for a constable.

Rachel was not at all sure that what he had done was legally correct. But no one argued with him, least of all the Crawleys. And it was clear to her that if they waited for the law to take its course, they would very probably never see their money again. Anyway, the general appeared to be a powerful, even domineering man who would simply overbear any magistrate who happened to learn of what he had done and had the temerity to question him on it.

'With your permission, Weston,' he said, cleaning off the quill pen at last, 'the jewels will remain as evidence. Money in itself is poor proof of theft since it is difficult to trace to its original owner. But the presence of these jewels here, especially since one of them was on the person of the female suspect when she was apprehended, will be incontrovertible proof that they are rogues and villains.'

Looking down at the jewels all heaped together in their heavy box, Rachel felt almost queasy. There were far more of them than she had expected. They must indeed be worth a vast fortune. Then she had a sudden thought and crossed the room until she stood looking down at Nigel Crawley.

'You did not intend to marry me at all, did you?' she asked him. 'You would have found an excuse to wait until after we had gone to Chesbury. You just wanted me to lead you to the jewels.'

He looked up at her with ill-concealed malice. But it was Miss Crawley who answered.

'Marry *you*?' she said with a scornful laugh. 'You think that just because you have all that yellow hair and those big, soulful eyes you are God's answer to every man's prayer? He wouldn't marry you if you were the last woman on earth. Anyway, he couldn't. He is married to *me*.'

'Oh.' Rachel closed her eyes. 'Thank heaven!'

Bridget tapped Miss Crawley – or Mrs. Crawley or whatever her name was – none too gently on the shoulder.

'You be quiet now,' she said, 'and speak when you are spoken to.'

It was the moment at which the door crashed open and Sergeant Strickland burst into the room.

327

'I got the message,' he said, looking at Geraldine, 'and here I am. So this is him, is it?' He bent a stern gaze on Nigel Crawley. '*Sitting* in the presence of ladies?'

'What ladies?' Mr. Crawley mumbled.

'That was not nice, lad,' the sergeant said, stepping closer, 'nor wise neither. On your feet, then.'

'You may go to the devil,' Mr. Crawley told him.

Sergeant Strickland reached out one massive hand to grasp him by the back collar of his coat, and lifted him to his feet as if he weighed no more than a small sack of potatoes.

'He called us all whores, Will,' Geraldine told him, 'in the middle of the yard outside the Pump Room. Rachel too. And then Sir Jonathan gave him a bloody nose and knocked him down. We all fairly swooned with joy. Jonathan looked as handsome as sin when he was doing it.'

'That was *very* unwise, lad.' Sergeant Strickland shook his head sorrowfully as he gazed at a now-cowering Nigel Crawley. 'Right, then. Stand at attention.'

Mr. Crawley gazed at him with uncomprehending eyes.

'*At-ten-SHUN!*'

He snapped to attention.

'Right, sir,' the sergeant said, addressing Jonathan, 'what is to be done with him?'

'A constable has been sent for,' Jonathan explained. 'The ladies' money has been returned to them, and Miss York's jewels have been recovered.'

'Right you are, sir,' Sergeant Strickland said. 'I will guard the prisoner until the constable arrives, then, and you and Lord Weston can take the ladies

328

back to the hotel for breakfast. Eyes *front*, lad.'

'Oh, Will,' Geraldine said, 'you are setting my heart all aflutter. If I had ever followed the drum with you, I would have been in a permanent swoon. I give you fair warning that I am falling in love with you.'

'You must be a sergeant,' the general said approvingly, 'and a damned good one too, if my guess is correct. I would be happy to have you serve in my battalion if I still had one, but Mrs. Sugden persuaded me to retire ten years ago.'

Sergeant Strickland saluted smartly. 'That is all right, sir,' he said. 'I was dismissed from the service anyway on account of I lost an eye at Waterloo, but I am a gentleman's gentleman now – until I can get my feet under me, so to speak. Eyes *front*, lad, and don't let me have to tell you again unless you wants to see me in a crotchety mood.'

Nigel Crawley stood like a soldier on parade, looking remarkably ridiculous. His nose shone like a beacon.

Rachel looked at Jonathan and found him gazing back at her, laughter and perhaps something a little warmer in his eyes. It had been a turbulent couple of hours, during which they had exchanged scarcely a word or a glance. But in that time he had been her champion. She abhorred violence, being of the opinion that there must always be a peaceful way of solving differences of opinion. Yet she would never forget the thrill of satisfaction she had felt when he drew blood from Nigel Crawley's nose after that man had called her a whore.

If she had not already been in love with Jonathan before then, she would have tumbled headlong at that moment.

But now their association was very nearly at an

end. There was nothing to keep her and her uncle in Bath now that Mr. Crawley had been apprehended and her jewels recovered. There was nothing to keep Jonathan from going to London. Today was perhaps all they had left.

She smiled back at him and felt a tightening of grief in her bosom.

Two constables arrived soon after that, and there was a great deal of noise and confusion again as several people tried to tell the story at once. But they left again eventually to take the prisoners before a magistrate, General Sugden, Sergeant Strickland, and the four ladies with them. Bridget would have stayed behind, but Rachel could see how wistful she looked and waved her away. She had her uncle to play the part of chaperon.

He was desperately weary again. He ordered breakfast in his own rooms after they returned to the hotel, and Rachel went with him, unwilling to let him out of her sight until he was settled quietly. Jonathan did not go with them.

Rachel could only hope that there would be a chance sometime later in the day for a private farewell. He would surely leave tomorrow – or perhaps even later today. She would not be able to bear a public leave-taking.

But how would she bear a private one either?

Her uncle was asleep within an hour after their return to the York House Hotel and Rachel got to her feet to leaf idly through the small pile of letters that had been sent on to him from Chesbury.

There was nothing to keep him here any longer, Alleyne realized. The charade was over and so was the chase. The thief who had been the cause of all Rachel's woes was caught and the money she had felt as a personal debt restored to her friends.

He could not claim much glory for the happy outcome for her, but it was pleasing anyway to know that she was going to live the life she ought to have been living since her father's death. She was Miss York of Chesbury Park, she was a considerable heiress, and, best of all, she had an uncle who loved her as a daughter.

He had nothing to stay for.

No further excuse.

By tomorrow night he could be in London. By the next day he might have found someone who recognized him, or he might have tracked down some information about himself. It was an exciting, happy prospect. Surely once he did see a familiar face he would recognize it and everything would come flooding back to him.

But as he looked out the window of his hotel room onto a street turned wet with a sudden downpour of rain, he felt neither excited nor happy.

In fact, he felt downright depressed.

She did not need him any longer. She did not want him. She was with her uncle, as she ought to be, and in time she would marry – how had she phrased it? – the love of her life. She would find such a man too. How could she not? Eligible gentlemen would flock to her side. She could choose whomever she liked.

He would go outside as soon as the rain stopped, he decided. If Strickland returned soon, perhaps they would even leave Bath today instead of waiting for tomorrow – if the sergeant wished to accompany him, that was. Perhaps he would prefer to stay with Geraldine.

Where would he begin his search? Alleyne wondered. And what clues did he have already that might lead him to his identity? He had not had any new dreams since the one about the fountain or any new feelings of familiarity like the one he had had after diving into the lake. At least, he did not *think* he had had either. And yet ...

Had he dreamed last night? There was something recent, something that had happened or something he had dreamed. But what was it? He frowned in concentration. Surely his memory of recent events was not about to start playing tricks on him.

He turned from the window in exasperation after a few minutes. He was going to have to go outside, rain or no rain. He would go mad if he remained here. But a knock on the door diverted his attention.

'Come,' he called, expecting that it would be Strickland or perhaps a chambermaid who did not know that he was in.

But it was Rachel. She came inside and closed the door behind her back.

'Rachel.' He smiled at her. 'I hope this morning's events did not put too much strain on your uncle's heart or distress you too much. But you must be very happy that all the stolen property has been recovered and that that husband-and-wife team will not have a chance to rob anyone else for a very long time.'

'I am.' But she looked decidedly pale, he thought. She did not return his smile as she came toward him, both hands outstretched, but she did look intently at him. 'Thank you, Alleyne. Thank you for everything.'

At first when he took her hands in his he thought the coldness in his head must be caused by the chilliness of

332

her hands. But then there was dizziness too.

'What?' He gazed blankly at her.

'Lord Alleyne Bedwyn,' she said softly.

He gripped her hands as if he were a drowning man and she his only lifeline.

'*What*?' he said again.

'Is the name familiar to you?' she asked him.

It was not. To his *mind* it was not. And yet his whole body was reacting to it in strange, uncomfortable ways akin to panic.

'Where did you hear that name?' He hardly even realized that he was whispering.

'There was a letter from one of my former neighbors in London,' she said. 'It was sent on here from Chesbury with Uncle Richard's mail. The only missing gentleman she knew of was Lord Alleyne Bedwyn, who died at the Battle of Waterloo, though his body was never found. She knew about it because she happened to be close to St. George's on Hanover Square when the memorial service the Duke of Bewcastle held for his brother was ending, and she stood watching the crowd leaving the church.'

Alleyne Bedwyn. Bedwyn. Bedwyn.

That is the greatest excitement we have seen in Bath since Lady Freyja Bedwyn accused the Marquess of Hallmere right in the middle of the Pump Room of being a debaucher of innocence.

That was what had been niggling at his mind a few minutes ago ... *Freyja Bedwyn*.

'Are you he?' Rachel asked him.

He raised his eyes to hers again and stared blankly at her. He knew that he was – he was Alleyne Bedwyn. But only his body knew it. His mind was still a blank.

'Yes,' he said. 'I am Alleyne Bedwyn.'

'Alleyne.' Tears sprang to her eyes and she bit her upper lip. 'It suits you so much better than Jonathan.'

Alleyne Bedwyn.

Freyja Bedwyn.

The Duke of Bewcastle – his brother.

They were all just words to his mind and churning panic to his body.

'You must write to the Duke of Bewcastle immediately,' she said, her smile suddenly radiant. 'Imagine how happy he will be, Jon— Alleyne. I will run down now and fetch pen and ink. You must—'

'No!' he said harshly, releasing her hands. He strode away from her to stand beside the bed, his back to her, his hands busily straightening the candlestick on the bedside table.

'He ought to be informed,' she said. 'Let me—'

'*No*!' he spun around to glare at her, his eyes blazing. 'Leave me. Get out of here.'

She stared at him, her eyes wide.

'Out!' He pointed at the door. 'Leave me.'

She turned sharply away and hurried to the door. But she did not open it. She stood for a few moments, her head hung low.

'Alleyne,' she said, 'don't shut me out. Please don't. *Please* don't.'

She turned her head to look at him, her eyes huge and wounded. And he knew that if she left the room he would go all to pieces. He reached out blindly for her, and they came together in the middle of the room, their arms coming about each other and clinging tightly.

'Don't leave me,' he told her. 'Don't leave me.'

'I won't.' She lifted her face from his shoulder. 'I won't ever leave you.'

334

He kissed her, straining her to him as if he would never let her go. And when he stopped kissing her he buried his face against her shoulder and wept. He would have pulled away from her then in horror and embarrassment, but she held him tightly and murmured unintelligible words to him, and he sobbed his heart out in great noisy, undignified gulps until he was spent and exhausted.

'Well,' he said shakily as he half turned from her in order to use his handkerchief, 'now you know what sort of person Lord Alleyne Bedwyn is.'

'I have always known him,' she said. 'I have just not known his name until today. He is a gentleman I like and admire and respect. He is a gentleman for whom I feel a deep affection.'

He put his handkerchief away in a pocket and raked his fingers through his hair.

'I always hoped,' he said, 'that if one small memory would return everything would come flooding back in an instant. But my worst fears have just been realized. Someone in the abbey yard this morning mentioned the name *Lady Freyja Bedwyn* and I felt as if I had been jarred by some shock even though I was too busy at the time to pay the feeling any attention. When you spoke the name *Lord Alleyne Bedwyn*, I knew immediately that it was my own. And I recognized the name of the Duke of Bewcastle. But the curtain has not fallen from my memory, Rachel. Freyja – how is she related to me? I know she is. I know who I am now. I know that I have at least one elder brother. But it is as if I know these things with my body, with a part of me that sits low in my stomach, rather than with my mind. I cannot *remember*.'

335

He was grateful that she did not say anything, did not try to offer comfort or hope in words. She merely stood beside him and set a hand on his arm and rested her forehead on his shoulder.

He took her to lie on the bed, and they lay there for a long time, his arm about her shoulders, his other hand over his eyes. She lay on her side, curled against him, her head on his shoulder, one arm thrown across his waist.

He felt infinitely comforted. She was Rachel. His love. His one anchor in a turbulent ocean of seething depths.

'I suppose there are not many people,' he said, 'who can say that they survived their own funeral. I have you to thank for that.' He kissed the top of her head.

She merely burrowed closer.

And then he saw the fountain again. But this time he saw it against the background of a great mansion that was a curious but not displeasing mixture of architectural styles, spanning several centuries.

'Home,' he said. 'It is my home.' He could not remember its name, but he could see it. And he described it to her – its outside, that was. He could not remember its inside.

'It will all come back to you,' she said. 'I know it will, Alleyne. Alleyne, Alleyne. I *do* like your name.'

'We all have strange names.' He frowned and then shook his head. 'I think it was my mother who named us. She was a famous reader of ancient romance and I suppose scorned naming us George or Charles or William – or Jonathan.'

She kissed his ear.

By the time they all gathered for dinner that evening, there was a great deal of excitement in the air.

Nigel Crawley and his wife had been bound over for trial, and the ladies were brimming over with eagerness to recount all the details that the others had missed when they returned to the hotel. Even Sergeant Strickland had found some excuse to be in the room, standing deferentially behind Alleyne's chair and occasionally unable to resist the temptation to interject a lengthy comment.

The ladies were also excited about having their money back, one thing they all admitted they had not expected to happen. Now they could declare themselves officially retired from their profession, an announcement that occasioned a toast to which everyone drank. And now they could revive their dream and decide exactly where in England they wished to settle so that they could go there and look about them for a suitable building in which to set up their boarding house.

Tomorrow they would leave for London to tie up all loose ends there and make their plans.

Rachel let them talk until they seemed to have nothing left to say. Then she looked all about the table, her hands clasped to her bosom.

'I have something to say,' she said.

Even Uncle Richard did not know yet. He had slept all afternoon. Anyway, she had lain on the bed in Alleyne's room all afternoon. She had even fallen asleep there. So had he, incredibly.

'Do you, Rachel?' Bridget said. 'We *have* been talking rather a lot, haven't we? But it has been a very exciting day, you must admit.'

'What is it, Rache?' Geraldine asked.

'I have someone to present to you,' Rachel said, 'someone whose acquaintance you have all been longing to make.' She laughed.

Alleyne was looking at her with bright, almost feverish eyes.

Rachel indicated him with one hand.

'May I present Lord Alleyne Bedwyn,' she said, 'brother of the Duke of Bewcastle.'

Flossie whooped inelegantly.

'God bless you, sir,' Sergeant Strickland said. 'I always knew you was a real nob.'

'Bewcastle?' Uncle Richard said, looking closely at Alleyne. 'Of Lindsey Hall in Hampshire? But that is not so very far from Chesbury. I ought to have seen the resemblance.'

'Lord love us,' Phyllis said, 'I am dining with a real live *duke's* brother. Catch me while I swoon, if you will, Bridge.'

'I *said* that was an aristocratic nose,' Geraldine declared. 'Now did I or did I not?'

'You did, Gerry,' Flossie said. 'And you were quite right too.'

'You *know* the Duke of Bewcastle and his family, Uncle Richard?' Rachel asked.

'I am acquainted with him,' her uncle said, 'but I cannot say I have met any of the others. There are a few brothers and sisters, I believe, but I do not know their names. But Lord Alleyne will be able to tell you.'

'My memory has not returned, sir,' Alleyne said. 'Only the merest fragments.'

There was a short silence while everyone digested that fact, but then everyone was speaking at once again, asking questions, making suggestions, offering

338

consolation, wanting to know how Lord Alleyne had discovered his identity if he still could not remember much.

It was Flossie who suggested another toast.

'To Lord Alleyne Bedwyn,' they all said.

He was to leave in the morning for Lindsey Hall. He said so in response to a question from Geraldine.

It was the question and the answer that somehow brought silence down upon all of them. Looking about the table, Rachel discovered that everyone had stopped smiling. Perhaps, she thought, she was not the only one feeling mortally depressed.

'I *will* miss the kitchen at Chesbury,' Phyllis said, 'and cooking for his lordship. I was happier there than I think I have ever been in my life. In fact, I *know* I was.'

'I never did give Mr. Drummond an answer,' Flossie said with a sigh. 'It didn't seem right to say yes when he is a gentleman born and I am what I am. But he knew about me and said he did not care a fig for my past. And I miss him something terrible.'

'I never did properly finish organizing the household at Chesbury,' Geraldine said, 'and doing an inventory. I could have done a good job as housekeeper there if I could only read and write.'

'I could teach you, Gerry,' Bridget said. 'But not yet. You had all better go on to London ahead of me. I had better stay with Rachel. She is going to need a companion and chaperon and it won't be any hardship to go back to Chesbury with her for a while. I have friends there.'

The other three ladies gazed wistfully at her while Uncle Richard cleared his throat.

'I *am* in desperate need of a housekeeper and a

339

cook,' he said. 'And I fear that if my steward cannot find himself a decent wife soon, loneliness may well drive him from my service. I would hate that. He is a good man. Rachel will certainly need a lady companion. Now far be it from me to destroy anyone's dream, but if you all *wish* to postpone it or even to change it entirely, then I would suggest that we all return to Chesbury together.'

There was a great clamor of voices then as all the ladies spoke together. It was almost impossible to distinguish individual comments, but they were all summed up, it seemed, when Phyllis rose from her place, swept around to the head of the table, wrapped her arms about Uncle Richard's neck from behind, and kissed his cheek.

The general laughter this time was a great deal merrier than it had been earlier.

'I suppose,' Uncle Richard said, 'that for the sake of my neighbors, Mrs. Leavey, we had better kill off Colonel Leavey in Paris. And I suppose we had better have him die impoverished, thus forcing you into taking employment as my cook.'

'And we are going to have to make up a story for Rache too,' Geraldine said. 'We will have to say that she has been abandoned by that monstrous, philandering husband of hers, I suppose. Unless someone can think of a way of making her single again so that she can receive suitors. Any suggestions?'

But no one had any. And melancholy descended upon the whole company again.

Tomorrow Alleyne would be going home to Lindsey Hall.

Chapter Twenty-Two

Alleyne did not take a private farewell of Rachel. He could have, perhaps, if he had knocked on the door of her room early, even though Bridget shared the room with her. Bridget would have taken herself tactfully off out of the way.

Instead he went down to breakfast in the public dining room only a little earlier than usual and then went strolling outside until he saw all the bustle of the Chesbury carriages being drawn out into the street and loaded up with baggage.

Weston had decided last evening to return home without further delay. Alleyne guessed that he was overjoyed to be taking his niece back with him, and only slightly less so to have the other ladies going with them. Chesbury Park was going to be a far more cheerful place for him to live out his life than it had been just a little over a month ago.

Perhaps good had come of his wild scheme after all, Alleyne thought, though he hoped he had learned his lesson that lies and deception were not the way to go about achieving any goal.

He had decided to see them all on their way before

leaving himself. Another delaying tactic? he wondered. But he would be on his way well before noon – to Lindsey Hall in Hampshire. He had remembered last night that there was a magnificent medieval banqueting hall just beyond the front doors, complete with carved wooden screen and minstrel gallery, huge oak table, and weapons and coats of arms on the walls.

Geraldine came out first. Strickland was with her, carrying a bag that must be hers. He was looking stoic, and she was looking like a Latin tragic queen. The other ladies followed them out into the yard, and then came Rachel with Weston.

He ought to have gone to the Pump Room, or, better, yet, on a long walk, Alleyne thought. Farewells were an abomination. Nobody ever wanted them, yet they seemed a necessary evil.

Weston shook his hand, bade him a hearty good day and good wishes for his own journey, and was helped into the first carriage by his valet. Bridget hugged him and followed the baron inside, and then it was the turn of Flossie and Phyllis, who was weeping copious tears. Geraldine was huddled with the sergeant outside the second carriage, which she entered after the other two were already inside.

That left Rachel. She did not hug him. Neither did she scramble to get into the carriage with her uncle and Bridget. She stood pale and dry-eyed and unsmiling until he looked at her, sorry then that he had not gone to her earlier. But when his eyes met hers, she smiled brightly, took a few steps forward, and held out both hands to him.

'Alleyne,' she said, 'good-bye. Have a good journey later. And don't fear. Once you have arrived at Lindsey Hall, once you have seen the Duke of Bewcastle and the rest of your family again, everything will come back to you. It may take a little time, but give yourself that time. Good-bye.'

It was a cheerful, polite, *rehearsed* little speech.

He took her hands in his and bowed over them. He raised them one at a time to his lips. And suddenly he could not remember why he was allowing her to leave him like this – except that he had nothing to offer her, perhaps not even his freedom, and that after the life she had lived so far in her twenty-two years she deserved the chance to be Miss York of Chesbury, free to consider the suit of a wide range of gentlemen.

It was only natural that they feel sentimental and all choked up with emotion at a moment like this. They had been through a great deal together in the past two months. They had meant a great deal to each other.

'Be happy, Rachel,' he said. 'It is all I wish for you.'

And he released one of her hands, helped her up into the carriage, watched her arrange her skirts about her before shutting the door, and stepped back so that the carriage could proceed on its way. He raised a hand in farewell and smiled.

There was a great deal of noise and bustle as the two carriages, followed by a baggage coach, moved out into the street, turned the corner, and disappeared from sight. There was a great deal of waving from inside the carriages – except for Rachel, who leaned back in her seat and did not even look out. Geraldine had rolled down the window of the second carriage and waved a handkerchief out of it, her eyes on Strickland. She was crying.

And deuce take it, *he* felt like crying too, Alleyne

thought, deliberately not turning his head to look at his valet.

He loved her, damn it. He *loved* her.

'I'll finish packing your things, sir,' the sergeant said after heaving a great, soulful sigh. 'You got to love them all, haven't you, sir? They have hearts as big as the sea no matter what they used to do. Not that I care about that. I never did look down on that sort of lady like some fellers do, even the fellers what uses their services. They got to earn their daily victuals the same as the rest of us. And I can't say as killing for a living is any better. I'll have the carriage come round in one hour's time, shall I?'

'Yes,' Alleyne said. 'No, make it noon. I need to take a walk and blow away some cobwebs. Better yet, leave it until I get back. There is no big hurry, is there?'

He did not even go back inside the hotel. He strode off down Milsom Street in the direction of the city center. Then he wove his way through the abbey yard, past the abbey itself, and onward to the river. He stood gazing down into its waters for a while, but then he walked along beside it past the weir until he reached the Pulteney Bridge. He crossed it and set out at a brisk pace along Great Pulteney Street, in the direction of Sydney Gardens.

At first his thoughts were all centered on Rachel. He wondered exactly where she was at every moment, whether she was cheerful and busy conversing with her uncle and Bridget, whether she missed him – whether her heart was back here with him.

And then without any warning that it was about to happen he remembered Morgan. His sister. The woman who had been waiting for him at the Namur

344

Gates. She had been tending wounded soldiers there when he left Brussels, and he had been intent upon returning to her as soon as possible so that he could take her home to the safety of England.

At first he could not remember why she had been in Brussels in the first place or why she was there at the gates. And he could not remember why he had ridden through the gates away from her instead of taking her home without delay. But then he recalled that she was eighteen, that she had made her come-out in London back in the spring and had then gone to Brussels with a friend of hers and the friend's parents. He could not recall their name – though the father was an earl. Then he had a flashing image of Morgan's face, stopped walking in order to close his eyes, and brought it back into focus. It was a dark-complexioned, oval face with dark eyes – like his own – and dark hair. A beautiful face. She was the loveliest of them all. She was the only one who had not inherited the family nose.

How many of them were there?

Freyja must be one. She must be his sister. What had been said in the abbey yard yesterday morning?

That is the greatest excitement we have seen in Bath since Lady Freyja Bedwyn accused the Marquess of Hallmere right in the middle of the Pump Room of being a debaucher of innocence.

Freyja Bedwyn. The Marquess of Hallmere. Hallmere.

And then he remembered that they were married. He had been at their wedding not so long ago. Last summer? Yet Freyja had accused Hallmere quite publicly, in the middle of the Pump Room, of being a debaucher of innocence?

Quite unexpectedly Alleyne chuckled aloud. Yes, that sounded just like Freyja – good old Free, small and fierce and quite ready to use her sharp tongue or her fists or both at the least provocation. He could suddenly picture her, strangely handsome with her fair, unruly hair, her darker eyebrows, and her prominent nose.

He sat in Sydney Gardens for hours, absently watching the squirrels, occasionally nodding to other walkers, and slowly piecing together a few random pieces of his life. There were still huge chunks of it missing, but his panic was beginning to recede. If some things had come back to him, then obviously his memory had not been wiped out beyond recall. Other things would come back too – perhaps everything in time.

Was there a wife hidden away somewhere in the darkness of the memories that had not yet returned?

Where was Rachel now?

When he finally got to his feet to make his way back to George Street and the York House Hotel, he was amazed to see from the position of the sun that it must be late afternoon. Where had the day gone?

But it would be too late now, he thought, to set out for Hampshire today. He would wait until tomorrow. There was no real hurry. They all thought him dead. They had held a memorial service for him in London. One more day could not matter a great deal to them.

He could not bear to face them without knowing them.

He remembered lying on the bed in his room yesterday afternoon with Rachel curled up beside him as he assimilated the knowledge that he was Lord Alleyne Bedwyn.

346

He missed her with an ache that felt like a real physical pain.

He doubted he had felt lonelier in his life than he felt at that moment.

Rachel had been home at Chesbury Park for five days. *Home*. It must be the most wonderful word in the English language, she thought. She belonged here. She could live here for the rest of her life if she wished. Even after Uncle Richard's days were over it would be hers.

She hoped it would be a long time before that happened. He was tired after the journey home from Bath, though he recovered faster than he had after the journey there. He was, she realized, a happy man. He loved her. And his home had suddenly come alive around him again. Geraldine had been named officially as housekeeper and had thrown herself into the task with great energy. She seemed to be quite a favorite with the other servants, especially the men. Bridget had already started to teach her to read. Phyllis was permanently ensconced as cook and soon discovered what Uncle Richard's favorite dishes were so that she could spoil him with them every few days. Mr. Drummond had announced his betrothal to Flossie and had been granted his employer's blessing. Bridget had made the weeding and tending of the parterre gardens her personal project, and they were blooming gloriously despite the fact that the end of August was drawing near.

Rachel kept herself busy, reading and mending and embroidering and keeping her uncle company. On one rainy day she spent an afternoon alone in the portrait gallery, gazing again at the likenesses of all her ancestors on her mother's side, reminding herself of the exact relationship of each to herself. She looked for ten whole minutes at the face and figure of the child who had been her mother. On the other, finer days she walked outdoors a great deal, sometimes with Bridget or Flossie, sometimes alone. She rode a couple of times, a groom a few paces behind her, and was proud that she could do it alone. She even took the boat out once, though she did not row anywhere close to the island.

Uncle Richard was determined to be well enough to take her to London next spring to be presented to the queen and to be given a come-out ball there before participating in some of the entertainments of the Season. She thought she would rather like that, old as she was to be making her debut into society.

She did not intend to hide away in seclusion merely because her heart was broken.

But that was a ridiculous, theatrical way of describing her condition. Her heart was not *broken*. It merely ached constantly, both night and day. She was sleeping in the same room as before. Although she had been in the other bedchamber only the once when Alleyne was there, when she had stayed for the whole night, it now seemed oppressively empty and silent. She avoided going into it, but she could *feel* it without having to go there. She wished there were a door she could close in order to shut it away from her memory.

She thought about him constantly. She wondered about his return to Lindsey Hall and tried to picture it in her mind. How would the Duke of Bewcastle have received him? Would there have been other family members there too? Would he have remembered them as soon as he saw them? Was he still struggling to retrieve his past?

Had there been a wife waiting there for him?

She supposed that she would hear of him again sometime, since it seemed that they now moved in the same world. Perhaps she would even see him again – perhaps next spring. Perhaps he would be in London.

She hoped not. Maybe in two or three years' time she would be able to see him and feel nothing but pleasure and a very mild affection. But not next spring. It would be too soon.

She had been strolling around part of the lake, where there was a tree-shaded path that the gardeners had recently cleared and tidied. She had found some shade in which to sit for a while, since it was a particularly warm day. She had gazed about her, breathing in the heavy smells of summer vegetation, drinking in with her eyes the beauty of this particular part of the park, squinting against the sun sparkling on the water of the lake. From here she could just make out the slate roof of the folly at the crest of the island.

But seeing it made her sad and broke her mood of near-contentment. She walked back to the house, taking a shortcut diagonally across the lawn. She stopped halfway and shaded her eyes with her hand. The doors stood open, as they often did these days, and someone was standing at the top of the steps. She did not think it was her uncle. A visitor, then? They had not had visitors since their return from Bath, and so no explanation had yet been given to the neighbors about her changed name and status.

And then her hand dropped to her side, she felt a great welling of emotion that escaped from her lips in a wordless cry, and she caught up the sides of her skirts and broke into a run.

'*Alleyne*!' she cried, her heart so bursting with joy that it did not even occur to her to wonder why he was here.

He met her halfway and caught her up in his arms and swung her twice about before setting her back on her feet and putting enough distance between them that she could see he was grinning, his eyes alight with laughter.

'Dare I hope you are glad to see me?' he asked her. 'You are a sight for sore eyes, Rachel, though there ought to be a better way of saying it than with that sad old cliché. I have missed you.'

Somehow she found that she was looking beyond his shoulder to the window of her uncle's room. He was sitting there, looking down at them. She took a step back, and Alleyne looked over his shoulder and then back again.

'You were not here when I arrived,' he said. 'I have had a word with your uncle.'

'But what are you *doing* here?' she asked him. And now that her mindless joy was past, she was sorry he had come. All that she had suffered during the past five days would have to be repeated when he went away again. 'How could your family have been willing to let you go again so soon? Was it a happy return, Alleyne? Did you recognize them all? And remember everything?'

With every word she drank in the sight of him as if she had forgotten and would commit every detail to memory for future reference. He was hatless. The slight breeze was ruffling his hair and lifting that errant lock from his forehead.

350

'I have not been there,' he said.

'What?' She raised her eyebrows.

'I am the world's worst coward, Rache,' he said. 'I stayed in Bath, making excuses every day to wait one more hour or one more day. I could not face them until I had remembered everything or at least enough that I would not just stand there like a mindless dolt after knocking on the doors of Lindsey Hall and asking if anyone there knew me.'

She tipped her head to one side and reached for his hands, without thinking.

'And have you remembered?' she asked him.

'A reassuring amount,' he said. 'More and more each day, in fact. I have no more excuse not to go to Lindsey Hall. And I *want* to go almost more than I want to do anything else in this life.'

'But you came here instead?' She looked inquiringly at him.

'I turn weak at the knees,' he said, flashing her a grin again, 'at the thought of going there, of presenting myself to Bewcastle and any other member of my family who happens to be there, and of announcing to them that their brother has come back from the dead. I think one of the worst experiences of the past week was discovering from you that they had held a memorial service for me – a *funeral*, except that there was no body. To be treated as dead when one is still alive – no, I cannot begin to explain how it feels.'

She squeezed his hands more tightly.

'I cannot go there unless you come with me,' he said. 'Now, is that not a totally unmanly thing to say? The old Alleyne Bedwyn would not have said it or felt it. He was an arrogant, devil-may-care, independent, rather hard-edged man. I have changed since his days.

351

I cannot do this without you, Rachel. Come with me?'

'To Lindsey Hall?' Her eyes widened.

'If for no other reason,' he said, 'then because you are the one who saved my life, Rache. Bewcastle will want to thank you. If you do not go there, he will come here, I daresay, and that would be a daunting experience for you. He is as high in the instep as it is possible for any aristocrat to be.'

His grin, she realized when he flashed it again, did not denote amusement. He needed her. He desperately needed her.

'I will come,' she said, 'if Uncle Richard says I may.'

'He has already said it,' he told her, 'and Bridget has agreed to accompany us – but only if you agree of your own will. I can do this alone if I must, Rachel. Of course I can. But I would rather do it with you.'

He raised one of their clasped hands to his lips, and she smiled at him.

'One thing you ought to know,' he said, 'is that I am not married, Rachel. There is no wife, and there are no children. There is no betrothed, no romantic attachment at all.'

Her gaze slipped from his, and for the first time a painful hope was born in her. Why had he come back? Why was it so important to him that she accompany him to Lindsey Hall? Was it just because she had saved his life?

'I want to hear about everything you have done during the last five days,' he said. 'Is it possible that it has been only five days? It seems like an eternity. And I want to tell you everything I have remembered in that time. I want to tell you who I am. Will you walk with me?'

She nodded and took the arm he offered and wondered if the sun had somehow affected her mind. Could this possibly be happening? But his arm was solid beneath her hand and she could feel his body heat all down one side. If she chose, she could close her eyes and rest her cheek against his shoulder.

He was real, and he was here. And he was not married.

They did not take any conscious direction. They went around the house and strolled along the back lawn, which had been cut since that first morning when she had ridden across it with him, though daisies and buttercups and clover bloomed gaily again.

She told him about the journey home and about the past few days because he seemed genuinely interested. He looked down into her face as she talked, and laughed when she told him about riding alone and taking the boat out.

'I hope,' he said, 'you are as proud of yourself as I am of you, Rache. You have turned yourself into an intrepid country lady.'

She *was* rather proud of her accomplishments.

'But I have still not perfected the art of standing on a horse's back on one foot twirling hoops,' she said.

'It has to be a *galloping* horse,' he told her, and they both laughed.

But he did most of the talking, because there was so much she wanted to know, and so much he was eager to tell her.

The Duke of Bewcastle was a powerful man, aristocratic hauteur bred into his very bones. He ruled his world like a despot, and yet he never had to raise anything more violent than his eyebrows and his quizzing glass in order to enforce his will. His name was Wulfric. The second brother was Aidan, a former cavalry colonel who had married last year and settled on the land with his wife and their two foster children. Then there was Rannulf, usually called Ralf, who looked like a Viking warrior and was married to a gorgeous redhead – Alleyne's own words. Freyja – the name he had overheard in Bath – was his elder sister, a formidable spitfire married to the Marquess of Hallmere, who somehow seemed able to handle her without having to throttle her every day of their lives. Then there was Morgan, the youngest of them all, only eighteen years old.

'She is the lady who was waiting for me at the Namur Gates,' he explained. 'The lady of my recurring dream. Her chaperon had not taken her away from Brussels when the battle loomed, and they had allowed her out to tend the wounded on the day Waterloo was fought. I had promised Bewcastle to keep an eye on her even though she had not gone to Brussels under my care. I was desperate to get back to her.'

'What was your regiment?' Rachel asked.

'Ah,' he said, 'I ought to have started with that. I am not a military man. I was going to be a diplomat. I was attached to the embassy at the Hague, under Sir Charles Stuart. I was sent to the front with a letter for the Duke of Wellington and was carrying a reply back with me – the infamous letter of my dreams. I have changed so much, Rachel. I could not go back to that life now even if I were to be offered the whole embassy.'

It had taken him five days to remember, and even now there were gaps and blanks in his memory that puzzled him and kept him struggling for total recall.

'But what I am missing the most,' he told her, 'is , if that is the right word. I know all these things about myself and my family and my life dispassionately, rather as if they are things I have learned about someone else. I have a feeling of disconnection, as if I do not quite belong to it all. I feel almost embarrassed about going back, as if I will need to apologize for not having died after all.'

He took her hand from his arm and clasped it instead, lacing their fingers as he did so.

'And look,' he said, 'we have walked all the way out to the trees and I have hardly allowed you to squeeze a word in. What sort of gentleman am I not to observe the niceties of polite conversation?'

'This is not a polite conversation,' she said. 'I am your friend, Alleyne. I *care* about you.'

'Do you?' He smiled at her. 'Do you really, Rache? I have been pretty self-centered lately, though, haven't I?'

'With good reason,' she said. 'But it only seems that way to you because you have been alone with your own thoughts and returning memories for five days. Before that you concentrated upon helping me even if we did go about it in a thoroughly misguided way. And then you were my champion when we found Nigel Crawley. I sometimes think I should be ashamed to feel a thrill at the memory of you knocking him down and drawing blood from his nose, but I am not.'

'Shall we walk through to the cascades?' he suggested.

It was very warm among the trees. But the sun was in such a position that the rock on which they had sat before was in shade. They sat on it again, Alleyne lounging on his side, Rachel with her knees drawn up and her arms clasped about them.

'I was born to wealth and power, you know,' he said. 'It is not necessarily a good thing, though I suppose it is infinitely preferable to being born to debilitating poverty. I am independently wealthy even now. I would not have to do a hard day's work in my life if I chose not to. I was a restless, aimless, careless, cynical man with no deep feelings for anyone or anything. I do remember that about myself. And yet I knew there was an emptiness in my life. I thought of going into politics but went into the diplomatic service instead. I suppose it seemed more adventurous.'

'But you will not go back,' she said.

'No.' He shook his head. 'I belong on the land. I know that now. Strange – I can remember now that Ralf discovered that too last year when he went to stay and then to live at our grandmother's. Good Lord, I have just remembered her – my mother's mother. She lives in Leicestershire – a little bird of a woman. And Aidan discovered it too when he decided to retire from the cavalry and live with Eve in the country. Maybe once we learn to strip away the trappings of wealth and power, that is what we Bedwyns are at heart – a family devoted to the land, to the basics of life and contentment. And love.'

He was staring into the water, Rachel could see, his eyes half closed. She wondered if the time would come when she would be alone again and would sit here remembering today. Or if . . .

His eyes were on her.

'That is it, of course,' he said, but he did not say it as

356

if he had just made the discovery. He spoke as if he had thought this through before but had only now worked it into his full understanding of himself. 'It is love that makes all the difference. One might say that losing my memory was the best thing that ever happened to me, since it totally disconnected me from my past and gave me the chance to start again, to make the same sort of mistakes again, and to learn the proper lessons from them this time. But they are lessons I have been able to learn because there has been a new dimension to this new life of mine, one I have never experienced before, and one that has made all the difference to me.'

Rachel rested her cheek on her knees and kept her eyes on him.

'It has always been a tradition with our family,' he said, 'that we tend to marry late but that when we do so we marry for keeps and for love. Fidelity within marriage is expected of even the most rakish of us. I watched it happen last year to Aidan and Ralf and Freyja, and I was somewhat incredulous and somewhat skeptical. I really did not understand. Now I do.'

Rachel hugged her legs a little more tightly while he smiled directly into her eyes.

'I know you are enjoying the first real freedom of your life, Rachel,' he said. 'And for the first time you are in the milieu that is yours by right of birth. You owe me nothing – quite the contrary. And though love centers upon one person when it also qualifies as being in love, it is not a possessive or a dependent thing. I do not want you to feel trapped or pity-bound. If I must live without you, I will. Even if I must go to Lindsey Hall alone I will. Ah, there is that dimple again. Have I said something funny?'

'No,' she said, 'but you really *do* talk too much, Alleyne. You must have caught it from Sergeant Strickland.'

He laughed and she gazed at him, amazed that a man who was so very handsome and charming, who had lived a life of privilege and power, his every whim catered to, women doubtless falling all over their feet for one of his smiles – it amazed her that such a man could be so unsure of himself with her that he was babbling.

'Yes,' she said.

'Yes?' He raised his eyebrows and immediately looked arrogant.

'Yes, I will marry you,' she said. 'And if you now tell me that that was not what you were leading up to at all, then I will jump in the river and allow it to carry me out into the lake and oblivion. *Was* it what you were about to say?'

She gazed at him in horror then, her cheeks aflame, just as if the sun were beating down on their heads.

He laughed again, sat up, took her face in his hands, and kissed her.

'No,' he said, 'but it is not a bad idea, is it?'

She shrieked and pushed at his chest.

He cupped her chin in one hand and kissed her again.

'In fact,' he said, 'it is downright brilliant, Rache. Will you marry me, my love? You *are* my love, you know. You are my new life, and though I could live it without you, I would really rather not. *Will* you marry me?'

She pressed her mouth against his.

'Is that a yes, Rache?'

'Yes,' she said.

He drew back his head and smiled at her, but totally without mischief this time. What she saw in the depths of his eyes took her breath away. She set a hand that was curiously trembling against the side of his face.

'I love you,' she said. 'I could live a contented and productive life here at Chesbury alone except for my uncle and my friends if I had to. But I would really rather you lived here with me, my love.'

They gazed at each other with wonder and the beginnings of laughter.

'I spoke to your uncle before I came out looking for you,' he said. 'We will have the first banns called next Sunday, Rache, and think of some tale to tell the locals. We will set Strickland and the ladies to dreaming up something suitably hair-raising and convoluted. But it will be a month before we can celebrate our nuptials and I can carry you off to a respectable bridal bed. Can you wait that long?'

She shook her head and bit her lower lip.

'Good girl,' he said, one hand against the back of her head. 'Neither can I.'

He kissed her again and brought her over on top of him as he lay back on the warm stone. It probably was not the most comfortable bed in the world – in fact, it undoubtedly was not – but they scarcely noticed any discomfort as they lost themselves in the sensual pleasure of making love.

And yet it was not quite a mindless encounter either. Rachel was very aware that just a few hours ago she had been telling herself that she could learn to be content without him, that perhaps in a couple of years she would be able to see him again without feeling too much pain. And she was very aware too of the heat of the day, of the rushing sound of the cascades, of birds singing.

They made hot, hungry, swift, lusty love. And afterward they lay side by side, warm and panting and relaxed, his arm beneath her head as they gazed up at the treetops and occasionally turned to smile at each other.

'How did you know I was alive?' he asked her.

'I touched you,' she said. 'I touched the side of your face and felt a slight warmth. And then I touched your neck and felt a pulse.'

'You gave me life,' he said. 'New life. I said from the start, did I not, that I had died and gone to heaven and found a golden angel waiting for me there.'

'But that was the second version,' she reminded him. 'In the first one you had died and gone to heaven and found it was a brothel.'

He laughed and rolled over on top of her and kissed her breathless again.

Chapter Twenty-Three

Alleyne had decided upon morning as the best time of day to return to Lindsey Hall. Bewcastle was most likely to be at home then – if he was at home at all, that was. But it was late August, and he was unlikely to be in London.

They had stayed the night at an inn several miles away, since Alleyne did not want to be recognized, and so they had to leave soon after breakfast, he and Rachel. Bridget remained behind at the inn.

It was late in the morning of a lovely sunny day when their carriage approached the house. He felt a stab of recognition as soon as they entered the straight driveway with its elm trees lined up like soldiers on parade on either side. Setting his head close to the window, he could see the great house up ahead, and before it the circular flower garden with the fountain at its center.

He wished then that he had not eaten any breakfast. It sat uneasily in his stomach. It would not take much, he thought, to make him turn around and flee, never to return. It was really quite absurd, this reluctance to come home, to show himself to Bewcastle. It was as if he felt that because they had held a memorial service for him he ought to remain dead.

What he *ought* to have done was write to Bewcastle first, as Rachel had wanted him to do back in Bath.

And then he felt her hand warm in his own and turned his head to smile at her. Bless her heart, she did not say a word. She merely looked back at him with eyes so filled with love that he felt suddenly calmed. His old life was beginning to close about him again – the carriage had turned to circle around the fountain – but here was his new life beside him, and nothing could ever be the same again. Nothing and nobody could mean more to him than Rachel.

He vaulted out of the carriage as soon as it had drawn to a halt and the coachman had opened the door. He turned and handed Rachel down and tucked her hand beneath his arm. But he did not have to knock on the great double doors. They opened back, and Bewcastle's butler stepped out and to one side with great dignity and a deep, reverential bow and a look on his face that was almost, but not quite, a smile. And then he looked up and directly at Alleyne.

The half-smile vanished, his face turned sallow, and his jaw dropped.

'Good morning, Fleming,' Alleyne said. 'Is Bewcastle at home?'

Fleming had not been Bewcastle's butler for the past fifteen years for nothing. One could almost have counted the seconds – there would not have been more than ten of them – while he recovered from his silent shock. In the meantime, Alleyne was leading Rachel up the steps and into the great hall.

'Not at present, my lord,' Fleming said.

But Alleyne had come up short just inside the

doors. The great medieval hall, which had been one of his first returned memories, was being set for a banquet. Servants were bustling about, setting out dishes, arranging flowers, straightening chairs. More than one stopped to gawk at him until a silent signal from Fleming sent them scurrying back to work.

'His grace is—' the butler began.

But Alleyne held up a staying hand.

'Thank you, Fleming,' he said. 'He will be home soon?'

'Yes, my lord,' the butler told him.

Something was about to be celebrated in grand style. There was a state dining room at Lindsey Hall. The great hall was used only for the rarest of festal events. The last time it had been used was for Freyja's wedding.

A wedding?

Bewcastle's?

But he would not take the simplest course of asking Fleming. He stood where he was, looking about him, more than ever thankful for the quiet comfort of Rachel at his side, her arm still through his.

They thought he was dead. They had held some sort of funeral for him. And then life had carried on for them. Today, only two and a half months after Waterloo, there was some event grand enough to be celebrated in this sort of style.

He asked himself if he felt hurt. How could life have continued on for them just as if he had never existed? But how could life have stood still for longer than two months? It had not for him. His life had moved on, and it seemed to him as if he had done more living, more growing, since Waterloo than he had done in all of the almost twenty-six years before it.

363

He had found Rachel during those months. He had found contentment and happiness and roots. He had found love.

He looked down at her.

'It is all very magnificent,' she said. 'I am quite awestruck.'

He opened his mouth to say something in reply. But they both heard it together, over and above the bustle in the hall – the sound of horses' hooves clopping up the driveway and the rumble of carriage wheels. He closed his eyes briefly.

'I'll stay in here,' she said. 'Go out there alone, Alleyne. This is something you need to do alone. It will be something you will look back upon as one of the happiest days of your life.'

It seemed unlikely to him when even now, several hours after he had eaten breakfast, he felt as if he were in danger of losing it. But he knew she was right. This was something he had to do alone.

He stepped out onto the terrace.

It was an open barouche, and there were two people sitting inside it, a man and a woman. At the same moment as they wrapped their arms about each other and kissed, heedless of anyone watching from the house, Alleyne saw the colored ribbons fluttering behind and the old boots dragging along the ground. It was a wedding carriage.

Bewcastle?

But as the conveyance turned onto the terrace and the couple drew apart, he saw that the man was not Bewcastle. He was – good Lord, he was the *Earl of Rosthorn*, the man who had hosted that picnic in the Forest of Soignés that Rachel had mentioned, the man who had been dangling after Morgan none too discreetly.

364

But that realization and that suddenly returned memory came and went in a flashing moment. For his eyes had alit on the woman, on the *bride*, and she was Morgan, all decked out in white with lavender trim.

He could no longer think at all. He could scarcely breathe.

She looked at him with bright, laughing eyes as the barouche drew to a halt – and then the smile froze on her face, her complexion turned deathly pale, and she scrambled to her feet.

'Alleyne,' she whispered.

He had had a couple of weeks to prepare for the shock of this moment. But it was doubtful he felt it any less than she did. He opened his arms, and she somehow launched herself out of the barouche without first opening the door. His arms closed about her and held her to him for long moments. Her feet were not even on the ground.

'Alleyne, Alleyne.' She kept whispering his name over and over as if she did not trust the evidence of her senses sufficiently to speak out loud.

'Morg,' he said, setting her on her feet at last. 'I could not miss your wedding, could I? Or the wedding *breakfast* at least. So you have married Rosthorn?'

The earl was descending from the carriage the more conventional way. But Morgan was still holding Alleyne and gazing into his face as if she could never look her fill.

'Alleyne,' she said aloud. 'Alleyne.'

Perhaps in a few moments more she would have recovered sufficiently to say something more than his name. But the bride and groom had not been given much of a head start from the church. A whole cavalcade of carriages was proceeding up the driveway. The first of them was already circling the fountain and taking the place of the barouche, which the coachman had drawn away from the doors.

Everything was going to be all right after all, Alleyne thought. All the unfamiliarity, all the sense of disconnection, all the impersonality of his memories, had fallen away the moment Morgan had landed in his arms. He was back in his boyhood home, and by some strange chance he had arrived at a festive moment in his family's life, at a time when they would surely all be here.

He peered almost eagerly into the leading carriage and saw his grandmother with Ralf and Judith inside, and Freyja and Hallmere crowded in with them. Strangely, though, despite the fact that both Freyja and his grandmother looked fondly out at Morgan, neither of them looked at him. Ralf vaulted out and turned to hand down their grandmother, and Morgan called his name. He looked over his shoulder with a cheerful grin – and froze just the way she had done a minute or two ago.

'My God,' he said. '*My God. Alleyne!*'

And he left their grandmother to fend for herself, closed the distance between himself and Alleyne, and caught him up with a whoop and a great bear hug.

There was a great deal of noise and confusion then as Rannulf's strange behavior drew everyone's attention to the man he was hugging with such enthusiasm. There were hugs and exclamations and questions and a few tears. Alleyne hugged his grandmother gently. She looked frailer and more birdlike than ever as she patted his cheek with one gnarled hand and gazed at him in wonder.

'My dear boy,' she said, 'you are alive.'

Only Freyja had not been a part of that first flurry. But the others stood aside to let her through. She was looking at Alleyne with pale cheeks and haughty gaze. She strode toward him, and he opened his arms. But instead of coming right into them, she drew back her right arm and struck him hard on the jaw with her fist.

'Where have you *been*?' she demanded. '*Where have you been*?' And she launched herself at him, headfirst, and hugged him hard enough to squeeze the breath out of him. 'I'll kill you with my bare hands. I swear I will.'

'Free,' he said, flexing his jaw, 'you don't mean it. And if you do, I won't let you. I'll get Hallmere to protect me.'

But suddenly Aidan and Eve and the children were there too, alighting from the second carriage, and both children launched themselves upon Alleyne with shrieks of delight while Eve stood with both hands over her mouth and her eyes huge. Aidan was not far behind the children.

'By God, Alleyne, you are alive,' he said, stating the obvious as he drew his brother into his arms.

Alleyne did not believe he had ever been hugged more in his whole life.

He laughed and held up both hands as if to stave off the myriad questions that were being directed at him.

'Later,' he said. 'Give me a moment to enjoy the sight of you all again and to recover from Freyja's blow. You still throw a mean one, Free.'

He could see his Aunt and Uncle Rochester pulling up in a carriage with two ladies Alleyne did not know, and the look of shock on his aunt's haughty, aristocratic face was almost comical.

Where was Bewcastle?

But then he was there, standing on the terrace some distance away, and such was the power of his presence that everyone seemed to sense it and fell back away from Alleyne even as they stopped talking. There was still all sorts of noise, of course – horses, carriage wheels, voices, the water spouting out of the fountain – but it seemed to Alleyne as if complete silence fell.

Bewcastle had already seen him. His gaze was steady and silver-eyed and inscrutable. His hand reached for the gold-handled, jewel-studded quizzing glass he always wore with formal attire and raised it halfway to his eyes in a characteristic gesture. Then he came striding along the terrace with uncharacteristic speed and did not stop coming until he had caught Alleyne up in a tight, wordless embrace that lasted perhaps a whole minute while Alleyne dipped his forehead to his brother's shoulder and felt at last that he was safe.

It was an extraordinary moment. He had been little more than a child when his father died, but Wulfric himself had been only seventeen. Alleyne had never thought of him as a father figure. Indeed, he had often resented the authority his brother wielded over them with such unwavering strictness, and often with apparent impersonality and lack of humor. He had always thought of his eldest brother as aloof, unfeeling, totally self-sufficient. A cold fish. And yet it was in Wulfric's arms that he felt his homecoming most acutely. He felt finally and completely and unconditionally loved.

An extraordinary moment indeed.

He blinked back tears, suddenly ashamed. And it was just as well he had not given in to the mortifying temptation to weep. Bewcastle took a step back and possessed himself of his quizzing glass again. Perhaps he too was feeling embarrassed by such a public display. He was looking his usual cool, haughty self again.

'Doubtless, Alleyne,' he said, 'you are about to offer an explanation for your long absence?'

Alleyne grinned and then chuckled.

'When you have an hour or three to spare,' he said, looking about at them all – his family, with more acquaintances and other guests arriving every moment. 'But it looks as if my arrival has taken the focus of attention away from the bride, and that is unpardonable of me. I must beg your indulgence for a moment longer, though.'

He looked toward the open doors of the house and could see Rachel standing just inside, in the shadows. He smiled at her as he strode toward her and held out one hand for hers. She was horribly frightened, he could tell, but she was outwardly calm as she set her hand in his and allowed him to lead her out onto the terrace.

She looked incredibly beautiful, he thought, even though her pale green carriage dress and hat did not nearly match in splendor all the wedding finery about them.

'I have the honor,' he said, turning back to face his family, 'of presenting Miss Rachel York, niece and heir of Baron Weston of Chesbury Park in Wiltshire, and my betrothed.'

There was a great deal of noise and fuss as Rachel smiled, her eyes bright, her cheeks flushed. But it was

Bewcastle, as usual, who had the final word.

He made Rachel a stiff, very correct bow.

'Miss York,' he said, 'I am acquainted with your uncle. Welcome to Lindsey Hall. Doubtless Alleyne will be able to regale us with many stories during the coming hours and days. But this morning there is a wedding to celebrate and guests to entertain and a breakfast that is awaiting us all. The Earl and Countess of Rosthorn will lead the way inside.'

The Earl and Countess . . .

He was referring to *Morgan*, who, now that the first shock of her brother's return from the dead was over, was smiling radiantly at Rosthorn, and that gentleman was looking back at her with an answering look of adoration and offering her his arm.

Wulf was bowing and offering his to Rachel.

And she had been right, Alleyne thought as his grandmother took one of his arms and Freyja grabbed the other as if she intended never to let go. He would surely remember this day as one of the happiest of his life.

But only because Rachel was with him, by Jove. Without her he might have procrastinated until he was in his eightieth year or beyond.

Some of the trees about the lake were beginning to turn color. Rachel looked down on them from the window of her bedchamber. September had been a wet and chilly month, but yesterday had finally been sunny again, and today it felt almost as if summer had returned just for the occasion.

Her wedding day would have been glorious in drizzle or thunderstorm or blizzard, but she supposed that every bride dreamed of blue sky and sunshine to

370

greet her as she stepped out of the church with her bridegroom.

She was ready to leave for the church. But she was early, of course. Geraldine had arrived in her dressing room at the crack of dawn, followed by two footmen carrying the hip bath and a whole stream of maids following with pails of hot water. Geraldine had insisted upon staying to wash her back and then help dress her in the ivory lace and satin confection of a dress Uncle Richard had insisted she have made for the occasion, in addition to a dizzying number of bride clothes.

It was not fitting for the housekeeper to play the part of her maid, Rachel had said with a laugh. But Geraldine had insisted anyway.

'Rache,' she had said, 'I am going to be the bride of a valet – or a gentleman's gentleman, as Will prefers to call himself – before Christmas, so that makes me more or less a maid by marriage, doesn't it?' She stopped to laugh. 'Did you hear what I just said? A *maid by marriage*. And me a maid. Anyway, no one can do your hair as well as I can, and today it has to look extra special for Lord Alleyne to look at all day and take down tonight when the two of you go to bed. I don't suppose you need any advice for the occasion seeing as you don't have a mother, do you?'

The other ladies had ended up in her dressing room too before the morning was well advanced, though Phyllis had not been able to stay long because there were guests staying at the house and, in addition, she had insisted upon catering the wedding breakfast herself.

'It should go well, Rachel,' she had said as she was leaving, 'if I can just keep my mind off the fact that

371

I am feeding a real live *duke*. I have seen him. He looks like Lord Alleyne except that it seems to me that if someone were to put an icicle in his hand it would just sit there and never melt.'

'He bowed to me when I went to Lindsey Hall after Lord Alleyne summoned me there,' Bridget said with a sigh, 'and asked me how I did. I nearly fell over, but of course he didn't know who I really was, did he?'

Flossie had arranged the veil over Rachel's bonnet after Geraldine had set it carefully in place over her coiffure, and had stood back to assess the effect.

'You are the loveliest bride I have ever seen, Rachel,' she said, 'even though I thought I looked pretty good myself two weeks ago.'

Rachel had hugged them all when it was time for them to be on their way to church. She could not go downstairs too soon. Alleyne was staying at Chesbury, though not, of course, in his old room. All his family was staying here too. She did not want to see any of them before she entered the church. Doing so would invite bad luck.

Carriages were being brought up onto the terrace below, and she turned from the window before any of the intended passengers could step out of the house.

She had spent almost a week at Lindsey Hall before returning with Bridget to prepare for her wedding. She had been horribly uncomfortable at first, and that was an understatement. The Bedwyns seemed to ooze aristocratic hauteur from every pore. And they were a forthright, boisterous family into the bargain. But she had grown comfortable with them. She had come to like them and even to be fond of them.

Including the Duke of Bewcastle.

He was powerful and autocratic and reserved to the point of coldness in his manner. He never laughed or even smiled. But Rachel had seen his face during that long minute while he had held Alleyne in his arms out on the terrace. Probably she was the only one who had seen it since he had had his back to everyone else.

There had been raw and naked love in that face.

Rachel had felt a particular fondness for him ever since.

She had got to know them during that week, and they had accepted her without any apparent qualms. Of course, she thought, they would probably have accepted anyone under the circumstances. They had their brother back after believing for two long months that he had died while bringing the Duke of Wellington's letter back to the ambassador in Brussels. The letter had been found abandoned in the forest.

Alleyne had made it clear to them all almost from the first minute that she had saved his life.

She could hear the sound of voices below and then the slamming of doors followed by the clopping of horses' hooves and the rumbling of wheels. A few moments later there was a tap on her door and Sergeant Strickland answered her summons.

'Everyone has gone to the church,' he said, 'and the baron is waiting downstairs for you. My, you do look as fine as fivepence, missy, even if it is not my place to say so on account of I am only a gentleman's gentleman.'

'You may say so anytime you wish, Sergeant,' Rachel said, smiling and crossing the room impulsively to set her arms about his neck and kiss his cheek. 'I will always, always be grateful to you. It

373

was you who saved his life. I could not have done it without you. Thank you, my friend.'

He beamed at her and looked horribly embarrassed.

And then, just a few minutes later, she was sitting in the carriage beside her uncle, her hands tingling with pins and needles, her heart thumping, her head spinning. Even now – especially now – she could not quite believe in her happiness.

She had gone into the forest to raid dead bodies. Then she had agreed to a scheme full of lies and deceptions. Then they had gone tearing off to Bath and he had recovered his memory – and left her. And then – oh, and then she had walked back from the lake and ended up running into his arms and into her present state of happiness.

Her uncle took one of her hands and squeezed it.

'I suppose I cannot say I am the happiest man in the world this morning, Rachel,' he said, 'since it would be strange indeed if Bedwyn did not have that distinction. But I lay firm claim to being the second happiest.'

She turned her head to smile at him. He was not looking exactly robust and in the best of health. But he had improved so enormously since that afternoon when they had arrived at Chesbury that it was almost difficult to realize that he could be the same man.

There was a crowd of villagers about the church-yard gate. There would be several neighbors among the guests inside. Explanations had been tricky. They had been told of the memory loss, of Sir Jonathan Smith having been chosen as a suitable name until Lord Alleyne Bedwyn remembered his real identity. And since there was some question of the validity of a marriage in which the groom had signed the wrong name, and since both families had missed the first wedding anyway, then the decision had been made to repeat the ceremony. No one had asked about the estate in Northumberland and so no explanation had been made.

And then they were inside the church, and Bridget was waiting there to straighten Rachel's hem and make sure her hair and bonnet had suffered no catastrophe during the journey from house to church.

'You are ready, my love,' she said, standing back and smiling, her eyes suspiciously bright. 'Go and be happy.'

Someone must have given a signal to the organist. Music filled the church, and Rachel moved into the nave, her hand on her uncle's sleeve. The pews were all filled, and everyone turned a head to see her come. But though she was aware of them, she did not really see them. She was aware only of Alleyne, standing at the front, Rannulf beside him.

He was not smiling. But his eyes were dark and intent upon hers, and in them she read pure worship. He was all in black and ivory and white and looked quite astonishingly handsome.

And then she was close to him, and then she was beside him.

And he smiled.

She blinked back sudden tears and smiled back.

'Dearly beloved,' Mr. Crowell said.

It would have been nothing short of a miracle if the Bedwyns had not slipped out of the church while the register was being signed and prepared a suitable welcome for the bride and groom.

Alleyne laughed when he saw them all as he came

out of the church with Rachel on his arm. The open carriage had been decorated much as Morgan and Rosthorn's had been last month, though it looked very much as if a couple of old kettles had been tied to the back of this one. And they were lined up on either side of the path armed with flower petals and colored leaves – Aidan and Eve, Davy and Becky, Freyja and Joshua, Judith, Morgan and Gervase, and Rannulf just dashing into place.

'I am afraid, my love,' Alleyne said, 'we are going to have to run the gauntlet of the Bedwyns' idea of fun.'

'I suppose,' she said, 'you did this for *their* weddings?'

'Except Morgan's,' he admitted, 'and Aidan's. He married by special license and did not let any of us know until later.'

'How unsporting of him.' She laughed and looked so startlingly lovely that he felt the breath catch in his throat. 'I *love* the Bedwyns' idea of fun.'

And she took his arm, lifted her chin, and sauntered down the path with him, laughing into the faces of all of them as they passed until her delicate wedding outfit was dotted with every color of the rainbow.

'You see?' Alleyne called out. 'I have married a woman worthy of the Bedwyn name. She does not simply put her head down and run for it.'

He helped her into the carriage and followed her in, standing for a moment while she arranged her skirts about her, not making any attempt to brush away petals and leaves, and he threw handfuls of coins to the village children, who ran shrieking and squealing to retrieve them.

And then he sat down beside Rachel and took her hand in his, lacing his fingers with hers as the carriage rocked on its springs and moved away in the direction of Chesbury. He ignored the cheering and the catcalls behind them, though he was suddenly aware of the joyful pealing of the church bells – and of the metallic clatter of two kettles being hauled along in their wake.

'Well, my love,' he said.

'Well, my love.'

They laughed together and he squeezed her hand.

'Whoever would have thought,' he said to her, 'that I would ever come to be eternally thankful for that musket ball I took in my thigh and that fall from my horse and that loss of memory? Whoever would have thought that such seeming disaster would turn into the best thing that had ever happened to me?'

'And whoever would have thought,' she said, 'that I would ever be thankful for dreary employment as a lady's companion and the disaster of a betrothal to a rogue and the theft of all the money I owned and all the money my friends owned? Whoever would have thought that my foray into the forest in order to find riches with which to pursue the thief would lead me to you?'

'I'll never ever say that I do not believe in fate,' he said, 'or in a definite path that our lives take in order to lead us to fulfillment if only we will take it without wavering.'

She lifted her face and he kissed her lightly on the lips.

'And listen to me,' he said, 'spouting philosophy when fate has given us these few moments to be alone together before the onslaught of the wedding breakfast. Tonight seems eons away, but there *are* these moments.'

He released her hand in order to set his arm about her shoulders and draw her closer.

'I have told you before,' she said, 'that you sometimes talk too much.'

'Insubordination,' he said, rubbing his nose against hers. 'You are my wife now, Rache. You are Lady Alleyne Bedwyn and have to be polite to me and obey me.'

'Yes, my lord.' Her eyes laughed into his.

'Kiss me, then,' he said.

'Yes, my lord.'

She laughed aloud. But then she obeyed him, turning on the seat and wrapping both arms about him in order to do so more thoroughly.

His golden angel.

His wife.

His love.

About the Author

Best-selling, multi-award-winning author Mary Balogh grew up in Wales, land of sea and mountains, song and legend. She brought music and a vivid imagination with her when she came to Canada to teach. Here she began a second career as a writer of books that always end happily and always celebrate the power of love. There are over four million copies of her Regency romances and historical romances in print. She is also the author of the Regency-era romantic novels *One Night for Love*, *No Man's Mistress*, *More Than a Mistress*, *A Summer to Remember*, *Slightly Married*, *Slightly Wicked*, *Slightly Scandalous*, *Slightly Tempted*, and *Slightly Dangerous*, all available in paperback from Dell. Visit her web site at www.marybalogh.com.

Slightly Dangerous

Most of the guests were weary from traveling and used the time between tea and dinner to rest quietly in their rooms. Wulfric took the opportunity to slip outdoors for some fresh air and exercise. He did not know his way about the park, of course, but he instinctively sought out cover so that he would not be seen from the house and thus invite company. He made his way diagonally across a tree-dotted lawn and took a path through denser trees until he came to the bank of a man-made lake, which had clearly been created for maximum visual effect.

He should have gone home to Lindsey Hall.

But he had not, and so there was no point in wishing now that he had made a different decision.

He was still standing there, content for the moment to be idle, when he heard the distinct rustle of footsteps on the path behind him – the path by which he had come. He was annoyed with himself then that he had not moved off sooner. The last thing he wanted was company. But it was too late now. Whichever of the side paths he took, he would be unable to move out of sight before whoever it was emerged onto the bank and saw him.

He turned with barely concealed annoyance.

She was marching along with quite unladylike strides, minus either bonnet or gloves, and her head was turned back over her shoulder as if to see who was coming along behind her. Before Wulfric could either move out of the way or alert her to impending disaster, she had collided with him full-on. He grasped her upper arms too late, and found himself with a noseful of soft curls before she jerked back her head with a squeak of alarm and her nose collided with his.

It seemed somehow almost inevitable, he thought with pained resignation – and with the pain of a smarting nose and watering eyes. Some evil angel must have sent her to this house party just to torment him – or to remind him never again to make an impulsive decision.

Her hand flew to her nose – presumably to discover if it was broken or gushing blood or both. Tears welled in her eyes.

'Mrs. Derrick,' he said with faint hauteur – though it was too late to discourage her from approaching him.

'Oh, dear,' she said, lowering her hand and blinking her eyes, 'I am so sorry. How clumsy of me! I was not looking where I was going.'

'You might, then,' he said, 'have walked right into the lake if I had not been standing here.'

'But I did not,' she said reasonably. 'I had a sudden feeling that I was not alone and looked behind me instead of ahead. And of all people, it had to be you.'

'I beg your pardon.' He bowed stiffly to her. He might have returned the compliment but did not.

More than ever she looked countrified and without any of the elegance and sophistication he expected of ladies with whom he was obliged to socialize for two

381

weeks. The breeze was ruffling her short curls. The sunlight was making her complexion look more bronzed even than it had appeared in the drawing room. Her teeth looked very white in contrast. Her eyes were as blue as the sky. She was, he conceded grudgingly, really quite startlingly pretty – despite a nose that was reddening by the moment.

'My words *were* ill-mannered,' she said with a smile. 'I did not mean them quite the way they sounded. But first I spilled lemonade over you, then I engaged you in a staring match only because I objected to your eyebrow, and now I have run into you and cracked your nose with my own. I do hope I have used up a whole two weeks' worth of clumsiness all within a few hours and can be quite decorous and graceful and really rather boring for the rest of my stay here.'

There was not much to be said in response to such a frank speech. But during it she had revealed a great deal about herself, none of which was in any way appealing.

'My choice of path appears to have been serendipitous,' he said, turning slightly away from her. 'The lake was unexpected, but it is pleasantly situated.'

'Oh, yes, indeed,' she agreed. 'It has always been one of my favorite parts of the park.'

'Doubtless,' he said, planning his escape, 'you came out here to be alone. I have disturbed you.'

'Not at all,' she said brightly. 'Besides, I came out here to walk. There is a path that winds its way all about the lake. It has been carefully planned to give a variety of sensual pleasures.'

Her eyes caught and held his and she grimaced and blushed.

'Sometimes,' she added, 'I do not choose my words with care.'

Sensual pleasures. That was the phrase that must have embarrassed her.

But instead of striking off immediately onto her chosen path, she hesitated a moment, and he realized that he stood in her way. But before he could move, she spoke again.

'Perhaps,' she said, 'you would care to accompany me?'

He absolutely would not care for any such thing. He could think of no less desirable a way of spending the free hour or so before he must change for dinner.

'Or perhaps,' she said with that laughter in her eyes that he had noticed earlier across the drawing room after he had raised his eyebrow and so offended her, 'you would not.'

It was spoken like a challenge. And really, he thought, there was something mildly fascinating about the woman. She was so very different from any other woman he had ever encountered. And at least there was nothing remotely flirtatious in her manner.

'I would,' he said, and stepped aside for her to precede him onto the path that led back in among the trees though it ran parallel to the bank of the lake. He fell into step beside her, since the person who had designed this walk had had the forethought to make it wide enough for two persons to walk comfortably abreast.

They did not talk for a while. Although as a gentleman he was adept at making polite conversation, he had never been a proponent of making noise simply for the sake of keeping the silence at bay. If she was content to stroll quietly, then so was he.

'I believe I have you to thank for my invitation to Schofield,' she said at last, smiling sidelong at him.

'Indeed?' He looked back at her with raised eyebrows.

'After you had been invited,' she said, 'Melanie suddenly panicked at the realization that she was to have one more gentleman than lady on her guest list. She dashed off a letter to Hyacinth Cottage to invite me, and, after I had refused, came in person to beg.'

She had just confirmed what he had been beginning to suspect.

'After I had been invited,' he repeated. 'By Viscount Mowbury. I daresay the invitation did not come from Lady Renable after all, then.'

'I would not worry about it if I were you,' she said. 'Once I had rescued her from impending disaster by agreeing to come after all, she admitted that even if having the Duke of Bewcastle as a guest was not quite such a coup as having the Prince Regent might have been, it was in fact far preferable. She claims – probably quite rightly – that she will be the envy of every other hostess in England.'

He continued to look at her. Then an evil angel really *had* been at work. She was here only because he was – and *he* was here only because he had acted quite out of character.

'You did not *wish* to accept your invitation?' he asked her.

'I did not.' She had been swinging her arms in quite unladylike fashion, but now she clasped them behind her back.

'Because you were offended at being omitted from the original guest list?' She was normally treated as a poor relation and largely ignored, then, was she?

'Because, strange as it may seem, I did not want to come,' she told him.

'Perhaps,' he suggested, 'you feel out of your depth in superior company, Mrs. Derrick.'

'I would question your definition of *superior*,' she said. 'But in essence you are quite right.'

'And yet,' he said, 'you were married to a brother of Viscount Elrick.'

'And so I was,' she said cheerfully.

But she did not pursue that line of conversation. They had emerged from among the trees and were at the foot of a grassy hill dotted with daisies and buttercups.

'Is this not a lovely hill?' she asked him, probably rhetorically. 'You see? It takes us above the treetops and gives us a clear view of the village and the farms for miles around. The countryside is like a checkered blanket. Who would ever choose town life over this?'

She did not wait for him or mince her way up the rather steep slope. She strode up ahead of him to the very top of the hill, though they might have skirted around its base, and stood there, spreading her arms to the sides and twirling once about, her face lifted to the sunlight. The breeze, which was more like a wind up there, whipped at her hair and her dress and set the ribbons that tied the latter at the waist streaming outward.

She looked like a woodland nymph, and yet it seemed to him that her movements and gestures were quite uncontrived and unselfconscious. What might have been coquetry in another woman was sheer exuberant delight in her. He had the strange feeling of having stepped – unwillingly – into an alien world.

'Who indeed?' he said.

Mrs. Derrick stopped to regard him.

'Do *you* prefer the countryside?' she asked.

'I do,' he said, climbing until he was beside her and turning slowly about in order to see the full panorama of the surrounding countryside.

'Why do you spend so much time in town, then?' she asked.

'I am a member of the House of Lords,' he told her. 'It is my duty to attend whenever it is in session.'

He was looking down at the village.

'The church is pretty, is it not?' she said. 'The spire was rebuilt twenty years ago after the old one was blown off in a storm. I can remember both the storm and the rebuilding. This spire is twenty feet higher than the old one.'

'That is the vicarage next to it?' he asked.

'Yes,' she said. 'We practically grew up there, my two sisters and I, with the old vicar and his wife. They were kind and hospitable people. Their daughters were our particular friends, and so was their son, Charles, to a lesser degree. He was one boy among five girls, poor lad. We all went to the village school together, girls as well as boys. Fortunately my father, who taught us, was not of the persuasion that girls have nothing but fluff to keep their ears from collapsing in on each other. Louisa and Catherine both married young and now live some distance away. But after the old vicar and his wife died, within two months of each other, Charles, who had been a curate twenty miles from here, was given the living himself and married Hazel – the middle sister of my family.'

Yes, he thought, she really was from a different world – the world of the lower gentry. She had indeed made a brilliant marriage.

She stretched out one arm and moved a step closer to him so that he would be able to see just what it was she pointed at.

'There is Hyacinth Cottage,' she said. 'It is where

we live. I have always thought it picturesque. There was a moment of anxiety after my father died, since the lease was in his name alone. But Bertie – Baron Renable – was kind enough to lease it to Mama and Eleanor for the rest of their lives.'

'On the assumption,' he said, 'that you will not outlive the two of them?'

She returned her arm to her side. 'I was still married to Oscar at the time,' she said. 'His death was not predictable, but even if it had been, Bertie would have assumed, I suppose, that I would remain with his family.'

'But you did not?' he asked her.

'No.'

He looked at Hyacinth Cottage in the middle distance. It looked a pretty enough home with its thatched roof and sizable garden. It looked like one of the larger houses in the village, as befitted the home of a gentleman by birth, even if he had also been the schoolmaster.

Mrs. Derrick, standing quietly beside him, chuckled softly.

Wulfric turned his head to look at her.

'I have done something to amuse you again, Mrs. Derrick?' he asked.

'Not really.' She smiled at him. 'But it has struck me how like a doll's house Hyacinth Cottage looks from up here. It would probably fit into one corner of the drawing room at wherever you live.'

'Lindsey Hall?' he said. 'I doubt it. I perceive that there are four bedrooms upstairs and as many rooms downstairs.'

'Perhaps the corner of your *ballroom*, then,' she said.

'Perhaps,' he agreed, though he doubted it. It was an amusing image, though.

'If we follow the path right around the lake at this pace,' she said, 'we may arrive back at the house in time to scrounge a biscuit or two with our late-evening tea.'

'Then we will move on,' he said.

'Perhaps,' she said, 'you did not intend to walk so far. Perhaps you would prefer to return the way we have come while I continue on my way.'

There it was – his cue to escape. Why he did not take it, he had no idea. Perhaps it was that he was unaccustomed to being dismissed.

'Are you by any chance, Mrs. Derrick,' he asked, grasping the handle of his quizzing glass and raising it all the way to his eye to regard her through it – simply because he knew the gesture would annoy her, 'trying to be rid of me?'

But she laughed instead.

'I merely thought,' she said, 'that perhaps you are accustomed to riding everywhere or being conveyed by carriage. I would not wish to be responsible for blisters on your feet.'

'Or for my missing my dinner?' He lowered his glass and let it swing free on its ribbon. 'You are kind, ma'am, but I will not hold you responsible for either possible disaster.'

With one hand he indicated the path down the other side of the hill. For a short distance, he could see, the path then followed the bank of the lake before disappearing among the trees again.

She asked questions as they walked. She asked him about Lindsey Hall in Hampshire and about his other estates. She seemed particularly interested in his Welsh property on a remote peninsula close to the sea. She asked about his brothers and sisters, and then, when she knew they were all married, about their spouses and children. He talked more about himself than he could remember doing in a long while.

When they emerged from the trees again, they were close to a pretty, humpbacked stone bridge across a stream that flowed rather swiftly between steep banks on its way to feed the lake. Sunshine gleamed off the water as they stood at the center of the bridge and Mrs. Derrick leaned her arms on the stone parapet. Birds were singing. It was really quite an idyllic scene.

'It was just here,' she said, her voice suddenly dreamy, 'that Oscar kissed me for the first time and asked me to marry him. So much water has passed beneath the bridge since that evening – in more ways than one.'

Wulfric did not comment. He hoped she was not about to pour out a lot of sentimental drivel about that romance and the gravity of her loss. But when she turned her head to look at him, she did so rather sharply, and she was blushing. He guessed that she had forgotten herself for a moment – and he was delighted that she had recollected herself so soon.

'Do you *love* Lindsey Hall and your other estates?' she asked him.

Only a woman – a sentimental woman – could ask such a question.

'*Love* is perhaps an extravagant word to use of stone and mortar and the land, Mrs. Derrick,' he said. 'I see that they are well administered. I attend to my responsibilities for all who draw a living from my properties. I spend as much time as I can in the country.'

'And do you love your brothers and sisters?' she asked.

389

He raised his eyebrows.

'*Love*,' he said. 'It is a word used by women, Mrs. Derrick, and in my experience encompasses such a wide range of emotions that it is virtually useless in conveying meaning. Women love their husbands, their children, their lapdogs, and the newest gewgaw they have purchased. They love walks in the park and the newest novel borrowed from the subscription library and babies and sunshine and roses. I did my duty by my brothers and sisters and saw them all well and contentedly married. I write to each of them once a month. I would, I suppose, die for any one of them if such a noble and ostentatious sacrifice were ever called for. Is that love? I leave it to you to decide.'

She gazed at him for a while without speaking.

'You choose to speak of women's sensibilities with scorn,' she said then. 'Yes, we feel love for all the things you mentioned and more. I would not want to live, I believe, if my life were not filled with love of almost everything and everyone that is involved in it. It is not an emotion to inspire contempt. It is an attitude to life directly opposed, perhaps, to that attitude which sees life only as a series of duties to be performed or burdens to be borne. And of course the word *love* has many shades of meaning, as do many, many of the words in our living, breathing language. But though we may speak of loving roses and of loving children, our minds and sensibilities clearly understand that the emotion is not the same at all. We feel a delighted stirring of the senses at the sight of a perfect rose. We feel a deep stirring of the heart at the sight of a child who is our own or closely connected to us by family ties. I will not be made ashamed of the tenderness I feel for my sisters and for my niece and nephews.'

He had the distinct feeling that he was being dealt

a sharp setdown. But as with many people who argued more from emotion rather than from reason, she had twisted his words. He directed one of his coolest looks at her.

'You will forgive me if I have forgotten,' he said, 'but did I say or imply that you *ought* to be ashamed, Mrs. Derrick?'

Most ladies would have looked suitably chastised. Not Mrs. Derrick.

'Yes,' she said firmly. 'You *did* imply it. You implied that women are shallow and pretend to love when they do not know the meaning of the word – when, indeed, there is no meaning to the word.'

'Ah,' he said softly, more annoyed than he normally allowed himself to be. 'Then perhaps you *will* forgive me, ma'am.'

He moved back from the parapet, and they walked on, in silence now, back among trees, though there was a clear view of the lake, which they circled about in order to return to their starting point. She set a brisk pace back to the house from there.

'Well,' she said, smiling brightly at him when they stepped inside the hall, breaking the lengthy silence in which they had completed their walk, 'I must hurry if I am not to be late for dinner.'

He bowed to her and let her run – yes, run – up the stairs and disappear from sight before making his way to his own room. He was surprised to discover when he arrived there that he had been out for well over an hour. It had not seemed so long. It *ought* to have done. He did not usually enjoy the company of anyone whom he had not chosen with care – and that included all strangers.

The Duke of Bewcastle did not, Christine was relieved to find, feel obliged to escort her up to her box of a room. Doubtless he was sagging with relief that he had survived such a tedious hour, she thought as she ran lightly up the stairs, forgetting all of Hermione's teaching about running being an ungenteel way of moving from one place to another.

She hurried along to her room. It would not take her long to dress for dinner, but she had left herself precious little time.

She could scarcely believe what she had just done. She had allowed herself to be goaded by a couple of silly girls, that was what. She had dashed out of the house after tea in order to steal some quiet time alone, she had run headlong into the Duke of Bewcastle – *ghastly* moment – and then, just when she had been about to scurry away from him, she had conceived the grand idea of winning the wager right there and then, almost before it had been made. Just to prove to herself that she could do it. Right from the first moment she had had no intention of dashing back to the house after the hour was over to claim her prize. She did not need the prize or the envy of her fellow-conspirators. It was just that she was at the nasty age of twenty-nine, and all the young ladies, almost without exception, had looked on her with pity and scorn as if she were positively ancient.

She still could not quite believe she had done it – and that he had agreed to accompany her. And that, even on the hill, when she had been assaulted by conscience and had given him a decent chance to escape, he had chosen to continue on the way with her.

She was enormously glad the hour was over. A more toplofty, chilling man she had never known. He had talked of Lindsey Hall and his other properties, and he had talked of his brothers and sisters and nephews and nieces without a single glimmer of emotion. And then he had spoken scathingly of love when she had asked him about it.

If the full truth were told, she would have to admit that she did find him fascinating in a shivery sort of way. And he did have a splendid profile – and a physique that more than matched it. He ought to be cast in marble or bronze, she thought, and set atop a lofty column at the end of some avenue in the park at his principal seat so that future generations of Bedwyns could gaze at him in admiration and awe.

The Duke of Bewcastle was a handsome man and easy on the eyes.

She stopped suddenly in the middle of her small room and frowned. No, that was not his appeal. Oscar had been a handsome man – quite breathtakingly so, in fact. It was his looks that had bowled her right off her feet and right out of her senses. She had been a typically foolish girl nine years ago. Looks had been everything. One glance at him and she had been head over ears in love. Only his looks had mattered. She had been quite unawakened to any other appeal he might, or might not have had.

But she was older now. She was awakened, knowledgeable. She was a mature woman.

The Duke of Bewcastle was definitely handsome in his cold, austere way. But he had something else beyond that.

He was sexually appealing.

The very thought, verbalized in her mind, set her breasts to tightening uncomfortably and her inner passage and thighs to aching.

How very embarrassing.

And alarming.

He was a dangerous man indeed, though not perhaps in any obvious way. He had not exactly tried to have his wicked way with her out there in the woods, after all, had he? The very thought was ludicrous. He had not even tried to charm her – even more ridiculous. He had not even cracked a smile the whole time.

But even so, every cell in her body had pulsed with sexual awareness while she had walked with him.

She must have windmills in her head, she thought, giving herself a firm mental shake as she sat down before her dressing table mirror, to be feeling a sexual attraction to the Duke of Bewcastle, who could be placed bodily atop that lofty column at the end of that avenue in the park at Lindsey Hall and passed off as a marble statue without anyone's ever knowing any different.

And then she slapped a hand over her mouth to muffle a shriek. Windmills in her head? She looked very much as if windmills had been busy on her head. Her hair was in a wild, tangled bush about her head. And her cheeks were like two shiny, rosy red apples after being exposed to the wind. Her nose was like a cherry.

Heavenly days! The man must be made of marble, all funning aside, if he had been able to look at her like this without breaking out into great guffaws of mirth.

While her cells had been merrily pulsing away with sexual attraction, his must have been cringing with distaste.

Mortified – and far too late – she grabbed her brush.